PRAISE FOR BILL YENNE

Bill Yenne writes "with cinematic vividness."

ROGER MCGRATH, *THE WALL STREET JOURNAL*

I can guarantee that you will be engaged by [Bill Yenne's] master storytelling from his opening words to the very last page.

COLONEL WALTER BOYNE, SMITHSONIAN NATIONAL AIR & SPACE MUSEUM

Bill Yenne is a perfect example what happens when a child reads too many books and doesn't watch enough television. He ended up with an imagination.

JOHN SMITHERS OF MONTANA'S *MISSOULIAN*

GHOST ARMIES OF THE NĀPALI COAST

GHOST ARMIES OF THE NĀPALI COAST

JIM HAMMER
BOOK 3

BILL YENNE

Ghost Armies of the Nāpali Coast
Paperback Edition

Rough Edges Press
An Imprint of Wolfpack Publishing
1707 E. Diana Street
Tampa, FL 33610

roughedgespress.com

Paperback ISBN 978-1-68549-638-8
Ebook ISBN 978-1-68549-637-1
LCCN 2026936056

GHOST ARMIES OF THE NĀPALI COAST

INTRODUCTION

So many people, from cruel Taliban warlords to duplicitous Pentagon bureaucrats, have learned the hard way that it is a fool's errand to find themselves on the bad side of Jim Hammer when he sets his mind to righting a wrong. After twenty years in the US Army, he left the service, imagining he would be taking time off from all those wars. He was mistaken. There was more work to do. This is one of his war stories.

NOTE TO THE READER

With the exception of Hemolele`auwai Valley, which figures prominently in this narrative, as well as some of the businesses in the town of Kekaha, all of the named places are real, and the author has been to most of them. The unnamed tiki bar in Hanalei is real, though it is described as it was in earlier years when the author first frequented it. All of the military and electronic hardware is either real or depicted as a fictitious later variant of a real system. The phenomena known as *huaka`i pō* and *oi`o,* which play an important part in this story, are both genuine elements of Hawai`ian folklore.

Certain words in the Hawai`ian language (including "Hawai`ian" itself) are properly spelled with the use on an *okina* (`) a glottal stop between adjacent vowels. The name of the famous cliff-studded northwest coastline of Kaua`i is seen in various media spelled in various ways. We employ the spelling used by the Hawai`i Department of Land and Natural Resources, the stewards of this coastline, and spell it Nāpali.

PROLOGUE

JIM HAMMER GLANCED up from the Western novel into which he'd been submerged most of the way from Seattle. It was the 1870s and Gideon Safford, a westering man on the run from his past, had just accomplished the impossible. He had crossed the Continental Divide on the cusp of a Montana winter as flakes of a raging blizzard stung the back of his neck.

Despite being deeply engrossed in the distant past through the yellowed pages of his book, Hammer had long ago trained himself to read subtle changes in his here-and-now surroundings. He'd sensed none of those for hours until he felt the 737-800 bank slightly as it turned into the landing pattern for Honolulu International Airport.

He looked around. Most of his fellow passengers were staring at screens or napping. Across the aisle in 14D, Lauren Stahling was deeply engrossed in her own book, gently tapping a yellow number two pencil on her chin as she waited to pounce on a page to scribble a note. He smiled. He found her gorgeous and liked the way she reacted when he worked that phrase into conversation from time to time.

She was one of those strong and confident women who embodied those qualities rather than asserting them. Today, with her pencil and her long dark hair tied back loosely, she looked more like a schoolteacher than the boss lady of a county assessor's office.

He liked having her at his side, even if there was an aisle between them, but he'd much rather they were side-by-side *outside* this hundred-and-twenty-foot aluminum tube. They were both looking forward to a month off the grid on the island of Kaua`i, the most lightly populated of the main Hawai`ian islands. Hammer's old friend Rob had a house on the remote North Shore that he'd inherited from an uncle, and he had offered it to them. He hardly ever got over there, and he explained that it would be a favor to him to have someone look in on the place.

Lauren glanced up from her own book and gazed across the aisle. Seeing Hammer's long legs folded and twisted into the space under the seat ahead, she was glad that they'd paid extra for the exit row and that she'd booked them both into aisle seats. Mostly, she was glad to look forward to some uninterrupted time alone with this man with whom she was been reunited last fall after twenty years.

They had been best friends in high school—until that one night just before graduation when they became a lot more than friends. Then he'd gone off to the Army and wound up in special forces. She went off to college, had a life, had plenty of ups and downs, and then suddenly, he walked back into her life—through the door of the Logan County, Montana Assessor's Office.

They both had spent a lot of years blaming themselves for destroying a friendship by pushing things too far, but now realized, after all that time, they both really wanted it to go that far—and farther.

Since he'd been out of the Army, though, Hammer had been getting into trouble.

First, he jumped headlong into taking down an international human trafficking machine, and he had dragged Lauren—more willingly than she could have imagined—into freeing slaves and erasing slavers.

A couple of months ago, after he'd gone to help out a couple of friends in Louisiana—and wound up derailing a billion-dollar Taliban gunrunning scheme—she decided he needed a break. They *both* needed a break. A month off would do.

It was around the time of this deciding that Lauren had found a curious old book in a used bookshop in Billings.

In 1888, an archaeologist named Annison Cutts had written about a spectacular ancient waterworks that he'd discovered in a steep mountain canyon on the remote and inaccessible northwest coast of Kaua`i. It was like the pyramids. Nobody could figure out how it could have been built there. Even the nineteenth century Hawai`ians whom he showed it to had no idea that it even existed. They simply assured him that it was erected by the Menehunes, the legendary "little people," who are said to be responsible for all sorts of remarkable prehistoric building projects.

When she told Hammer they ought to take a look at this place, he said "let's go."

Their interest was further piqued when she figured out by reading every old book on Kaua`i archaeology she could get through interlibrary loan that *nobody* had been to this place since before 1903. It had been forgotten. She did find an ancient *heiau*, or stone temple, in the area that Cutts had visited. This appeared on a 1931 topographical map, but on no maps since. This was their only clue for where to look.

It was not hard to get away. Lauren was in charge of her department and had many years of sixty-hour work weeks behind her. As for Hammer, he enjoyed pointing out that after twenty years of twenty-four-seven in the field with the US Army, he was *retired*.

They both raised their heads with relief when they heard the disembodied voice of the captain saying, "Flight attendants, please take your seats for landing." Within an hour, they'd be on their connecting flight to Kaua`i.

He glanced to his left, the plane was in a steep turn now, leaning toward final approach and he could look straight down into Pearl Harbor. Amid the scattering of gray warship hulls were two huge, flat-topped vessels marked with the white numerals "73" and "76," which he knew to be the massive US Pacific Fleet nuclear carriers USS *George Washington* and USS *Ronald Reagan*.

Suddenly, the monotony exploded into discord.

Someone ran up the aisle past him. It was a passenger. The cabin crew was already seated.

Hammer looked around. There were two more people in the aisle. One of them started shouting something about "striking a blow against the American war machine."

The jetliner was being hijacked on final approach.

One man was trying to get through the door to the flight deck. The thought flashed through Hammer's mind that their plan was to crash this aircraft into one of the carriers in Pearl Harbor taking a hundred-seventy or so people into a fireball death in a horrendous suicide publicity stunt.

It all happened in slow motion after that.

Time unwound to a crawl.

Hammer looked across into Lauren's eyes and saw an expression of dread. He tried to return an expression of reassurance but found that difficult.

A hijacker lunged down the aisle, followed by a second one. The first man carried a pale-gray pistol that looked like one of these that are fabricated by a 3D printer—so they're short on metal parts that ring bells at TSA. The second had a wooden stake, this material also chosen for its lack of metal.

Hammer's right hand snapped out into the aisle and seized the right hand of the would-be gunman. Hammer's grip being what can only be called vise-like, the man came to an abrupt and unplanned halt as the bone and ligament of his hand was crushed inward against the plastic pistol grip.

In that endless, time-lapse split second that followed, the other man stumbled against his co-conspirator whose forward motion had suddenly been interrupted.

At this moment, Hammer watched Lauren Stahling, her fear turned to anger, fiercely drive her number two pencil deep into the thigh of the second man, then jerk it out, releasing a torrent of blood.

While this was happening, Hammer violently twisted the arm of the first hijacker whose hand he had crushed, brutally and completely dislocating his shoulder, so that arm and body were now connected only by skin.

As the gun tumbled uselessly to the floor, Hammer kicked it under the seat next to him and released the injured hijacker, who was now shrieking helplessly, consumed by horrific pain.

His next move was to seize the stake in the hand of the hijacker with the bleeding thigh, and to repeat what he had done to the first hijacker. Within seconds, these two men, high on ambition when their day began, had been crippled with disabilities that would remain with them for all of their future days.

With two hijackers disarmed and incapacitated in the space of a couple of seconds, Hammer found himself surrounded by the bewildered expressions, mainly of fellow passengers, but the bewilderment also extended to the hijacker fourteen rows forward at the door to the flight deck.

Hammer leaped to his feet and covered this distance in no more than a few seconds, running as fast as anyone can run up the narrow aisle of 737-800.

The challenges he had overcome with the first two pirates paled by comparison to this impasse which he now faced.

Between Hammer and the hijacker, the way forward is blocked by a flight attendant crouching on her hands and knees, her face bleeding from his having clobbered her as she vainly attempted to stop him.

Seeing Hammer, she started to edge out of the way, but this was not the obstacle that most vexed Hammer.

In the man's hand, Hammer recognized a Breachmaster MkIV thermal cutting tool. Only about seventeen inches long and weighing about six ounces, these things are carried by first responders for use in getting through metal obstacles.

Hammer and his team had used these to breech metal doors in Afghanistan, and he well knew what they could do. They burn at five thousand degrees and can cut through two inches of steel. Hammer knew that when this jerk lit it up, he could be inside the cockpit in seconds.

He lit it up.

The glare was blinding.

The flight attendant screamed.

The man began cutting, confident that Hammer could not, and would not, try to interfere.

The man had gloves and Hammer did not. At five thousand degrees, skin does not burn. It evaporates.

As he watched the steel around the door lock turn into a bright orange river and dribble down the bulkhead, Hammer knew he had one chance, and it was a chance sliced minutely thin.

He lowered his head and waited for that split second when the man glanced back at the cut he was making.

Hammer seized this mistaken moment and pounced.

The man's other mistake was that there was only one other man on this airplane with any experience using a thermal cutting tool, and this was the man who he had discounted as a serious threat.

The man's adversary knew where and when the thermal tool could be touched or grabbed at a reasonable temperature, and this was what happened.

Again, it was Hammer's vise-like grip, now fueled by an afterburner of adrenaline as it crushed the bone and nerve and sinew of the man's hand and wrist.

Hammer took him by the force of two vise-like hands and held both of his hands rigid. The Breachmaster MkIV, now glowing with the fire of the sun, was away from anything that it could harm, but barely. For anyone watching, and there were dozens of sets of eyes now watching, it all looked frighteningly dangerous, but it was actually safe—until the pilot banked the plane!

The man lost his balance and began to fall, but Hammer braced his own feet and kept his balance.

Experience told Hammer that the Breachmaster would burn for twenty to thirty seconds. How long had it been? How long would he have to hold this man firm before the damned thing went out?

It seemed like they had been standing there for thirty

minutes or more, but those were "time-stands-still" minutes. Hammer had no idea of the actual time.

Finally, the Breachmaster sputtered and spat and the sun went out.

Behind him in the cabin, he could hear a riffling of applause, but Hammer did not turn away. The thing was now cooling, but the time between five thousand degrees and room temperature is not quick.

He waited and waited, with the hands of the groaning hijacker in his crushing grip. Again, twenty seconds can be an eternity.

The passengers watching the spectacle of this broad-shouldered, six-foot-two man methodically saving their lives were speechless.

Finally, Hammer turned to the flight attendant, who had now gotten back to her feet.

"Could I get some water?" he asked with a cheerful smile.

Her initial expression was one of bewilderment, but she quickly understood why he was asking, and she produced a metal pitcher. He nodded toward the Breachmaster, and she slowly doused it with cold water.

As the hissing steam billowed up, the applause from the cabin was deafening.

It was, admittedly, a pretty dramatic sight.

The big man who was the object of their ovation finally released the hijacker, who crumpled to the floor in agony. In his intolerable pain, and with his hands now both permanently crippled beyond any future usefulness, he was no longer a threat to anyone. Hammer then took the metal pitcher and dropped what was left of the breaching tool inside. He then looked at the flight attendant and nodded to the phone on the wall that connected her with the pilot.

"Tell him everything is okay now and then let me talk to him for a minute."

"Captain...this is Judy...it's all over back here. A passenger took care of it. He wants to talk to you."

With that, she passed him the phone with a shaking hand.

"Captain, this is Captain James Hammer, US Army Special Forces...*retired*. The threat has been neutralized. All three of the hijackers are incapacitated and down."

"I know," the pilot said. "My first officer was watching through the peephole in the door. We sure felt the heat...and by the way *thank you*."

"I'd say no problem," Hammer replied with a laugh. "But as you saw, that's not *exactly* true."

"And from what we figured out from what just happened, Pearl Harbor owes you a colossal 'thank you.'"

"I'd say all in a day's work," Hammer joked. "But I'm retired."

"Are we safe for landing?" the pilot asked.

"I don't see any reason why not," Hammer replied. "There was no damage done to the aircraft, except to your door, which is probably still hot to the touch. I'd suggest that you go ahead land wherever Air Traffic Control may have diverted you...and tell them to have somebody on standby to take these clowns into custody."

CHAPTER ONE

LAUREN STAHLING WATCHED as a convoluted dream slipped from her fingers and spiraled into oblivion. After a long while, she realized she was awake now, and the silence was filled only with the calls of birds. There was even the incongruous distant crowing of a feral rooster.

She opened her eyes slowly and found herself in a room where one wall was covered tastefully with *lauhala* matting framed in dark wood, and the others were painted the color of coffee with a lot of cream. The earth-tone, tropical-print curtains covering the windows on the opposite wall ruffled slightly in a timid breeze. The red numbers on the digital clock read five-fifty-eight.

High above, there was a ceiling fan, but it was not running. There was no need. The temperature was perfect. Lauren kicked off the sheets. The soft, delightfully cool draft caressed her body. Back home in Montana only a few days ago, she had been wearing a flannel nightgown—and socks. This morning, she wore nothing.

She glanced over at the man lying next to her, his shoulder rising and falling gently as he slept. With mixed feelings, she let him sleep. The devilish Lauren wanted to touch that shoulder, that body. This Lauren wanted to wake him up because she knew what would happen next, and she selfishly craved for this to happen.

On the other hand, the kind and compassionate Lauren wanted to let him sleep. After what he'd been through, he deserved to sleep for days. Of course, they had *both* been through it, but him more than her.

After he had tossed the expired breaching tool into the metal water pitcher and the applause had died down to a low rumble, he remained at the front of the cabin while the jetliner made a second, and this time successful, final approach. Meanwhile, the aisle had been blocked by a half dozen men who piled onto the two hijackers, pinning them to the floor, so Hammer couldn't make it back to his seat. He waved to Lauren, and she gave him a thumbs-up.

They touched down on one of the intersecting runways shared by Honolulu International and Joint Base Pearl Harbor-Hickam and then taxied to a remote corner of the Air Force side of the base.

What she saw outside looked like overkill to Lauren. She lost count of the number of Humvees and police cars that swarmed around the 737-800 after it rolled to a stop. Air stairs were rolled out to forward doors on both sides of the cabin. After the flight attendants opened these doors, dozens of armed men in tactical gear flooded inside.

"No need for all this, boys," Lauren whispered with irony. "That *one guy* up front already started *and* finished the job. Nothing left for you to do here."

From the fourteenth row, none of the tactical boys heard what she had said, but the woman sitting next to Lauren laughed out loud. She knew that Lauren was "with" that "one guy," and it was obvious that Lauren was right.

Indeed, the situation was secured. A passenger who had identified himself as a deputy police chief from somewhere had taken charge of the passengers who wanted to help out by sitting on the first two hijackers and stopped them from beating the bandits to death. Lauren showed him where Hammer had kicked the hijackers' weapons, the 3D-printed pistol and the stake, and he showed these to the tactical team.

Within a minute or two, they had gotten the hijackers off the plane, while up front, Hammer was escorted off along with the pilot and copilot and the flight attendant who had been up there helping him with the water pitcher.

When this was done, the situation had melted into a confusing blur. As children wailed and passengers tried to stand, the tactical people in the narrow aisle seemed unsure whether to continue to search the plane or get everyone off. Finally, the latter course, which had seemed obvious to Lauren, was chosen.

After the tac squad had all withdrawn from the crowded plane, the situation was the usual chaotic, every-one-for-themselves scene. Under any circumstance, the process of retrieving luggage from the overhead bins and exiting a jetliner is an example of disorganized mayhem, but today the jumble and tumble was magnified tenfold. To their credit, the tactical people let the tumult take its own course. Like a raging river, the momentum was in one direction—*out*.

The passengers were herded into the Air Mobility Command waiting room, which was a stripped down variation on a civilian airport waiting room, with the same lines of barely comfortable seats, and with a large 515th Air Mobility Wing insignia on the wall instead of an airline logo. This was to be their home for the next several hours.

Lauren parked hers and Hammer's roller bags in the corner, got rid of her bloody number two pencil in the bathroom, and sat down to wait. She had no idea where Hammer had been taken.

Replying to a frantic "Are you all right!?!?" text message, she phoned her mother in Montana.

"Yes, everybody's fine."

"No, they always make it look more dramatic on the TV news."

"Yes, James took care of things and it's all fine."

Yes, "James," as Linda Stahling called Jim Hammer, was always taking care of things. Linda was pleased that her daughter had finally reconnected with that nice boy from high school.

Oh, boy, if she only knew *half* of the adversaries Lauren had seen the "big guy" defeat in the past year since he got out of the Army! Lauren chuckled, asking herself what her mother would have thought about the night that she and James made love in a Virginia field in the raging firelight of a burning business jet full of slave traders that Hammer had just *shot down*!

Hammer was an acquired taste, and one Lauren was immensely pleased to have acquired.

She looked around the room at all the people who owed their lives to this man and phoned his Aunt Charlotte in Montana to let her know that the situation was under control, and that her favorite nephew was behaving himself.

Of course, not all those who owed their lives to Charlotte's nephew were happy about the hours they'd spent in the waiting room. As might have been expected, there was a knot of indignant passengers complaining loudly and demanding that they be released immediately, but this was to no avail.

Eventually coffee and juice boxes were wheeled in, and before the day was through, there would be stacks of pizza boxes.

A small battalion of agents had been dispatched from the FBI Hawai`i Field Office in Kapolei, a half hour west of the air base, and they set up tables in an adjacent room to begin doing witness interviews. When they finally got to Lauren, and she identified herself as the County Assessor of Logan County, Montana, she found them mildly more courteous as that they realized they were speaking with a fellow public servant.

A television set on the wall was already carrying sensational cable news channel reports about the "near-miss hijacking," with "breaking news" headlines about a "Pearl Harbor Attack." The fact that today was a Sunday, just like that *other* Pearl Harbor Attack in 1941, was not lost on those who were writing news copy.

The cell phone videos of Hammer with the hijacker and his torch had already gone viral and these too had been picked up and used repeatedly by the networks.

After a very long time, Hammer himself finally emerged from behind a door on the opposite side of the room. When Lauren crossed the room to greet him, he unreeled his story of what had happened in there.

Initially, they were skeptical, even suspicious, that one man could have done what the copilot and the flight attendant said Hammer had done, so they proceeded to grill him.

However, when they pulled up his DOD files and begin reading through his twenty-year service record, the two young FBI agents began exchanging incredulous glances. It was not so much the five Silver Stars and the three Distinguished Service Crosses and everything else, it was the stories, many of them classified, of what he had accomplished from Afghanistan to South America to Southeast Asia, that had them calling other agents over to gawk at their laptop screens.

As he left the room where they had sequestered him, he noticed they were jostling one another to shake his hand. When the people in the waiting room saw him and recognized him from the cell phone videos on television, there was more than a mere ripple of applause.

The murmured comments going around the room agreed that they and Pearl Harbor really *were* lucky to have had him in the right place at the right time.

He had found this amusing, and Lauren found *that* amusing.

It was after dark when they finally sent over some shuttle buses to take the hundred-and-seventy-some impatient passengers to airport hotels, and Lauren went to work trying to get them on a Monday flight to Kaua`i.

After replaying the chaos of Sunday in her mind, and pushing it *out* of her mind, Lauren stretched her body, smiled, and basked in the tranquility of a Tuesday morning in a place that a lot of advertising copywriters like to call "paradise."

She opened the dark wood wardrobe and took out one of the light cotton sundresses she had hung there last night. She had bought several of these for the trip. They rolled up small and didn't take up much room in her bag. She slipped on her flip-flops, stepped out the back door, took a deep breath of the clear, clean tropical air, and decided to take a walk.

The house was on a gravel road in the midst of a forest of tall trees partially enveloped with vines. There was a scattering of other houses on the road, and by the looks of the cars and pickups parked at them, the people who lived here were locals. With the residue of red-dirt mud on its tire rims, and a scattering of fallen leaves on it, the old silver-gray Ford Taurus they had driven in here last night fit in nicely. When he flew out, Rob always left it parked in a lot near the rental car lots at the Līhu`e airport. He had mailed Hammer the car and house keys.

Arriving here last night in the dark, after what seemed like forever on a narrow rural highway with one-lane bridges, made the place seem all that much farther off the grid. With feral roosters chasing feral chickens through the underbrush, it was the same this morning.

She remembered her first trip to Hawai`i long ago when the early-twenty-something Lauren and her early-twenty-something college friends had come to Waikīkī for surf, sand, throbbing nightlife, and drinks with paper umbrellas—a lot of those. Too many. That seemed a hundred years ago and a million miles from this place.

Heading toward the sound of the ocean, she was pleasantly surprised to discover that it was much closer than she expected. He found herself stepping out of the jungle onto a sandy beach on a broad, crescent-shaped inlet that merged into the sea only a hundred feet away. The sound toward which she had been heading was the surf breaking against a reef about a quarter mile offshore. The waves on the water between her and there were quiet and gentle. She felt like she had walked onto a movie set.

As she crossed the sand, she counted a half dozen other beachcombers on the whole expanse of the inlet, and several people snorkeling. She waded into the water up to her knees and enjoyed the sensation of warmth, which was a contrast with the familiar feel of the glacier-fed lakes in Montana.

She looked down and watched a pair of bright yellow

butterflyfish chasing one another around her legs. She was glad that she had insisted they bring snorkels on this trip.

On the way back to the house, she took a different trail. On the way, she passed through a glade with a most curious aroma. It was sweet and fruity, and as she was trying to figure out what it was when she heard something fall from a tree a short distance from where she stood. She looked up, then down, and realized she was standing under a tall mango tree from which ripe fruit was falling to the ground. Again, she felt like she had walked onto a movie set.

When she came back into the small house, Hammer was standing in the kitchen in his swim trunks making coffee.

"Good morning, island girl," he said with a smile, nodding to the hem of her skirt, which was still wet with seawater. "I see you found the ocean…ready for coffee?"

"I'll trade you," she said, returning the smile and handing him a mango.

"You've been shopping," he said.

"I got these straight from the source," she replied, kissing him on the mouth with mango-flavored lips. "Let's go swimming."

CHAPTER TWO

HAMMER AND STAHLING returned to the beach that she had found, made a vigorous swim nearly out to the coral reef where the waves were crashing and ended up lying on their beach mats soaking up the sun, which was dodging in and out from behind the cumulus that was drifting across the island.

They tried snorkeling and enjoyed swimming through the schools of multicolored fish. These mostly steered away from the humans, often swimming faster than they could in the shallow water that washed over the coral and lava rock outcroppings at the ocean bottom in the bay. However, they discovered one species, an eight-inch, white-faced triggerfish with a black band across most of its body and a distinct yellow and black chevron on both sides, that liked to chase human intruders.

After a couple of hours in the water, the humans abandoned these playmates for dry land, toweled off and decided they were ready for lunch. They had more mangos and some of the pastries that Rob's neighbor had left for them, but they decided they wanted something more substantial.

"We went through that little town last night," Lauren remembered. "It was closed then, but there was a little market there. It's only about a half mile back down the main road. We could walk."

The road was a lot busier in the middle of the day than it had been last night—Rob had warned them about the daytrippers who came up from the resort strip south of Līhu`e—but there was a parallel trail on the ocean side that kept them away from traffic.

As they reached the edge of the little town, their eyes were captured by the sight of a farmers' market in a large meadow across the road on the inland side.

"Let's check this out," Lauren said, taking Hammer by the hand. "This looks interesting."

"It's sure *colorful,* like the fish back there in the water," he said, looking around at the flower stands nearest the entrance to the place. "Look…they got those flower necklaces. I thought they only sold those at the airport, but I didn't see any when we got in."

"They're called leis," she explained impatiently, knowing he knew that, "and we got in pretty late last night."

"You'd look good with one of those," he said. "Want one?"

"How romantic," she said, pecking him on the cheek.

The girl at the nearest stand smiled when she overheard this interaction. For her, it was just another day in paradise with the off-islanders.

"I recognize the plumeria," Lauren said as she leaned over to sniff the girl's flowers. "But what's this one? It smells amazing."

"That's 'cause it's *puakenikeni*…from the perfume flower tree," the girl said in a "take one home" tone of voice.

Hammer opened his wallet as Lauren slipped the delicate flowers over her head.

They moved on, passing the handmade crafts, which interested them only insofar as Hammer wanted to inspect how some model outriggers were made.

At the fruit stands, they both chuckled at the sight of mangos marked with a sign that said "local," and sampled the star fruit, whose slices are a five-pointed yellow star. They bought some mountain apples, a juicy, pear-shaped thing that's the same color as an apple, inside and out.

The last stand in the row was presided over by an older woman with a lined face that looked like that of someone who knew next to everything, but whose eyes sparked and sparkled like those of a teenager. Her wares consisted of baskets of herbs and powders, little dropper bottles, and tiny jars. She even had jars hand-labeled as "herb-infused honey." There were no signs identifying this stuff as "local." With only one glance at her, you *knew* she needed no such sign.

"When I saw you two walking this way," she said with a perceptive smile, "I plucked this little tincture off my top shelf. I call it my 'love potion.' But I'm putting it back."

Lauren looked at her quizzically.

"Your expression asks 'why,'" the woman said cheerfully. "This is something I offer to young couples…we get a lot of honeymooners on this island…and I like to give them a little something to keep them in the mood. But you two? No way. As soon as you got close enough for me to see your eyes and the way you walk together and move together, I knew. You kids don't *need no* love potion. If I was one of those girls who looks at auras and chakras and that sort of thing, I'd say that the aura that encircles the both of you is as bright and as hot as a phosphorous torch. You don't *need no* love potion."

The way she winked when she said "phosphorus torch" struck Lauren as uncanny. She doubted whether this woman would have recognized Hammer from cable news, or that she even *watched* cable news.

"Well then, what *would* you recommend?" Lauren asked, staying on topic.

"I see that you're wearing *puakenikeni,* so you must have good taste...and I can tell you're both straightforward people...no gobbledygook."

Hammer smiled. He liked the way she said "gobbledygook."

"Maybe a tincture of *liliko`i*? You know, passion fruit? It sooths...takes the edge off fretfulness and hurt. I can tell that you have both had some high anxiety lately. I can tell that you're processing it better than most people do, but why not add something that sustains peacefulness and restful sleep?"

"Okay," Lauren said. She was naturally averse to a hard sell, but she found herself mesmerized by the old woman, and like the woman said, "Why not?"

"By the way, my name is Anise," the woman said. "Yes, like the herb, but I've been Anise a lot longer than I was Margaret. My friend who long ago suggested that I 'looked like an Anise' was probably right. I've grown into it."

"I'm Lauren...I've always been Lauren...never Laurie, and this is...Jim."

She knew he preferred to be called by his surname, but in this instance, first names seemed to fit the occasion.

He smiled as he shook Anise's hand.

As Lauren opened her purse to pay for the tincture of *liliko`i,* Hammer picked up a jar of the honey.

"Cacao-ginger," Anise said with a playful smile that belied her age. "It's a naughty intermingling of pungent and basic flavors that are fun for the taste buds and cannot help but promote peacefulness."

It was the phrase "fun for the taste buds" that reeled Hammer into a purchase decision.

As Anise slipped the honey jar into a paper bag, her cheerful expression turned serious.

"One more thing," she said. "And this one is on the house...I can tell that the pair of you have a taste for the type of adventure that invites danger."

The motherly look in her eyes, and the pause in her dialogue asked the question, "Am I not right?"

They looked at one another.

"I can tell that you, Jim, more than Lauren, but *both* of you have encountered...and will continue to encounter... malevolent people. You are magnificent people. I like you very much...but you are people, because of your often reckless affinity for excitement often swim with sharks. You *know* what I mean."

There was no disguising the expressions on their faces.

"I want to give you this," she said, bringing a bag out from beneath her table. "This is an herb that is native only to the mountains of this island. It has grown here since before the first Hawai`ian people came here. Some say the Menehunes planted it. Some say the gods put it here. I won't tell you the name, but I'll give you this bag."

"What...how?" Lauren asked, taken aback.

"You burn it like incense. You burn it around people who are evil...truly and diabolically evil. It will create confusion and bewilderment, impairing, but not eliminating, their will to do harm."

After a long pause, Anise continued.

"It's not to be used impulsively...haphazardly...willy-nilly...or maybe even *ever*. You may go through your entire life without using it. Most people never use it. But I know you are good people who sometimes swim in dark waters, so this may be helpful. How do you know *when*? I believe that *you*...either of you...*will* know."

CHAPTER THREE

"IT LOOKS like grass seed with a few cast-offs from an everything bagel mixed in," Hammer said as he turned the plastic baggie over and over in his hand. "She sure gave us plenty of it."

"Don't mess with it," Lauren admonished. "It's only for serious business and if we're lucky, we'll never have to open that bag."

"I'm just trying to figure out what it is," he said defensively. "But I guess I don't know anything about the high country of this place."

"You soon will," Lauren said happily.

They had spent the hour since their Wednesday morning swim and beach time nibbling bread with cacao-ginger honey and discussing the hike they were planning for Thursday morning along part of the Nāpali Coast and up to Hanakapi`ai Falls. Strenuous for many, this hike was intended by them as a warm-up for their expedition to Lauren's forgotten Menehune waterworks.

They had spent their first day and a half behaving like vacationers, and they were ready for some serious exercise. After their session with Anise on Tuesday, they had bought some chicken sandwiches at the deli inside the little roadside market for lunch. There was no sign reading "local," but the number of hens free-ranging all over town left little to the imagination.

When they got back to the house, they had discussed afternoon naps, but only in the abstract. However, they each tasted a drop of Anise's tincture, and the next thing they knew the sun was coming up on Wednesday. Anise would have been the first to say they "probably needed their rest."

After their morning swim, Lauren had unrolled her 1931 topographical map, the last map that showed the ancient *heiau,* the stone temple at the foot of the valley that Annison Cutts had visited. The paper was old and slightly crispy, and it spelled of age.

"Where did you get this thing?" Hammer asked.

"I'm a county assessor," she said smugly. "I know how to get maps of *anywhere.*"

"Here's the *heiau* that Cutts said was at the base of the canyon with the waterworks," she continued. "See here... that canyon is labeled Hemolele`auwai. I looked it up... an *auwai* is a waterway...you see it on irrigation ditches and flood control ditches. The word '*hemolele*' means perfect or without fault...even *holy.*"

"Sounds like the place," Hammer agreed.

"Now look at these," Lauren continued. "These are copies of maps of the same place from later years. The names of ridges and stream valleys, like Kawaula, Po`opo`oiki and Miloli`i and so on, also show up on the later maps, but Hemolele`auwai is not there anymore."

"It's like they decided it wasn't important any longer," Hammer suggested. "Or they got lazy and decided not to bother to send anybody out to field check the location. You can see by the closeness of the contour lines that it's steep country, and by the lack of trails in this whole area that it's borderline inaccessible."

"That's why I brought you along," she said with a wink.

"I'll take that as a challenge." He laughed. "How do we get there?"

"This highway, number 550, goes up through Waimea Canyon into Kōke`e State Park which is up here on in the mountains at about 4,200 feet. Along the way, there are a lot of turnouts…trailheads for hiking trails. I've looked at it with Google Earth. We can park here at the Miloli`i Ridge Trailhead and walk part of the way on that trail, then cut over to Hemolele`auwai."

"Have you looked at the 'perfect ditch' on Google Earth?"

"You can see it, but it's a deep canyon, so it's always in shadow and you can't really see *into* it."

"That keeps it mysterious," he said with a wink. "What's that other book you were reading? Is that another copy of the Cutts book?"

"Nope, this is even older. This is a fifties reprint of the original 1878 edition of *The Ancient History of the Hawai`ian People*. It's by a Swede named Abraham Fornander. Cutts is practically unknown, but Fornander's name crops up a lot in Hawai`ian history circles and in Hawai`ian ethnography writings. He wrote or contributed to dozens of journals and bulletins and scientific yearbooks."

"Sounds all very academic," Hammer said.

"You might have liked him," Lauren said. "He got shanghaied as crew on a whaling ship, then apparently jumped ship in Hawai`i in the 1840s and got himself hired as a surveyor by a coffee planter on Oahu. He became a pal of King Kamchameha III, who later appointed him as a judge. He lived in the islands for forty years, started a newspaper, and was once the governor of Maui."

"Interesting…" Hammer said thoughtfully.

"He married a woman named Pinao Alanakapu, who was a tribal leader on Molokai, and they had three kids."

"What does Pinao's husband have to say about your secret waterway?"

"There's two related stories," Lauren said paraphrasing from the printed page. "There was a shaman called Aukelenui`a`iku, who traveled to a place where the water of life…it's spelled *ka-wai-ola-loa-a-Kāne*…is kept. *Kāne,* which is pronounced *kah-neh,* is the Hawai`ian word for 'man.' You've seen it on bathroom doors over here next to '*wahine,*' pronounced *wah-heenie,* which is the little girl's room. But *Kāne* is also the name of the god of light and life. Fornander also tells the legend of Ke-alii-waha-nui, the king who conquered the Menehune people. Kāne stepped in to rescue the Menehunes and sent them off to a place called *Ka aina momona a Kane,* which is the 'abundant land of Kane.'"

"Sounds like we're on the right track," Hammer said.

"You betcha."

"Speaking of 'water of life,' I was thinking about the Irish translation of those words," Hammer said with a smile.

"*Uisce beatha,*" Lauren replied with a grin.

"You know your Irish Gaelic."

"Especially when that phrase is the one that the word whisky is derived from!"

"Speaking of which, I noticed an interesting bar in that bigger town about six or seven miles back down the road."

"Hanalei," Lauren said. "That reminds me of that place in the song about 'Puff the Magic Dragon.' I think that's the town where he frolicked...the land called Hanalei?"

"Do you want to go down there? We could have a couple of drinks and probably get dinner somewhere."

"Are you asking me on a date, mister?"

"Not just *any* date...this one will be in the 'land called Hanalei.' Maybe we'll see magic dragons?"

At some point around the midpoint of the twentieth century, when the celebrated drifter and beat poet Jack Kerouac was driving cross-country and scribbling the notes that became his well-remembered book *On the Road,* he stopped into the notorious city of Butte in Montana, the home state of Hammer and Stahling. He wrote that his visit to the infamous M&M "was the end of my quest for an ideal bar."

It was in Hanalei that Hammer and Stahling found their ideal of a Hawai`ian bar.

The place was unassuming in the extreme, but far from being rundown, it was more well-worn, like a comfortable t-shirt you never want to throw away, even though your significant other says you should.

This place checked all the boxes. It was a tiki bar, but not one from the "tiki revival" of the late nineties, or the later revivals a couple of decades later. It had been one in the early fifties, or maybe earlier, long before Elvis first sang "Blue Hawai`i."

There was *lauhala* matting on the walls, but it had the patina of age. It had been there forever and looked it. There were no windows, just large rectangular openings over which *lauhkala*-covered awnings were lowered after closing time. The barstools were all on kitschy "tiki-god" wooden pedestals—but they were each individually hand carved a long, long time ago.

Best of all, the clientele appeared to be mainly locals, and as with any good watering hole, there was a cluster of who appeared to be "regulars" at one end of the bar.

There were tables in the room, but in a place like this, if you want to be *part of the room*, you sit at the bar. They each ordered a beer from under a tap handle with a logo they didn't recognize. Like the mountain apples, the *liliko`i* tincture and the guys at the end of the bar, all the draft beer sold here was local. That fact was all the two adventurous mainlanders needed in the way of introduction. And it was pretty good.

They met a guy who had moved to Kaua`i from Salt Lake City about eight years earlier. He said he was a day trader and could work from anywhere. He'd decided that the North Shore was the best "anywhere" he could find in the world. When he left, they got to talking with a couple from LA who were halfway through two weeks in a nearby Airbnb. They had liked it at first, but the pace was too slow for them.

It started raining, then raining hard. Even though the room was open to the outside, nobody seemed to notice. An hour later, as patrons came and went, Hammer and Stahling gradually became old-timers themselves—at least among the people perched on the hand-carved stools.

When the LA people left, Hammer and Stahling struck up a conversation with the last of the end-of-the-bar crowd, who introduced himself as Virgil. He said he'd been here since the seventies, which he described as being in the slot between the sixties, of which he spoke with reverence, and the "new-agey" nineties. He had the same relaxed sparkle in his eyes as Anise, but they were not nearly as sharp and perceptive. Anise was a very high bar in this department.

"Back then, people came to the North Shore to get away from places all over," Virgil said, sipping his beer. "They come looking for peace or looking for themselves. Up here, there was no connection to anywhere. The phones were all landlines and the lines didn't go most places. You still can't get cell service most places. There were hippie camps up there and around here that lasted for years. Still are. When they talk about the 'end of the road' up at Ke`e Beach, it still really *is* the end of the road. Then you take the trail out along the Nāpali Coast for a couple of days to Kalalau and you're *really* at the end of the world."

"That's what I've heard," Lauren said, urging him to keep unreeling his yarn.

"It's like the Garden of Eden out there...with fruit just dripping off the trees and marijuana growing wild all over the hills. People living out there for months and years at a time without cell phones...electricity...clothes. Some people go into the Kalalau Valley and never come out."

"You could almost say it's a tropical paradise around *here,*" Hammer said, trying not to sound too much like a tourist.

"This is the land called Hanalei," the old guy said with a wink as he finished his beer and wiped the last residue of foam off his long, gray beard before he slipped away into a night washed clean by the brief but furious tropical rainstorm.

The place through the door in the back of the bar made

pizza, so Hammer and Lauren ordered one and ate it in the spot where they'd been sitting. It was pretty good.

When they'd finished, a couple who looked to be slightly younger, maybe early thirties, sat down next to them. They introduced themselves as Rachel and Brandon and said they lived in Kapa`a, the mainly working-class town about twenty-five miles back down the highway—the *only* highway on the north and east sides of the island—toward the airport. She worked for the school district and he was an electrician. They had met at Arizona State, but soon discovered they both were born and raised on Kaua`i.

Rachel and Brandon said they had been on the Nāpali Coast Trail that day and they had the red dirt on their legs to prove it. When Lauren and Hammer explained they were planning to do the hike tomorrow, Rachel suggested they all move to a table where it would be easier to talk.

"Don't try to do it in flip-flops." Rachel laughed, pointing to her own flip-flops. "Our boots are in out the trunk...they're a whole lot too muddy even for in here."

"Yeah," Brandon added. "I'll have to get 'em hosed off before that stuff hardens too much."

"How far are you planning to hike?" Rachel asked. "All the way to Kalalau Valley?"

"No," Lauren said. "That's a rugged eleven miles and we just want a day hike. We're just warming up for some longer hikes up in the mountains above Waimea Canyon...but we're going to hike up to the falls from Hanakapi`ai Beach to add a little distance to our day."

"That's pretty steep," Brandon cautioned. "It's a thousand-foot elevation gain both coming and going to Hanakapi`ai and another seven-sixty to the falls."

"We're from Montana," Hammer said.

"You'll be fine." Brandon laughed. "I bet you'll find the views comparable...*different*, but comparable."

"So I've heard. Can't wait."

"Besides, we heard that you gotta get a day use permit to hike the Nāpali Coast past Hanakapi`ai," Lauren interjected.

"Don't get me started," Rachel said, although it was clear from her tone that this ship had already sailed. "In the past several years, demand to hike that trail has gone off the charts. The Department of Land and Resources doesn't make it easy to get permits. You used to be able to drive right up to the trailhead at Ke`e Beach, leave your car for as long as you wanted and hike as far as you wanted. Now you can't even drive to Ke`e and it's impossible to get a reservation to park in the lot that's *near* Ke`e. You gotta park down here and make reservations for a shuttle bus."

"We're staying about halfway up there, and there's a shuttle stop out there. The guy whose house we're at gave us his park-and-ride shuttle passes."

"Those things are golden," Brandon said. "But get out to the shuttle stop early...like sevenish."

"I've seen the pictures, it seems like the hike will be worth it," Hammer said.

"We live here and we *still* go," Brandon said.

"Do you ever camp up at the Kalalau Valley?" Lauren asked.

"We did once," Rachel said. "It's another world out there. You supposedly need a permit to camp there, but I don't think rangers go out there all that often, or maybe *ever*. I doubt that most of the people living out in Kalalau...and there are people camped full time out there...even know what a permit is."

"This was worth it," Lauren Stahling said, pausing in the still cool Thursday morning air to take a sip from her water bottle.

Hammer just nodded as he moved his sunglasses to his face from their perch on the front of his ball cap.

The Nāpali Coast Trail kicks off with a steep winding climb through the jungle, but eventually you can look through the Hala trees and catch views of the Pacific from hundreds of feet above it.

About an hour into the hike, the line of huge cliffs that lie westward for miles along the Nāpali Coast comes into view. Knife-like ridge after knife-like ridge, each rolling into the crashing surf over three-thousand-foot cliffs and interspersed by deep valleys filled with raging torrents rolling into waterfalls. It was not just like the pictures in the travel brochures, the Montanans were standing in place where they *take* those pictures in the travel brochures.

They had seen only a few people on the red-dirt trail, but they had been among the first on the trail that morning and with their practiced experience, they moved more quickly than most hikers. When they descended into the valley at Hanakapi`ai Beach where the swift-moving, boulder-strewn stream flows into the ocean from the falls, there were a few more people. Many of them looked like they'd camped here last night.

When they had climbed the thousand steps to Hanakapi`ai Falls, they were almost alone again, and they *were* the first to strip down to their swimsuits to plunge into the pool at the bottom.

"It's weird to lie here floating in the water and staring up at a waterfall," Hammer said.

"You couldn't do this in Montana," Lauren replied. "Most days it's freezing."

"That's what you get," Hammer teased before being

splashed for his insolence. They were still unwinding from Sunday's fiasco.

By the time they'd finished their swim, there were quite a few more people around, some of them also jumping into the water.

As they were sitting on the rocks, drying off, an old man wandered by in a deep muttering conversation, apparently with himself.

"Can you feel it?" he asked.

They weren't sure he was talking to them, or someone in his imagination, but then he sat down and looked at them.

Another local character, they thought, though instead of a sparkle in his eye, his twitching expression reminded him of that of the roosters that wandered everywhere back in the more populated area of the island. Before they could ask what it was, they were supposed to have seen, he continued.

"It's the vortex...it's strong out here...can't you feel it?"

He didn't wait for an answer.

"Kaua`i is the most special place on earth...it's got a direct connection to Lemuria, you know."

Lauren looked quizzically at Hammer, who whispered, "Imaginary lost continent."

Their new friend didn't notice.

"The most potent vortex in the world," he continued, "maximum sensations of radiance and power obtainable...you can cure your spirit here...higher dimensions ..."

"Looks more like a swimming hole," Hammer said after the man had wandered off.

"It's kind of in the spirit of what I've been reading about the ancient Hawai`ians," Lauren said. "But it's curious to see the new age crowd grafting their philosophy onto a place that already has its own native mythology. I've noticed this in advertisements for pricey new age retreats that are posted on bulletin boards around in the places we've been."

"Cashing in on the Garden of Eden," Hammer said.

"Or the land called Hanalei," Lauren replied with a chuckle.

"At least the *town* called Hanalei has a good bar," Hammer said as Lauren smiled. She sensed another date night developing.

CHAPTER FOUR

"THERE IT IS," Lauren said as she slid her sunglasses to the top of her head and squinted at the Ocean Breeze Motel.

"It has to be," Hammer deduced. "It's the only place in town."

"And we thought the North Shore was off the beaten path," he said. "This town reminds me of someplace on the highline in Montana or North Dakota. It's not a place where tourists want to linger."

"Right down to the climate," she said. "I looked it up. The west side of Kaua`i gets less than a third of the rainfall as the North Shore."

"What a difference in sixty miles," he said.

After an early start on Thursday, they were in no hurry on Friday. After another leisurely morning at their nearby beach, they made an equally relaxed, two-hour clockwise drive over halfway around the perimeter of the island.

They stopped for lunch at a place that Lauren deemed cute and even stopped for samples at a coffee plantation. She said they were acting like tourists and he realized she was right. With him in an aloha shirt and her in one of her tropical pattern sundresses, they even looked to part. Thanks to the fridge at Rob's place, her *puakenikeni* was still good so she wore that too.

They agreed that the residual anxiety of the hijacking had dissipated. Maybe it was Anise's *liliko`i* tincture or Thursday's hike to the falls, or maybe it was just that they had been through tense times before. They wondered out loud how the other people on the plane were getting on. Narrowly missing the suicide crash of a jetliner was never the best way to begin a Hawai`ian vacation.

Their plan for the day was to position themselves on the far west of the island in order to get a very early start on their hike into the valley of the ancient waterworks on Saturday. Lauren had booked a motel room in Kekaha because it was the closest place to the highway into the mountains—*and* they had vacancies. It was obvious why. Kekaha is not a tourist destination.

"At least they have a promising bar," she said, pointing to a place that called itself Huna's Hideaway. The building was what might be called "fifties modern," with walls of glass blocks flanking the entrance and a neon sign with the name in script lettering.

"Probably the place where the guys from the mill hung out," Hammer said, pointing to the rusting remnants of the long-ago-padlocked Kekaha Sugar Mill.

"Hikers or sailors?" Shirley Ono asked cheerfully as they stepped into the motel's lobby.

"Well…I guess we're in the first category," Lauren said. "We're checking in. Last name is Stahling. I phoned Monday."

"Gotcha right here," Shirley said in a lighthearted way. "Welcome to the Ocean Breeze."

She was an older, well-tanned woman wearing a colorful mu`umu`u and a hospitable smile. "Sorry to catch you off guard. I'm just waiting for some other thing that would bring folks out this far from civilization. Ninety-nine percent of our business comes from people heading up to hike in the canyon, or overflow from the Navy base."

"That would be Barking Sands…the missile range… right?" Hammer asked.

"You bet. Mainly the Navy people stay on base, but sometimes if they've got something going on over there, they run out of room for people coming in for whatever it is and they stay with us. We're less than ten minutes from the main gate."

The room was nothing fancy, but it was cleaner than the average mid-market motel room, and it had a view of the mountains to get them in the mood. Lauren flopped down on the bed and deemed it comfortable.

"I saw that Navy base on the map, but I didn't think much about it," she said. "What kind of ships do they have over there?"

"It's not ships," Hammer said. "It's missiles."

"*Missiles*? What kind of missiles?"

"Anything they want, really. It's a test facility. It's the base for the Pacific Missile Range. They call it the Pacific Missile Range Facility…PMRF. It's only a few square miles on land here, but the range extends for forty or fifty thousand square miles out over the Pacific and a thousand square miles under the ocean for submarine-launched missiles."

"Wow. Not something they share with the average tourist."

"It's not really a secret, but like Shirley said, tourists don't come out this way much unless they're just passing through on their way to the mountains."

"Why do they call it Barking Sands?" Lauren asked.

"I don't know," Hammer said. "I've heard that was

the name of the beach before the sugar company built an airstrip out there. I think it was called that when the Army had it. The Navy calls it PMRF, but everybody I've met who's passed through there just calls it Barking Sands."

The sun was going down when they woke up from their naps, so they got dressed again and went to look for a place for dinner. Shirley recommended a place "down toward the Big Save market." It was good that she gave them directions. The place was just a hole in the wall, but it turned out to have exceptional BBQ pork and rice.

Compared to the rest of the main street, Huna's Hideaway glowed like a Las Vegas casino, with the colored lights inside spilling through the glass block walls. It could not have been more different from the tiki bar in Hanalei, but it matched that place in authenticity. Instead of aging hippies and the well-heeled Airbnb crowd, the clientele was a mix of working-class locals and young people in military haircuts from PMRF.

The jukebox was playing Jawai`ian Reggae, and like all bars in the proximity of military bases, there were a lot of squadron insignias and similar memorabilia on the walls. There were framed photos of missile launches, and of the sugar mill in its glory days.

The place was about half full, but there was room at the bar, so Lauren and Hammer took a seat. There were some tap handles from a place that was known as the "westernmost brewery in the world." They did a quick calculation of what places there were between Kaua`i and the international dateline and ordered a couple of pints of "the last beer before tomorrow."

"I got a question," Lauren said when the man delivered the pints.

"Shoot," he said.

"You probably get asked this a lot...but they say, 'when in doubt, ask the bartender'...why do they call that place out there Barking Sands?"

"I've heard that that's the sound that the sound made that the sand makes when you walk on it."

"Have you walked on it?"

"Yeah," he said. "But there's better beaches around here, and Barking Sands has a powerful riptide."

"You wanna know the *real* story?"

Everyone turned. A woman sitting a couple of seats down from Lauren had plowed into the conversation.

"What's the real story, Rhonda?" the bartender asked impatiently.

"There was an old fisherman...this was a long time ago before your time or mine...and he lived out there," Rhonda explained. She was a woman in her late forties, still attractive despite having had too much sun through the years. "This guy, y'know, he had nine dogs. Anybody you ask will tell you he had *nine* and no other number. When he went out in his outrigger to fish, he tied up the dogs and they barked all day. Because the wind carries to sound, you couldn't always see where barking was coming from, so people thought it was the sand that was barking."

"You know you're in a pretty laid-back place when the big debate is what makes the sand bark," Lauren said with a smile.

"As Jimmy Buffett might have said...'wastin' away again in Kekaha Town, searchin' for my noisy shaker of sand,'" Hammer hummed. "Some people claim..."

"There's a woman to blame," Lauren said, picking up the train of Buffett's lyrics, "But it could be *your* fault."

This broke the ice. Even Rhonda and the bartender were laughing and humming along.

"And now it's a missile base," Lauren mused.

"Time was, I didn't pay much attention to all that Navy stuff out here on this end of the island," Rhonda admitted. "But I do get some customers at my jewelry shop from the base, and I have come around to believing that they do have a purpose."

"What happened to soften your outlook?" the bartender asked.

"Well, I'll tell you," the shopkeeper replied in a deliberate manner, sipping that frozen concoction that helped aid her practiced storytelling. "It was way back in 2018… January. You were here then. You remember that. It was Saturday the thirteenth. Trouble always finds me on Saturday the thirteenth, never a Friday the thirteenth."

"It scared everybody in the state," the bartender said, nodding in agreement. "Everybody's cell phone in the whole state started beepin' and chirpin.' I'll never forget how freaked out I was."

"What happened was…" Rhonda said as she watched Hammer and Lauren twisting their heads back and forth to follow the conversation. "What happened was that everybody in the whole state got this emergency alert telling 'em that a nuclear missile was headed for Hawai`i and this was 'not a drill.' What it *was like* was a scene from a bad movie."

"For months, the news had been full of all these stories about North Korea and their nukes and missiles, and their nut-case leader," the bartender said. "We figured that this was it. The end. Lights out!"

"Everybody was coming unglued," Rhonda continued, energized by the recall of an exciting story. "It turned out that somebody pushed a wrong button somewhere but it took an hour or so for them to let us know it was a false alarm. People were running all over looking for a place to hide."

"You know, Kaua`i is the closest place it Hawai`i to North Korea," the bartender interjected. "We figured if that whack job over there wanted to hit somebody, Kaua`i would be the easiest."

"So now you know why I learned to like the Navy base?" Rhonda said. "I'll tell you why. They got missiles out there that can *shoot down* missiles. Did you know that?"

"So I've heard," Hammer said.

"They do," Rhonda said. "We see 'em shoot those things off every so often. If they can protect me from that crazy guy's missiles, I'm happy they're there. Ever since that Saturday the thirteenth."

"Then just last week, those guys hijacked that airliner over Pearl Harbor," the bartender interjected, looking at Hammer and Lauren. "Did you guys hear about *that*?"

"Yes, we did," Lauren said. "That could have been really bad too. Good that it wasn't."

"What's the world coming to?" Rhonda asked rhetorically, indicating to the bartender that she was ready for another margarita.

At a table across the room, unnoticed by Hammer or Lauren or Rhonda, three men were deep in conversation. Among them, Master Chief Petty Officer Anthony Karboli was definitely the most ill at ease. This was unfamiliar ground for a senior enlisted US Navy Master-at-Arms, or security man. Karboli was used to being the one in control of any situation. He was among those at the top of the enlisted food chain at PMRF. He not only had three stripes and a rocker on his sleeve, but as an MA, he carried a *badge*.

Karboli was a cop. A federal cop. A *tough* federal cop. He was not used to being the one at the interrogation table doing the sweating, but to paraphrase Jimmy Buffett's lyrics, the fault lay entirely on *his* shoulders.

One might be tempted to continue the analogy and add that there was also "a woman to blame," except in this case, he was being told by the other two that the female involved was just *seventeen* and legally still a child.

"This is really, really bad, Master Chief Tony," Han jong-sok said with a tone of exaggerated false sincerity as he let Karboli stare at the photo of himself in a very naughty and compromising bedroom encounter with a young blond in a very revealing dress. She had assured him when she was twenty-one and he had believed her. Even in the picture, she *looked* twenty-one, although Karboli had neglected to do an ID check.

If she *was* underage, Karboli was looking at serious Navy disciplinary action, and maybe even Kauai County criminal charges. If anyone decided to get nasty, it could be a dishonorable discharge, but Karboli had too many friends in high places for that.

"It would be a shame if..." Han said provocatively, as Cho ho-jin, his loyal factotum, and a man of few words, just smirked.

"Screw you, Han," Karboli growled. "What do I have to do to make this crap all go away?"

"Thank you for asking," Han said. "As it happens, we could really use your professional help. Our company is doing a little research work in the outback of this island, and we'd like to be able to call you if we are stopped to be questioned by the local police."

"What kind of 'research work' are you talking about?

Why would a sugarcane company like yours get into trouble with the police?"

"You just never know. We would hate to have our progress in developing a sugar-growing model compromised."

"Compromised by *what*?" Karboli asked. "What are you concerned about specifically?"

"In business, one must always prepare contingencies against the unforeseen," Han said cryptically. "I would really like you and your federal badge on *our* side."

Karboli cursed the day he met this group of Korean businesspeople—there were three men and a woman. They were with a company called Sweet Harvest out of Seoul. They were in Kaua`i, they said, researching the growing of small-batch sugarcane for small-batch rum. How sweet, he thought.

It had been that night at the private card club at the Royal Pacific, that exclusive new five-star resort on the South Shore. Karboli liked his cards and thought of himself as one of the most astute poker players on the island. When Han and Cho had invited him to sit down with them, he was feeling pretty cocky.

It was getting late, but he decided he'd clean them out real quick and go home. However, as they say about the best laid plans, things started to go wrong. Was he making stupid mistakes, or were they really that good?

He was just one hand away from an empty wallet when his luck turned. He won that hand and then the next. It was then that he started to realize they were carefully and subtly *letting him* win back his losses. He decided to fold and call it a night. Weirdly, they parted on good terms, with Han and Cho behaving as if they had met a new friend.

They crossed paths at the club again and even sat down once for a couple of hands. Then there was that fiasco one week ago. It was a few days before that failed attack on Pearl Harbor that put everybody on edge. The Royal Pacific was hosting a meet-and-greet and lavish dinner for local movers and shakers to mingle with the top brass from PMRF.

As a senior enlisted man, Karboli was on the guest list, and who should he find tapping him on the shoulder during the black-tie cocktail soiree, but Han jong-sok. Somehow, through somebody he had met, the Korean rum-maker had gotten onto the guest list. They started talking, but this time, it was not cards on Han's mind, nor in Han's hotel suite, but *girls*. Would Tony like to "meet" one?

"I really don't think I can make any promises, Han," Karboli said at last, mustering his confidence. "I don't think I can promise to compromise the integrity of the PMRF security establishment to help you out of hypothetical scrapes with the police."

The man who had bested him at the poker table two weeks ago and who tricked him a week ago with this woman, was threatening to *extort* him. What if that girl really was twenty-one? She *looked* twenty-one. She certainly *acted* like she was older than seventeen. Karboli decided to call Han's bluff.

"Oh Chief Tony," Han said in a mocking, pleading way, "I thought we were friends."

Han placed his phone, now displaying a video of a nude Karboli with the same woman, now no longer clothed, on the table in front of Karboli. The petty officer watched as the video depicted them entangling themselves with one another and doing what unclothed couples often do.

"Okay," Karboli said after a minute as he pushed the phone away. "I see it, but there's no way she's seventeen. *No way.*"

"Cho, do we have that other picture?" Han asked his associate.

Cho took out his phone, thumbed it for a few moments, found what he was looking for, zoomed in and placed his phone alongside Han's.

Karboli studied the image, which showed a close-up of a young, smiling woman—the *same* young, smiling woman.

"*Now*...zoom out," Han told Cho.

As he did so, the full image that appeared was of a young woman in a formal dress standing next to an older man in a uniform—that of a naval officer.

"Tony, this is a picture of Lynsee...did she even tell you her name? We *know* that she neglected to tell you her correct age?"

They could tell by the look on Karboli's face that her age had not come up in their conversation.

"Did she tell you the name of her daddy?"

Karboli couldn't believe what he was seeing. He recognized the man in the uniform as Vice Admiral Hardgrove Kinkaide, the COMABMPAC, the Commander of Naval Anti-Ballistic Missile Operations in the entire Pacific. His headquarters were currently at PMRF ahead of classified live-fire tests of a key component in the US Navy's Aegis Ballistic Missile Defense System. Very serious stuff. Nuclear war defense serious.

"Daddy's here on business and he brought his family with him to Kaua`i," Han said, almost cooing. "Wasn't that nice of him? Sun and fun? Too bad he's too busy to keep an eye on the trouble that little Lynsee is getting herself into."

Hardgrove Kinkaide!

Karboli felt a lump in his throat as big and as deadly as an Aegis warhead.

Hardgrove Kinkaide's nickname said it all. He was simply called "Hard." He was the hardest, strictest, most inflexible, most demanding admiral in the Pacific. As an officer, he made officers like George Patton or Curtis LeMay or William Tecumseh Sherman seem as cuddly as kittens.

A few minutes ago, Karboli had been weighing the likelihood of avoiding a dishonorable discharge. Now he was looking at the certainty of decades behind bars in a place where child abusers don't fare very well.

He was a cop; he knew the statutes. He knew that Article 120 of the Uniform Code of Military Justice offered little mercy to anyone convicted of the sexual assault of a child. He knew that with Hard Kinkaide's thumb on the scales, there would be *no* mercy.

Karboli glanced across at Han jong-sok.

He was smiling beatifically in a way that confidently communicated the idea of "checkmate."

CHAPTER FIVE

WORDS FAILED them as they emerged from the dense koa-tree forest and looked out across a vast open panorama.

If there is anything more visually magnificent than a tropical sunset, it is a tropical sunrise. It washes into the cool, deep indigo blueness of night, causing the retreating stars to seem to sparkle with its fire as it chases them away, one by one.

Lauren and Hammer were hiking north by northwest, and the sun was coming up over their right shoulders, but they didn't bother to look, the scene ahead of them was so visually spectacular that they could not turn away.

The colors were rapidly changing as the brilliant orange-gold light gradually crept down the jungled cliffs, with the scene framed against the deep sapphire of a limitless ocean beneath a limitless sky.

"It never gets old," Hammer said. They were used to scenes like this in Montana, with vast snowfields instead of an ocean.

They had been awake in Saturday's wee hours and

had driven up through Waimea Canyon on Highway 550, the only car on the only paved road leading all the way up into these mountains. They started their hike on the Miloli`i Ridge Trail in the dark, knowing from their map that it started out as a wide vehicle track that was easily navigated with the headlights they clipped to the brims of their caps.

A short distance into their hike few miles into the hike, they discovered that the wider track had been washed out, turning the trail into a mere foot trail, but the sky was starting to get light, and they could easily see their way. They had descended a thousand feet from the road but were still nearly three thousand feet above the ocean.

With the Nāpali Coast spreading out before them, Lauren pulled her topo map from of her backpack and oriented it to the scene ahead. Several miles off to the left on Makaha Ridge they could see the antennae and blinking red lights of the remote PMRF instrumentation facility, about fifteen miles as the shearwater flies north of the base itself.

Between Makaha Ridge and the Kalalau Valley, a dozen or so miles around the coastline, was a vast and rugged wilderness area. In all that vastness, there was almost no level spot, only a kaleidoscope of steepness. As they had seen on their hike on Thursday from the side, and now saw from above and behind, the Nāpali Coast is a series of knife-like ridges interspersed by deep valleys.

As Lauren had shown Hammer, all the names on those to the ridges and valleys to their left and their right were named on both the 1931 topo map and the modern map—except Hemolele`auwai, the "Perfect Waterway" of Annison Cutts. The contour lines were there, but not the name. In the distance to their right, Lauren could almost see it.

This wilderness ahead was bisected by only a handful of human trails, but there were also animal trails, created and used mainly by the wild goats who populate the Kaua`i outback. Lauren and Hammer often used animal trails in the Montana mountains, especially during hunting season, so these were a familiar feature.

Using a satellite photo app that Hammer had left over from his special forces days—like Google Earth, but far more detailed—they had already penciled in their route from Miloli`i Ridge to the mysterious valley of Hemolele`auwai.

It was a perfect day for a walk in the woods. The place exploded with the sounds of birds, a cacophony of calls and warbles that serenaded hikers. They crossed a ridge called Pokuakini, descended into the valley of the same name and climbed another ridge under the watchful eye of a small group of goats. They were smaller than the goats of the Rockies but were likewise adept at navigating steep terrain.

"According to your map, your valley is just past this ridge," Hammer said, pausing to take a sip from his water bottle. "Are you excited?"

"Yup," she said, taking the bottle as he handed it to her.

He had deliberately stopped a little way down from the crest of the ridge, because he guessed that when she saw the valley beyond, she would be unstoppable. He was right. She paused only to look once at her map, as though to confirm that she had finally found the land of her El Dorado.

It was a deep valley, but not wide, more like a narrow canyon. The stream running through the valley was mainly obscured by vegetation, such as large-leaved vines and the native Hala trees that grow everywhere on Kaua`i, but they could hear it gurgling. Because of the narrowness of the valley and the steepness of the sides, they were in shadow. This was why no detail in the valley was visible in satellite imagery, even with Hammer's fancy app.

He followed her as she followed the valley, picking her way downstream through the jungle, about six yards from the stream. She moved carefully but purposely, studying every detail of the terrain, looking for something that would tell her she had arrived.

After about ten minutes, she stopped, stood up straight and cocked her head.

"Hear that?" Lauren asked cautiously.

He stopped and listened. Birds. Stream. Lauren's heart rate climbing?

"Hear that? It's the stream. It's not the sound of a wild stream anymore, there's a rhythm to it. Hear that? *Whish, whoosh…whish, whoosh…whish, whoosh…*"

He heard what she was talking about, but it did not sound distinctly rhythmic to him.

Without waiting for further comment from him, she pressed forward quickly, so quickly that he almost lost sight of her red tank top in the jungle ahead.

Moments later, he caught up with her. Again, she had come to a stop, this time she was staring down the course of the water.

"Hemolele`auwai," she said elatedly as he stood at her side.

Looking down at what she was seeing, it took him a moment to process it.

A few feet ahead of where they stood, the stream was flowing into a circular basin whose diameter was a little greater than the length of a large bathtub. It was made of hewn and fitted black lava rocks, clearly constructed by human hands. The stream poured into this basin to a depth of about three feet, then exited through an opening about a foot wide near the far rim of the basin.

Carefully, they made their way around the basin to see where the water went from there. If the sight of the basin, high up in the mountains so far from anywhere that humans normally walked, was astonishing, what they next saw was inconceivable.

The water entered a fitted stone trough about two feet wide, descended for around fifteen feet and entered another basin, just like the first. Then, there was another trough and another basin below, and then another and another.

As Lauren snapped pictures with her phone, they counted nine troughs before the succession of basins and troughs was obscured by the dense foliage. The stonework was moss-covered and heavy-worn by years of water running through it, but it was surprisingly precise, and surprisingly intact.

"It seems to be in good shape for something this old," Hammer said in amazement. "How old do you suppose it is?"

"It was ancient when Cutts saw in the 1880s," Lauren said. "Archaeologists claim that the stone *heiau*s on this island date back eight or nine hundred years…so that's a guess."

"Unless it was the Menehunes who built it," Hammer suggested with a smile.

"Then it's a *lot* older," Lauren said, playing along, "but who's counting?"

With both of them sharing the triumphant mood, they enthusiastically followed the Hemolele`auwai water course down the slope and through the jungle.

They had just counted the sixteenth basin, when the sound of the water began to grow significantly louder. As they went, it became clear that somewhere up ahead through the jungle, there was a roaring waterfall. Having learned from experience to be wary of unseen waterfalls, they slowed their pace.

Suddenly, as Lauren worked her way through the leaves of a mokihana tree, she felt the stones beneath her feet *slide out* from beneath her feet!

For a split second, she beheld the waterfall—a raging, spitting, crashing, white column that descended downward hundreds of feet.

She felt herself floating, flailing in space, helplessly hovering over a void.

Just as suddenly, she felt her left wrist clamped in a vise, the same vise that had been felt by hijackers over Pearl Harbor six days ago.

Above her, Hammer had not lost his footing, and his left hand gripped a branch of the mokihana tree. As she looked upward, she saw him carefully lifting the weight of her body with his right hand.

Slowly, but without stopping, she felt herself inching upward.

As in all situations like this, it seemed like an eternity, but at last, she was able to grab another mokihana limb with her own free hand.

Another eternity ensued before she felt him placing her feet on solid ground.

"Don't let go," she whispered.

He just nodded. He could tell she was a little wobbly.

It was another eternity before she was able to stand, and at this point, they both began moving at a deliberate pace back up the way they had come.

When they had reached back up to the seventh or eighth basin, she stopped.

Breathing an exaggerated sigh of relief that she'd obviously been holding in, she dropped her backpack and pulled Hammer into what a romance writer might describe with phrases such as "passionate embrace."

After yet another eternity, this one recapturing the triumphant mood of earlier, Lauren announced she was "hot and sweaty," as she removed her hiking boots and began peeling off her clothes. Her two-piece swimsuit was the last onto the pile.

She glanced at him with a subtly provocative smile as she stepped into the nearby basin. She did not have to invite him twice.

While the previous eternities might actually have been measured in seconds or minutes, this next one took a good deal longer. A lot longer.

It ended with them reclining in the cool, but not cold, water, bodies intertwined and looking up at the jungle and jumble of mokihana leaves that arched above the water course.

"Do you suppose that the Menehunes had this in mind when they built this thing?" Hammer asked.

"I'd like to think they thought about this," she replied with a smile, kissing him on his lips. "But I have no idea what it's actually for. Somehow, though, I don't think we're the first to use it for this. It's just the right size."

It was a very long time before either of them moved from this spot, but at last Lauren got to her feet. He was always captivated, even mesmerized, by the sight of her perfectly proportioned body in motion. To him, she looked like one of those marble statues of the perfect female form that you see in fountains all across Europe—but much more graceful. And much warmer to the touch. When he said something to this effect, she splashed him playfully.

He was in the midst of fashioning a witty retort when he saw her face suddenly take on an expression of horror.

"Oh...my..." she gasped, looking at something above and behind him.

Imagining a predator encroaching upon their idyll, he turned quickly to confront it. What he saw was as much of a shock as it had been for her. Staring at them from about five feet above and behind was a human skull.

"Look at what's been watching us," she said as she regained her composure. "Or rather *who*."

"This thing really breaks the mood," he commented.

With the mood thus broken, they both got dressed before they approached the skull for closer examination.

Without touching it, he stepped in for a close look. After twenty years of special operations and combat actions all over the world, this was not new for Hammer, but it was definitely not something one sees every day.

"It's not fresh," he observed. "It's been here for a long time. At least thirty years...maybe fifty."

"You're not gonna believe this," Lauren said. She was crouching at a spot uphill on the opposite side of the watercourse. As he watched, she brushed some fallen leaves from a thing on the ground over there—a *second skull.*

"And what do they have in common?" Hammer asked rhetorically.

Lauren just nodded. They each had a hole squarely in the middle of the forehead.

Neither of them said "bullet hole," but this was obvious.

"Well," he said, almost reluctantly. "Let's take a look around and see if we can figure out what might have happened."

"*Fifty* years ago?" Lauren interjected.

"The wild pigs have probably scattered the bones... even maybe *ate* the smaller ones...but there might be something."

Because it was afternoon, and they wanted to get out of this canyon to find a level camping spot before dark, they gave themselves ten minutes to look around but took a little longer.

"I guess we'll have to report this," Lauren said.

"No doubt," Hammer said. "This place is, as they say on the TV cop shows, a 'crime scene.'"

They found the two lower jaws near, but no longer connected to, the skulls, so Hammer decided to take these to the county medical examiner for identification. There were teeth for dental records and cartilage that might yield DNA.

Taking pictures of the skulls and other artifacts, they walked back and forth over a wide area that had been ruffled and rifled by pigs and water for decades. Their grisly discoveries included a not-yet-disintegrated ribcage, and a human pelvis that Lauren was sure belonged to a woman. Their not-so-grisly findings included fragments of a canvas coat with metal buttons attached, which Hammer identified as originating with the US Army.

She knew that he'd been through this before with battle deaths, often those of people he knew, and she hoped that the anonymity of age would make this time easier.

An hour later, they found a level, dry place to camp on a shoulder of Pokuakini Ridge just as the sun was about to sink into the Pacific. The colors and the shapes of the cumulus that drifted across the sky invited them to stare transfixed for a little while before they rolled out their sleeping mats and Hammer set up his little thirteen-ounce Jetboil stove with its built-in cooking pot.

After a dinner of freeze-dried macaroni and meat sauce, they lay down to enjoy the explosion of stars that spread across the sky. They picked out a few familiar constellations and commented on how different they looked twenty-six degrees closer to the equator than their usual haunts.

"I'd say this was an exciting day," Hammer said at last.

"One that I'll never forget," she said, wrapping her arms around him. "Traveling with you is *never* monotonous."

"I was just about to say the same thing about you," he replied as she rolled over and sat up to look at him in the starlight.

Once again, as earlier in the pool, he watched as her gaze was distracted.

"What's that?" Lauren said, pointing into the distance.

"Not again," he said with mock despair as he rolled over to look where she was pointing.

"That's the lights of the PMRF outpost on Makaha Ridge," he said. "We saw that this morning, it's five or six miles away."

"Not that," she said impatiently. "I'm talking about *that.*"

He rose to his knees and looked more carefully at where she was pointing.

"There, on that spur of this ridge we're on," she said. "About a mile or so closer to the ocean."

He could make out a very, very faint pinprick of red light.

"What *is* that?"

"I don't know," he said, reaching into his backpack for his powerful Oberwerk 10x42 HD II binoculars. He handed them to her.

"Wow, this gets you close," she said. "I always forget how good these are. Okay, I see three distinct red lights. Small red lights, like you see on cable boxes and that kind of thing. There's a fourth light that's going in and out, like it's behind a bush that'd moving slightly in the breeze."

"Anything else?"

"It's too dark," she said, straining to see. "Even with a zillion stars, there's not enough ambient light to make out anything. What do you think it is?"

"It's too far out to be a cell tower," he postulated. "My guess it's some kind of gadget that PMRF has stuck out there. Maybe we should go check it out in the light of day tomorrow?"

Morning comes at first light when you're camping under the stars, especially in places where the birds are early risers. Nevertheless, as she often did, Lauren Stahling pulled her lightweight sleep sack over her head until she smelled the coffee that Hammer had cooked up on his Jetboil.

They'd finished their breakfast and had packed up before the morning sun crested the mountains to the northeast. With his binoculars, Hammer was studying the location, far down Pokuakini Ridge, where they'd seen the red lights last night and reported that he could see "something…but mostly trees."

In the first rays of the morning sun, any chance of distinguishing faint red lights was washed away.

Following the goat trails to avoid wallowing in brush, it took them a little over a half hour to reach the place. Had they not known something was there, it would have been easy to miss. There was a large, low canopy tent whose camouflage pattern had been picked to closely match the low trees and bushes into which it was crowded. The whole thing blended together fairly seamlessly. Hammer gave the owners a "B plus" for obfuscation, but Lauren knew he was being strict.

From the air, it was effectively invisible to the tourist helicopters that cruised the Nāpali coastline, even if they came this close to the PMRF site, which they were not allowed to do. From the ground, it was perched at the crest of a two-thousand-foot cliff, so it was unlikely that anyone would be casually walking past.

The sides were open, and the red lights could be seen on a number of black consoles that lurked in the darkness. Power was drawn from solar panels that were even better camouflaged than the tent. Because they had missed these at first glance, Lauren gave them an "A" for this but didn't share her grading scheme with her companion.

"What is all this stuff?" Lauren asked as they entered the tent and looked around. There were two dozen pieces of equipment and a like number of red lights, with a few green ones mixed in. She was an admitted techno-peasant —at work she had a geek who took care of this stuff—and she looked to Hammer as an interpreter.

"Is this some kind of spying operation?" Lauren suggested. "The Navy is nearby."

"I don't see any surveillance gear, like I'd expect at an espionage setup," he said. "I see tracking hardware, jammers..."

"Where is Tim Tommis when you need him?" Lauren quipped. She had met Tommis, the communications man from Hammer's old special forces team, who had reinvented himself as a tech wizard so far beyond the charts that half of what he did seemed to mere mortals like black magic.

"Tommis is at the other end of the email with the pictures I'm about to take," Hammer said. "The email that gets sent as soon as I get back to someplace with a semblance of internet connection."

"Too bad you couldn't use the internet connection of this place," she said facetiously. She knew that the last thing they'd want to do is leave their electronic fingerprint in this place.

"They never bothered to give me their password," he replied, equally facetiously.

"Are you seeing what I'm seeing?" she asked as she leaned close to study the gear.

"Yup," he said. "Most of this stuff is Russian."

"Right," she agreed. "And a lot of what I'm seeing in these manuals is in *Korean*."

They looked at one another. Their minds went back to their conversation with Rhonda and the bartender about incoming North Korean missiles. On their lips was the not-so-rhetorical question, "*Who* is Russia's best friend on the Korean Peninsula?"

CHAPTER SIX

IT WAS SUNDAY, and Dr. Kimberly Graihr really should not have been at work. However, Sundays were generally slow days for routine business, and a good time to wade through a backlog of paperwork, and an excuse to take next Thursday off to go surfing on the North Shore with her boyfriend.

Next door on the main highway through Līhu`e, at the Wilcox Medical Center, Kaua`i's largest hospital, it was twenty-four-seven, but the patients here at the Kaua`i County Medical Examiner's Office were in less of a rush.

The medical examiner was surprised when her land-line rang. It was reception.

"Dr. Graihr, this is the front desk, I have someone to see you."

"I'm not expecting anyone. Tell them the office is closed. They can come back on Monday morning."

"They're insisting."

"Did you tell them that I was here?"

"Yes…you *are* here."

"Please tell them to come back on Monday morning."

"They're insisting…and they have body parts."

That got the doctor's attention.

"I'll be right out."

The couple in the lobby, wearing shorts, flip-flops and a patina of trail dust, looked like fugitives from the Nāpali Coast—unwashed and unkempt, like they had just walked off a mountain trail, but there was a cool confidence to their bearing and a sharpness in their eyes.

"I'm Dr. Kimberly Graihr," she said, extending her hand, first to the woman. "I'm the Kaua`i County Medical Examiner. We're closed today, but I'm told that you have…um…body parts?"

"I'm Lauren Stahling," the woman said, producing her picture ID from her purse. "I'm the County Assessor of Logan County, Montana. The gentleman is Captain James Hammer, US Army Special Forces…"

"Retired," Hammer added, smiling as he shook the doctor's hand.

"I see," Dr. Graihr said as she tried to square their disheveled appearance with who they actually were. "Now…about those…body parts?"

"Is there a place where we could sit down?" Lauren asked.

They were shown through the nearby double glass doors, down a hallway and into a conference room.

"Let me start with the backstory," Lauren said, remaining on her feet. She knew how to take charge of a meeting in the world of civic bureaucracy. "We were hiking yesterday up in Nāpali Forest Reserve, specifically in the vicinity of the Miloli`i Ridge Trail."

The doctor nodded. She had lived on the island for fifteen years. She knew where that was. She was a woman about Lauren's age, with shortish strawberry-blond hair and the build of someone who surfed for fun and to stay in shape, not that of someone who surfed every day.

"We were in a ravine near that trail when encountered two sets of human remains."

"What were you doing in that ravine?"

"Enjoying one another's company," Hammer interjected with a deadpan expression, winking at Lauren.

"Like he said," she replied, laughing as she winked back. "Initially, we were surprised to discover two human skulls. We surveyed the scene and found other items, all of which I photographed and I have the pictures that I can show you and email to you."

"Was there any indication of cause of death?" Dr. Graihr asked.

"As you'll see in Ms. Stahling's pictures, there was a bullet hole in the center of the forehead of both skulls," Hammer replied. "I'd guess a .45."

"Are you sure?"

"Based on my experience…from my line of work… *former* line of work."

"He's retired," Lauren interjected with a smile and another wink. The doctor noted the playfulness between them.

"And the body parts?" Dr. Graihr asked.

"Yes, ma'am," Hammer continued. "We tried to leave the presumptive crime scene intact, and not to touch anything, but I retrieved both lower jaws, which had become disconnected from the rest of the skulls."

At this point he reached into a paper bag he was carrying and produced the bones, each in a separate ziplock bag.

"I thought they'd be useful for identification with dental records, or with DNA through the dried cartilage that you can see here and here," Hammer explained. "In my former line of work I've seen this done successfully, but admittedly with samples that are a lot newer. These are quite old. I'm guessing fifty years or more, but this part is *your* line of work. And no…we did not touch these with our fingers, so you won't find our DNA."

"Plan on wild pig DNA, though," Lauren interjected.

The doctor was pleased, and even amazed, by their apparent professionalism, but she knew this was not the Army captain's first rodeo.

"Well," Dr. Graihr said, staring at the baggies. "I'll admit that this is not how I'd planned to spend my Saturday afternoon."

"We're sorry to do this to you," Lauren said. "This sure is not how *we* were planning to spend our vacation here on your island, either…but we thought you should be the first to know what we found."

"Thank you," the doctor said. "I guess you've come to the right place, especially considering the age of the remains…which I agree are at least fifty years old and quite possibly older. It's hard to tell. Obviously, they've been exposed to a lot of weathering and other degradation. But moving on, I think that to close the loop, the police should be included in the conversation. Would you mind if I call—?"

"Not at all," Lauren interrupted. "Go ahead. We'll wait."

"Kaua`i Police Department," a woman's voice answered when the doctor dialed out on the conference room landline. The phone was on speaker and the doctor left it that way.

"Kai, it sounds like you're working today too."

"Yeah Kim, my lucky week to spend my Sunday on the major crimes desk. What's up?"

"Well, this is going to sound strange, but I have a couple of hikers who just walked in with some human remains. I think you might want to pop over and take a look."

"What? What kind of remains?"

"They have two sets of mandibles...fifty-year-old human jawbones."

"The jawbones of a fifty-year-old?"

"No, the bones themselves have been on the ground up in the mountains for at least this long," the doctor explained. "It's definitely a cold case...*very cold*."

"I'm on my way."

"That won't take long," the doctor said, almost apologetically. "This is a small county and an even smaller county seat. All the county offices are five or ten minutes apart. The police station is just this side of the airport."

"Sounds like *my* county seat," Lauren said, smiling a county official to county official smile. "Obsidian has almost exactly the same population as Līhu`e. All of our offices are five minutes apart too...but we don't have a commercial airport."

Detective Kai Nialani walked into the room about twelve minutes later. She was dressed in blue, with sergeant's shoulder stripes and a badge, a tactical belt on her hip and a Glock 19 in her holster. She looked a little younger than Lauren and her hair was tied back in a tight bun.

"Detective Nialani," the doctor said, speaking more formally than the first-name basis she had used earlier on the phone. "This is Lauren Stahling, she's the Assessor of Logan County, Montana...and Captain Hammer, who's retired from US Army Special Forces."

She shook their hands perfunctorily, conveying the reserved feel of someone who worked hard to be taken seriously.

"Now, what's this about the jawbone?" Kai asked, getting to the point of that for which she'd dropped everything.

Lauren and Hammer repeated everything they had told Dr. Graihr as Detective Nialani scrutinized the bagged bones. They showed her the pictures they'd taken of the two skulls with the suspicious bullet holes, and of the coat with metal buttons attached that Hammer identified as an Army uniform.

"We'll have to send these over to the state crime lab in Honolulu," Kai said. "Our crime lab doesn't have the means for this sort of DNA testing. HPD's Scientific Investigation Section is the only full-service forensic testing lab in Hawai`i that's accredited by the National Standards Institute, so we'll put it in their hands."

"Sounds like it'll be in good hands," Hammer said.

"We'll get this out to them right away," Kai said. "We're actually sending them some ballistics samples on the late flight this afternoon...things I want in their laps first thing Monday morning...so I'll stick these in the same package. I'm sure this case will pique their interest."

"Do you have any fifty-year-old cold cases involving missing persons up in that area?" Dr. Graihr asked.

"I'd have to check the files," Kai said. "There have been a lot of missing persons through the years...especially up in the Kalalau Valley. Some people who later show up telling about how they dropped out and never wanted to be found. I can't think of any with an Army connection...especially when you add in what looks like a homicide."

Kai asked for contact information, and Lauren handed the detective her business card, pointing out her cell phone number. She gave one to Dr. Graihr as well.

"We'll let you know what we find," the medical examiner promised in a cheerful voice.

"We'd be curious," Lauren said with a smile.

After a cordial round of handshakes, the two mainlanders were back in their borrowed car and headed into the rest of their interrupted vacation.

CHAPTER SEVEN

"I SAW your note about the human bones," KPD Lieutenant Richard Faralaco said, poking his head into Detective Kai Nialani's office mid-morning on Monday. "So you got 'em off to the lab in Honolulu already. Tat's good work."

"Thank you, Lieutenant. I had the ballistics on that shooting up in Kapa`a last week so I just added the bones to the box."

"Good thinking," her immediate superior said, giving her a verbal pat on the back. "That saves money on our courier budget."

"Of course that's still cheaper than expanding the KPD crime lab," Kai said. Both she and the other two major crimes detective sergeants had long been nagging for a beefed-up lab.

"As I keep telling you, we don't have that much need for DNA testing when Honolulu is only an hour away," Faralaco insisted. "Besides, wouldn't you rather we put the money into detective overtime?"

"Yessir."

"You mentioned in your note that you think this is a

cold-case murder," Faralaco continued. "What makes you think so?"

"It's a cold case because the medical examiner thinks the bones are at least fifty years old," the detective replied. "And a murder because of what looks like bullet holes in the skulls...right in the centers of the foreheads."

"Okay, now you've got my attention," the lieutenant said. "I thought you only had jawbones."

"The people who brought them in took a lot of pictures. I can show you. I downloaded all of their pictures on my desktop machine."

As Faralaco crowded into her cubicle, she began slowly clicking through the photos. There were pictures of the skulls from various angles, other random bones, a partial ribcage still hung together with cartilage and the pelvis, which the medical examiner confirmed to be female. Finally, there was the fragment of an Army uniform.

"So you've got at least one woman and at least one soldier," the lieutenant said thoughtfully.

"Maybe the woman *was* the soldier," Kai suggested.

"What have you done on missing persons?"

"I've gotten a start on it," she said. "I started with thirty years ago and I'm working back. I'm looking for people who went missing up in that part of the island."

"Good work," Faralaco said. "Let me know what you find."

Jim Hammer and Lauren Stahling had spent Monday having resumed their itinerary of putting the rest of the world out of their minds.

Leaving their cell phones tethered to their chargers at the house—and *untethered* to their owners—those owners got an early start with their morning swim, put in a couple of hours snorkeling with the kaleidoscope of tropical fish, and fell asleep in the sand under the shade of an ironwood tree.

It was deep into the afternoon when they finally wandered—by way of the mango tree—back to the house. Neither of them was ready to power up a cell phone, so they didn't. That bit of passive disobedience felt almost good as the idea of taking a shower together, which they also did.

An hour later, they were still lying on the bed staring lazily at the ceiling fan spinning hypnotically when Lauren announced:

"It's nearly seven in Montana. I'm going to check my work messages. At least I won't have to deal with whatever happened until tomorrow."

"It feels good to be retired," Hammer said, laughing. "Seriously, though, now that you've been the first one to blink, I think I'll power mine up and scratch this itch I have to know whether Tim Tommis has had a chance to look at that pile of pictures I sent him of all that Russian gear."

"I'm sure he's at least taken a peek," she said. "I can't help but think that this is the kind of stuff that would light up his curiosity enough to push it to the top of his list. I'll bet you a drink at that bar in Hanalei that you've got something from him."

"You win," Hammer said a couple of minutes later.

"What did he say?"

"He says to call him and that he's going to be up late...I guess it's nine on the East Coast. How's your 'ankle monitor.' Anything important?"

"Just a couple of quick things," she said. "Go ahead and call him...put it on speaker."

"Aloha, buddy," Tommis said, answering his phone.

"Are you still on the Garden Isle? Why aren't you in the water...or are you?"

"Just got back."

"How did you guys make out with Lauren's Menehune archaeological site? Did you find it?"

"It's every bit as impressive as advertised," Hammer said. "Maybe even more incredible when you actually see it and realize that it's been there for what...maybe eight hundred or a thousand years."

"Is it intact?"

"There are sixteen sets of stone basins and troughs running down a steep slope through the thick jungle. They carry all the water of this stream, and it looks like it still works like it was meant to work except the bottom part of it, however long that was, has collapsed and it'd just waterfall a couple thousand feet high. I'll send pictures."

"Speaking of pictures, I got those that you sent," Tommis said, getting down to business. "How far was that from your basins and troughs?"

"A few miles and more than a few centuries," Hammer said. "We saw the red lights from where we camped on the way out. Couldn't resist taking a look."

"You know what curiosity did to the cat, right?" Tommis joked.

"This cat just filled your heavily fire-walled inbox with pictures from a Russian electronics swap meet. What do you see in there?"

"Where do I start?" Tommis said with a laugh. "Actually, the first thing that hit me after I'd picked through everything was what I did *not* see."

"You've got my attention," Hammer said.

"What you stumbled into is a pretty sophisticated electronic command center with a lot of advanced hardware. You're right that it is not a listening post. These are not spies. What else they lack, though, is communications gear. This means that whatever goes on here, goes on *here*...with no connection to any other unit or command center *anywhere*. Totally autonomous."

"Like Pokuakini Ridge is the center of its own little universe?"

"Yup...but it's a very *serious* little universe based on what I do see."

"It did *look* serious," Lauren interjected.

"Hi Lauren," Tommis said in greeting. "Okay, let's run through it. At the top of the list is a Russian 29B6 Konteyner over-the-horizon VHF bi-static radar system. This is the same system that they've got installed at Kovylkino and in Nizhny Novgorod Oblast to cover western Russia and Moscow to provide early warning of threats originating inside NATO."

"How does that work?" Lauren asked. "For a layperson."

"Well, most radar systems are line-of-sight, meaning the radar signal needs to be able to see the target or have a straight line to it to detect it. An over-the-horizon radar station like a 29B6 acquires a target beyond the horizon by bouncing a shortwave signal off the ionosphere. The echo signal bounces back the same way. Both the Russians and us and a lot of others have had this capability for air and missile defense going back to the Cold War."

"This place is just sitting there isolated from the rest of the world, but it's set up with this capability," Hammer observed. "Theoretically, this could detect a North Korean missile launch?"

"Oh yes, but as you probably know, the US Navy has got exactly that same capability just a few miles away at the Pacific Missile Range out of Barking Sands."

"I do," Hammer said. "This *has been* a topic of conversation. You get people talking over here, and you'll quickly learn that they're well aware that Kaua`i is the closest piece of the US to North Korea. People have stories about that false alarm back in 2018 when that alert went out that a missile was headed for Hawai`i."

"I remember that," Tommis said. "I'll bet they were freaked out! The DPRK, the so-called Democratic Republic of North Korea, had just tested their Hwasong-17 ICBM. It had the range to hit the mainland US, never mind Hawai`i. Now they've got the Hwasong-19 and Hwasong-20 with GPS guidance that can travel more than nine thousand miles. They also got an arsenal of about fifty nukes."

"At least we can see them coming."

"And Barking Sands is only one of the places where we've got missiles that could shoot them down...theoretically."

"I like the way you say 'theoretically,'" Hammer replied. "But why would somebody have this super high-tech radar just perched on a cliff out there?"

"That's not the troubling part," Tommis said.

"What's that?"

"It's some of their other gear. They also got 1RL257 and 1L269 broadband multifunctional *jammers*. They transmit radio frequency signals to overwhelm radar systems by inundating their receivers with noise and bogus input."

"It sounds like these people got radar to watch what they're doing while they're blinding the other side so they won't know what's going on, right?" Lauren recapped.

"Right," Tommis agreed. "But there's more. Your friends out on the cliff have also got an R-330Zh *short-range* jammer like the Russians have used in Georgia and Ukraine and other places to jam guidance on missiles and smart bombs. This thing has a range of at least twenty or thirty miles, and it has been used to knock out GPS, satellite communications, and even cell phone networks."

"The Pacific Missile Range outpost on Makaha Ridge is less than five miles away," Lauren said. "And the whole base at Barking Sands is less than twenty."

"Yup," Tommis said.

"Who would do this?" Lauren asked rhetorically. "As if all of those notes all over that were written in Korean weren't a clue. What were they about? I can recognize Korean, but I can't read it."

"Well, my translator tells me they were just crib notes on how to use the stuff," Tommis said. "There's nothing to indicate who's doing this, but my paranoid first guess is that it's the DPRK Reconnaissance General Bureau, their version of the KGB or FSB. Hammer and I and our team crossed paths with them once. They're a spy outfit that runs covert ops in South Korea and beyond. They have a cyber division that used to be called Bureau 121. It hacks and disrupts anywhere and everywhere. They're also infamous all over the dark web for hacking banks and big-time theft."

"I guess we better keep an eye on this Korean camp," Hammer said.

"I'm sure there's more to this than meets the eye," Tommis replied.

Thoughts of North Korean spies building an electronic warfare hive on a cliff overlooking the Nāpali Coast kept them awake and staring at the ceiling fan for a while before they finally dozed into their afternoon naps. When Hammer and Lauren finally woke up, the light of day was fading, so they decided to head over to the tiki bar in Hanalei for pizza and beer.

The place was not crowded, but they saw their friend Virgil, the old guy who they'd met here ten days ago. They waved. He waved them over to his end of the bar, and Hammer offered to buy him a beer when he ordered a first round. Virgil accepted.

"Did you take your Nāpali Coast hike?" Virgil asked.

"Only as far as Hanakapi`ai Falls," Lauren said. "We had a nice swim up there."

"Since then, we've taken a couple of walks out to the cliffs from up on the Kōke`e Park road," Hammer added.

"I haven't been up there in years," Virgil lamented. "Wish I could, but these knees keep gettin' less cooperative. They haven't invented the words yet to tell about those sunsets up there…but you gotta stay and watch it get dark."

"We did," Hammer said, sharing an insider's smile.

They ended up sharing some pizza with Virgil and had a good conversation of the kind that you always enjoy anywhere you get a local talking about a locality that he's devoted to.

Finally, Virgil headed into the night, and Lauren and Hammer decided on one more for their followed suit. Just as their beers arrived, a young Asian couple sat down near them at the bar. They were dressed in stylishly baggy T-shirts and overall shorts that looked like something expensive that was made to look cheap—like those jeans with the knees ripped out that young people buy in designer shops. He wore a ball cap turned backward and was more animated than his girlfriend, though they both seemed to be in a good mood.

"Let's get this party started," he said, glancing over toward Hammer.

"I think you just did," Hammer said with a smile, raising his glass slightly.

"That's what I'm slammin'," he said, moving his body as though listening to an inaudible bass track. "If you know what *mean*!"

Hammer just laughed. Lauren joined him, shaking her head.

"Teddy," the woman said. "Cool yourself out."

"Hi," she said, reaching over to shake Hammer's hand. "I am Pak Mi-Rae, you can call me Rae…and this Jong Nam-ho."

"*Please*," he said. "Call me Teddy."

After a round of introductions, Rae and Teddy ordered a couple of Mai Tais and they all started talking. It turned out that Teddy wasn't quite as drunk as he seemed. He was just a show-off.

After a few minutes of banter, when Lauren asked what they were doing on the island, their answer came as a surprise.

"We are here on business," Rae said.

"We're in the sugar business," Teddy added, touching his companion suggestively, but playfully.

"We are with a sugar company from Seoul called Sweet Harvest. We are in Kaua`i researching the growing of small-batch sugarcane for small-batch rum," Rae said, swatting his hand away.

"Sugarcane?" Hammer queried. "That used to be a big deal on this island, but long before my time. I thought all that stopped years ago."

"It is coming back for small-batch artisanal applications," she said as though quoting from a brochure. Her English, while fluent, was more stilted than Teddy's. "Our company hopes to apply this practice back in Korea."

"We're tasting rum at the moment," Teddy said,

holding up his glass. "It's a hard job but somebody has to do it."

The playful Teddy did like to toss around American clichés.

"What brings you to the North Shore?" Lauren asked, looking at Rae as Teddy went to find the bathroom.

"We are working on the South Shore near Kekaha, but we heard of Hanalei and took a night off from our work colleagues to come all the way over here. We are happy to get away from farm fields. Teddy and I are very urban in our styles."

"Hanalei is not exactly 'urban' is it?"

"But it's different…and you do not have to have red dirt under your nails. How can they stand this?"

After a boisterous, but entertaining conversation, Lauren and Hammer were getting ready to leave. It was Rae's turn to find the bathroom, and when she had left, Teddy leaned over toward Hammer as though wanting to take him into his confidence.

"Can I tell you a secret?" Teddy whispered.

"Okay."

"The sugarcane…it's just a *front*. You know what I'm sayin'?"

Hammer nodded.

"It's all fake news…we're really *secret agents*."

"*Oh really*?" Hammer said, certainly surprised, but not taking him too seriously.

"We're here to do a clandestine secret op. You know what I'm sayin'?"

"Yeah, you're secret agents here in Kaua`i to do a secret thing?"

"I can't tell you any more," he said, continuing the whisper. "Otherwise I'd have to kill you."

"Right," Hammer said, replying to the cliché, but surprised that Teddy didn't suddenly break into a laugh as was his pattern after making one of his absurd comments.

"What did he say?" Lauren asked as they were walking to the car.

"He told me a secret," Hammer said, shaking his head.

"Don't tell me that he said he'd have to kill you if you told anyone."

"Well, actually, he did," Hammer said, laughing.

"Oh brother," Lauren said with a grin. "I'll kill if you *don't* tell me."

"His secret is that they're secret agents sent to Kaua`i to do a secret thing."

"Weird..."

"An overactive imagination fueled by an overabundance of tropical drinks, I think," Hammer said, smiling.

"How can you say this after we just spent part of the afternoon discussing a nest of North Korean spies here on this island?" Lauren reminded him.

"What are the odds that an actual DPRK spy would glibly admit this to a total stranger he met in a bar while he was in the midst of running an op?"

"Are you saying it's a coincidence?" Lauren asked pointedly. "I thought you didn't believe in coincidences."

CHAPTER EIGHT

POLICE LIEUTENANT RICHARD Faralaco had no sooner stepped off the elevator after his Tuesday morning budget meeting than he saw Chief George Audhus glance at him with a strained expression on his face. The chief was standing in the hallway with his cell phone to his ear. He had apparently been on his way somewhere when his caller ID told him this was a call he could not ignore.

"Yes sir," Faralaco heard the chief say. "Yes sir, we're making progress...no sir. I'll keep you in the loop...yes sir."

"I've just heard from the top," Audhus said, looking at Faralaco and using his usual euphemism for the mayor of Kaua`i County. "The mayor's office is getting some heat from the County Council, who are getting some heat from the visitors bureau over this shooting up in Kapa`a last week."

The incident had involved a couple of locals in a petty drug deal gone sour, but one of them ended up in the hospital and a tourist from the mainland was treated but released.

"We've got one man in custody and the other perps in the hospital," Faralaco said. "I've got officers interviewing witnesses, so we ought to be able to hand the DA a solid..."

"We need to get this buttoned up," Audhus said. "If it hadn't been for that hijacking attempt over Honolulu on Sunday before last, this would have been top of the news cycle all week. Even still, the media won't let it go. Whoever said that there's no such thing as bad publicity didn't live in a tourism-dependent county with a wounded mainlander who happened to be a high-profile Silicon Valley billionaire. This is as big as a damned international incident. It's all hands on deck until the DA files charges."

"Yessir," Faralaco said. He knew that when his boss's boss was mad, that's all there was to say.

Faralaco had three detective sergeants in major crimes, and he had talked to two of them that morning. They were each headed up to Kapa`a in a separate car to work on witnesses and beat the bushes for possibly overlooked evidence. That left Detective Sergeant Kai Nialani.

He found her in her cubicle looking at her computer screen. A quick glimpse at what she was looking at told him that it was the cold case of the two skeletons.

"You're working that cold case, huh?"

"Yes, Lieutenant," she replied. "I've been through the records back to early forties, which is as far back as we have missing person files, and I've looked at unsolved murders where the bodies were not found. I'm not giving up yet but I haven't found anything that matches a *pair* of people up in the mountains around Kōke`e or Waimea Canyon. Of course, they could have come from anywhere on the island.

"Look, Kai," he said sympathetically. "You've done a good job, and I know you're starting to take this case personally, but maybe you ought to give it a rest until the DNA comes back. In the meantime…"

"I'd like to go take a look at the crime scene," she said abruptly, looking up at him.

"*What*? Way up in the mountains? You said it took those people a couple of days to walk in and out."

"I'd like to go up there and visit the crime scene, I think…"

"Listen, I can appreciate the interest that you're taking in this, but I've just talked to the chief, and he's under a lot of pressure from the mayor on the Kapa`a thing. It's what you might call very high profile. He said, 'all hands on deck.'"

"Lieutenant, let me remind you, my hands were the first KPD hands on the deck of the Kapa`a case when it happened," she said defensively. "I pulled an overtime shift up there that day while everyone down here was glued to the TVs with the Honolulu hijacking. I still haven't looked at any of that. I also was the one who processed the scene and finally recovered the cartridges…and got them off to the Honolulu crime lab on a Sunday."

"I understand," Faralaco said. It was his turn to be defensive. "I know you did, but humor me on this. The visitor's bureau is on the Council, and they're nagging the mayor, so we have to get this wrapped up."

"If you're talking about this being about politics and public relations, how do you think it will look to the media when KPD solves a fifty-year-old *double homicide*? I think that would earn the chief a lot of points with the mayor *and the media*…don't you?"

"Okay, Kai," the lieutenant said after a long pause. "Take two days and go visit your crime scene. Get an early start tomorrow and be back here Friday morning."

"Thank you, Rich," she said, using his first name. "You won't be disappointed."

"Okay…but one more thing…would you mind using your personal vehicle? I'd rather not have a KPD car offline for two days…not at a time like this."

"Okay…"

Kai stared at her screen for a moment, then clicked into a map app. She pulled up the Kaua`i map and started zooming in on intersecting state parks and forest reserves on the northwest side of the island. She looked at all their straight-line boundaries drawn by somebody who had probably never actually seen the natural topography of the deep valleys and steep cliffs in that area.

Gradually, she realized that she had absolutely no idea where the crime scene was, nor how to find it. The valley that the woman hiker named was nowhere to be found.

Her eyes fell on the business card she had tossed on the corner of her desk. She picked it up and stared at the Area Code 406 cell number. For some reason she had always remembered something her auntie had told her long ago—"If you don't know, ask somebody who does."

Lauren Stahling picked up on the fourth ring.

"Ms. Stahling, this is Detective Nialani of the Kaua`i Police Department, I hope I'm not catching you at a bad time."

"Oh, hi, Detective…no, we just got back from the beach. What can I do for you?"

"I'm calling with a follow-up on our conversation on Sunday. I'd like to go out and take a better look at the crime scene, and I'd like to get a better idea from you as to *where* you discovered the remains."

"Oh boy," Lauren said hesitantly. "That's a hard one. It's in a valley called Hemolele`auwai that shows up as a named feature on a 1931 topo map, but not on any other later maps."

"Hold on a second," the detective said. "I have a huge wall map here in the office, I'll walk over and look at it... okay, now...where is this?"

"We hiked out toward the Nāpali Coast on the Miloli`i Ridge Trail from a small parking area off Highway 550... you know, the road that leads up to Kōke`e Park. From there we navigated overland on a north-northeast heading using game trails."

"There's a lot of unnamed canyons...even on this large-scale map," Kai said, running her finger across the big wall map. "But nothing that says Hemolele`auwai. I don't know how I can find..."

"Why don't we just *show you,*" Hammer said, barging into the conversation he'd been listening into on speaker. "We've *been there*...we know the way...and Lauren was saying the other day that she wouldn't mind going in there again. I'm always up for a good hike."

"Sure," Lauren said. "We'll just *take you* there."

"Umm..thank you."

"When?" Lauren asked. "How about an early start tomorrow?"

"Perfect," the detective said. Tomorrow was not only ideal for her, it was the *only* option that Faralaco had given her. "We can take my personal car."

"How about we meet you at the police station parking lot in Līhu`e at eight?" Hammer said. "Wear good hiking boots. It's rough terrain...and come prepared to camp out tomorrow night. It's a long way into Hemolele`auwai Valley and back."

"There's one thing I've been wondering about," Kai

said. "What took you so far off the beaten track to this out-of-the-way valley the first place?"

"It's a long story," Lauren said with a laugh. "I'll tell you *all about it* tomorrow."

What have I done? Kai Nialani asked herself as she set her phone down on her desk.

Her idea of visiting a crime scene on a junket from which her boss tried to dissuade her had turned into a two-day backpacking trip with a pair of total strangers—or at least people she'd only met once.

What could possibly go wrong?

The easy answer was "anything."

The cynical answer was "everything."

Better late than never, she told herself as she decided to launch into a background check on tomorrow's hiking companions.

The Stahling woman checked out, right down to her headshot on the Logan County government website and a few glowing reports in local papers. She was a strong, competent and well-spoken woman who looked much more reputable in a business suit headshot than she did after a two-day hike.

Captain James Hammer, US Army, retired, was another matter. His special forces career put a lot of things behind classified firewalls, but everything else painted a picture of a consummate and effective officer who had accomplished much. Then she got to the part with the five Silver Stars, three Distinguished Service Crosses, Legions of Merit, a couple of Bronze Stars, and the list went on and on. He was someone for whom the term "hero" was an understatement.

The only thing negative came from a major general

who had complained that Hammer could have retired as a full colonel if he had accepted a desk in Washington instead of volunteering to go back into the field over and over.

Kai decided that if she was going camping in the obscure backcountry, this pair would be good companions.

Then she started Googling Hammer. To her astonishment, the first thing that popped up was the Honolulu hijacking. She had been embroiled in the Kapa`a investigation on the day that this had happened and had missed the news cycle. Everything she'd heard had been secondhand. She had no idea that it had been *him* who took down the three hijackers and prevented a suicide plunge into Pearl Harbor.

Kai felt her chin drop as she watched the video of Hammer calmly crushing the hijacker's hands as he waited for the breaching tool to burn out. The hairs on the back of her neck stood up as she watched him casually drop the thing into the metal pitcher and heard the applause.

Early Wednesday morning, Detective Kai Nialani was waiting when Hammer and Stahling pulled in next to her compact Ford C-Max in their borrowed full-size Ford. She had arrived early and so had they. Kai took this as a good sign.

"Let's take our car," Hammer said after all three of them had digested the size comparison between the two vehicles. All agreed.

"You didn't tell me that you were on that Seattle to Honolulu flight a few days ago," the detective told

Hammer as he helped her squeeze her gear into the trunk of the Taurus.

"Not much to tell aside from what you've probably heard," he replied. "The threat was neutralized, and the FBI got their bad guys."

"I've heard that there are a bunch of Honolulu newspapers and national news channels that are still really anxious to talk to you," Kai said.

"Not much to be said," Hammer replied. "The FBI got our statements. There's really not much to add."

"There were a hundred-and-seventy-odd other people who saw the whole thing," Lauren said. "I'm sure the networks talked to them."

"But you were the hero of the moment," Kai countered. "Those hundred-and-seventy-odd other people are alive because of what you did."

"Well, it wasn't just me...Ms. Stahling shoved a number two pencil straight through the thigh of one of them," Hammer pointed out. "But we came all the way over here to your state to be off the grid, not talk to TV cameras."

"And so you have, and have not," Kai said.

"I see you're planning to do some detectoring," he said, changing the subject as he helped load the thin canvas case containing her metal detector into the trunk.

"There could be...probably *are*...some important pieces of the puzzle under several inches of dirt and plant matter. I'm going to take my time and thoroughly process the scene."

"Speaking of the scene, you asked why we went there in the first place and I promised you a long story," Lauren said as they climbed into the Taurus. "As Hammer will confirm, I like looking for, and looking at, prehistoric sites on the hikes we take in the mountains back home."

"She never met a petroglyph that didn't speak to her,"

Hammer interjected with a grin, happy not to be talking about himself. "We've seen some amazing stuff."

"This is what got me started on this one," Lauren said, handing Kai the 1888 leather-bound book. "I found this in a used bookstore a few months ago. It's by an archaeologist named Annison Cutts...he writes about an amazing, handmade structure whose name means 'Perfect Waterway.' I figured it was probably a tourist attraction by now...but I found no other mention of it anywhere. It's a big mystery. I just had to see it."

"I've never heard of it," Kai said, opening the book on her lap in the back seat as Hammer pulled into traffic on the main highway. "My family...most of them...have been on Kaua`i forever and I've heard countless stories of the old days from grannies and aunties."

"You're not alone," Lauren said, leaning over the front seat. "Like I said, there's no other mention in any of the other books and I've read Thrum's *Hawai`ian Folk Tales* and Fornander's *Ancient History of the Hawai`ian People.* Also Martha Beckwith's huge book on Hawai`ian mythology from the thirties, and a lot of others. I figured it was all just a myth until I got this 1931 topo map that had a valley marked Hemolele`auwai, the same name Cutts used."

"Then the mystery got deeper," Hammer interjected. "None of the later maps she dug up had it. The really detailed maps showed it, but none of them had the name. Only the 1931 map."

"Where did you get all these maps?"

"Tell her what you told me," Hammer said, laughing.

"I just said that I'm a county assessor...so I know where to get maps of anything. It's true...not meant to be funny."

Kai smiled. She was enjoying the banter between this pair.

"These are photocopies of the area from the 1931 map," Lauren said, handing the detective sheets in page protectors. "The map is too big to take on a hiking trip… and here are some satellite pictures of the area where you can see the goat trails that we used."

"How can you even see…?" Kai asked, squinting.

"We're used to this," Lauren said reassuringly. "We use game trails a lot on backpacking and hunting trips back home."

"You do a lot of that?"

"Yup. We like being off the grid…together."

CHAPTER NINE

HAVING GOTTEN an early start that morning, they had beat the tourist traffic on the congested southeast corner of Kaua`i and passed only a handful of vehicles as they climbed up Highway 550 above Waimea Canyon. It was still refreshingly cool as they unpacked the car in an otherwise empty Miloli`i Ridge Trail parking area with a sign mentioning a 3,900-foot elevation.

Hammer offered to carry Kai's metal detector, and she accepted. Her backpack, crammed with crime scene processing gear, was much larger than the packs hefted by the others. Such outings were clearly second nature to these two mainlanders and they traveled light. Kai hadn't hiked in these mountains since she had been on an outing in high school, but she was not about to announce this. She stayed in shape and was sure she could do well.

The scene that unfolded as the Miloli`i Ridge Trail broke out into the open from the heavy forest was spectacular—for both the Montanans who had seen it four days ago, and for the detective who had been born on this island. It was later than sunrise this time, but the sun was still low enough that the colors—the greens, golds and sandstone reds of the land and the deep blue of the Pacific—were almost unnaturally rich.

The trio paused to take sips from their water bottles and to make the sorts of inspired comments usually expected from tourists.

"It's like Montana, only backward," Lauren said. "Instead of starting our hike at the base, we drove to the mountaintops. We're at three or four thousand feet, half the height of Montana mountains, but there, the valley floor is three or four thousand feet. Here the valley floor is at sea level, so the overall effect is similar."

As they pressed on, Kai was startled when Hammer suddenly left the trail, but then she saw they were now following a narrow track cut over the years by the small hooves of wild goats. A few moments later, Hammer paused to point out a small group of these light-colored animals in the distance.

"I guess you know where you're going," Kai said as Hammer made an occasional abrupt turn to follow a slender path she could not see until she was walking on it.

"We were here over the weekend," he said.

"He's just showing off," Lauren said, chuckling. "It's second nature for him. Take him anywhere and he remembers the way in and out like he's got Google Earth map wired into his brain. That's part of what made him good at his old government job."

"Special Forces?" Kai said.

"Yeah…that."

When they made their Wednesday lunch stop, Kai Nialani breathed a sigh of relief as she dropped her pack.

"Let's trade off carrying the mission gear," Hammer

suggested casually, nodding to her pack, which was certainly the largest of the three. "I'll take the next shift after lunch."

"Okay," Kai said. Part of her wanted to say no, because her Glock 19 was in that pack, but she had already developed a rare high level of trust for these people whom she had known for barely three days.

Mainly she hesitated because she wanted to present herself as up to the challenge of the hike, but she *did* have the largest pack, and she felt tired while the others had yet to break a sweat.

Lauren read what Kai was thinking, and as Hammer wandered off to find himself a makeshift latrine, she leaned over and whispered, "Don't mind him. He's not showing off by offering to trade packs. He's used to team ops and teams share the load. He's used to carrying stuff. He once carried a wounded soldier in full battle gear most of the way across the Hindu Kush. Your pack is no big deal for him. Really."

Even though they had just met, Kai could easily believe this.

"Where did you find a guy like that?" Kai asked.

"We were best friends in high school," Lauren said.

Kai smiled the kind of knowing smile that women often exchange when discussing such matters among themselves.

"*No,* it actually wasn't like *that* back then," Lauren said, reading what Kai was thinking. "It didn't become like *that* until we got together again after being out of touch for twenty years. Now it's like that…but we're best friends again too."

"So I can see."

Less than an hour later, they crested a small ridge and dropped down into a narrow valley with an inviting little stream rushing through it.

"Listen to the water," Lauren said, looking at Kai.

"Sounds like a stream."

"Listen to the rhythm," Lauren said. "It's not wild as it descends into that vegetation. Listen to the rhythm, the *whish, whoosh…whish, whoosh…whish, whoosh…*"

"Yeah, I guess I can hear that."

"Now," said Lauren. "Come look at this."

Hammer smiled as he watched Lauren take the detective through the tangle of foliage up ahead to show off her earlier discovery.

"There you go," Lauren said. "There's Hemolele`auwai…the so-called Perfect Waterway."

Kai stared in disbelief as she looked at the series of chutes and pools arrayed at perfect increments down the course of the stream as it descended through the narrow valley, *whishing* as it dropped through a trough and *whooshing* as it swirled in a basin.

"How far does it…?"

"Through that jungle down there it keeps going… there are sixteen pools, then it suddenly falls off into a two-thousand-foot waterfall. I discovered that the hard way, but he grabbed me before I had a chance to check out the bottom."

Kai glanced at Hammer who was out of earshot.

"How old is it?" Kai asked. "I guess you're *the* expert since nobody else knows about this place."

"Cutts couldn't find anybody on the island who knew about it either, and that was back in the 1880s, so it was old then. We were guessing eight hundred years based on the age of the *heiau*s on Kaua`i. Does that sound right?"

"In school, they said eight about hundred years ago,

but that's just a guess. There were probably Polynesians on this island over a thousand years ago."

"How old are the Menehune fishponds on the south side of Kaua`i?" Lauren asked.

"They say five or six hundred years," Kai said. "But you're not saying that Menehunes built *this*, are you?"

"I'm just saying that when you get into stuff that's prehistoric...before anything was written down...then folklore and oral tradition...you know, storytelling...is a big part of explaining the past. It's like leprechauns in Ireland. I doubt that most people actually believe in them, but they've been intertwined with the folklore since anyone can remember."

"Same with Menehunes, I guess," Kai said. "It's not something I spend a lot of time thinking about...until I see something like this. I grew up listening to stories of all the myths and legends, but I mostly put it out of my mind a long while ago. The investigator in me wants to find an explanation for this, but I wouldn't know where to start. I guess they still can't figure out exactly how the Egyptian pyramids were built."

"Basically, we're looking at the *what* and the *where* of Hemolele`auwai," Lauren said. "None of us have much of an idea of the *who, when* and *why*...but that's a mystery for another day. You're here to see a crime scene."

"Right," Kai said. She had just started having fun with the discussions of folklore, and this amazing, yet inexplicable, structure. It was strange talking about the history of her own island with mainlanders, but Lauren Stahling had not only a keen interest, but an involved familiarity, and a key rarity among armchair academics—an open mind.

"We'll show you what we found and where we found it, and then you can go to it," Hammer said, handing over Kai's pack.

"We found the first skull down there near the eighth basin under that short mokihana tree," Lauren explained. "The second one is uphill and a little farther away from the watercourse, but also on the far side. We didn't touch either one, but we brushed leaves off both with a stick. Hammer can show you the pelvis and ribcage, and the place where he found that piece of uniform. Then we'll get out of your way."

"I guess I'll get to work then," the detective said as she unpacked her gear and started setting up a search grid with sticks and string. "I have to say this is the oldest murder scene I've ever worked. That's not to say that I've worked a lot of them. We have a very low crime rate here on Kaua`i. Way below the national average...or Honolulu average. We get only one or two murders a year here. Sometimes none. Not that any of them are ever easy, but almost all are easy to figure out."

"What about missing persons?" Lauren asked. "We've heard that there's a lot of people who disappear voluntarily up in the Kalalau Valley and who don't want to be found."

"Yes, there's a lot of that," Kai admitted. "It does eat up a lot of our time, but most of these people show up eventually. That's a whole other world from where most visitors go. Have you been up there?"

"Only as far as Hanakapi`ai Falls."

"This over here is even more other worldly than Kalalau," Kai continued. "I went through all the old missing persons files we have and couldn't find anything with two people lost in this area at one time. That's why I'm anxious to work the scene and find *something*. The DNA is good only up to a point because nobody collected DNA on people back then. The best we'll do is find relatives that are in the database somewhere."

"How long have you been with the KPD?" Hammer asked.

"I studied criminology at Colorado State, and my first cop job...believe it or not...was a few years on the mean streets of Chicago. There was a time when I just had to get off-island, but I was glad to come back. That was a dozen years ago."

As her cohorts lounged on the hillside making occasional small talk, Kai Nialani put on her surgical gloves and sifted through the grid she'd set up, logging and photographing her findings on the surface and near the surface. There were more bone and more shreds of fabric, but after several decades, much it was scattered. She gathered all the bones she could find. At least the lab could distinguish male from female.

At last, she took a break, a long drink of water, and broke out the metal detector. After a few moments of beeping and calibrating, she began at one corner of the grid and worked through it methodically, circling from the periphery of the grid toward the skulls, which were near the center. More buttons turned up, along with a zipper.

A particularly loud chirp turned up a brass belt buckle with a "US" monogram embossed on it and a rotten fragment of canvas webbing attached, which she bagged and handed to Hammer.

"Can you identify anything about this?"

"It's Army-issue and issued a long time ago," he said. "It's a web belt from as far back as World War II. The buckle is old...formed metal not stamped metal like you see in more recent buckles."

"That thickens the pot," Lauren said.

"Sure does," Kai agreed as she went back to work.

A few minutes later, there was a chirp so slight that she almost ignored it, but Kai was quickly on her hands and knees, scratching carefully into a small patch of ground covered with vegetation.

"*Oh*...look at this...so tiny," she exclaimed.

Lauren and Hammer paused and stared, unable to see the little thing she had picked up with the aid of a stick and flicked into a baggie.

She stepped toward them and held up the object for them to see.

"Can you identify anything about *this*?"

"A million years and you never would have found *that* without your metal detector," Lauren said, staring at the minutely delicate ring.

"It's gold, because gold never corrodes," Hammer said. "Any jeweler could probably ID the stone, but I'd guess it's a diamond, because who would bother putting a rhinestone that small into a ring?"

"And now, the skulls," Kai said.

"I know what you're hoping for," Hammer said with a smile.

She smiled. They both hoped, and Lauren caught on immediately, that the bullets might still be lodged inside.

Kai and her audience were not disappointed.

She picked up the first skull, which had a vertebra attached by some long-dried-out gristle, turned it over so that the bullet wouldn't fall out on the ground, and shook it slightly. They could all hear the rattle of lead on bone.

"I'll let the lab open them," she said, taking some large, heavy plastic bags from her pack. "I guess we're done here."

"If I might be so bold as to make a suggestion," Hammer said.

"Sure."

"I knew a man once, who wrote a law that's never been repealed. His name was Murphy. If he was here, I know he'd suggest that you step outside your grid with your detector, spiral outward for a couple of spins, and then work back and forth on both sides of the waterworks and go downstream at least twenty feet. You've had decades of floods and rainstorms up here that could have carried stuff away from your basic grid area."

"Wouldn't that have affected something as small as the ring?" Lauren asked.

"Not to be morbid," Hammer said, "but I bet that ring was still on a finger until very recently."

Kai immediately returned to the spot where she'd recovered the ring, dug down a little farther and came up with a number of proximal and intermediate phalanges, which she bagged. As Hammer had suggested, they were partially connected by dried cartilage. The ring had still been on a finger until *very* recently.

It was after nearly an hour of going back over the grid site before she started down the slope with the metal detector. She was about twelve feet below the grid when they heard one of the loudest chirps of the day.

"This is deep," she said as she started digging down through the dirt and plant matter.

Lauren and Hammer had stepped closer to watch when she carefully brought up a small aluminum thing.

"Ladies and gentlemen," she said, looking at the dog tag and pointing toward the largest of the two skulls, "please meet Captain Glenn Alan Dexsen, US Army."

CHAPTER TEN

"I'D SAY that you had a reasonably successful day," Hammer put forward to Kai as he finished cleaning up from their Wednesday evening meal.

After all those years in the Army, setting up and running bare-bones campsites in remote locations had become second nature. Freeze-dried ready-to-eat meals have improved considerably in recent years, and the prep time is quick. Lauren had grown to appreciate this. All she had to do on their camping trips was eat what he cooked on his little Jetboil backpacking stove, which was usually good.

"I wish I'd found his other set of captain's bars, but that one that I found just as we were packing up was a huge deal," she replied. "It was your idea to search downstream that netted the dog tag, though. Thank you. That was a game-changer. Identifying him goes toward breaking the case."

"A step in the right direction," Hammer said as he stepped away to get some more firewood.

"Now that we know who *he* was, I wish we had an

idea of who *she* was," Lauren said. "Maybe the ring... how old is the oldest jeweler on Kaua`i?"

"I don't know, but it ought to be easy to figure out," Kai said. "By the way, that's a nice ring you're wearing."

"Thank you," Lauren said, holding up her hand to show off the curious and delicate little silver ring with the interesting, intertwined design. Its bouquet of small sapphires sparkled in the firelight. "I love it. He bought it for me late one night in a weird little 'voodoo jewelry' store in an alley off Royal Street in New Orleans."

"I like the design."

"I'd never seen anything like it," Lauren said, admiring her ring. "You know, the funny thing was, we walked by there the next day taking a shortcut to a coffee place, and it was not only closed, but it looked like it hadn't been open for years. All cobwebs and dust inside the windows."

"Very strange."

"New Orleans is a ghostly place," Lauren said. "Kind of like *this* place, these valleys and ridges over here where nobody goes and you find skeletons. It almost feels like we're surrounded by ghosts here tonight. I admit that I *am* a little thankful that we were able to hike a couple of ridges away from Hemolele`auwai before it got too dark to keep on those scant trails."

"It sure got dark quick," Kai said, looking up at the sky. "I admit that I haven't camped out since high school. I forgot how many stars there are. And there's nothing else in all that blackness except this campfire. It's a strange feeling when you're used to car lights and house lights and street lights everywhere you turn."

"Wait 'til the fire dies down," Hammer interjected.

"When you were camping as a kid, did you ever tell ghost stories?" Lauren asked.

"Always," Kai admitted. "Doesn't everybody? I

hadn't thought much about it until you started talking about leprechauns and Menehunes and folklore this afternoon."

"Tell us a Hawai`ian ghost story," Lauren said.

"I don't know…do you believe in ghosts?

"I don't know," Lauren said. "Does anybody categorically *not* believe in ghosts? Isn't that the point of telling ghost stories?"

"Do *you* believe in ghosts?" Kai asked Hammer.

"Depends on which ghosts," he replied, only half joking.

"Well put," Kai said, smiling. "In Hawai`i, there are a lot of kinds of ghosts. The word *lapu* means ghost, as in an apparition, like a specter. Just like with Western ghosts, the spirits haunt the places where they were on Earth, and they are said to appear to people."

"Like in a haunted house?" Lauren asked.

"Or like a haunted mountain valley. *Kupu`ino* is a name for an evil spirit or a bad person. The word *kapu,* which you sometimes see on 'no trespassing' signs in out-of-the-way places on the island, means 'forbidden.' It's like the Polynesian word *tapu*…the English word 'taboo' comes from that. Ignoring a *kapu* is how a soul gets into trouble and becomes an evil spirit, or a *kuewa,* a wandering spirit."

"Wow," Lauren said, "and all this from somebody who said she didn't think much about folklore."

"It stays with you," Kai admitted. "I guess I remembered for longer than I thought I did. I'll tell you a popular ghost story that was always guaranteed to frighten the kids. Have you ever heard of the 'night marchers,' or the 'spirit ranks'?"

Both of the mainlanders shook their heads.

"Okay," the Hawai`ian detective said, reaching into an aspect of her experience that was not often tapped. "Like the name says, they are spirits of dead warriors who form into a procession. They march through the night, sometimes carrying weapons, sometimes playing musical instruments like a New Orleans funeral. Sometimes they pass through walls. Some people claim to have seen them, but it's supposedly very precarious to get mixed up with them. The Hawai`ian words *huaka`i pō,* literally means 'marchers in the night,' and the word *oi`o* translates as 'spirit ranks,' or 'ghost columns.'"

"Like the old country song, 'Ghost Riders in the Sky,' Johnny Cash covered," Hammer interjected.

"That's right," Kai said. "Just like that, but they're herding souls, not cattle."

"A ghost army in the sky," Lauren said.

"Exactly," Kai agreed.

"Where are the souls being herded?"

"Just like any culture, I guess, if you're lucky, it's *papa lani,* the upper spaces, the heavenly place. If you're not so lucky, it's the realm of Milu. He was a chief who violated a *kapu* of some sort on Earth and wound up being flushed into the underworld, the world of the dead, where he became its boss. The gateway to Milu's netherworld is supposedly an opening on a bluff above the ocean."

They looked around. Each knew where they had camped, and they could hear the faint sound of crashing waves in the distance.

Kai Nialani awoke Thursday morning in the purple light of the predawn world. Most, but not all the stars had faded from the heavens, and the air was filled with a concerto of bird songs and the smell of coffee. It was a surprisingly comforting sight to watch Hammer kneeling next to his small, but efficient, gas stove making coffee.

Lauren Stahling was sitting up but still wrapped in her tropical weight sleeping bag as she sipped her coffee and looked out over the ocean.

"Ready for coffee?" Hammer asked, and Kai nodded.

They had both enjoyed the tales of night marchers she had spun, but they were both snoring before she got the ghosts tucked back onto the back shelves of her own imagination.

After a breakfast of packaged oatmeal that tasted far better here than at the table in her Līhu`e condo, Kai gathered up her personal gear and was ready to join the others for the hike back into the outside world.

"Thank you for giving me such a great escort into this place," she said with genuine appreciation.

"It was our pleasure," Lauren said. "Thank you for sharing all those stories that we'd never have known about. It's also great to know that somebody other than us in the twenty-first century has seen the valley of Hemolele`auwai."

"It's good to know that you've made a good start toward giving names to some of the lat people who came here in the *twentieth* century," Hammer added.

Nearly an hour later, they were about one or two narrow valleys away from reaching the Miloli`i Ridge Trail that would lead them back to civilization. They had divided the load of forensic gear and samples equally among their packs, but Hammer was still carrying the metal detector.

Suddenly, they heard a raucous commotion boiling up from the valley below. There were the shouts of men, the yelping and barking of dogs and series spine-chilling shrieks.

Looking down into the valley, they could see movement through the Hala trees. Out of habit, Hammer kept his Oberwerk HD II binoculars at the top of his backpack and had those out at the first bark. He took a long look, then handed them to his companions.

"The dogs have a wild pig cornered down there on the stream," Lauren said, passing the field glasses to Kai.

They all watched as the shouting men entered the fray to finish it off. This was easier said than done, but at last the squealing came to an end.

"That's how the locals hunt pigs on Kaua`i," Kai explained. "Dogs and knives. Sometimes without the dogs. You can't have *kalua* pork without the pork, and this way it's already partially sliced. Seriously, though, wild pork isn't that good. They do it for sport, mainly. There are some people who do it a night under a full moon when the visibility is good."

"I guess if you're using knives, you don't have to work about shooting somebody by accident," Hammer said. "Is pig hunting regulated?"

"Wild hog hunting is legal on all the main islands except Lanai," Kai explained. "Licenses for locals are ten bucks. If you want to give it a try, the non-resident fee is ninety-five."

"Except under moonlight, it would be easier with a rifle," Lauren commented.

"But that would mean missing half the fun," Hammer added. Then turning to Kai, he asked what method she used.

"I haven't...at least not yet."

It was only a short time when they stepped off the nearly invisible goat rail and were back on the much wider and well-defined Miloli`i Ridge Trail. After where they'd been, this felt like a highway.

Soon, they started to meet other hikers, who were

happy to exchange pleasantries. There was a young couple from Bend, Oregon, who said they were honeymooning, and a pair of old men from Wisconsin who admitted to being taken off guard by the steepness of the terrain.

Next, while Kai, Lauren, and Hammer were taking a water break, a group of unsmiling men emerged from up the trail and marched purposefully past them without a word. Leading the way was a well-built man in his late thirties with a US Navy Surface Warfare School t-shirt and bright red hair, trimmed in regulation haircut. With him were two Asian men. They were each a large and obviously heavy pack—much larger than the modest daypacks of the other hikers, and larger even than Kai's equipment pack.

They each did a double-take when they saw Kai's KPD uniform shirt.

"Great day for a walk," Lauren said cheerfully.

"Yes, yes," the man bringing up the rear said in accented English as he turned slightly.

"Where you from?" Lauren asked. "We're from Montana."

"Korea," he said, apparently taken off guard by her friendliness.

"Well, have a great day!" she shouted as he hurried to catch up with his hiking partners.

She noticed that Hammer had turned to watch the exchange. She returned his raised eyebrow when the man said, "Korea."

They both knew that the Miloli`i Ridge Trail also led to Pokuakini Ridge, with its puzzling piles of Russian electronic warfare hardware, and manuals translated into Korean.

They had most of the long drive back to Līhu`e behind them when Kai Nialani's phone beeped. It was Lieutenant Richard Faralaco.

Nearly an hour ago, when they had returned to the world of cell service for the first time in more than a day, she had taken it as a relief to have checked in to her KPD office and discovered she had missed nothing outside the normal routine in her time off the grid. This was about to change.

"Detective Nialani," she answered.

"Hello, Detective, did you get to that crime scene?" Faralaco asked with unexpected urgency.

"Yes, sir," she said, surprised to hear him showing so much interest in an errand that he had agreed to almost patronizingly. "I spent yesterday afternoon processing the scene and gathering more evidence. I'm on my way back. I'll be there in thirty minutes."

"Good," he said. "We got the DNA back."

"That was fast," she said. "I figured with the lab's backlog, an outer island cold case it could take two or three weeks if we were lucky."

"Well, somebody…meaning *you*…put it in the package with the ballistics from the Kapa`a debacle, and that envelope was marked as high priority."

"My bad," Kai said with no trace of contrition. "What did they say?"

"It's just like you guessed…one male and one female, and they date back to the middle of the twentieth century. There's no DNA hit on the male…yet…but the woman is a genetic match to the Mattochs family."

"That sounds familiar…why do I know that name?"

"They were a very prominent family here on Kaua`i back in the middle of the twentieth century. Very high society at a time when high society was a thing. They owned a couple of sugarcane refineries and a bunch of land. There are streets named after the Mattochs people. They were a big deal…and that makes this case now a big deal."

"You don't hear that name much today," Kai commented. "I wonder which Mattochs this woman was."

"There was a Gladys Mattochs who went missing back in 1946," Faralaco said.

"I didn't see that name in missing persons," Kai said.

"Technically, she wasn't reported as missing," Faralaco said. "There's a one-page document in the file. Case closed without an investigation. The family was convinced she had eloped with her boyfriend and left the island."

"Apparently they didn't make it," Hammer said when Kai had hung up her phone.

"And apparently it was a lot longer ago than fifty years," Lauren added.

Fifteen minutes later, the Ford Taurus was in the KPD parking lot and the others were helping Detective Nialani unload her gear and the bags of samples. She waved to a couple of patrol officers to lend a hand while she said her goodbyes to Stahling and Hammer. She promised to let them know how things turned out.

"Where to now?" Hammer asked his companion when the detective had disappeared into the building. "I can see the wheels spinning in that head of yours."

"You know me too well," she replied.

"Nope…still learning…but the learning curve is a helluva ride."

Eight minutes later, they were pulling into the parking lot on Hardy Street of the Līhu`e Public Library, the island's largest library. Eight minutes after this. Lauren was filling out a request slip for microfilm rolls of the local daily newspaper—from the summer of 1946.

Using an index, they found a lot of entries for "Mattochs" that year, but they were soon able to narrow down the week that the society pages were buzzing with the supposed elopement of young Gladys. Reading the old pages on the microfilm reader was like watching a syrupy rom-com on a black-and-white television set.

The Mattochs family had high aspirations for Gladys and were naturally thrilled when the twenty-year-old was on the threshold of an engagement to the socially well-positioned Clarence Flaunsin of Los Angeles, whom she had met while attending UCLA. There was a visit by the Flaunsins to Kaua`i and talk of a Beverly Hills wedding.

As in any good, syrupy rom-com, there were complications—the kind where the hometown girl falls for somebody else. In this case, the somebody else was a soldier named Glenn Dexsen, who Gladys met at a dance at Barking Sands when it was still an Army Air Forces base.

There was tension, a fistfight, and angry posturing between Dexsen and Flaunsin the families. Dexsen's car was found, but Glenn and Gladys disappeared without a trace. Dexsen was formally listed as AWOL, an elopement was supposed, and the story faded into oblivion with no further mention in the local paper.

Lauren took photos of a half dozen salaciously headlined articles, and emailed these to Kai Nialani. Soon the Taurus was on the road to the North Shore.

"Now that we've put that mystery in Detective Nialani's capable hands, I can't help thinking about those Koreans we passed on the trail," Hammer said as they drove.

"Have you forgotten about the Korean 'spy' who we talked to at the bar on Monday night?" Lauren asked. "Do you still think that was a coincidence?"

"I think it's pretty much obvious from the size of those packs that those two on the trail today are part of whatever's going on at the Korean camp we found up there," Hammer said. "But our friend Teddy and his girlfriend weren't with them."

"Rae, the girlfriend, did say they had colleagues on the island," Lauren pointed out. "Those two could easily have been them."

"I guess that sometimes when the drunk at the bar claims he's an international spy, he really *is* an international spy," Hammer said, shaking his head.

CHAPTER ELEVEN

TWO MEN HAD BOARDED a Friday morning flight from Honolulu to Kaua`i and took seats eleven rows apart. Ryu Myong-su wore a gaudy aloha shirt as befitting a Korean tourist bound for a Hawai`ian vacation on an island less crowded that the one with tourist-clogged Waikīkī beach. Zachery Preneu wore a suit, although he loosened his dark blue-gray tie as soon as he sat down. As a special agent with the US Army Criminal Investigation Division, he was not traveling for sun or fun. He was on business.

Ryu stood on the doorstep of the climactic moment in an audacious scheme which he had planned with meticulous precision for years. It was intended to change the course of world history forever, and there was no reason to doubt that it would.

Preneu had received orders barely four hours ago to set out on this undertaking for which he had barely been briefed.

The two men had never met and did not meet today, but they did share a shuttle bus to the rental car lots. Getting off the bus at different agencies, Ryu rented a bright-blue Mustang convertible, while Preneu had reserved a white Toyota Corolla—flamboyant versus virtually invisible. Ryu had a drive of about an hour to the five-star Royal Pacific Resort, while Preneu's destination was practically across the street—the headquarters of the KPD.

Chief George Audhus was on hand to greet Special Agent Preneu. The speed with which CID had gotten involved in this cold case from the middle of another century was not only startling; it gave everyone at KPD a case of whiplash.

When Kai Nialani had walked into KPD headquarters yesterday afternoon, Audhus and Lieutenant Faralaco were standing in the bullpen with a group of about a dozen others wondering out loud about how the Mattochs DNA could have made this cold case unexpectedly important.

When Kai had handed over Glenn Dexsen's dog tag on Thursday, this was immediately treated as a pivotal breakthrough.

Fueled by excitement and propelled by the momentum of the day, she sat down and phoned the US Army Human Resources Command. Luckily, since it was nearly quitting time in Kentucky, her law enforcement caller ID got her through to a senior someone who took an interest, and who logged in Glenn Dexsen's name, rank, and serial number. He said he would get back to her. This earned her a metaphorical pat on the back from both Audhus and Faralaco.

None of the three of them expected that the "getting back" would take the form of four o'clock Friday morning phone calls from Army CID in Quantico, Virginia. The time difference between there and Hawai`i seemed to be an alien—or at least ignored—concept.

However, for some unexplained reason, the Criminal

Investigation Division had taken an intense interest in Captain Glenn Dexsen. They were sending someone from their Honolulu office right away. Everyone at KPD assumed they would eventually hear from the Army's Mortuary Affairs people, and that there would be no particular urgency, given the age of the remains.

They were wrong. It was as though Dexsen had disappeared only yesterday.

Preneu walked into KPD headquarters purposefully, his necktie now tightened and dramatically took off his aviator-style sunglasses.

"We're happy to cooperate with CID in any way we can," Audhus promised, handing Preneu the evidence bag containing the dog tag. "This is the evidence that identifies one of our deceased as Captain Dexsen. We have DNA results that confirm the other as a female member of a local family, and there was a young woman from that family who disappeared in 1946."

"Is there DNA evidence from Dexsen's body?" Preneu asked. "Who has it?"

"It's with the state crime lab in Honolulu."

"Okay, I'll notify our people over there," Preneu said. "We'll take charge of that. As you know, the Defense Department has the DPAA forensics lab in Honolulu. They're the best lab in the world for identifying remains. I'll take the dog tag with me."

"We're curious as to why CID took such an interest in a cold case this old that they sent you over to see us so fast," Audhus said. "Who is this man, this Captain Dexsen? Why is he so important?"

"He's one of our own," Preneu said without saying why or how this made the Dexsen case a matter of such urgency. "We want to know how he died."

Audhus and Faralaco looked at one another. They

imagined that remains of service members turn up frequently without this triggering an immediate CID intervention.

"Speaking of which," Preneu continued. "Do you have a theory of what happened or who the assailant might have been?"

"Not as yet," Faralaco answered. "Do *you*? It would be helpful if you could tell us why Dexsen is so important."

"I just got here," the CID man replied. "I haven't got a theory...I haven't seen the rest of the evidence you collected yet...may I have a look?"

Audhus nodded to Faralaco to handle this, and the lieutenant nodded to Kai to join them as they made their way to the KPD crime lab.

Preneu scrutinized the evidence bags, which were arrayed on two tables, but the center of attention was the pair of skulls.

"What's your assessment of the entrance wounds?" Preneu asked the lab tech after staring at the skulls for the better part of a minute.

"The bullet holes being in roughly in the same place in the centers of the foreheads suggests an execution-style killing," the tech explained in a calm, almost deadpan tone. "Obviously, after exposure to the elements over more than half a century, there's no gunshot residue. Neither bullet penetrated all the way through the skull, and we've recovered both."

"Looks like nine millimeter," Preneu said, leaning over the table for a closer look. "Why would a nine-mil not go through a skull from the range you'd expect for an execution shot?"

"Depends on the powder load," the tech answered. "We're used to six or eight grains in nine-mil ammo. This could've been less. Who knows how they loaded cartridges way back then?"

"May I see?" Preneu asked.

The tech produced two metal pans containing misshapen pieces of lead.

"They look a little small for nine millimeter," Kai suggested.

"Let's take a look," he said, picking one up with his forceps and putting it under his microscope.

"I see what you're saying," he said. "They are small for nine, but they're too big for 7.62mm or .38 caliber. It's hard to tell. The lead is very soft and they deformed considerably when they hit the bone."

"What about eight millimeter?" Kai asked.

"That caliber is impossibly rare," Preneu said dismissively.

"Bag both of those for me," the CID man said as the tech replaced the slug in the pan. "I'll see what our lab has to say about them."

The tech looked at Faralaco, who nodded. The KPD people were not expecting to hand over their evidence so abruptly, but they knew that federal agents always trump local police departments.

"Is there anything else we can do?" Faralaco asked with a measure of sarcasm.

"I think I've seen enough for the time being," he said. "I need to get out to the Pacific Missile Range at Barking Sands naval base to pick up what they may have in their files about Captain Dexsen's time at that facility."

"Why would there be any records pertaining to an Army officer at a naval base?" Faralaco asked. "I know that it was an Army Air Forces base back in the forties, but it was transferred to the Air Force, and then to the Navy in the sixties. Wouldn't the Army have taken their stuff?"

"I've spoken to personnel at the base who have identified certain materials that may still be in storage."

"I'll go with you," Kai said abruptly, surprising Preneu, as well as Faralaco, who hadn't expected own of his officers to be so assertive with a federal agent. "As you said, you're investigating the death of one of *your* own…but this was a double homicide and it's our job to continue our investigation of the other victim. Gladys Mattochs was one of *our* own."

When he drove into the Royal Pacific Resort, his 5.0-liter V8 engine rumbling loud enough to turn heads, Ryu Myong-su let the valet park the Mustang, and stopped in at the bar for a Mai Tai before he even went to his room. The man from Korea, the "Land of Morning Calm," took a deep breath and relaxed, enjoying his moment of serenity on Hawai`i's "Garden Isle."

"You look like you just got to the island," the bartender said, grinning. "Hope you're having a good time so far."

"Yes, I did," Ryu said, returning the grin. "Now, I'm going to live it up…*like there is no tomorrow*."

"Oh yeah?"

"What I mean is that tomorrow I must work…business meetings."

"I'm sorry to hear that."

Ryu nodded. He enjoyed a Mai Tai and a hot car, just like the next guy, but his work was more important. His work was his life. It didn't hurt that in his work he was the *sajangnim*, the big boss who demanded and received the respect of others.

In this position, it had never hurt his professional career in South Korea that his name sounded like that of

General Ri Myong-su, once the Chief of the *North* Korean General Staff, and a close confidant of the late supreme leader, Kim Jong Il. Ri was the archetype of the toughest of Korean tough guys, and Ryu cultivated the rumors that they were related—maybe even an illegitimate father-son relationship.

He had been leveraging this alleged "bad guy" connection for years. It had been especially useful during his stellar career as a senior operative with the Gukga Jeongbowo, the South Korean National Intelligence Service.

He finished a Mai Tai, watered down in the tourist trade tradition, and had a second before going up to his room to unpack. At the bottom of his roller bag was a notebook with a bright green cover. It was an innocent-appearing notebook, like a child's school notebook, with Korean characters in red and yellow printed across the cover at an angle. Inside, it was anything but innocent. In carefully written script, it was Ryu's manifesto, his outline for his history-altering plan.

By the time that Ryu had showered, changed into business attire, and gotten back to the bar, Han jong-sok and Cho ho-jin were waiting for him. They had taken a table at the far side of the bar where it opened to the outdoors and far from where their conversation could be overheard.

Ryu's colleagues had been on the island for a couple of weeks now, visiting boutique rum distilleries and small-batch sugar-growers to craft their bona fides in that field. After his parallel career on the deep, dark side of international banking, Ryu could easily afford to bankroll the endeavor. Thanks to his clandestine conduits into that world, he had deftly skimmed thin slices from countless wire transfers and other transactions that were so negligible as to be impractical to trace.

Through the years, they mounted up into billions of Korean won.

Both Han and Cho stood as their boss entered and bowed slightly.

"*Annyeonghaseyo, sajangnim* Ryu," Han said, using the formal greeting and the honorific in Korean that one uses with one's superior.

"Please," Ryu said. "American language and American customs. We must fit in here. Not attract attention. What do you have to tell me?"

"We have spent time with four rum distillers," Han began. "Who knew there were so many on this small island? You know that South Korea has a hundred cities with more people than this island?"

"And we have gotten our fingers dirty in the fine, sugar-growing red dirt," Cho said, holding up fingers with rust-colored stains. "It's hard to get clean. Can you imagine a place that is so proud of the redness of its dirt?"

"This is a strange place, it is true, and I am proud of you gentlemen for your diligence in pursuing our declared purpose in this place," Ryu said politely. "But now that we are able to speak freely without disguising our words as we must do in emails. Now, tell me where are Pak Mi-Rae and Jong Nam-ho? Why are they not here for this meeting?"

"They're coming," Cho promised. "I got a text message…any moment."

"I worry about their lack of discipline," Ryu said, shaking his head. "I always have. I wonder about their commitment to the plan."

"I don't worry about Pak," Han said. "Her commitment is solid. If anything, she is to be praised for keeping 'Teddy' Jong in line. He may be not so good with discipline, but he is fully committed to our plan."

"We need Teddy," Cho reminded them. "He may be a bit of a 'K-pop party boy,' in his private life, but he is a technology genius that the plan depends on."

"Tell me about the installation that you have erected," Ryu asked.

"It is located on a cliff up in the mountains overlooking the ocean. There is nothing between it and Korea but the ocean. It is hidden and well-camouflaged. No one can see it or tell that it is there."

"Good. And the equipment?"

"The last gear came into Honolulu with a shipment of televisions last week and arrived here on Wednesday. We installed it on Thursday. We are all ready for whatever day the US Navy picks for their missile test."

"How will we know?" Ryu asked.

"They will publicize it, as they always do," Han said. "But we have also taken an American naval person into our employ as what the Americans call a freelancer. He is the US Navy's Master-at-Arms Chief Petty Officer Anthony Karboli. He is a senior enlisted man in the security apparatus of the Barking Sands base...the Pacific Missile Range."

"Han calls him 'Master Chief Tony,' which he resents," Cho interjected.

"Having a security man in our service is proving to be important in our work," Han explained. "The Pacific Missile Range has a remote radar and radio facility up in the mountains on a ridge very close to our place. American military people come and go up there all the time, and they will be busier as the 'X-Day' approaches. Chief Tony will arrange guard schedules to keep prying eyes away from our post. There are no questions asked when Chief Tony is with us."

"I congratulate you on finding a man of such importance to help you," Ryu said cautiously. "How can you be certain of his loyalty?"

Han had been itching to share pictures of young Lynsee Kinkaide.

"This is him?" Ryu asked in disbelief. "Who is the woman?"

"Technically, she is still a girl," Cho said. "She is *barely* seventeen."

"So you have him with an underage girl," Ryu asked skeptically. "Is that enough? It is so uncommon in America for a man to have underage girls."

"Yes, but Vice Admiral Hardgrove Kinkaide, the Commander of US Naval Anti-Ballistic Missile Operations in the entire Pacific has only *one underage daughter*," Han said with a broad grin. "This could easily land him in a military prison, where the admiral would make like unbearable for Chief Tony."

"*Chukahaeyo*," Ryu said with a slight nod, using the Korean word for "congratulations."

Just then, Rae Pak arrived with the roguish Teddy Jong, who conveyed their apologies for arriving late for the first meeting with their important *sajangnim*.

After the bowing of heads, the boss waved off the tardiness, but all could tell by his expression that he was irritated.

"What has your Master Chief Tony told you about the missile tests?" Ryu asked.

"It will be even more important than we expected," Cho said. "There will be four launches from here of a new extended range anti-missile missile, which is the newest part of the American Aegis Missile Defense System. Very important."

"That sounds dangerous," Ryu said with a wink, captivated by the technical details."*When* is this test? When will we know?"

"It has been changed several times, but Chief Tony will learn this and we will know before almost anyone else," Han said with reassurance as Karboli glowered.

Kai Nialani had not expected to be headed back to the west side of Kaua`i again so soon, but if there was anything out there which might help explain the murders, she couldn't let the eyes of the CID to be the only eyes to see it. She was glad she had worn her full uniform today.

She had thought of insisting they take a KPD squad car, but she let Zachary Preneu drive. He was one of those who liked to be in charge, and she decided to let him think he was.

As they reached the main gate of PMRF, Kai noticed that security was more robust than she had seen on other visits to the base. There were more guard dogs than one would normally expect and they were using mirrors to peek under some of the vehicles lined up to enter the facility. The color-coded threat level sign near the gate was at "orange," which seemed intimidating.

"Special Agent Preneu and Detective Nialani here to see Master-at-Arms Chief Petty Officer Anthony Karboli," he said, handing over his own badge and ID, followed by the same for Kai. The guard unconsciously stiffened, recognizing Karboli's name, that of his own superior—a senior enlisted security man at PMRF.

When they walked into the security office, Kai immediately recognized the well-built man in his late thirties with bright red hair whom she had seen on the trail only yesterday. She could tell by the flicker of recognition on his face that he too remembered.

"I see that your security level is up to FPCON Charlie," Preneu observed as Karboli introduced himself.

"As you probably know, the DOD baseline level has been set at FPCON Bravo, threat level yellow," the master chief explained. The force protection condition levels were set by those up the feed chain, but it was Karboli's job to enforce them. "But we're at FPCON Charlie and ratcheting up for a test op soon…a big one. I can't really elaborate further."

"I understand," Preneu said. "Let me introduce Detective Kai Nialani of the KPD. It was a double murder, and KPD is investigating the death of the Kaua`i resident who was killed along with Captain Dexsen."

"Hello, Chief," she said, shaking his hand. "But I believe we've met one another before…on Thursday on the Miloli`i Ridge Trail. You were out for a hike with your friends."

"Oh, that's right. Yes, Detective, we did cross paths on the trail."

"Coincidently, I was returning from the crime scene with evidence of *these* two homicides at the time."

"They were killed up *there*?"

"Yes, the skeletal remains were found in a valley near Miloli`i Ridge," Kai confirmed.

Karboli seemed uneasy to learn of skeletons being found near where he'd been hiking. Kai thought it odd. Preneu didn't seem to notice.

"You told me on the phone that you still have US Army records here at PMRF?" Preneu reminded him.

"Yeah, it was an Army base that became an Air Force base that the Navy now owns. The Army took everything they wanted, apparently. Whatever's left, they didn't seem to miss it, but the Navy can't dispose of it because it's Army property. Since you're with the Army, you're welcome to it. Since they don't want it, you can both take anything you want since it's for official investigations."

The warehouse where this material was stored was an unremarkable metal structure tucked in among other ordinary buildings about three city blocks from the security office. Karboli unlocked the door, turned on the lights and took them to a stack of cardboard boxes in one corner of a building that was filled with many piles of boxes that seemed long untouched.

"I'll leave you to it," he said. "If you need anything else, contact the security office, and check in there before you leave the base...make sure this door's locked on your way out."

Kai stepped over to a four-deep stack at one corner of the pile and started reading the markings, while Preneu peeled off his dark-blue suit coat and hung it on a folding chair.

The boxes smelled musty, but this being the dry side of the island, they were probably not as compromised by humidity as they might have been.

Reading main subject headings of the labels out loud as they went, they worked methodically. There were routine maintenance records for vehicles and machinery that was all long-since sold off or scrapped. There were even things such as the records of an intra-base volleyball league dating to the nineteen-fifties.

"Here's something from Army days," Kai announced at last as she read a label out loud. "Records of the 494th Bombardment Group, USAAF, from 1944."

Preneu was at her side in moments, and it was he who descended on the box and pulled it open. The aging yellow masking tape had lost its adhesive properties and flaked off like so many fallen leaves.

"Was Dexsen in the Army Air Forces?" Kai asked as

she took a step back to let Preneu have his way with the musty old cardboard box.

"It's Army, and it's the right time period…that is, if we go with the theory that the shooting took place in 1946," he said without directly answering her question.

"Let's see…there are B-24J aircraft…867th Bombardment Squadron, 864th, 865th," he muttered.

"Here's this in that folder that you just tossed aside," she said, opening the brittle old manila folder. "It says here that the 494th Bombardment Group left Barking Sands for Angaur Island in the Caroline Islands in October 1944. The war was going on. They were going off to go fight it."

Preneu studied the page and then took the folder. Finally, he said he guessed she was right, and they both went back to digging.

The next time, it was the turn of the CID man to make an interesting discovery, and that of the KPD detective to look over his shoulder.

"What do you have there?" Kai asked when she saw him open a box and sit down to dig in.

"Transient Personnel Records, 1945 to 1947," he read from the label.

"I guess that means people who were just passing through," she said.

"Right."

Kai went back to the likes of "Removal of Temporary Wartime Barracks," and "Issues Pertaining to Food Refrigeration in the Tropics," while Preneu silently perused the personnel files, studying each list of names and dates.

She was looking over his shoulder when he found it. There it was in black and white. Dexsen's name rank and serial number, along with the date of his arrival in early 1946. The war was over by then, and she guessed he was on his way back to the States from the Pacific Theater. She scribbled notes in her notebook each time that Preneu tossed a page aside.

For a few weeks, the files contained no entries for Dexsen. Then came an increasing number of motor pool requisition requests. Kai realized—and she wondered if Preneu did as well—that this was probably the courtship of Gladys Mattochs. He was taking out vehicles to go see her, and to take her on dates. He was stuck in Kaua`i on his way home, and a chance meaning had blossomed. This was like watching a Hallmark movie.

Preneu kept flipping through the box, out of 1946 and into 1947, but Dexsen was gone, and Preneu grew noticeably bored.

Finally, he stood up and stretched.

"There's nothing there but routine stuff," he said. "I suppose seeing it and knowing it was nothing made this trip not such a waste of time. Why don't you go ahead and put all that back in the box while I go find a bathroom?"

He then walked away, leaving the KPD detective in the middle of log sheets he had scattered, and having been told to clean up his mess.

As she looked through the papers that Zachery Preneu had tossed aside, she had not seen the "nothing" he saw. She had seen a pattern that was more than just the dating history of Glenn and Gladys. She picked up the last page on which Glenn was mentioned. It was the last week of June, the week that Glenn and Gladys disappeared.

Then she looked at his unit. All the soldiers in all these log sheets had their units listed. Most of them were squadrons and regiments, all numbered, the 494th this or the 103rd that. Dexsen, though, had a three-letter acronym. It meant nothing to Kai and she had not bothered to note it at first. Then, she detected that during that same last week of June, another man had arrived at Barking Sands who belonged to that same outfit.

She stared with deep interest at his motor pool records. He too, requested vehicles while he was at Barking Sands—including one on the same day that Glenn Dexsen made his last request. Then, a few days later, he left for the mainland.

His name was Lieutenant Frank Striden, and he also belonged to this unit called "OSS," whatever that was.

CHAPTER TWELVE

LIEUTENANT RICHARD FARALACO was glad that it was Detective Kai Nialani's idea because he didn't want that job himself. He could, and would, let her do it.

Nobody likes to do next-of-kin death notifications. They are never easy and they never get any easier. This was Kai's fourth time, and it was the oldest homicide she and Faralaco could remember being reported in all their time in the KPD.

The "preferred protocol guidelines" say that death notifications to survivors be made as soon as possible. That wouldn't be possible. No current member of the Mattochs family had yet been born when Gladys died. This only served to make it all that more strange.

The guidelines say you should notify the survivors in person, not over the phone. This was exactly where Kai was headed this rainy Saturday morning in Līhu`e. At least the weather fit the mood.

The years had scattered the Mattochs family. Gladys had been an only child, and her devastated parents had moved to the mainland, a hard move for people who had actually been born in Kaua`i. Her father had a brother, and his granddaughter was the only Mattochs heir left to preside over what little was left of the family estate after most of the land and property had been sold off.

Cynthia Mattochs—she used her maiden name—did not look like an heiress. She looked like one of those people who you saw at Costco or Target and never even noticed. She was shorter than Kai, with shoulder-length white hair.

"May I help you?" she asked, obviously startled to have a uniformed police officer on the porch of her home on this leafy street in an upscale Līhu`e neighborhood.

"Cynthia Mattochs?"

"Yes..."

"I'm afraid that I have some bad news."

"Oh no! *Oh no*! Please tell me it's not Jeffery!"

"It's not Jeffery, ma'am. It's Gladys. I'm here to inform you of the passing of Gladys Mattochs. I'm sorry for your loss."

The fluttering of eyelashes suggested relief that it was not Jeffrey, whoever he was, and Cynthia's mind not yet reaching back far enough for a memory of Gladys.

"*Gladys*," she exclaimed at last. "I have not heard that name spoken for so long. It must be...I don't know."

"It was 1946, ma'am. Gladys went missing in 1946..."

"That's right," Cynthia said. "Would you like to come in?"

They sat in Cynthia's living room, with its picture window view of a large flowering tulip tree. It was an old house. Kai wondered whether Gladys had walked these halls back then. Cynthia offered "coffee or something stronger." Kai declined, but Cynthia poured herself two fingers of gin and splashed in some soda.

"She eloped," Cynthia said with assurance. "She and her soldier boy caught an Army flight to the mainland

and never looked back. She had a big fight with her parents and dropped them like a hot potato."

"And you know this how?"

"It's what *everybody* said. Everybody knew about the fights. It was before my time, obviously, but that was what everybody said. Of course, by the time I was old enough to care, nobody talked about it that much anymore. That's why I had to rack my brain at first when you said her name. Where did she end up?"

"She and Captain Dexsen never made it off this island. They died in a canyon in the mountains up above the Nāpali Coast."

"*No*, I can't believe it!"

"I recovered the remains myself," Kai assured her. "The DNA was done at the state lab in Honolulu."

"They were here all along?"

"Yes."

"You said there was DNA, so that must mean there are remains?"

"Yes, but..."

"I know there's not much after all that time in the mountains, but we could arrange for a burial...right?"

"Yes, we'll arrange for them to be returned after we complete our investigation."

"Investigation?" Cynthia asked. "Why? How did it happen?"

"I'm afraid that I have to inform you that they were murdered."

"*Murdered*? Can there be any other explanation?"

"No, ma'am. Fatal bullet wounds were visible, and bullets were recovered."

Cynthia just sat and stared, obviously in shock. The guidelines say to give the next-of-kin as much information as possible, but even after all this time, mention of bullets was deeply disquieting.

"Who could have done this?" Cynthia asked.

"I was about to ask you that."

"I have no idea. I guess the jilted lover is always a suspect, right?"

"Often that's the case."

"Then Clarence Flaunsin jumps to mind. He assumed that *he* would marry Gladys. Both families assumed he would marry Gladys."

"That was in the newspapers," Kai told her.

"I never saw the newspapers."

"They're on microfilm at the library on Hardy Street."

"Oh, how convenient," Cynthia said sarcastically. "I'll take a pass."

Kai just nodded.

"This may also be in the newspapers, but Flaunsin and that soldier got into a fistfight," Cynthia added. "That was part of what the family whispered about."

"I suppose we should probably look into Mr. Flaunsin," Kai said.

"I heard he was killed in a car accident in the sixties, but I don't know. The Flaunsin family used to be very important in Southern California, but I don't know about now. The Mattochs family used to be very important on Kaua`i. That's the funny thing about the newspapers. Your name is in there nearly every week for years, and then decades later, you're at a point where there's no institutional memory that the family ever existed."

"I'll follow up on Flaunsin," Kai said, already thinking that this family was a dead end.

"Thank you for doing this," Cynthia said, touching Kai's knee for emphasis. "Murder…*murder*. Now that you say it, all these memories are flooding back. All the things the family talked about. *Everything*. Please do find out who did this to Gladys. I thought we had closure, accepting they ran away, but now, it's like a wound ripped open. Please find out what happened to Gladys."

"I'm certainly going to try," Kai said, biting her tongue. She had been told in her early days in law enforcement never to make promises to victim families that could not be kept, and she always thought about that at times like this.

In this case, she was not lying when she said she would try. It was personal for her too. She had held the skulls in her hands in the middle of nowhere. She had seen the bullet holes, and she had seen the bullets.

Kai Nialani *had to know* who killed Gladys Mattochs.

On Saturday morning, as Kai Nialani was stepping into the soft rain in Līhu`e, Manter-at-Arms Chief Petty Officer Anthony Karboli was on a concrete pad next the dry red dirt of a sugarcane field on the far west side of Kaua`i.

His day job, the one that had him in command of a contingent of security personnel enforcing perimeters ahead of an unprecedented series of missile launches at PMRF had him on the run for the past week, but his side jobs kept interfering. The visit by Army CID and the local cop on Friday was a distraction, but his unexpected commitment to a strange Korean sugar company had become a serious complication.

He was between the rock of being a security cop dealing with the highest security level exercise in a few years, and the hard place of the threat of dishonor at the least, and prison at the worst. He had no choice. He had to thread the needle and make all this work.

He was surprised at first to see them roll up in a

bright-blue Mustang convertible with the top down. He didn't know the full extent of what they were doing, but he knew it was covert, and he wondered how driving around in a vehicle this conspicuous aligned with a covert operation.

Then it dawned on him. It was the "hide in plain sight" principle.

How does a foreigner with surreptitious purpose hide in plain sight on a tourist island? *As a tourist.*

As Han, Cho and their boss, whom Karboli was about to meet, all piled out the car in their tropical shirts and flip-flops, they looked more like they belonged in Kaua`i than Karboli did, with his spit-shined shoes, his khakis and insignia, and his badge.

"Aloha, Chief Tony," Han jong-sok said. "Our *sajangnim* is anxious to meet you. This is Ryu Myong-su."

"Chief Petty Officer Karboli," he said, extending his hand. As Ryu recognized, it would have been easy to belittle this important man, as Han seemed to want to do, but Ryu saw nothing useful to be gained by treating him with disrespect.

"I would like to thank you for your kindness in helping my associates with our important work here. As the day approaches, the security of our installation will be critical. I understand you have personal weapons for us?"

"Yes, I do," Karboli said, picking a small canvas bag up them the ground and setting it on a low stack of shipping pallets to open it. "As you requested, I have several automatic handguns, all chambered for 9mm, and several boxes of ammo."

He opened the bag and unwrapped three pistols from a dark-colored hand towel. The three weapons had a familiar appearance but were somehow different.

"These are weapons that were confiscated by security services at the base," he explained. "They've been locked up and untouched for years, so they won't be missed. They were logged in, but because none of them have serial numbers, they're untraceable."

"No serial numbers?" Ryu asked in surprise.

"None," Karboli confirmed. "They're what are known in the civilian world as 'ghost guns.' They're handmade with random parts from 'buy-build-shoot' kits. This one may look like a Glock G17, and it's got a few Glock parts, but mostly polymer parts. It has no Glock serial number. Criminals like these because they can't be traced. They're like ghosts."

"You have done well, Chief Karboli," Ryu said, picking up the Glock G17 lookalike and sighting it.

"I've tried to do everything that Mr. Han and Mr. Cho have asked. This includes helping them carry some gear to your place up there on Thursday."

"Thank you for that," Ryu said warmly.

"Yes," Han added. "That was very helpful. There was a lot of equipment."

This visit to the outpost, of which Han had taken many photos, also served to establish Karboli as having been present at the site. If anything went wrong, this could be used to incriminate him, and Karboli knew this.

"On our way in to the site, we passed a woman in a Kaua`i Police Department uniform shirt," Karboli told Ryu. "I saw her again yesterday. She's a homicide detective. When we saw her up in the mountains, she was on her way back from recovering the remains of two murder victims."

"*What*?" Ryu asked, startled. "What kind of remains?"

"Human remains...skeletons. People were murdered a few miles from your site."

"*Skeletons*?" Han asked, sounding worried. "Dead persons?"

"Yes," Karboli said. For an instant, he found himself with a ploy with which to annoy Han. "Bullet holes in the middle of each skull. Execution style."

"You saw this same policewoman yesterday *again*?" Ryu asked, sounding concerned.

"Yes, I did," Karboli confirmed. "She came to our security office at the base with a US Army CID agent, that's the Army Criminal Investigation Division."

"What did they want?"

"They wanted to look at old personnel records that are left from when the base belonged to the Army back in the forties."

"Why/" Ryu asked. "What were they looking for?"

"One of the murder victims was a soldier," Karboli explained. "He and a civilian were murdered up in the mountains in 1946. The civilian was a local woman who may have been his girlfriend. The skeletons had been there ever since. Some hikers discovered them and the police recovered them."

"Were other people murdered?" Han asked. "Are there other skeletons up there?"

"Maybe," Karboli said, realizing that talk of skeletons was making Han squeamish—and anything subtle that he could do to make Han uncomfortable was a way of getting back at him for his mocking.

"I don't know," Karboli continued. "It's out of our jurisdiction. The PMRF instrumentation site is on Makaha Ridge, a very narrow swath of the ridgeline. Everything else up there is state land. It's out of our control, so we would not have been briefed. They were looking through a lot of records, so it may be that there were other killings and the skeletons are still up there. I can't say anything, one way or another."

"Will this investigation interfere with what we are doing?" Ryu asked.

"I don't think so," Karboli said thoughtfully. "Not unless you believe in ghosts."

CHAPTER THIRTEEN

"DO you know what our job is here?"

Dave Altbeck, a journalist from *Defense Up Front,* the print and online monthly, wondered if this was a trick question, given that it was being asked by the COMABM-PAC, the Commander of Naval Anti-Ballistic Missile Operations for the Pacific. He knew that the answer was complicated, and that it could take ten minutes to answer. He also knew that Vice Admiral Hardgrove Kinkaide was a complicated man given to being succinct when he wanted to be.

"I think you'd say that your job here is a straightforward mission to shoot down incoming ballistic missiles, sir," the journalist answered, assuming the admiral was in a mood to be concise.

"Our job," the admiral replied, "is to protect the United States of America from Armageddon, if it comes from out of western skies."

Okay, add the adjective dramatic, Altbeck thought to himself as he scribbled in his notepad.

Kinkaide was one of the most powerful American naval officers in the Pacific at this moment. The admirals who skippered Carrier Battle Groups or Ballistic Missile Subs had more lethal hitting power at their fingertips, but Kinkaide's field of operations was the *entire* Pacific Ocean.

This week and last, and for as long as it took, he now was the OTC, the "Officer in Tactical Command," of an operation called codenamed Vigilant Basilisk, which involved thousands of personnel and dozens of air and sea assets spread across a swath of the PMRF that stretched all the way to Kwajalein Atoll, twenty-five hundred miles away.

It was hard not to compare this to Vigilant Wyvern, that anti-ballistic missile weapons system flight test of a number of years ago that was the biggest of its kind up to that time. Basilisk would dwarf Wyvern in every way.

"If you had to summarize what you hope to accomplish with Basilisk on the eve of the test, what would you say?" the journalist asked. He had been extensively briefed several times, but he was always looking for a quotable quote or two.

"Basilisk? *Hmmm,*" Kinkaide replied. "Between you and me, I'm not so big on these mythological nicknames, but I guess if you have to use one, the name of a serpent king who can kill an enemy just by looking into its eyes is a good one. Here at ABMPAC we're in the unambiguous business of killing enemies."

Hard to beat a quote like that, Altbeck decided.

He was embedded with Kinkaide for the duration, confirmed to PMRF until Vigilant Basilisk concluded. The whole base was on FPCON Bravo, but even without, there was no way that the Navy could have a journalist out in the world talking about what he was seeing before Basilisk was over. After a successful test, telling the world was *exactly* what they wanted—good publicity.

Nobody knew when this would be, because the day

and time of the launch was classified, unknown to all but the handful at the top with need-to-know clearance. Altbeck didn't know, although he did know from what he'd picked up from various conversations that it had been postponed several times since the weekend. What he *did know* for certain was that he was close enough to the action that he'd be one of the first to know.

In the meantime, there were far less exciting places to spend a Saturday than to be sequestered within Kinkaide's inner sanctum, PMRF's Battle Management Interoperability Center. This place veritably crackled with anticipation and adrenaline.

Kinkaide always maintained his headquarters wherever he needed to be. Wearing the three stars of the second-highest rank in the US Navy, he could easily operate from a fixed location well back from the action, but Kinkaide preferred to lead from the front. This week and last, and for as long as it took, this was at Barking Sands, here inside the BMIC. Bathed in the soft red light, Kinkaide was like a hero on the set of a movie, surrounded by eighty-six-inch PN-LA862 AQUOS 4K interactive touchscreen LCD displays and every other technical system necessary to communicate and coordinate the intricate actions involved in firing a barrage of missiles across this vast slice of ocean.

"These are the launch batteries," Kinkaide said, pointing to brilliantly illuminated icons on the screen. "Have you seen these in person?"

"No, sir," the journalist replied. "I was met at the gate by a lieutenant commander and a captain, who said they didn't have the authorization to show me anything."

"We'll see about that." The admiral smirked. Nothing within a radius of thousands of miles was above *his* pay grade.

"Do you know what this is?" Kinkaide asked, walking to another of his bank of giant PN-LA862 touchscreens.

"It says Kwajalein, so I'd guess that's the ICBM launch site. That's where you'll launch the target for the Aegis Ballistic Missile Defense System interceptor missiles that you'll launch from here at Barking Sands."

"Right. In Vigilant Wyvern we confirmed the capability of the Aegis Combat System, in a ballistic missile defense configuration, to detect, engage and intercept two inert short-range ballistic missile targets, but Basilisk gets two ICBM targets. Almost nobody will know this until launch. This is part of the exercise. You get to know because you won't talk to anybody until it's over."

"I see..."

"This time, the targets are a pair of LGN-30G Minuteman IIIs and they're *not inert.*"

"You mean...?"

"No," the admiral said with an uncharacteristic laugh. "We *did* pull out the W87 *nuclear* warheads, but these were replaced by a ton of one of the powerful explosive chemical combinations ever cobbled together. It's a mixture of PETN, *pentaerythritol tetranitrate,* combined with RDX, a nitroamine explosive with twice the energy of TNT by weight."

"That should be an extraordinary blast."

"You're probably wondering why we went to the trouble, since the point of the exercise is just to evaluate the intercept?" Kinkaide asked.

"Sure..."

"Because the Chinese will be out there watching," the admiral said. "They watch everything we do, and we want to astound 'em with a 'big bang' this time."

"I see..."

"I promised to show you some missiles," Kinkaide

said, changing the subject as he started walking toward the door. "Let's go look at some missiles."

What Vice Admiral Hardgrove Kinkaide failed to share with his shadowing journalist was the Achilles heel of Vigilant Basilisk. For all his bravado about the seamless systems inside his Battle Management Interoperability Center, he and his team were wrestling with the heart of the Aegis Ballistic Missile Defense System itself.

As they drove out toward one of the remote hangars adjacent to the 6,002-foot main runway at Barking Sands, an Air Force C-17 was unloading some thirty-foot containers, and the admiral was subconsciously chewing the inside of his cheek. One of the most powerful American naval officers in the Pacific was nervous, and the object of his nervousness was inside these huge containers.

The US Navy had good luck with its RIM-161 SM-3 missile-intercepting missiles, and with its successor, the RIM-174A SM-6 Extended Range Active Missile. In addition to its extended range, the ERAM had a more potent processor, running more precise targeting software that helped it hit ballistic missiles that were untouchable by SM-3 missiles.

The A-Model SM-6 ERAM was a better weapon. However, as is so often the case, when engineers set out to make something better into something *even* better, things don't work out as hoped. When the first batch of the "new and improved" RIM-174F ERAMs arrived ten days ago, they *were* new, but anything but improved.

What Kinkaide could have told them is that at least half of what made up the newness of any "new" variant of any system was *never* improved.

Somebody at the Missile Defense Agency had decided to "upgrade" the Mk104 dual-thrust solid-fueled rocket sustainer—the rocket engine that remained with the missile after booster separation—with a Mk109B. Just to be on the safe side with new equipment he had not used before, Kinkaide had ordered the sustainer to be test run. It failed.

Kinkaide demanded a list of fixes be done, and the results were arriving now.

This fiasco had resulted in the original test firing being canceled, but because the date was top secret, only Kinkaide and a handful of his ABMPAC team knew that it had come and gone without a launch. Of course, there had been rumors, including those which had fallen on Altbeck's ears over the weekend.

Altbeck, like the majority of Navy personnel at Barking Sands, was clueless about the exact nature of the snafus as he and Kinkaide watched one of the twenty-eight-foot replacement ERAMs was unpacked from its crate.

"Same diameter, but longer than the A-Model," the admiral said, ticking off attributes of the weapon. "It's got a Mk125 blast-fragmentation warhead like the 'A.' You don't need much to blow a hole in an ICBM. The 'F' has a bigger solid rocket booster, though. This will push it up around Mach four. You want that speed when you've got a DPRK Hwasing-19 or 20 bearing down on you, or headed for the US of A."

"You are assuming that North Korea is the most probable threat that you're countering?"

"Wouldn't *you*?"

Kinkaide also did not share that another aggravation causing him to lose sleep this week was another Kinkaide.

As with the bugs eating the RIM-174F program alive, the presence of Lynsee Louise Kinkaide at Barking Sands was an unanticipated complication. When the admiral had first come over to Kaua`i a couple of weeks ago, his wife and seventeen-year-old only daughter had come along.

There was a meet-and-greet and a dinner at the five-star Royal Pacific Resort for local bigwigs to meet the Barking Sands brass. He thought his wife would like this, and the admiral figured they could stay on at the resort for a few days of sun and surf while he ensconced himself at PMRF.

As with the RIM-174F, things did not go as planned. Mrs. Kinkaide suddenly had a work emergency on the mainland, and they decided that "Lynsee Lou," as her mother called her, could stay on with family friends for a couple of days, then fly home to San Diego. Another scheduling snafu, and the early departure of the family friends made it so that she wound up with Dad at Barking Sands a day before threat level FPCON Charlie descended, effectively trapping her on base.

While the Battle Management Interoperability Center was her dad's true home away from home at PMRF, Lynsee had the run of the on-base admiral's quarters, where he appeared only for a few hours of sleep each night. The quarters were pretty lavish by Navy base housing standards. There was even a pool.

It's probably axiomatic that teenagers find a great deal of entertainment in their personal handheld devices, but after a couple of days of texting her friends back home about how bored she was, Lynsee got bored of doing this. The base hugs the shoreline, so there is a long beach, but it was windy, with heavy surf, so she soon grew bored of this as well.

As hangouts, there were the O-Club and the NCO Club, but she was neither an officer nor an NCO, so that left a pizza and burger place called Shenanigans. It had a "single sailor vibe" with karaoke and the like. Lynsee was not a single sailor, but she was of the demographic with whom they liked to flirt, and she soon fell in with a group of other young women, mostly single sailors themselves, who had great fun flirting back.

She was seventeen, though her father thought of her as twelve, but she had an ID—with a name other than Kinkaide—that said she was twenty-one. Lynsee also a fashion sense, and skills with cosmetics, that allowed her to easily make herself *look* twenty-one.

Saturday afternoon found her meeting some of her new friends at Shenanigans, wearing Rouge Dior lipstick and a stylish, sparkly top that was the right mixture of cool sophistication and daytime-appropriate. She was there to turn heads but not expecting to turn that of Master-at-Arms Chief Petty Officer Anthony Karboli.

Nor was Karboli expecting this either. He had come in here looking for Petty Officer Second Class Joel Dyallic, a master-at-arms in Karboli's MA chain of command. Dyallic was technically off duty, but with Vigilant Basilisk looming, and the base at threat level FPCON Charlie, nobody was *really* off duty.

Karboli and Dyallic, like nearly everyone else at PMRF, were in that familiar limbo of military life known as "hurry-up-and-wait." It was the indeterminate state of knowing something big was imminent but not knowing when. As the people tasked with base security, this was particularly tense time for MAs. No wonder, Dyallic was in here unwinding. The PMRF MAs were banned from drinking during FPCON Charlie, but at least he could take a few hours off to hang out and *pretend* it wasn't happening.

Karboli saw Lynsee before he recognized her.

His eye caught the long blond hair, the evocative curve of her body and her long, perfect legs; then they narrowed in on the lips, a color he liked without needing to know it was Rouge Dior.

He saw a beautiful woman in her twenties, just as he saw such a person when he first met Lynsee at the Royal Pacific. It was only when he did a double-take that he realized he was seeing the *same teenager* he first met at the Royal Pacific.

He turned his head, but it was too late.

"*Anthony*," she shouted across the uncrowded room.

Before he could move, she was moving toward him, a broad and seductive smile on those Rouge Dior lips.

What was she still doing here on the island?

When Han had told him she was Kinkaide's teenage daughter, Karboli had assumed she would have left the island after the big soiree. What was she still doing at Barking Sands? Why had she followed him to the base in the middle of a missile launch exercise?

Lynsee Kinkaide had no idea that their nude romp in that suite at the Royal Pacific had been captured in explicit detail on video by Han jong-sok's cell phone. She did not know that this video was being used to blackmail Karboli, nor that he now knew her true age.

As she reached him and embraced him provocatively, she only knew that this was a man with whom she believed she had fallen in love. Nothing else mattered to this teenager in love.

Part of the thing that made Han's video sizzle to such a degree was that both of those in it were having what might be called "the time of their lives." For Lynsee, whose young life had witnessed so few such times, the

Royal Pacific tryst was beyond special. It was life-changing. She had met the love of her life.

"Oh Anthony," she said, leaning in for a kiss. "You don't know how much I've missed you."

Most of what she knew about these moments had been learned from the Hollywood interpretation, and for her, this was a true Hollywood moment. She had been reunited with her soul mate, a man she had feared she would never see again. Now fate had handed her another chance.

For him, being caught in the blast of a RIM-174F warhead would have been preferable to this.

"I'm on duty," he said almost pathetically. "I can't be seen..."

"I understand, Anthony," she said. Having been raised in a Navy family, she knew how things worked in the Navy without wanting to admit it at this moment. "But I want us to be together. Can't we just..."

"I'm on duty," he repeated, feeling his voice quavering as he pushed her away.

He saw people staring at them, and among those he saw Petty Officer Second Class Joel Dyallic. His expression was a mixture of bewilderment and the amusement that a bystander might take in the display that was unfolding.

Karboli just gestured for Dyallic to come with him *now* and backed away from Lynsee.

It may have been a twenty-something's lipstick on them, but they were the lips of a seventeen-year-old that spoke as the two men left the room, and the eyes of a seventeen-year-old that began to shed mascara-damaging tears.

"Anthony...I *need* you," she whispered quietly. "I *love* you. Please say that you *love me*."

CHAPTER FOURTEEN

LESS THAN EIGHT miles from where a love-struck teenager and a troubled chief petty officer slept fitfully, but a mile apart, Pak Mi-Rae stared into Sunday's predawn darkness from the kitchen window of the modest mid-century bungalow on the edge of Kekaha that the Sweet Harvest Sugar Company out of Seoul had rented for its staff a couple of weeks ago.

In Ryu Myong-su's bold and extraordinarily deadly plot, what more sarcastic cover could he have chosen for his mad designs than the imaginary Sweet Harvest? What, he had asked himself, as he had filtered his team of sugar company executives into Kaua`i, could be nicer, friendlier, or sweeter?

Outside the bungalow was the brown Hyundai Palisade SUV that Han jong-sok had rented when the Sweet Harvesters had first landed. He picked brown, thinking that it wouldn't show the dirt from the farms they would visit. He was wrong. The dirt was red.

Ryu's blue Mustang was not here. It was with him at the Royal Pacific, where his accommodations were much more luxurious than at the bungalow. He was the *sajangnim*, the big boss man. It was only right that he set himself apart from his minions.

As Kai sipped her *nok-cha* green tea and listened to the fitful snores of her three male companions in the other rooms, she saw, without really noticing them, the headlights of a handful of the cars driving past on the main highway, Highway 50, a block away. One of them, now signaling for a turn onto Highway 550, the road up into the mountains, was a certain older model silver-gray Ford Taurus.

Jim Hammer and Lauren Stahling had talked about, and wasted beach time discussing, what could possibly be going on at the place up on Pokuakini Ridge. Most of the rhetorical questions were variations on whether it was a threat to PMRF or a creation of and by PMRF. Were the people who set up this place *North* Korean spies? If not, why Russian hardware? When they met those two Koreans, hiking with a redhead who looked like active-duty Navy, and saw all of them lugging huge packs, this brought on more questions.

Should Hammer and Stahling report what they had found as they had reported the bones? *Who* would they report it to? They couldn't call the cops over what had the earmarks of a military exercise.

Should they report it to the Navy? What if the people involved were *South* Koreans, and this was part of a legitimate, if covert, exercise? In this case, would Hammer and Stahling get themselves busted for disrupting it?

"We need to go back up to that Korean camp and have another look," Lauren had said at last. "If we don't figure this out, this will continue getting in the way of our beach days."

"You're just saying that because you're an adventure junkie," Hammer said with a laugh. She was. She thrived on it.

"Listen, mister," she said with a smile as she wrapped her arms around him seductively. "You're not supposed to tease people about their addictions. Especially when *you're the one* who hooked me in the first place."

It was still dark when they reached and passed the turnoff for the PMRF remote facility on Makaha Ridge, and the parking area for the Miloli`i Ridge Trail. They had parked here on their previous visits, but not this morning.

Today, out on an abundance of caution, which they refused to call paranoia, they continued driving for a quarter mile to the *next* parking turnoff. For the Koreans or anyone to see the same Taurus frequenting the same parking area over the space of a few days might raise suspicions. By now, it was light enough that they could easily hike cross country and intersect the trail.

As on their previous visits, there was nothing disappointing about the sunrise across the top of the Nāpali cliffs, which exploded into view as they broke out of the dense koa forest at the higher elevations. Just as this pair were obsessive adventure junkies, they were easily seduced by intense scenery, whether it was in the Montana Rockies, among Southwest mesas, or here on this island.

Pausing a time or two to climb to a high spot to check the trail behind for other hikers coming along behind them, they made it to the place where the goat trail to Pokuakini Ridge and the Korean camp peeled off from the main Miloli`i Ridge Trail by mid-morning. They had made good time, but they were both strong hikers and it *was* downhill.

They paused about forty yards from the tent, at which distance most people would have been unable to see it for the camouflage. Hammer went in alone to make sure no one was there. Twenty years of eluding the enemy in places like Afghanistan had made this second nature for him. Lauren enjoyed watching him as he moved like a shadow. As he got close to the site, she couldn't see him any longer, even with his Oberwerk binoculars.

At last, he appeared and waved for her to come down.

The scene inside the tent had changed. At the center of the side facing westward toward the ocean were three new LG flat-screen monitors that made the Russian gear look antiquated. Most curious were two large flat things that looked like refrigerator doors without the refrigerators. They had been folded down so they could be carried in, and now they were unfolded and set up.

"What are these things?" Lauren asked, trying to figure them out.

"They're scanned array radar antennae."

"What do they do?"

"Warning or control, or both," Hammer said. "Depends on this other hardware they've brought in here. They're only the antenna part. They can serve either defensive or offensive electronics. They can serve hardware that either tracks or attacks...or both."

"Sounds serious."

"This whole place is getting more serious all the time," he said. "I'm going to run this by Tim Tommis, but I think our next visit out here will be to shut all this down."

Ryu Myong-su and his crew of faux cane-growing researchers from Sweet Harvest met no other hikers on their own Sunday morning walk along the Miloli`i Ridge Trail. There was a family of four getting out of their car in the parking area with plans to hike out for the unforgettable views, but they would be hiking more slowly and less purposefully. For them, this was not a business trip. Maybe they would see one another later in the day, or maybe not.

As the people from the Korean Peninsula guided their *sajangnim* on his first visit to the unforgettable views at the top of the Nāpali Coast, they soon left the main trail for a less traveled route that led to their carefully constructed site. On this route, they could be certain they would be seen by no prying human eyes—or could they?

In fact, two sets of such eyes, belonging to humans well-practiced in the arts of backcountry concealment, were calmly watching as they passed.

Ryu Myong-su's plan was at last coming to its culmination. He was about to resolve the world's most difficult geopolitical dilemma. For well over half a century the Korean Peninsula had been the scene of a dangerous, but almost comedic, poker game. For most, it was accepted as endless. For Ryu, who was most skilled at the tables himself, no games of chance are endless.

It was no game of chance that he picked as the core of his team, two skilled and successful former military officers who were also skillful card players. Han jong-sok and Cho ho-jin were hardcore tactical masterminds who became so dangerous at the tables in their retirement that they had been banned for life at certain casinos from Macau to Singapore. They were anxious to accept the challenge of stepping up from green felt to a game of global dimensions, a game with blindingly high stakes.

Han and Cho, ever-vigilant and hyperaware, lived in a real world, while Pak Mi-Rae and Jong Nam-ho lived in cyberspace, a limitless world that you can neither see nor touch, except through the magical looking glass of a computer screen.

Typecast within the group as a sort of K-pop cutup, Teddy Jong was recognized in this parallel universe for being beyond all measures of genius. If the dark web was a real place, there would be streets named after him, and he'd live in a hundred-room palace at the top of the hill.

Rae was a near match for Teddy in technical prowess, but in her introspective personality, she was the diametric opposite. Whereas Teddy was hot, even white-hot, Rae was cool, so cool that ice often seemed to hang on her words. He typically dressed like he had stepped from an all-night disco, but she dressed in subdued tones, not the black on black of a "goth girl," but the hues of a shadow that you might see without noticing.Ryu didn't see their destination until they were practically upon it, and he congratulated the team on their diligent camouflage work. Inside the well-concealed canopy tent, the contrast was stark. He passed from the rugged wilderness of imposing cliffs and timeless terrain into the winking and blinking lights of an impressive electronic operations center.

Rae and Teddy stood by quietly as Han and Cho explained the new scanned array radar antennae they had just installed. Like Hammer and Stahling, Ryu thought they looked like refrigerator doors. Cho then went on to housekeeping details of the construction and placement of the installation itself, and of the all-important, and well-concealed, solar panels that delivered the electrical power required for all the electronics.

"These, Sajangnim Ryu, are the 1RL257 and 1L269 multifunctional tactical battlefield jammers," Han explained as he began to show his leader around the place. "The Russians call this system Deadly Nightshade, which explains why it's so useful for our purposes."

"What does this 'deadly' system do for *our* purposes?" Ryu asked.

"It broadcasts radio signals to kill radar systems. Our

Russian friends have used these in their wars with great success against the best Western equipment."

"You got this from our Belarusian friend in Busan?" Ryu asked, referring to a certain furtive black market arms dealer who operated out of on a back alley warehouse on South Korea's largest port city waterfront.

"Yes, we did," Han confirmed.

"What's the range of these?" Ryu asked.

"Up to fifty kilometers, but remember, the main Pacific Missile Range base at Barking Sands is half that distance from here. Their important instrumentation station at Makaha Ridge is only about eight kilometers from where we're standing. You can see it from that little hill outside. I can show you!"

"I noticed as we walked in," Ryu said. "What else do you have to show me?"

"Our prize purchase from the man in Busan was this," Han said proudly. "This is our own 29B6 Konteyner over-the-horizon VHF radar system," Cho said proudly. "It's the same type of early warning system our Russian friends use to protect Moscow from NATO. It is very powerful and comprehensive radar. We can see everything with this."

Ryu nodded, he had been briefed before on the 29B6 and now he was running an operation that *had one.* Having a "Konteyner" of his own was as much fun as renting a bright-blue Mustang convertible. He adored this hardware that was the offensive military equivalent of his V8 muscle car.

He was not disappointed when Cho directed him to another ominous-looking console.

"I recognize this friend," Ryu said. "This is that R-330Zh tactical jammer that I got from my old friends at South Korean Intelligence. We got these from Ukraine, who had captured them from the Russians. The range should be sufficient to cover all the American bases and everything across this whole side of the island."

"We have no reason to believe any different," Cho interjected, pleased by Ryu's knowledge of their equipment. "The Russians call it 'Zhitel,' which means something that is at home in a place, but it makes *this place* inhospitable to others. It jams guidance systems and wipes out all satellite communications receivers...GPS, cell phones, everything...military and civilian. It pokes out their eyes and ears!"

"Very good," Ryu said proudly. "Now, tell me about this in the middle. The rest of this room looks like it might be straight out of the Reconnaissance General Bureau in Pyongyang, but with these LG monitors, this looks like we're in an office building in Seoul...or New York."

Teddy Jong practically exploded with pent-up enthusiasm. Teddy was ready, ready to show off his part of the show.

"This is my baby, or what I like to call the *heart* of our sweet electronic warfare nest," he effused with no trace of modesty. "I built her by hand back home, and she was shipped here in a container of LG television sets. Under these flat screens, she is a C-band active electronic scanned array radar system that can both detect and neutralize anything radar-guided. I call her 'Kitty,' because when she says 'Hello,' you no longer have a mouth. Get it, the Hello Kitty dolls have no mouth."

"Tell us how you designed your Kitty," Han said, steering Teddy back on message.

"I started with a TPQ-76 Cloud Mirror system with active electronically scanned array technology for detection, which is *very* leading-edge South Korean equipment. Then, I gave her some teeth, but she's sneaky. You don't see her, and you *don't know you don't see her*. She attacks by spoofing your global navigation satellite systems. You think you're seeing *real* GNSS or GPS data, but you're actually seeing what I send you, which is all fake news, fake data. Everybody depends on GPS, but Kitty and I will give you *counterfeit* data!"

"How does that work?" Ryu asked.

"In their exercise, the Americans are planning to launch ICBMs from Kwajalein as targets for their Aegis missiles," Teddy began, "Kitty and I can 'mirror' that data and tell North Korea that it is coming for them. In North Korea, they will think they see a real Minuteman coming toward them, so they will react and launch one or more Hwasong-20 ICBMs against the United States."

"The Americans will have already launched their Aegis missiles from here at Barking Sands," Han interjected. "They will be unable to reload to respond in time to stop the Hwasong."

"The Americans in their heartland, at the US Strategic Command's own Command and Control Facility, will see the incoming Hwasongs," Ryu said, paraphrasing his own manifesto which lay between the covers of his bright-green notebook. "They will have sought authority from their president to strike back...and POTUS will have given the green light for a withering and overwhelming American counterstrike against the DPRK, the wicked *North*."

Ryu then stepped toward the edge of the cliff, put his hands on his hips and stared westward toward the broad blue Pacific.

"It will be a world war," Teddy said proudly. "It will be a world war started by a spoofing Kitty."

Ryu Myong-su and his enthusiastic troops left their tent on top of its Nāpali cliff feeling on top of the world. He had convinced them that a hot war on the Korean Peninsula—even a hot war as hot as the 100 million degrees Centigrade of a nuclear blast—was a *good* thing. They were convinced that reordering the geopolitical landscape of the Far East was worth it.

People have been using wars for reordering landscapes since the dawn of geopolitical history, but not all of those who dreamed the big bellicose dreams had means and opportunity to see them through. Julius Caesar and Alexander the Great did. Napoleon and Hitler *thought* they did— until they realized they didn't. Ryu intended that he would be one of the rare few who did.

Ryu and the others slipped away believing that their outpost to be so well-camouflaged that their eyes were the only human eyes ever to fall upon it, but other eyes were watching.

As Hammer and Stahling passed the Oberwerk binoculars from one to the other in their invisible perch on a ridge above the trail, any chance Ryu had of executing his plan without serious opposition had slipped through his fingers without him even knowing it.

CHAPTER FIFTEEN

AFTER HER MEETING with Cynthia Mattochs on Saturday, Kai Nialani couldn't stop thinking about Clarence Flaunsin, the man who would've, and thought he *should have,* married into the Mattochs family. That is, if Captain Glenn Dexsen hadn't gotten in the way.

Was that motive enough for him to kill them both? Sure. "If I can't have you nobody can" shows up as a reason to kill in countless whodunits and an equal number of police reports.

Did he kill them? Kai had no way of knowing.

She came into the office on Sunday and ran a background check on Flaunsin. He'd married someone else six years later and was never divorced. He had apparently never returned to Hawai`i.

Meanwhile, he'd had a number of pretty serious traffic citations in Southern California through the years, but he always scraped by. Until he didn't. In 1963, the woman he was with when he piled up his late-model Corvette doing ninety on Sunset Boulevard just past North Whittier was not his wife. There were no survivors.

When Kai arrived at work Monday morning, she took her usual shortcut from the parking lot, which took her past the crime lab. The door was open, so Kai decided to look in.

"I don't see the skulls from my double homicide," she said to the lab tech.

"They were released to Army CID," he replied.

"You shouldn't have done that. Only *one* of those belonged to one of theirs," she said indignantly. "And the family is going to want remains to do the burial."

"I don't make the rules," he said, using an excuse that is as old as bureaucracy itself.

"Who authorized this?"

"Lieutenant Faralaco and the chief."

"When?"

"Saturday morning."

Kai then realized that at the same time that she was talking to the descendant of Gladys Mattochs, all that remained of Gladys was being spirited away and off the island where they had lain for most of a century.

Kai Nialani's next stop was the office of Lieutenant Richard Faralaco.

"Lieutenant, what's this about the remains of Gladys Mattochs being handed over to Army CID?"

"Yes," he said. He could tell she was angry. "The chief and I met with Agent Preneu on Saturday and had a long talk about the case."

"Why wasn't I told about this meeting? It was *my* case."

"It was kind of spur of the moment," Faralaco said. "Preneu phoned the chief and said he wanted to talk before he flew back to Honolulu, and when they got together, I happened to be here."

"What was this talk about?" Kai asked. "What was said about *my* case?"

"Now listen, Detective," he said. He always called her by rank when he was using his "official" voice. "First of all, this is not *your* case any longer. CID has taken jurisdiction. Second, it's an old, cold case that has nothing to do with the safely of Kaua`i residents and visitors today."

"What about that press release that you were planning to issue about the case today?"

"Scratched," Faralaco said succinctly. "There will be no press release. The media will never know. There's no reason to start rumors about unsolved murders."

"*Why*?" Kai was incredulous, and her expression showed it.

"Between you and me, CID wants the whole story under wraps, and as the chief and I see it, there's no reason for it to be otherwise."

"What about the family?"

"Oh that's right…you were going to do the death notification. You didn't, did you?"

"Yes I did…on Saturday about the same time you were handing everything over to Mr. CID."

"Oh, I wish you hadn't," Faralaco said, a pained look on his face. "I didn't realize there were any of them left on the island. What did you them?"

"There's one still alive and well here, and I told her we were sorry for her loss and looking for the killer."

"You didn't tell her we had any leads, did you?"

"No, because we don't. She suggested the ex-boyfriend of Gladys Mattochs, but he died in a car wreck in 1963, so he's beyond being interview material."

"Could he have done it?" Faralaco asked.

"He *could have*, but the evidence is circumstantial and flimsy."

"Good," the lieutenant said. "If we get backed into a corner, he's the man, but we'll make sure it does not come to that. Listen to me, detective, this case is *over*. I don't want you doing or saying anything about this case. If CID wants it to go away, it goes away. Is that clear?"

"Yes, sir."

"I could get used to this," Lauren Stahling said as she nuzzled her head into Hammer's shoulder.

"I already am," he said as he lazily stroked her back.

"It's almost like the Garden of Eden out here," she said.

"When you got two naked people lying around eating mangos that fall from a tree outside their door," he added. "And don't forget these people making friends with all the colored fish out on the reef and the colorful characters in the tiki bar that time forgot."

"What day is it?" she asked.

"I think…Monday?"

"Right."

She began kissing him again, but only in places she could reach without moving her head, as though moving it was more work than she could muster in her relaxed state.

"Of course the Garden of Eden had a devil, and we got our own devil up on that ridge," he said.

"Don't remind me," she said. "I'm living in a daydream here."

"I almost dread hearing from Tim Tommis about the devil's nest up on that cliff."

"Turn off your phone," she suggested.

"I did when we went out for our reef swim this morning," he said. "Forgot to turn it back on."

"You're impossible."

"I know," he admitted.

"I kind of like it that way," she admitted. "What girl wants a guy who's 'possible?' What's the fun in that? Besides, you also asked Tim to look up what he could find in personnel records about Glenn Dexsen."

"He was happy with that. He said it gave him a break from all the Russian electronics."

"You're really piling it on him this week," Lauren admonished.

"He lives for this stuff."

Suddenly, it was her phone, not his, that started jingling.

She sat up, pushed her long hair back, picked up her phone, and tried to put on the voice of someone she was not a moment before.

"This is Lauren Stahling," she said in a businesslike manner.

"Lauren, this is Detective Nialani of the KPD. Am I catching you at a bad time?"

Bad time? I'm lying around naked making love with an impossible man and pretending we're in the Garden of Eden. Bad time? Arrrgh!

"No, not at all," she lied. "What can I do for you, Detective?"

"It's the murder of Gladys Mattochs, I'm afraid, and I could use some help. Off the record, if that would be okay?"

"*Off the record*? What do you mean?"

This got Hammer's attention and he too sat up and leaned over to listen as Lauren put her phone on speaker.

"I needed to talk to someone."

"*What happened*?" Lauren asked.

"Army CID showed up and took jurisdiction," Kai said.

"The feds always take priority over local jurisdictions," Lauren reminded her.

"I'm aware of that," Kai said. "But it was the *way* he did it, and the fact my bosses told me he wanted to bury it...including the death of Gladys Mattochs *after* I had made the death notification to the family. The lieutenant ordered me to say nothing more about this case. He said if CID wants it to go away, it goes away."

"But here you are talking about the case after you were told not to," Lauren said.

"I'd like to talk with you, and with Captain Hammer, if I may. I know this will sound funny...is there a way we could talk in person? Like I said, off the record."

"I suppose," Lauren said. "Do you feel like diving to the North Shore? There's this little tiki bar where we like to go for pizza and..."

"I know the place," Kai interrupted. "I could use an excuse to get out of Līhu`e. I'll see you there...sevenish?"

"It's a deal," Lauren said.

About an hour later, Lauren was just coming back into the house from gathering a few mangos to share with Kai Nialani when she heard Hammer's phone ring.

"Tim," he said. Having seen a caller ID that he knew belonged to his friend back east. "We were just talking about you earlier. That hardware up at the Korean camp has got us wondering what to do."

"You could just phone it in to the base and let the counter-intel agencies fight it out over jurisdiction."

"We could do that," Hammer admitted. "We did do that with the skeletons and the local cops."

"I sense a 'but' coming," Tommis said, chuckling. "Sorry, man, but I know you too well."

"Okay," Hammer said. "There's several reasons *not* to call it in. Let's start with *who* do we call? There is every indication, including our own eyes, that a certain master chief petty officer who's a senior part of the PMRF security machine working with these Koreans. Whether he's a loner or part of a group of traitors, we don't know. What if I call it in and wind up talking to him?"

"Understood."

"Like we found out in Afghanistan, when you're up against people in the shadows, like drug-dealing NGOs, and especially those double-dealing DOD bureaucrats, the best way to deal with a problem is to do it yourself."

"Now, *there's* the Hammer we've come to know and love."

"I especially don't plan to find myself sitting in an office somewhere telling some desk jockey all about *how* I know about all these things I've found out from you."

"Thank you for that."

"Another thing on our minds out here," Lauren interjected, "is that when we *did* report those skeletons to local cops, things didn't work out so well."

"For you guys?"

"No, for the detective who we took in to collect the bones."

"What happened?"

"Well, CID hopped on the first plane and raced over here to take charge of the case. Then he told the local chief and lieutenant to tell the detective that the case officially didn't exist anymore. Y'know, like it never, ever happened. Wow, was the detective pissed off."

"I'm sorry to hear about this," Tommis said. "I'll get back to you on IDs for those pictures you took of your Korean friends, but the skeletons, and your man Glenn

Dexsen, are the reason I'm calling. You wanted me to do some digging on him, right? Well, I did."

"What did you find?" Hammer asked.

"A lot," Tommis said. "I'll email it over right now. I got into a lot of spaces between spaces in old War Department and OSS files. I got into a lot of metaphorical dark rooms where the metaphorical single light bulb hadn't been turned on in decades."

"Sounds fun," Lauren said.

"But there's a sliver of good news in here," Tommis said. "When you see this, you'll understand exactly *why* CID is behaving like they are."

CHAPTER SIXTEEN

LAUREN AND HAMMER arrived first and got a table in a corner of the tiki bar that was away from the main flow of foot traffic. They had each taken a first sip of their beer when Kai Nialani came through the open doorway.

She had left her uniform and all indication of her being a police officer behind in Līhu`e. Like Lauren, and like around half the women in the place, she was wearing a floral-print sundress and she had her hair down, rather than tied up or tied back. Hammer was in his typical "uniform" of gray shorts and a gray ball cap, but at Lauren's insistence, he had traded his gray t-shirt for one of his aloha shirts, albeit one with a dark gray background.

After exchanging the typical pleasantries about "how was traffic," Lauren gave her a Tupperware container of mangos, a neighborly gesture which she appreciated.

When Kai had ordered a ginger ale and the threesome had agreed on a mushroom-sausage pizza, she thanked to two mainlanders for letting her bend their ears and got down to business.

"Well, let me give you the chain of events over the last few days," Kai began. "When I brought in the dog tag that we found on Thursday, we now obviously had a name for the previously unidentified male. Since he was Army, I reported this to the US Army Human Resources Command."

"Makes sense," Hammer agreed. He'd been through this drill before himself.

"I could have phoned the DOD Joint Mortuary Affairs Center, who we call sometimes with current deceased service people, but they're in Fort Lee, Virginia and I knew they'd be closed. That's why I called Human Resources Command. They're on Central Time. Anyway, I went and did my part, assuming that it would work its way through the bureaucracy back there."

"We figured that JMAC would send someone in a week maybe," she continued after taking a sip of her drink. "What none of us at KPD was prepared for was for the Army to send an agent from the Criminal Investigation Division over on the first flight from Honolulu on Friday morning."

"That sounds serious," Hammer said. "But he *was* a murdered soldier."

"It surprised all of us that they sent CID so *quickly*."

"This Captain Dexsen must have been a pretty important person," Lauren commented.

"I sensed this in talking with the CID agent, but he didn't talk much, and he refused to say anything about Dexsen or why CID had a special interest in him...but that's his business not mine. My business was investigating who shot Gladys Mattochs. By the way, I want to thank you for sending those microfilm copies. They were way valuable, and I admit I might not have gotten to that right way on my own."

"Sure, my pleasure," Lauren said. "I have to admit,

after being involved as we were; we're pretty interested in this case too."

"To make a long story short, I was able to make a death notification visit to Cynthia Mattochs. She's the only Mattochs still living on Kaua`i. Gladys was before her time, but she knew the stories of the disappearance."

"I guess you gave her some closure."

"Yeah, I guess. And a big surprise. Like it said in the paper at the time, the whole family have been convinced all these years that Glenn and Gladys had eloped."

"Oops."

"I was planning to hand over the remains when the investigation is done," Kai said. "You know, so that the family can have a service, and a burial or cremation, or whatever they want."

"That would be nice," Lauren said. "I'm sure they would appreciate that."

"But that's when I found out that when the CID man took over the case, he took the evidence...*all* the evidence. Both the skulls. *Everything*."

"*That sucks*," Lauren observed. "What did your boss say?"

"It turns out he and the chief had a meeting with the CID agent about what I thought was my case, *without me*, and handed it over."

"That *really* sucks."

"Well, it's the feds asserting their prerogative," Hammer reminded them. "That's what they do."

"What sucks even more was when Lieutenant Faralaco told me that it's not my case anymore, he added that it's *never even going to be a case* anymore. He said CID wants the whole story under wraps. Him and the chief agreed to this. There was supposed to be a press release about a cold case, but that will not be issued. He said the media would never know. He said that KPD didn't want rumors about unsolved murders."

"Even though there *is* an unsolved double homicide?" Hammer said.

"When he said CID wants it to go away, you can imagine, this makes me *really* want to solve it!"

"In spite of your lieutenant and your chief?" Hammer asked with an ironic grin. This was exactly the kind of thing for which he had been notorious.

"*Yes*!" Kai said. "They are both truly spooked by this CID dude, and it's not like either of them. They're scared of something."

"Sounds like it," Lauren said sympathetically.

"But this is only part of it," Kai said, reaching into her bag and taking out a folder. "On Thursday, when the CID man showed up, he said he wanted to go out to Barking Sands to look for personnel information about Dexsen, and I said that since I was investigating the homicide of a local citizen, I needed to go too. This guy, his name in Preneu, agreed, but you could tell he didn't want me along."

"Why would they have any Army records out there?" Hammer asked. "It's been a Navy base since the nineteen-sixties and the Navy was the main tenant since they started doing missile launches in the fifties."

"As it was explained to me, the Army took what it wanted when the base was transferred from the Army Air Forces to the Air Force. Their pull-out was gradual as the Navy moved in. A lot of what was left behind was outdated and nobody wanted it. As we saw, there's a stack of old boxes of abandoned records still in storage that haven't been touched since before any of us were even born. It is *literally* musty old paperwork. Preneu and I went through it for hours. Mostly you can see why nobody wanted it. Maintenance records of vehicles scrapped years ago? Volleyball tournament records from the fifties?"

"Point taken," Hammer agreed as the pizza arrived.

"Oh, there's one other thing I forgot to mention," Kai said as they sorted out the slices. "The security man who took us to the warehouse where the boxes were stored was the same man we saw on the trail last Thursday. Remember that red-haired guy who was hiking with the Koreans?"

"Oh yeah?" Lauren said, trying very hard not to look startled at the mention of "the Koreans."

"Yeah, his name is Karboli, he's a chief petty officer, and a master-at-arms, meaning that he's a badge-carrying Navy police officer. He was Preneu's contact at Barking Sands."

"So now he's aware of the murders and the investigation?" Lauren asked.

"Yes, he's aware of the murders and he was obviously looped in on the investigation, but I don't know whether Preneu has briefed him on the abrupt end of the KPD investigation," Kai said resentfully.

"Did he hang around while you were looking at obsolete maintenance records?"

"No, he had to go back to his security gig. They have a big exercise or missile test coming up soon. They've always got something going on out there, but it never affects the rest of the island. We just see the streaks in the sky."

When everyone had gotten through their first slice, and came up for a breath, Kai returned to her narrative.

"It wasn't all a musty, dusty waste of time, though," she explained. "Eventually, Preneu came across a box of Transient Personnel Records dated from 1945 to 1947, you know, records people who were passing through the base on their way home from the Pacific Theater of World War

II," she said. "In there, we found Dexsen's name. Or I should say, *he* found Dexsen's name, but it was me who figured out *why* it was important."

"You have our attention," Hammer said with an attentive expression.

"It was a log that showed when any of these people did anything official, starting with their arrival. For Dexsen, we see him coming in February, and then, through the spring, an increasing number of times when he requisitioned a vehicle from the motor pool."

"This is where he starts going on dates with Gladys," Lauren said, pleased to have deduced the pattern.

"*Exactly*," Kai said. "For me it was almost like watching a Hallmark movie, but I could tell that Preneu was *not* seeing this."

"He may not watch Hallmark movies," Hammer suggested sarcastically.

"For an investigator, he was surprisingly dismissive, and not very deductive," Kai complained. "He was the same way in the crime lab when we were looking at the two bullets. They were somewhat deformed, as you might expect with very soft unjacketed lead, but they seemed too small for 9mm or .38 caliber, and too large for 7.62mm. The lab tech confirmed this by measuring."

"Well, 8mm is right in the middle," Hammer said.

"That's what I suggested," Kai said. "But Preneu dismissed this. His exact words were 'impossibly rare.'"

"Rare, but far from impossibly rare," Hammer said. "I'll tell you one 8mm weapon that was far from rare in the early forties, and that's the Japanese Nambu automatic. Japanese Army officers used them as a standard sidearm. Later in the war, the powder load in the cartridges might have been a little light, which might explain why the bullets entered the skulls without exiting. There were hundreds of thousands on Nambus made, and for Americans coming home from the Pacific, it would have been a compact 'bring-back' trophy. Dexsen might have had one."

"Well, Preneu missed that one," Kai said smugly. "And he left all the personnel log pages. He told me to put it all back in the box while he went to look for a bathroom."

"What a guy," Lauren said derisively.

"Chief Petty Officer Karboli had told us that we were free to take anything we wanted. He said it was not Navy property, so go ahead. Preneu didn't, but I did. I grabbed the ones from the end of June 1946."

She then pushed aside her plate and opened the folder which she had brought.

"This page shows him requisitioning a vehicle on the date that the newspapers said he and Gladys disappeared. It was found in Līhu`e, so that's why everyone assumed they had hopped an inter-island steamer or whatever."

"Understandable assumption," Lauren said with a nod.

"Now, here's the point I've been getting to," Kai said. "You see how everybody on these log sheets is identified by their unit number? Well, Dexsen doesn't have a *number*, he has this acronym, OSS. I didn't know what that meant, but I do now."

"It was the Office of Strategic Services, top secret intel, and sabotage agency set up in 1942 by President Roosevelt and General Wild Bill Donovan," Hammer said. "Very colorful. Later very famous."

"Which I've learned," Kai said. "I also learned that a lot of people think it became the CIA, but actually, it was shut down completely, and the CIA was started later."

"With a lot of the same people, though," Hammer

added. "There are a lot of stories in the black ops world about the transition. Still very murky."

"I understand," Kai said. "I really hit a wall in trying to research files related to Dexsen's service file. It seems that a lot of files burned at the National Personnel Records Center fire in St. Louis back in 1973. They're just gone."

"Around eighty percent of Army records for both world wars," Hammer said, shaking his head. "They built the place without sprinklers because they were afraid of potential water damage."

"I'm sort of in the records business myself," Lauren added. "We talked about this fire at a convention once. One thing I do remember is they don't even know to the nearest *million* how many records they actually lost. A real disaster if you care about this stuff."

"It's going to make my work harder on this case," Kai said. "But I did find *this* in the transient personnel file from Barking Sands. Here in the last week of June, there's *another* OSS man arriving at Barking Sands. He requested a vehicle on the same day that Glenn and Gladys disappeared, and he left for the mainland a few days later. In and out in less than a week. His name was Lieutenant Frank Striden."

Kai paused, seeing that she had the riveted attention of her companions.

"He could have gotten his hands on one of these Japanese pistols just as easily as Dexsen," she said. "Could Striden have been involved in the murder?"

She watched the expressions as Lauren and Hammer glanced at one another.

"Am I crazy to be manufacturing a conspiracy theory in my head?" Kai asked. "This is why I wanted to talk to you two, especially you, Captain Hammer. Call it some kind of intuition, but I have a sense that *you* know a lot more about this kind of thing than you like to let on. I hope I'm not out of line with any of this."

"I think good detective work involves thinking *outside* the lines," he said.

"And I think we might be able to help you get around the lost records problem," Lauren said, taking an especially fat folder from her own tote bag. "We're lucky that the house where we're staying has a printer. This came to us this afternoon after you called...and before you ask, no, we don't believe in coincidences."

"I have a friend who's kind of a researcher," Hammer said. "He's good at ferreting out old and overlooked files like you found at Barking Sands. There's a lot of personnel information contained in files stored elsewhere than St. Louis. These are things that cross-reference information that may have been in files lost in 1973."

Hammer did not mention that Tim Tommis not only had his fingers on "overlooked" files, but on ones deliberately buried deep under multiple levels of secret classifications.

"You can take these with you, but we'll run through a few of the highlights," Lauren said, pulling out a thick sheaf of papers. "This is what Glenn Dexsen did in World War II."

As Lauren flipped through it, Kai Nialani found herself looking at page after page of typewritten letters and memos on OSS and War Department letterhead, most of them marked "Top Secret" or "Eyes Only."

"There are a lot of pages related to his service record early in the war," Hammer pointed out. "He was in the 34th Infantry Division before the war, but he was one of those who were transferred to the Rangers in 1942. They were the Army's original elite operators. He was with the 2nd Ranger Battalion in Normandy in 1944, and then things started to get interesting."

"Right after D-Day, the British Special Operations Executive cooked up Operation Foxley," Lauren explained, pulling out several pages. "This was a plot to assassinate Adolf Hitler at his lair in Berchtesgaden. You can look this up on Wikipedia. Dexsen was one of several American OSS men assigned to be part of that project."

"I've never heard of it," Kai admitted.

"Spoiler alert, it never happened," Hammer interjected. "It was about to happen, but Hitler had just left Berchtesgaden to go to his 'Wolf's Lair' command post in East Prussia. This was where his own generals tried to blow him up, and flubbed, less than a week later."

"I've heard of *that*," Kai said.

"It was a big deal at the time, but Foxley was classified for over half a century," Lauren added. "Later, there were a couple of TV shows about it."

"*Nobody's* ever heard of what happened next," Hammer continued. "Dexsen was one of eight OSS men who were recruited for something that was so secret that there is *almost* no record of it. What you're seeing here is the only thing *I've* ever seen."

"Operation Terminal Showa," Kai read from the page he handed her. "What was this?"

"It's 'Terminal' as in 'end of the line,' and 'Showa' is the name Emperor Hirohito had picked in the twenties for his own reign as emperor of Japan," Hammer said. "Terminal Showa was the OSS plan to assassinate Hirohito. From one Axis head of state in Europe, he set his gunsights on another in the Pacific. You can't read about *this* on Wikipedia."

"*Wow*," Kai said soberly. "Needless to say, we know this one didn't happen either."

"Up until August 1945, Hirohito and Japan were showing no signs of wanting to end the war," Hammer continued. "And they still had millions of undefeated troops in China and in Japan. This op was apparently one choice for putting an end to it before the ground invasion of Japan proper. Another option was to use those two bombs."

"As we know, *this* they actually did, and the rest is history," Lauren interjected.

"Then Hirohito ordered all his undefeated millions to surrender, and the war was over," Lauren continued. "But this left the OSS with a suddenly obsolete assassination plan."

"When MacArthur and the Allies decided to use Hirohito as part of their plan for the occupation, the emperor went from being an Axis villain to a useful partner," Hammer said. "According to these documents, even the existence of Terminal Showa as a plan became a liability. It had to be disavowed. Like it had never existed."

"This page is your smoking gun," Lauren said, handing it to Kai. "This is your *why*. Here's a list of the eight OSS agents who were part of the hit teams that were supposed to infiltrate into Japan to take out the emperor. At the bottom are the orders to terminate the *eight*. The smoking gun is not that there was a plan to kill an Axis head of state, but the *written plan* to assassinate the would-be assassins…to murder American servicemen."

"Nobody could be allowed to talk," Hammer said. "You'll notice that seven of the names are checked off on this page. You'll also see the date, and the one name *not yet* checked off as of that date."

"May 1946," Kai said gravely. "Captain Glenn Dexsen…and then, three weeks later, he and Gladys went for a drive and never came back."

"Striden, apparently it was him, took them to a place so far from anywhere that they would never be found," Lauren said.

"To a place in the mountains overlooking the ocean," Kai added. "Where the *huaka`i pō,* the ghost army of marchers in the night just marched them off into the oblivion of the netherworld."

Hammer and Lauren just nodded.

"What happened to Striden after this?" Kai asked.

"Nobody knows," Hammer said. "He got on a plane on that day noted in the log you found, and he flew back to the States. He disappeared after that. Our friend said his curiosity was piqued and he'll continue looking. Anything further is buried deeper and for almost as long as the skeletons up there at Hemolele`auwai."

CHAPTER SEVENTEEN

"SORRY TO CALL SO EARLY your time," Tim Tommis said when Hammer had struggled himself awake to answer his phone in the almost darkness of the leading edge of Tuesday's dawn.

"Not a problem, man," Hammer replied, his barely awakened voice croaking. "Retired life has got me going soft."

"I'm also sorry to have taken so long to get back to you on those pictures you sent me."

"It's only been less than two days," Hammer said generously. "I assume you need to sleep once in a while."

"The Shadow *never* sleeps," Tommis said with a chuckle, referencing the old-school radio drama. "You oughta know that."

"I stand corrected. What's up?"

"You've got a game-changer going on out there on your cliff top," Tommis said. "Based on what you sent me before Sunday, my assumption was that it was probably a *North* Korean op, based on the Russian gear. Also that it was some kind of interference op. That was based on seeing the jammers."

"It's not?"

"The new gear that they've added changes everything. They've got a *South* Korean TPQ-76 Cloud Mirror system which they've heavily modified to spoof control data, and those big, scanned array radar antennae that extend their reach. The Russian Zhitel jammers allowed them to shut down anything or everything at Barking Sands if they wanted to. This other stuff would let them substitute selected jammed data streams with false data... not just at Barking Sands but across the entire Pacific."

"In layman's words?"

"In layman's words, they could spoof Barking Sands into believing something was happening when it wasn't, or vice versa, and then trick them into acting on phony information. In short, they could take over an ongoing op and create an international incident."

"Like what?"

"Like tricking North Korea into actually doing what everybody in Hawai`i thought they did in the 2018 false alarm incident," Tommis said soberly.

"Oh shit."

"I did some checking on current ops out there," Tommis continued. "It seems that they've got an Aegis anti-missile missile test called Vigilant Basilisk coming up within a couple of days."

"Vigilant *Basilisk*?"

"Yeah. It's not the first time they've named a launch op after an imaginary lizard. This one is rumored to be the biggest they've ever done out since Vigilant Wyvern, which was a number of years ago. It's been announced publicly, but not the exact date. That's still classified. The word on the street is that it was supposed to have happened about now, but they've had trouble with a new variant of the RIM-174 missile, which they're trying to fix."

"Who's doing this, if *not* the North Koreans?" Hammer asked.

"At first, the Cloud Mirror hardware threw me. It's made in South Korea and very hard to get your hands on. It almost looked like an official South Korean military op."

"If they had Russian stuff *and* South Korea stuff at the same spot, it could be either deliberate deception *or* it could be some freelance operators just patching it together with gear from wherever," Hammer suggested wryly.

"*How did you guess?*"

"*Guess*? I was just being facetious."

"You nailed it, man," Tommis said.

"*What?*"

"I ran a facial recognition check on those people in the pictures you sent. They're all South Korean civilians. There's not too much in the database on the two younger ones that you said you had met, but two of the others are former army officers. Their names are Han jong-sok and Cho ho-jin. They have a special forces background and spent time running covert ops in North Korea."

"And now a freelance covert op in Kaua`i," Hammer summarized. "What about the fifth one, the one who everybody was standing around looking at like he's the boss?"

"Well, he *is* the boss. His name is Ryu Myong-su. He's formerly with South Korean National Intelligence. He was kind of a prodigy, who was clever at what he did and he developed a good reputation for ultra ruthlessness in an organization where ruthlessness is part of the job description. He was very anti-DPRK, but he created this rumor which not *everybody* believed, but which nobody could disprove."

"Sounds intriguing," Lauren interjected.

"Since the spelling of the two names are so close, he cultivated the fake narrative that he's the illegitimate son of General Ri Myong-su, the head of the *North* Korean General Staff, and a bosom buddy of Kim Jong Il."

"The bastard son of an ultimate badass," Hammer summarized.

"It served him well, but this his reputation as a super-cool operator went to his head. He soon had a reputation for arrogance and for being too cold-blooded. They let him take 'early retirement.'"

"Not a team player," Hammer said. "We've all seen the type."

"They have a saying at the NIS that they 'serve in the shadows to light the way forward,'" Tommis explained. "When he left the service, he stayed in the shadows. He ran deals for corrupt politicians and illicit arms dealers all over the Far East and gradually became a sort of freelance megalomaniac."

"That can't be good."

"From what I've learned, he's been bent on tricking the American *and* the North Korean *offensive* ballistic missile organizations into some kind of a war for some time. The question is, how do start a nuclear war when you don't have any nukes?"

"You trick the guys with nukes, on both sides, into starting your war," Hammer suggested. "What's the worst that can happen? Apocalypse now?"

"Let's just say that the most dangerous man living on the Korean Peninsula is *not* the clown living the presidential palace in Pyongyang," Tommis said.

"He's the clown running the show up there on Pokuakini Ridge," Hammer replied.

"Yup."

"As I was saying the last time we were up at the

Korean camp," Hammer said. "I guess we better put a stop to it."

"What are you going to do?"

"We'll think of something."

"I know you will," Tommis said. "You always do."

"I'll put on the coffee," Lauren, who had overheard the conversation, said from the other room.

"Oh Daddy," Lynsee Kinkaide complained when she heard her father clattering the crockery in the kitchen at the Barking Sands admiral's quarters. "It's too early. It's not even light out."

Lynsee had barely seen her father in days, and this morning, like yesterday, their interaction was just voices through a closed door.

"Go back to sleep then," Vice Admiral Hardgrove Kinkaide barked from the kitchen. "I know you're bored stiff here. You need to get back to San Diego now that your mother's done with whatever it was that was so damned important. I'll have someone on my staff arrange transportation and escort you to the commercial airport in Līhu`e. Be ready to travel later today. Someone will contact you on your cell."

"*Oh no,* Daddy," she said, suddenly panicking. She had spent two whole days trying unsuccessfully to engineer another "chance encounter" with Chief Petty Officer Anthony Karboli, the love of her life. If she was suddenly ripped away and exiled to San Diego, she may never see him again. This just *could not be*!

"I don't mind, *really,* Daddy. I know you're busy, busy, busy. Don't worry about me. I'll be your good little sailor, just like always. You just go and worry about your missiles and whatever. I'll worry about me."

"Okay, I'll stand down then," he said. He sounded relieved. One less distraction. "My car is here."

Moments later the front door slammed.

Lynsee lay there for a long time thinking about Anthony, her Anthony of the sweet, serious eyes, and of their one magical evening together. Her mind flooded with memories of all the things he had told her as they made love, while her imagination flooded with a longing to hear his voice saying these things now and *forever*. She imagined his lips telling her he loved her and that they would go somewhere far away from all this Navy bullshit and be together forever.

She imagined his lips doing lots of things.

Lynsee dreamed the dreams of a romantic child, barely into her teens, even as she once again broke out the elements of the disguise that would transform her appearance into that of an adult.

"If you don't mind me saying, chief, that woman at Shenanigans the other day seemed like she was really into you," Petty Officer Second Class Joel Dyallic told his boss and they sat at their desks in the PMRF security command center awaiting confirmed orders to implement Vigilant Basilisk operational protocols. "Is she an ex-girlfriend? She was a real fox."

"I *do mind* you asking," Chief Petty Officer Anthony Karboli replied in an irritated tone. "And no, she is not an ex-girlfriend, and *no*, this is not a topic for further discussion, petty officer."

In the Navy, as in any branch of the service, you learn pretty fast that you don't discuss the romantic life of a superior, even if your relationship with that superior is usually cordial. Dyallic was young, but he realized he'd blown it. He had to learn.

"Message received and understood, Chief," Dyallic said. "I apologize."

"Apology accepted," Karboli said in an effort to end the conversation firmly and finally.

With this, the master chief stood and walked over to study the huge map of the base perimeter on the far wall. Life in the tense limbo of "hurry-up-and-wait," especially when waiting for something as potentially frenetic as Vigilant Basilisk spawned all sorts of uneasy small talk, and Karboli knew this. He just wanted to shoot down any and all talk about this particular terrible teen.

For the past two weeks, ever since Han had shared the video of Karboli and Lynsee, Karboli knew he was living on borrowed time, but for those two weeks he *did* have time. He was safe as long as Han *needed* him. Han would risk nothing, at least until the moment of the upcoming missile launch.

For the past two days, Karboli had the worst of all complications. Not only had the impending launch become a postponed uncertainty, the girl he thought was a woman had reappeared out of nowhere. Would she tell her father about them? Had she told him already? *Probably not,* but he couldn't know for sure.

What he did know for sure was that he did not want to discuss her with any of his subordinates. At least Dyallic did not know that her last name was Kinkaide.

In the Army, as in any branch of the service, you learn pretty fast that you don't question orders. You can wind up in a world of hurt for disobeying orders, but *questioning* orders is the start down that same slippery slope.

Army CID Special Agent Zachery Preneu was not quite ready to start down that slope, but the events of the past few days had him wondering to himself.

As he sat at his desk in the CID Pacific Field Office at Schofield Barracks, a thirty-minute drive north of Pearl Harbor, he had a momentary break after a lengthy email exchange about drug dealers at nearby Fort Shafter. This allowed him a pause to speculate in his mind about this decades-old homicide which had touched a raw nerve at the top of his chain of command.

The order to shut down the investigation had then come back down that chain of command and it was unequivocal. You don't question orders, and you don't ask why. Zachery Preneu was not about to question orders, but he had worked himself around to the point where he was about to ask *why*.

Preneu's boss, Special Agent in Charge Margo Motherwell, had suggested "national security" in her orders, but she had stopped short of using this phrase. Preneu sensed that he knew why. It was a term that was always guaranteed to feed the rumor mill. If the point is to quietly shut something down, that's the last bell you want to ring.

Motherwell was a tough, no-nonsense career agent who had put in almost three decades at several field offices and had a reputation for running things by the book. When her bosses, up there in the chain of command, had given this order, she had not thought to ask why. How would she react if Preneu asked? One way to find out.

"I have a question, ma'am," he said as he passed her in the hall. He wanted to make it appear casual, but he made sure that they were in a part of the office where nobody was within earshot.

"Yes, Agent Preneu," Motherwell said without impatience, which he took as a good sign. She was not in a hurry at the moment.

"Now that we've got that situation over in Kaua`i buttoned up, I was wondering if there was anything more you could tell me about why Quantico wanted a cold case that old to be closed without further investigation."

"There were a lot of classified programs during World War II which became immediately obsolete as soon as the war ended, but they had to remain classified to protect sources and methods," she said, using what sounded too much like a boilerplate disclaimer.

"I understand, but..."

"I'll say this only one time. Basically, when Quantico saw the name of this man Dexsen, they told me that it is imperative that this name be kept out of the media, and that we contain *all* mention of the name, even within law enforcement circles, do you understand?"

"Yes, ma'am."

"Quantico is adamant," Motherwell said firmly. "I'm adamant. The fewer people who know, the better. I don't care what happens to any of those civilian bones, or even soldier bones, but I do care about the dog tag and Dexsen's name. That name should never appear in any memo, and as of this moment, never again be spoken. Is there a problem with the people over there in Kaua`i?"

"No, not at all," Preneu said. "They have other fish to fry over there. They had a shooting that became a PR nightmare for them. The whole Dexsen story will blow over soon, if it hasn't already..it will go back to being a forgotten cold case."

"Good, we *absolutely* cannot have any embarrassments. Am I making myself clear?"

"Yes, ma'am."

CHAPTER EIGHTEEN

TUESDAY NIGHT at Huna's Hideaway in Kekaha this week was not nearly as lively as normal. The jukebox was playing Jawai`ian Reggae, and there were some people playing pool, but with PMRF at FPCON Bravo, most of the people at the base were on duty stations or standing by to *be* on duty stations, so they were not at the bar.

Rhonda, the vivacious forty-something jewelry shop owner who had regaled Hammer and Stahling with tales of barking dogs and intercontinental missile false alarms a week and a half ago, was at her usual spot at the bar, bantering with the bartender. He made a show of merely tolerating her, but he actually missed her on nights when she had something more important to do. Tonight, he had double the repartee, because Rhonda had dragged a friend along with her, although Selke was barely getting a word in edgewise.

All of this was unfolding when Han jong-sok and Cho ho-jin took bar stools near Selke's, caught the bartender's attention and ordered Mai Tais. Ignoring the others, they began talking to one another in Korean.

Growing bored with the topic that was consuming

Rhonda and the bartender, Selke allowed her attention to drift the opposite way.

"Excuse me," she said, interrupting them a few minutes later. "I don't mean to interrupt, but I hear you using the word *gwisin*. That's the Korean word for 'ghost,' right? My friend Yiecha, she's told me lots about Korean ghost stories and spirit lore. I find it *very* fascinating."

The two men stopped their conversation to look at this woman, both of them finding *her* fascinating. She was older than they were, but not by much, and she had riveting, though compassionate eyes. She wore necklaces and dangling earrings of soft light metal, and there was a faint, distant, tinkling sound as she spoke.

"My name is Selke, by the way," she said, extending her hand. Like Rhonda, she was in her fifties, but still quite attractive in a vaguely hippie-ish way.

"I am Cho ho-jin and this is Han jong-sok. As you can tell, we are visiting from Korea."

"I am happy to meet you gentlemen," she said, her voice soft and almost hypnotic. "I hope that you don't think me rude to interrupt your conversation about the *gwisin*."

"Not at all," Cho said. "It in unusual to meet someone who knows about *gwisin* is a ghost in Korean. The same thing…a spirit being. As your friend may have told you, a *gwisin* is sometimes, not always, the ghost of someone who remains on earth to take revenge on their murderer before they go on to the spirit world."

"That's what we were talking about," Han said.

"You *know* someone who was murdered?" Selke asked, trying not to appear to eager.

"We found out on Saturday," Han said. She could tell he was being serious. She was good at reading people.

"Was it someone you knew?" Selke asked empathetically.

"No, it was someone from long ago," Hȧn explained. "It was a soldier and a local woman who was his lover."

"Oh, I'm so sorry," she said, and they sensed she meant it. She was good at drawing people in with empathy.

"Sometimes there is a *cheonyeo gwisin*, the ghost of a young maiden who was murdered," Cho continued. "She haunts the world clutching powerful bitterness for her killer."

"Both of these people were shot in the head," Han interjected. "This happened many, many years ago, but the skeletons lay where they fell and were not found until last week."

"Where?" Selke asked.

"In a valley up in these mountains," Han said, gesturing toward the north.

"When we were hiking up there ourselves last Thursday, we saw a police woman," Cho said. "Master Chief Tony said he saw her again and she told him she was bringing out remains. He said that she said there are probably many more skeletons up in the mountains."

"Who's Master Chief Tony?" Selke asked.

"*Ohhh*...umm," Cho mumbled, caught off guard.

"He's our friend who talked to that police woman," Han said, jumping in to save Cho from his awkwardness.

"A soldier and a maiden?" Selke asked to confirm.

"This is what we were told," Han said.

She could tell they were deeply troubled by this. Cho especially. She was adept at reading between the lines.

"If they remain at the scene of the brutality, bodies of those killed violently, make for unfinished business for their spirits," Selke said. "This is what Hawai`ians believe, but it's the same everywhere...in all cultures. It's universal."

As Han and Cho were digesting this and nodding in agreement, Ryu Myong-su walked into Huna's Hideaway with Pak Mi-Rae and Jong Nam-ho—Rae and Teddy.

"We were just speaking with our friend here about the skeletons that Chief Tony told us about," Han told Ryu. "And *gwisin*...and the spirit world."

"I'm Selke," she said, speaking softly and directly to Ryu, who she correctly deduced was the leader of this group, as she warmly took his hand. "We were having a thoughtful conversation about these things."

"Come," Han said. "Let's take this table now that everyone is here. Selke, please join us. I'm sure that everyone will be happy to hear more of what you have to say."

Ryu was immediately skeptical, but he saw that both Pak and Jong were interested, so he went along with the momentum of his entourage as they moved to a large table with Selke as their invited guest. As with Han and Cho, he could not help himself. He was fascinated by this woman with the sharp and insightful eyes.

"The Hawai`ian people have their beliefs about places where bodies of those killed violently are allowed to lie where they have fallen," Selke explained. "The most awful destiny that can happen to a soul is to be forsaken by its *aumakua*, its ancestral spirit, and left to wander, a rootless ghost in some deserted place."

"We all heard the *gwisin* stories as children," Rae said. "But when you get older..."

"When you get older, you know it when you can *feel* the spirits," Selke said, smiling gently. "The *aumakua* intercede between this world and the world beyond." Han was intrigued, Cho was enthralled, and Teddy Jong was mesmerized. Ryu remained dubious, but Selke had definitely gotten his attention.

"Again, you said that the skeletons that were found were those of a dead soldier and a maiden?" Selke asked. Cho nodded.

"Sometimes the restless souls of dead warriors are seen at night in ghostly human form," she continued. "In Hawai`i, many believe that ghosts come back to the places they lived in this world...and especially where they *died*."

"Like *gwisin*," Cho interjected.

"Like *gwisin*," Selke agreed. "There are processions of ghosts who come out on the nights of a full moon to go to the hallowed places. The Hawai`ians call them *huaka`i pō*, the 'marchers in the night,' and lots of Hawai`ians have seen them. Even some mainlanders and foreigners have seen this haunted spectacle of unsettled spirits."

"What do you do when you see them?" Teddy Jong asked. "Have you seen them?"

"I haven't, but I have talked to several people who have seen the *oi`o*, or the 'spirit ranks,' as they're sometimes called. They've seen them and heard the chanting voices, and the shouts. What do you do? Encountering such a parade is horrifying. They say it's incredibly dangerous. I would be terrified to experience something like that, and I am not normally a fearful lady."

"Why do you fear this army of ghosts?" Ryu asked.

"Because they're unsettled spirits," Selke said. "They appear at night...around midnight, often under a full moon. They can be heard, often screaming like banshees."

Selke had everyone's attention.

"*What? Why?*" Teddy stammered.

"They are often escorting the souls of the dead from the extreme darkness of the night to the extreme darkness of the underworld of Milu, the king of the netherworld. If the living are in the wrong place and the wrong time, they too will be swept into the infernal regions. Who wants to go *there*?"

"Nobody, of course," Ryu responded.

"When you said that the skeletons were found up in the mountains, the mountains above the Nāpali Coast, I remembered that the gateway into the underworld of Milu is said to be a crevice on a cliff above the Pacific," Selke said.

At the mention of the cliff above the Pacific, Ryu noticed the others glancing at one another with concerned expressions—except Teddy Jong. He looked absolutely *terrified*.

Ryu was especially concerned about Han and Cho. Jong was an undisciplined gamer-dude, but they were both solid ex-military men, the last people whom he could imagine as superstitious.

"Maybe the policewoman was exaggerating," Ryu said. "There were probably only the two bodies."

"Are you talking about the bodies they found a couple weeks ago up in the mountains?"

Everyone looked up. It was Rhonda. The bartender had become preoccupied—with tending bar, of all things—and was ignoring Rhonda, so she went looking for another conversation to join.

"Yes," Selke said. "We were speaking of ghosts and *gwisin*, and the restless souls of dead warriors who are seen as *huaka`i pō*, the 'marchers in the night.' The police told their friend that one of the dead people was a soldier."

"That's right," Rhonda said. "My friend's niece works in the medical examiner's office in Līhu`e. She said there were body parts brought in. They sent them to Honolulu for DNA. She heard that the cops also found some Army dog tags."

"Did she say anything about other bodies that have not been recovered?" Ryu queried.

"I don't remember," Rhonda said. "I didn't pay a lot of attention because it happened so long ago. When was it? The forties? Maybe there were more skeletons. I remember she said there was quite a big fuss in Līhu`e when these skeletons came in. She said she heard there were bullet holes in the skulls!"

"I feel so sad for their souls," Selke said sorrowfully. "Especially for the souls that are still trapped up there where they were so brutally murdered."

CHAPTER NINETEEN

"I'M glad you kids called ahead," Shirley Ono said from behind the counter, greeting Lauren Stahling cheerfully as she stepped into the Ocean Breeze Motel in Kekaha. "I'm afraid we've got a full house for a change. I've got you in the same room you had before, if that's okay."

"That would be perfect," Lauren said, pushing her sunglasses to the top of her head and signing the registration book. "It certainly *does* look crowded out there."

"That's an understatement," Shirley said. "We've got gawkers and reporters and we even have a TV crew from Honolulu planning to do a live national feed of this missile launch."

"Any idea when it's actually going to happen?"

"They're not saying. The rumor over the weekend was that it was going to be any minute, but here it is Wednesday and that obviously turned out to be wrong. I don't know why they're being so coy. They announced a couple of weeks ago that it's going to happen, so that's not a secret. I guess they don't want to tell us the time so they don't have to admit they were wrong when it gets postponed. Are you here to watch it?"

"No we came back over to the west side to do some more hikes up in the mountains. Maybe we'll get to see it from up there."

"These things are a real show," Shirley said. "We're only a few miles away, so when they do one from shore here at Barking Sands it sure shakes up the place. Sometimes they do these from ships offshore, but this one is supposed to be from land."

"Well, I hope nothing gets broken when they shake up the place," Lauren said.

"Me too."

Lauren Stahling and Jim Hammer had returned to Kekaha again as a base for their plan to shake up and shut down Ryu Myong-su's delusion of grandeur once and for all. This plan hinged on getting their work done before the missiles went up—but not *too long* before.

While Lauren checked in, Hammer strolled down the street a bit to chat with the guys at the television truck with the big dish on top. They had set up a tent next to the vehicle and were lounging in aluminum chairs drinking soda from cans and looking bored. As for many on the base up the road, it was hurry-up-and-wait time, the calm before the storm.

"Looks like you guys are ready," Hammer commented.

"All we need is for the countdown to start," one man said.

"And hope that it doesn't start at anything more than T-minus twenty-four hours," added another. "We're ready to go anytime. We'd be go for T-minus twenty-four *minutes*. I'm ready for 'em to get it over with."

"You want a Coke?" the first man asked.

"Sure," Hammer said, grabbing one from the ice chest as the man tipped up the lid. "How do you find out?"

"We take turns going up to the media tent at the main

gate at the base and hanging out. Our producer's up there now."

"I see you guys are from Honolulu," Hammer observed.

"Yeah, as you can see by the logo, we're also a network affiliate so we also shoot content that will go on the nightly news...whenever this happens. There isn't a huge media presence here, but we're not the only TV truck. All the networks like the visuals from a rocket launch. Viewers too. It's eye candy. Are you here for the launch?"

"No we're here to go hiking up in the mountains," Hammer said, nodding to Lauren, who had now joined him. "I guess we'll see it from there if it happens while we're up there."

"It'll be hard to miss," one of the men said. "The press release says it'll be a simultaneous launch of four missiles. That alone should be a real show."

The press tent to which the TV crew referred turned out to be the epicenter of what might be called a media circus. Out of more than passing interest, Lauren and Hammer decided to drive the few miles to the PMRF main gate to have a look.

Though heavily armed masters at arms on heightened security were just inside the fence, the media tent looked like something out of a county fair, with media people and curious locals milling around. The general consensus within the crowd echoed what had been said at the TV truck—people were anxious for the launch time to be announced.

They didn't have long to wait.

"Ladies and gentlemen," an ensign in a brilliant white

uniform announced as he stepped to the podium with a triangular PMRF insignia plaque and adjusted a crackling microphone. "I am pleased to introduce Lieutenant Commander Irv O'Malley with an announcement."

"Ladies and gentlemen," the slightly overweight public affairs officer said as he jiggled the same microphone. "On behalf of the US Navy Integrated Warfare Systems Program and the Missile Defense Agency, I'm pleased to announce that the countdown for Vigilant Basilisk, a joint Aegis Weapons System test, has begun. We are now at T-minus twenty-seven hours. For those of you who are doing the math in your head, the launch will be at 1602 tomorrow."

"Does that timetable include built-in holds?" shouted a man who was obviously familiar with launch protocols. Built-in holds were standard procedure.

"We have decided to forgo any built-in holds," O'Malley replied. "We are confident that we will be more than ready at 1602. We are pleased to say that we have set up an app, which you can download. This will give you continuous real-time updates on the countdown."

With this, the URL was displayed on a whiteboard, which the journalists hurriedly copied into their phones. At least everyone now knew that the launches would happen *no sooner* than four o'clock Thursday afternoon.

As they walked back to where they had parked Rob's Ford Taurus, Lauren and Hammer turned their heads at the low rumble of a 5.0-liter V8 engine and watched a bright-blue Mustang convertible, with its top down, drive away. It was the same car they had watched driving away from the Miloli`i Ridge Trail parking area on Sunday. In the open car, they recognized the notorious Ryu Myong-su and his ex-military henchmen, Han jong-sok and Cho ho-jin.

They too had come to town for the circus.

Dave Altbeck's first few days of being embedded within the nerve center of Naval Anti-Ballistic Missile Operations had been fascinating, even occasionally electrifying. Vice Admiral Hardgrove Kinkaide, the commander of the big show, was an engaging and colorful character, and he made life here interesting. He was also a rude, old-fashioned field commander prone to the kind of hyperbole that made good copy.

Since Saturday, though, when it became obvious without being spoken, that the launch date for Vigilant Basilisk had come and gone, the admiral had become edgy and preoccupied. Altbeck knew this had to do with the RIM-174F SM-6 missiles that were at the center of the action.

Four days ago, when Altbeck had personally watched a new batch of SM-6s arrive, he saw they were marked as RIM-174Gs. This was a different variant from the RIM-174F that was in all the early press releases, and which everyone expected. He had not wanted to ask the admiral what went wrong with the "F" model? He was afraid to. Kinkaide was that intimidating.

The journalist was in the Battle Management Interoperability Center digesting the countdown announcement when Kinkaide came into the room surrounded by his usual entourage of earnest-looking lieutenant commanders and captains from Naval Air Systems Command.

He caught Altbeck looking at him and waved him over. While many military commanders steer clear of the media, the showman in Kinkaide saw publicity as not only useful, but desirable—especially when congressional budget voting time rolled around. Why else would he have embedded the man from *Defense Up Front* within his inner sanctum during a largely classified operation?

"I'll bet you're wondering what it took us until now to start the countdown," the admiral asked. "Am I right?"

"The thought crossed my mind," Altbeck said, stating the obvious.

"It was the damned missile," Kinkaide asserted. "We had a reliable system with the RIM-174A, and then they sold us the RIM-174F. They decided to replace the Mk104 solid-fuel sustainer with the so-called 'new and improved' Mk109B. Let me tell you something, and you can quote me on this..."

Kinkaide paused for effect as Altbeck scribbled. His BMIC access didn't include using his recorder.

"When they sell you something that's 'new,' half the time it will not be *improved*. This damned Mk109B wasn't. They screwed the pooch on this one and I had to kick it back in their face. I kicked their anthill and had 'em scrambling. On Saturday, as you saw, they delivered their Mk109C, and the contractor fitted it in a new variant missile. All in record time."

It was clear that the admiral understood the nuances of his missile systems in the most minute of detail. His grasp of the details was far more comprehensive than one would expect from a three-star flag officer, but such was the case with Hard Kinkaide.

"We tore it apart, tested it and *now* we're ready to roll," the admiral continued.

Kinkaide waved over one of his lieutenant commanders, signaling he was done with the journalist for the moment, and Altbeck was left to wander the BMIC, his eyes inundated with heavily classified data that Russian or Chinese or North Koreans would pay millions to see.

Being embedded, Altbeck could see it all—for free. The price he paid was that he could tell no one what he was seeing—until it was over. He could not leave this place, but he could not file his story until after the launch.

This might be late Thursday, but if something happened to the countdown it could be after the weekend.

By then, the world would already know what happened from the footage shot live by the TV trucks, and from media content cribbed from official press releases. Most news consumers would be satisfied by dramatic color imagery of missile launches and of the "rocket's red glare" of missile intercepts.

This would leave Dave Altbeck as the only one with the *inside* story, the minute details of Vigilant Basilisk that only the gearheads who read magazines like *Defense Up Front* could understand and appreciate. But these readers were the true enthusiasts, the true technical aficionados. They would be eager to know things like the true story behind the new RIM-174G. Thanks to Altbeck, they would.

CHAPTER TWENTY

THE BLUE MUSTANG thundered to a stop outside the modest mid-century bungalow on the edge of Kekaha that the Sweet Harvest Sugar Company had rented a couple of weeks ago. As Ryu, Han and Cho came though the flimsy screen door, Pak Mi-Rae and Jong Nam-ho—Rae and Teddy—were lounging in the living room with the television on.

"What's the news, Sajangnim Ryu?" Teddy asked in Korean, using the formal honorific. Ryu couldn't tell whether the typically cheeky Teddy was being deliberately impertinent, but he didn't care. It didn't matter. He needed Teddy, and until the job was done, he would tolerate Teddy.

"The countdown was announced," Han said, answering the question. "They announced 'T-minus twenty-seven hours' at 1302 local time. This means that Operation Vigilant Basilisk will be initiated at 1602 local time tomorrow, Thursday afternoon."

"Don't forget built-in holds," Rae interjected. "Countdowns always have built-in holds and holds based on screw-ups which they find when they're fidgeting with their equipment."

"They announced that this one will *not* have a built-in hold," Han replied.

"I'm glad the launch will happen in the daytime," Cho interjected. "After what we heard last about the skeletons and the ghost armies, I would not want to be up in our hideaway after dark."

"Why did the Americans name this operation after a Basilisk?" Teddy asked nervously. "Why would they use the name of such a dangerous and evil creature? What do *they* know about this place?"

"Many years ago there was another test of the Aegis Missile System that they named Vigilant Wyvern," Ryu pointed out. "It's just the way they name things. It doesn't mean anything about this island."

"Even if you're correct about that, the skeletons are *real*, are they not?" Teddy asserted.

"Yes, it seems the skeletons were real," Han admitted. "And we have been told all our lives that angry *gwisin* haunt the remains of people who died violently."

"They said the remains were removed," Ryu reminded him.

"They also said that there might be *more* still up there," Han replied.

"No one knows this for certain," Ryu said.

"Like I pointed out last week, one of the dead was young maiden who was *murdered*," Cho said. "We learned about these when we were young. She is a *cheonyeo gwisin*, the ghost who haunts the world hanging on to potent animosity toward her murderer."

"I don't want to be where the angry *gwisin* are

"Here in Hawai`i, they have the ghost armies that haunt the night and frighten the people who see them,"

Cho said. "I don't especially want to see that if I can avoid it."

"You of all people?" Rea said, sounding annoyed. "A former military officer, unafraid of infiltrating the DPRK, afraid of ghosts?"

"These armies are said to be leading the spirits of the dead ... as well as unlucky people from the world of the living…into the underworld," Cho explained. "There was nothing in our experience in the Army that trained us to combat *this*."

"Where is the entrance to this underworld?" Teddy asked. "It's on a cliff above the sea. Right? Where will we be? On a precipice on top of the Nāpali Coast. I don't want to be where the angry *gwisin* are threatening to sweep me into *that* darkness!"

"I'm thankful that we will get in and out before nightfall so that you *men* will not have to be so frightened," Rea said skeptically, proud that the voice of reason on this point was that of a *woman*.

"I've started to think about the spirits of people who will die when Kitty spoofs those missile operators," Teddy said, raising an uncomfortable subject. "Rockets will be flying across the Pacific and turning people into angry and vengeful *gwisin*."

"You have programmed your Kitty to make the Americans hit the *North*, right?" Rae said demandingly. "They already have their ICBMs calibrated to strike the Hwasong launch sites in the DPRK. As soon as Kitty gives them fake news of a Hwasong launch against them, they will retaliate. They will attack the *North*, our enemy! They will destroy our *enemy*."

"You talk about ghost armies marching through the night and sweeping you into hell!" Han said angrily. "What about the *real* armies of the DPRK. They've had a million-and-a-half angry soldiers lined up on the DMZ…

barely fifty kilometers from Seoul…for years. Why? To sweep our *whole civilization* through the gates of hell!"

Ryu was pleased to hear Han say what needed to be said. This meant Ryu didn't have to.

As their *sajangnim*, Ryu could say it, and if necessary, he *would* say it, and they would always follow him. Yet to have a member of the team articulate it to the other members of the team was much more effective.

Wednesday night at Huna's Hideaway in Kekaha was livelier this week than it had been eight days ago when Ryu Myong-su and his entourage sat down with Selke and Rhonda for their tutorial an about an army of ghosts marching through the tropical night.

As it was last Tuesday, there were fewer people with military haircuts because PMRF was still at FPCON Bravo, and people at the base were on call, but this week the core crowd of locals was augmented by the journalists and the curious who had come to town for Vigilant Basilisk. With the countdown not climaxing until tomorrow afternoon, everyone could afford a few drinks tonight and still be clear-headed at T-minus zero.

Rhonda warmed her usual barstool near the end of the bar, and she had dragged Selke back to join her. Rhonda had an editor from online edition of a major network pinned down with her clever repartee about the "local" perspective on the Navy's arcane activities on Kaua`i. Chris was about her age and mildly attractive, and their body language suggested that there might be more to the conversation than talk about missiles and the missile range.

Chris was so enthralled with stories of barking dogs and spooks of all kinds in the mountains that he was actually taking notes. Clearly amused by all this, especially how seriously he took Rhonda, Selke was along for the ride. For the price of a round of drinks for the ladies, Chris was definitely getting some useful "color" he could use to enliven whatever he would write about the technical and strategic aspects of missile defense.

Pak Mi-Rae came in with Teddy Jong and watched with a weary smile as he searched the jukebox playlist for something by Pinktease, HumuHumu, or one of the other K-pop groups currently in fashion. A generation younger than the others in Ryu Myong-su's crew, they had opted *not* to spend the night before the big operation sitting around the bungalow obsessing.

When Selke caught Rae's eye and waved to her across the room, Rae walked over to the bar to say hello.

"Rhonda has a friend," Rae said with a grin, nodding to the intense discussion about the folklore of Barking Sands and the barking sands that were its namesake.

"Yes." Selke laughed. "He is really enjoying all she is doing to share a sense of place about the west side. Speaking of local stories, I'm sorry for scaring your friends with all those things about skeletons and ghost armies last week."

"Oh, that's okay, I wasn't scared...*really*," Rae said dismissively. "But Teddy really was worked up. He's very superstitious. Poor boy."

"All of the old Hawai`ian stories are not about evil and monsters," Selke said. "For instance, you know the little geckos you see crawling on your walls at night..."

"Oh yeah, we have those where we're staying. They're cute."

"Some people believe they're *aumakua*, they're ancestral spirits that act as protectors of the house and the family inside. That's a *good* thing."

"What's a good thing?" Teddy asked, joining them.

"Selke was just telling me that Hawai`ian legends are not all scary monsters," Rae said. "You should know that the geckos are actually guardians who watch out for the people in the house."

"Those little lizards?"

"Yeah, and they're the good thing. So stop dwelling on skeletons and basilisks."

"If you say so."

"Oh look," Rae said, looking past Teddy and toward the front door of the bar. "It's those people we met at the tiki bar over on the other side of the island last week."

Lauren Stahling and Jim Hammer, operating under the same assumption as many others, had decided that since the launch was not until tomorrow afternoon, they could afford a couple of beers at Huna's before making it an early night. Seeing Teddy and Rae as they walked into the bar, however, came as a surprise.

Moments later, Rae was introducing them to Selke, and there were "small world" comments as they told Rae they had already met Rhonda. In the next moment, all of them minus Rhonda and Chris were seated around a nearby table placing drink orders.

As Lauren allowed herself to be drawn into the ongoing dialogue between Rae and Selke, Hammer was left exchanging small talk with Teddy.

What Hammer hoped for was to loop the conversation back to the closing moments of their previous chat in Hanalei— this being Teddy's comment that he and Rae were "secret agents."

"Well how's the sugar business?" Hammer asked, making a "making conversation" reference to Teddy's cover story about them being overt, not covert, agents of the Sweet Harvest Sugar Company.

"Oh. It's fine. We're nearly through with our project here. We'll be going home soon."

Teddy seemed a bit reticent, so Hammer drew him into conversation about the weather, and whether he and Rae had been to a luau while on the island, as he waited for Teddy's first Mai Tai to begin loosening him up.

Midway through Teddy's second drink, as Hammer still nursed his first pint of beer, it was time to mention that Teddy seemed a little on edge tonight. Hammer said he guessed this was because Teddy would soon be leaving this "tropical paradise."

"You know, it's not such a paradise, Jimmy," he said, calling Hammer by the nickname Teddy had settled upon. "It's really a scary place when you dig deep. You can talk to our friend Selke there. When we met her last week, she told us all about ghosts that live in the mountains on this island."

"Ghosts?"

"In Korea, we have many stories about *gwisin,* which is a Korean word for such spirits who haunt you and chase you."

"They have those *here*?" Hammer asked, innocently playing along.

"You know...most people don't know...they found skeletons up there in the mountains."

"Skeletons?"

"A man and a woman. They were *murdered*. There were bullet holes in the skulls."

"That's awful."

"Spirits stay around in places where people are murdered."

"Are you sure?"

"I can tell you don't believe in ghosts," Teddy said,

working his way toward the bottom of his second Mai Tai while Hammer fingered a half-full pint glass.

"I have an open mind."

"Maybe I should have said I don't think you've seen ghosts, bit I *have*."

"Oh yeah?"

"When we children in Korea, they told us *gwisin* stories. We figured that it was their way to make us behave. I'm sure that was true, but this doesn't mean there aren't *gwisin* out there. I didn't believe in *gwisin* until one time when I was eight years old. I was out alone at night and I saw a ghostly specter following me. I watched very closely as it passed and it looked at me."

"You're sure?"

"I don't dare tell this to my colleagues."

"Why tell *me*?"

"Because I had to tell *someone*, and you're almost a stranger."

"I'm honored…I guess."

"Did you know that in Hawai`i, they have whole armies of angry spirits who march through the night?" Teddy asked earnestly.

"Angry spirits are not at the top of my list of worries," Hammer said. "But I'll consider myself warned."

"Selke told us they capture people and throw them through the gates of hell."

"How does she know this?"

"She's studied them. When you talk to her, you just *know*."

Hammer glanced at Selke who was engrossed in a conversation with Rae and Lauren. She had told Teddy the same story Kai Nialani had told, and Lauren had found it mentioned in her old books, so it was a genuine piece of folklore. As for Hammer, he'd heard Johnny

Cash's cover of "Ghost Riders in the Sky," so he understood the concept.

"You once shared with me that you're a secret agent," Hammer said. "I thought secret agents weren't prone to fear."

"Oh no," Teddy said. "I will be so glad when this is over."

"You told me you and Rae were on a secret op. Is that what you're talking about?"

"I'm just a techie doing a techie job," he admitted. "So is Rae. She pretends not to be afraid."

"Maybe you should just not do this op if you're afraid that the army of ghosts will throw you through the gates of hell?"

"It's not that simple," Teddy insisted.

"It never is," Hammer said, taking a sip from his almost-too-warm beer.

He smiled. Out of the corner of his eye, he saw Rhonda leaving the bar with the man with whom she'd been talking. By the way their arms were intertwined, he could tell their evening was only just beginning.

CHAPTER TWENTY-ONE

NEARLY TWO WEEKS had passed since Lauren Stahling and Jim Hammer first emerged from this dense koa forest and looked out across the vast panorama of a morning sunrise over the cliff tops of the Nāpali Coast.

Back then, they came following the trail of Annison Cutts, in search of an architectural masterpiece built half a millennium in the past. Today, it was the launch day for works of twenty-first century technology. For these two, it was the day of a sober rendezvous with a hive of evil which had existed for barely a month.

The dazzling orange-gold Thursday morning light gradually creeping down the jungled cliffs caught their eye as on previous visits, as did the deep azure of the vast Pacific beyond. Today, though, the sky was as troubled as their mood. On the distant horizon, storm clouds gathered, clouds not quite black, but darker and grayer than the familiar cotton-colored cumulus.

They had left the Ocean Breeze Motel in Kekaha in the Ford Taurus when it was still dark. Winding northbound on Highway 550, they had passed the turnoff for the PMRF facility, as well as the parking area for the Miloli`i

Ridge Trailhead, in the darkness. As expected, there was a Navy Humvee parked at the former. With all of the base on threat level FPCON Charlie, it would be routine to have security people dissuading casual motorists from exploring this road. The parking area for the Miloli`i Ridge Trailhead was empty, and they left it that way.

As they had done on Sunday, they continued for a quarter mile to the next turnoff, where they could park where the Koreans would not see the Taurus. From here, they could make their way cross country through the forest to meet up with the main trail. It was still dark and the forest made for tricky traveling, but the light of the nearly full moon on the pale white eucalyptus trunks made it fairly easy going.

"Tonight will be the full moon," Lauren had commented. "Last night when I was talking with those other women about skeletons and ghosts, Selke mentioned a couple of times about the night marchers marching under a full moon, but I'm not sure Rae realized that the moon was coming full now."

"I don't think most people these days, especially if they live in cities, really pay a lot of attention to the phases of the moon," Hammer suggested. "Unless you're a cop or you work the graveyard shift in an ER."

"But *not* if you work for a Korean sugar company," Lauren said wryly. "Sugar must be a high pressure business. Rae seemed especially stressed last night. I got the impression she and her friends had an important meeting today. I wonder what it could be."

As they stood at the edge of the mixed eucalyptus and koa forest looking at the sunrise, Hammer took out his Oberwerk binoculars and calmly surveyed the scene before them. He traversed from east to west across the rugged cliff tops, each one a study in challenging wilderness terrain, until his eyes fell on the dishes, antennae, and flashing red lights of the PMRF instrumentation facility on Makaha Ridge, five miles away.

He knew that over there under those antennae, especially today, eyes and binoculars would be looking back. Hammer had been looked back at under these circumstances before, but he was practiced in the art of not being seen by anyone looking back. When he and Lauren had come to this spot the first time, as tourists, they could not have imagined ever being here as part of a tactical operation—yet here they were.

On their first trip, Lauren was wearing a bright red tank top and Hammer a maroon t-shirt. Today, they were both wearing swim pants and long-sleeved swim shirts in various shades of dark gray. All of these were readily available at dozens of shops in Kaua`i, and ideal for the cool mountain air. The colors were ideal for going unseen.

He traversed back, slightly to the east and studied Pokuakini Ridge. The Oberwerk was a magnificent instrument, yet he could see utterly no trace of the Korean camp.

"I have to admire Ryu for picking wisely when he enlisted Han and Cho to situate his operation base over there," Hammer said. "It's not just the way they so perfectly camouflaged it, but the other thing that goes unnoticed, is how they picked the goat trails for access."

"Don't sell yourself short," Lauren said. "You picked the goat trails that took us to the ancient waterworks in Hemolele`auwai valley. You picked trails that Kai Nialani could not even *see* when we brought her up here, and she's a detective."

"Thank you, but I've seen *you* with a good eye for

game trails in the mountains back home, young lady," Hammer said. "No, what I was complimenting Han and Cho for was how they picked trails that are just out of the line of sight from the PMRF facility. Just like most people don't notice goat trails, very few people, present company included, can tell which of these trails are also used by humans."

"Two weeks ago we didn't care whether PMRF was looking at us, because we were just a couple of sight-seers," Lauren added. "And truth be told, back then, they probably weren't even looking at the hikers out here on the Miloli`i Ridge Trail."

"After my conversation with Teddy last night," Hammer said as they started down the Miloli`i Trail toward where the goat trails forked off, "I got to thinking."

"*Oh-oh,*" Lauren teased.

"Like I told you last night when we were recapping our conversations with all those people, Teddy is totally engrossed in the mythology of the ghost armies."

"Yeah, and so is Rea, but she insists that she's not superstitious."

"Well, I got to thinking a little bit poetically myself," Hammer admitted. "You know, with their choice of access trails, Ryu's gang is a little bit like a 'ghost army' themselves. They haunt these hills, completely unseen by PMRF...until they strike."

"You know who else is a ghost army, right?" Lauren said, "Who else is haunting the hills unseen, and *unknown* to their enemies?"

"Yup, I do," Hammer said with a smile.

———

The Korean camp seemed abandoned, as they had last seen it, but like on their previous visit, this ghost army of two approached it with great caution—just in case.

When they were certain that they were alone, Hammer found a vantage point where he could study the trail network behind them, all the way back to the tree line. He looked carefully to see whether anyone else was coming.

The trail was empty. They had at least twenty to thirty minutes before anyone could possibly interrupt them.

He looked at the Navy's countdown app on his phone. It was now just past T-minus eight hours, and they were still counting.

They had more than enough time for the opening action in their war against the ghost army from the Sweet Harvest Sugar Company.

It was going to be a different kind of war for Jim Hammer.

In his previous post-retirement campaigns against criminal gangs, he had carried his familiar Colt M1911 .45 automatic pistol, and his .338-caliber Barrett Mk22 sniper rifle. Today, he had neither. This adventure had started as a vacation, and he'd left his firepower at home—but Hammer had not survived in his trade without being a master of improvisation.

Rob was able to direct him to the place in the house where he had stashed the 50HRC Beta Titanium knife he used when scuba diving. The eight-inch full shank drop point blade might come in handy. Not to be outdone, Lauren had found a boning knife with a seven-inch saber-ground blade that was like the one she used at home when they went deer hunting.

Their biggest and best weapon, however, was that their ghost army had gone to war against another ghost army who didn't even know they were here. And now they *were* here, under the flaps of the tent containing the nerve center of Ryu's dark designs.

What next?

They could simply heave the mountain of electronics to crashing, splintering devastation on the lava rocks at the base of the adjacent cliff. That would have stopped the immediate threat, but as Hammer always said, you have to work your way to the top and cut off the head of the monster *behind* the threat.

In many ways, it was Ryu's own wicked inventiveness and resourcefulness that was the most lethal weapon in his whole endeavor. Just as an opera can never end until the fat lady's final solo, one of Jim Hammer's wars cannot end until the head of the mastermind rolls. Today, this was Ryu.

The plan devised by the two Montanans for the opening scene of today's final act was to treat this hub of iniquity with a light touch. The idea was for their presence to not be immediately felt.

Hammer preferred that his enemies believe that they were winning—all the way up to the moment when they suddenly realized they were *not*.

While Hammer carefully compromised the wiring connecting the solar panels to the batteries, so loss of power would be slow and barely perceptible, Lauren crawled in behind the center console over which they had watched Teddy preside when they were eavesdropping on Sunday. After their tutorial from Tim Tommis, they knew this was the centerpiece, the thing that could potentially spoof the world into some variation on Armageddon.

Lauren, like nearly anyone in the world, did not understand the technical nuances of a TPQ-76 Cloud Mirror system, nor how it could be adapted to spoof real-time GNSS or GPS data. Nor did Lauren, like most people, understand the technical nuances of a complicated cable television system, like the kind you need in out-of-the-way parts of Montana, but she had once spent a couple of hours successfully hooking one up for her mother.

What she had learned from that experience was if one or two sets of crucial wire connections are transposed, the whole setup behaves in unintended ways that are virtually impossible to troubleshoot without unlimited time and patience.

Lauren looked at her phone. It had taken only about ten minutes with small screwdrivers and needle-nose pliers to complete her work. The countdown app said it was now half past T-minus eight hours.

Lauren put her little toolkit back into her backpack and took out a plastic bag filled with what Hammer once irreverently described as looking like grass seed with a few cast-offs from an everything bagel mixed in.

"Remember Anise?" Lauren asked.

He nodded. Who could forget the engaging and somewhat mysterious woman they had met at the farmers' market two weeks ago, or this bag she had given them? She told them that if you burned it like incense around truly evil people, this would disorient them and weaken their will to cause harm.

"I remember her saying that we were good people who sometimes swim in dark waters," Hammer said. "I wonder where she got that idea?"

"I think she knew a lot more than met anyone's eye but hers," Lauren said, spreading some of the mixture on a flat rock under a camp table toward the back of the canopy tent.

"She told us not to use it haphazardly…or willy-nilly," he said as she took out the key-chain-size ferro rod she always carried in her backpack. "I can still hear her voice saying 'willy-nilly.' That's not something you hear much these days."

"I don't think this is willy-nilly, do you?" Lauren asked as a spark from the ferro rod ignited the powder.

"I think that what you're doing is *exactly* what she had in mind," he agreed. "She said we'd know when the time was right…and I guess we *do*."

As the burning powder filled the tent with a subtle, but strangely pleasing aroma, and as Lauren and Hammer slipped out into the clear mountain morning, Master-at-Arms Chief Petty Officer Anthony Karboli and Petty Officer Second Class Joel Dyallic were northbound on Highway 550 believing they had gotten an early start.

It was nearly T-minus eight hours, or 0754, and Karboli had expected to find the Miloli`i Ridge Trailhead parking area empty. He was not disappointed. It was.

"Pull in here and park nose out," Karboli ordered. "We'll set some cones and make sure we get names and ID for anybody who tries to hike on this trail today."

For the rest of the day, a Navy Humvee and a half dozen orange cones should be enough to dissuade almost anyone from stopping here. Unlike the Makaha Ridge Road, which led to PMRF property, Miloli`i Ridge was state park property, so they couldn't overtly *stop* would-be hikers. But they could intimidate them. A Humvee and a pair of armed men with badges were enough to intimidate casual hikers.

"Glad you knew where you're going," Dyallic. "I almost missed that little brown and yellow sign in the dark. I've never been up this road before."

"How long you been on the island?"

"Nine months, chief. I guess I'm not much on mountain sightseeing. I'm more of a beach guy."

"Nothing wrong with beaches."

"No, Chief."

"Are you a surfer?"

"No, Chief, but it's on the list," Dyallic said. "I do like beach volleyball."

"Keeps you in shape."

"And obviously, it's fun watching the ladies beach volleyball, if you know what I mean."

"Yes, I do," Karboli said.

Of course he knew. The sight of young, shapely women in peak physical condition in motion it tiny two-piece swimsuits was a dream for most males Dyallic's age. *Oh to be a young, enlisted man with nothing to lose.*

"Yeah," Dyallic continued. "We...me and my friends...we like to go over to Poipu, you know this side of Līhu`e, where there's all those resorts. Good way to meet the young ladies. Lotsa fun."

"I hope you're being careful. Remember, sometimes when something seems too good to be true, it *is*."

"Yes, Chief."

Dyallic remembered the young woman at Shenanigans who was a source of great embarrassment for Karboli. The young petty officer decided it prudent to say no more.

CHAPTER TWENTY-TWO

"*T-MINUS FIVE HOURS AND COUNTING*!"

Dave Altbeck glanced up impulsively at the sound of the disembodied voice booming from the speaker bar at the top of the front wall of the Battle Management Interoperability Center.

It was late Thursday morning, and he had been listening to these proclamations every hour on the hour since T-minus eleven. Nevertheless, against the backdrop of launch-day tensions, their sharpness and volume still made him flinch. Out of the corner of his eye, he could see that he was not alone. Even naval officers with a lot of stripes on their shoulders were caught off guard.

Altbeck would have it no other way. In future years, he knew he would remember this experience like no other. It was a dream come true to be a fly on the wall of Hard Kinkaide's command center. He would be at the epicenter when the admiral lobbed Aegis missiles like they were buckshot and took out ICBMs loaded with PETN in full view of Chinese spy ships—and this was Altbeck's *day job*.

Twenty-two hours down. Only five to go.

How could one man be so lucky?

Those hours, so long on excitement, had been low on the scale of creature comfort, but he did not care about that. He was young and he'd soon forget what it felt like to crawl into an anteroom to curl up on a dusty floor under a desk for a scant three or four hours of sleep.

As he looked up at the wall from where the voice had originated, his eyes fell on the digital clocks—a whole bank of them—and all of them with red numerals moving with breathtaking speed. Each one had digits down to milliseconds, and these changed faster than his eye could follow. The countdown clock was flanked by a local time clock, a Zulu Time clock, and a Kwajalein Time clock, which looked like it was four hours ago, but it was across the International Dateline so it was not even today, it was *tomorrow*.

Altbeck marveled at the unprecedented access that he'd had to Admiral Kinkaide over the past days. He was hearing things from the admiral that no one else from the outside world could hear. Everything he heard that was top secret *now* would be unclassified in five or six hours, and he, Dave Altbeck was hearing it first—and he was hearing most of it from the admiral *himself*.

How could one twenty-something gearhead be so lucky as to be in a place like this?

As Altbeck haunted the BMIC, seeing everything there was to be seen, Kinkaide had been in and out countless times. Those who kept track of him and his entourage reported him on the move from the engineering hangar to the launch area from which the missiles would soon arc into the sky.

Since the countdown had begun, he had been thundering hither and yon, fueled by black coffee. The rumor was that he could stay awake for a stretch of forty-eight hours or more during an exercise like this.

In fact, the admiral was just as engrossed in the excitement of the day as was the journalist. For both of them, *this* was what they lived for.

Lynsee Kinkaide hadn't seen much of her absent, obsessed father in the more than a week since he had moved her into the Barking Sands admiral's quarters, but she had not seen him *at all* in two days. She knew there was a big-deal exercise going on, and she had long ago learned that he cared more about his big-deal exercises than he did about daddying.

It was not that she still wanted to be daddied, like she did when she was a child. She really, *really* did not. She merely wished he'd make an effort so she would have the pleasure of rebuffing him.

It was almost noon Thursday on the clock in her bedroom as she rolled out from under the covers. Everywhere else at the Barking Sands base, and indeed across the tens of thousands of square miles of the Pacific Missile Range, it was T-minus four hours.

She looked at her phone for text messages. She looked at Instagram and all the other places where people her age interact, and she was disappointed in that way that people who cannot be satisfied are *always* dissatisfied.

What she really wanted, what she wanted even more than a chance to disdainfully repulse her father, was any communication of any kind from the gorgeous, handsome Chief Petty Officer Anthony Karboli.

Sadly, she had no way of contacting him. She had no numbers, no email, no social media URLs of any kind for him. In her mind, she was starting to believe that the universe had conspired to keep them apart.

She ate a Pop-Tart, drank some increasingly stale

orange juice out of a plastic jug that had been in the fridge for a long time and decided to go out. It was too early to go to Shenanigans, so she just went for a walk. With the way that everyone else was running around the base in their excitement over the big-deal exercise, Lynsee felt like she was in slow motion.

She was so damned tired of these self-important people and their exercises.

She thought about taking the car and driving somewhere. She had seen the videos. She knew that beyond the purgatory of Barking Sands, Kaua`i had beach life, a nightlife, and *fun*. She knew they had surfing and surfers and bars and all the places that the twenty-one-year-old behind Lynsee's fake ID would enjoy.

She knew where the keys were, the keys to the Lexus RX civilian rental car that her mother had left behind when she flew home. It was parked behind the admiral's quarters just waiting. The twenty-one-year-old behind Lynsee's fake ID obviously had a driver's license, and so did seventeen-year-old Lynsee.

She could do this and her father would never even notice. He never noticed anything she did unless it embarrassed him. What if she got busted for a DUI somewhere off-base? What if her father had to bail her out? It would serve him right. *Screw him.*

Saving her island-wide ramble in the white Lexus as a backup plan, she decided she would go find Anthony Karboli. She knew that with the exercise going on he would certainly be working, so she decided to go to his workplace. She walked over to the Barking Sands base security command post. It was only about a city block from the admiral's quarters.

It was surrounded by people wearing camo and packing heat. She always thought it was silly when they camouflaged themselves in camo-patterned clothes while they were standing around in cream-colored buildings or on asphalt pavement. Some even had assault rifles, but this had never intimidated her. Were they going to shoot a woman with long, blond hair wearing a tank top and cutoffs? *I don't think so*!

She walked straight up and straight in.

A young, uniformed man barely older than the woman in her fake ID stopped her.

"Wait a minute, miss," he said firmly. "You can't be here. Can you show me some ID."

"Okay," she said slowly, looking at the man with a smile she used when she wanted to be equal parts innocent and seductive.

Tipping her sunglasses to the top of her head, she opened her purse and produced her "Lynsee" ID, the one that allowed her to tap her last name with a carefully painted thumbnail, while covering the line that told her date of birth. She had been through this many times before.

"Kinkaide?" the young man said uneasily. "Are you, umm…?"

"The admiral's daughter? Yes, sir. I am."

"What can I do for you?"

"I'm looking for Chief Petty Officer Anthony Karboli," she said with authority.

"Are you…?"

"A friend? Yes. You might say we know one another *intimately*."

Her confident smile and her surname told the young MA to take this situation seriously. He started asking around.

"Is Chief Karboli in the building?"

"No? Then do you know where he can be found?"

She heard the other man promise to go find out and

she cast a teasing glance at the first man as they waited. Finally, the second man returned.

"He's with Dyallic. They're on security stakeout up at the Miloli`i Ridge Trailhead," he said. "They'll be up there 'til after the launch."

"They're up at the Miloli`i Ridge Trailhead," the first man repeated, turning to Lynsee. "Do you know where that is? Up on Highway 550, just past the turnoff for PMRF at Makaha Ridge."

"Yes, I do," Lynsee said, continuing to smile. She had never heard of the trail, but she knew the highway and that a Navy vehicle would be easy to spot. "Thank you."

She turned away and walked out with a plan.

The countdown clock was running in the security command post, so she knew they were going to be shooting off their rockets in only three hours. That would be around four o'clock. Her father would be so busy for hours around that time and after, so he would forget she existed. Anthony would be on duty until then for sure.

Her plan was simple. She would take the car and go to him. She would meet him just after the launch. Dyallic could take whatever vehicle they had used to drive up into the mountains and go away.

She and Anthony would find a meadow up in the mountains and make love, wild passionate love, all the rest of the day. They would make love like they did that night at the Royal Pacific.

He would tell her *again* how much he loved her. Then, they would take the white Lexus rental car and get away —far, far, away from the world of Hardgrove Kinkaide and his ridiculous rockets.

High in the mountains into which Lynd see planned to drive, up here next to the sign mentioning the 3,900-foot elevation, the sun was warming a day that had begun cool. Anthony Karboli and Joel Dyallic had been on duty for more than four hours and had nearly another four to go until T-minus zero, the crucial moment of the Aegis Ballistic Missile Defense System launch.

"It's getting a bit hot, Chief," Dyallic commented, less as a complaint, and more as a means of making conversation on a pretty boring day.

"Permission to find a spot in the shade, petty officer," Karboli replied, telling Dyallic that he could make himself comfortable.

For most of the tourists driving up Highway 550 toward Kōke`e State Park, the sight of military personnel with SIG Sauer M18 sidearms and a Humvee guarding the Miloli`i Ridge Trail parking area was surprising and a bit intimidating. A few slowed to gawk for a few seconds, but most hardly noticed. Across most of Kaua`i, the impending Vigilant Basilisk operation was virtually unknown, and it would remain unnoticed.

A family of four from Kansas stopped to curiously ask what was going on, but they decided the Waimea Canyon overlooks were much more interesting. Two backpackers from Arizona with the westward-leading Miloli`i Ridge Trail on their wish list inquired whether that trail was open.

Without answering directly, Karboli referred them to an alternate trail whose parking area was a short distance up Highway 550 and on the *opposite* side of the highway, the east side, away from the top of the Nāpali Coast. When he mentioned they could hike eastward to take a look at eight hundred-foot Waipo`o Falls, they decided that would be fun, thanked him, and drove on, heading toward the place where Karboli said they could park for this hike.

It was nearly one o'clock when the brown Hyundai SUV that Han jong-sok had rented three weeks ago drove past for about fifty yards and turned off into the same parking area as the Arizonans' car. Karboli and Dyallic watched as the five people climbed out, crossed the road and walked back to where the Humvee was parked.

Having watched Karboli's approach to the other cars that stopped, Dyallic decided to show his boss some initiative, and he leaped into action.

"What are your plans today?" Dyallic asked in the officious man-with-the-badge tone of voice he had heard Karboli use.

"We are planning to do a hike here today," Han said, confused not to see Karboli taking the lead.

"The US Navy is conducting an exercise today involving the Pacific Missile Range," Dyallic said, gesturing westward with his hand. "We're recommending that people not use the Miloli`i Ridge Trail today."

Han looked confused, as did Cho ho-jin.

Ryu Myong-su was glowering at Karboli with a what-the-hell? expression.

Karboli decided that it was time to take charge and smooth things over. The unsuspecting young petty officer had never seen these five people before and did not know that Karboli knew them intimately—*more intimately than he had ever wanted*. Dyallic had no idea that making this part of the day go smoothly for *these* five Koreans was exactly why Karboli had gotten them assigned to *this* red-dirt parking area on *this* particular day.

"What the petty officer is saying," Karboli said, stepping forward, "is that because of the Pacific Missile Range exercise we can't have people going off-trail out there. Technically, the Miloli`i Ridge Trail is *not* closed, but we're asking people to stay on the trail today. We have a facility on Makaha Ridge that you will see to the south when you are out there."

"Yes, sir, we understand," Han said, grasping the fact that Dyallic was not in the loop and deciding to play along with Karboli's misdirection.

"We appreciate your cooperation," Karboli said. For Dyallic's sake, he betrayed no indication that he knew Han or any of the others.

"Yes sir, we understand," Han said with a barely perceptible smirk. "We will cause no trouble."

You already have, damn you, Karboli thought to himself as they disappeared into the forest on the trail.

"That was an interesting bunch," Dyallic said after the group had gone. "That older one was a real serious thinker, you could tell. The young guy almost looked like he was going to some kind of a dance club...with that shirt and the way he had his cap turned sideways. I also think it's strange that they parked way over *there,* if they were going to hike a trail over *here*."

"You're a profiler now?" Karboli replied sarcastically.

"When we were in A-School at the Tech Training Center in San Antonio, they taught us to size up people. You know, like in crowds?"

"Right," Karboli said. "But I did not see these people, any of them, as constituting a threat to Vigilant Basilisk. Did you?"

"I didn't mean to say they were a threat," Dyallic said defensively. "I just thought they seemed like they were from a pretty wide selection of walks of life."

"They're just tourists out for a stroll. This is a tourist island. Some people like beach volleyball. Some people like to hike. Tourists come in all shapes and sizes."

"Yes chief. You're right."

CHAPTER TWENTY-THREE

"I KNOW it says this is the best rum on the island, but it's actually the best rum in the *world*."

Rhonda and Selke looked around quickly to see who had come up behind them.

The two women had been standing next to a display for Island Fire Rum in the Big Save Market in Kekaha idly discussing how they trying to get some grocery shopping out of the way ahead of the weekend.

"*Judy*!" Rhonda exclaimed as she saw who had ambushed the conversation. "I haven't seen you in weeks. Where have you been hiding?"

"Work mostly," Judy said as the women took turns hugging. "You know I work for Island Fire, at their distillery in Port Allen?"

"Yeah, I remember," Rhonda said. "How's that going?"

"Great, but it's still weird to see our point of sale signs out in the world. You know, we got our rum into the Honolulu Airport last month, and we're in Costco on three of the islands…and Maui next month."

"Girl, look at you go!" Rhonda said, feeling proud for

her friend. "When are you going to invite your *ohana* sisters over for a rum tasting?"

"*I know*!" Judy said. "I will. I promise. It's just been sooo busy."

"What are you doing playing hooky on a Thursday?"

"We've got a big retail chain from the mainland coming in on the weekend, so they gave us Thursday-Friday off this week...wait a minute! Why don't we step over to Huna's right *now*! They serve Island Fire over there. It's only two o'clock. It won't be crowded. I'll buy you a drink...or two."

"You don't have to ask me twice," Rhonda said, putting the milk and cottage cheese from her shopping cart back into the cooler.

Rhonda's friend, the bartender, was impressed when he learned that Judy worked at Island Fire, so he bought the first round.

"So you've got a big-time buyer from the mainland coming in?" Rhonda said, touching her glass to those of her two friends. "They're coming all the way here to the west side to drink rum. You'll have to learn to make Mai Tais. Mainlanders love Mai Tais."

"We've been getting a lot of off-island visitors lately," Judy said.

"You're on the map now," Selke commented.

"We've had this bunch from Korea hanging around a lot," Judy continued. "They say they're really interested in growing sugarcane in small batches for rum over there."

"They *say*?"

"Yeah, but you would think their company would send people who know more about sugar growing."

"What do you mean?"

"These guys...and there's one woman...don't know the first thing about growing anything. I've practically had to teach them."

"Wow."

"It's not so bad. There's one guy who's taken an interest in...well you know."

"Oo, la, la."

"He's kinda cute. A pretty buff ex-soldier, but he's added a lot to his waistline since he stopped being a soldier."

"So what?"

"So I'm not going to date anybody who I know through work," Judy said emphatically. "That's a gateway drug to all kinds of would-be problems. Anyway, they're all going back to Korea in a couple of days, so there."

"What's their company called?" Selke asked.

"Sweet Harvest," Judy replied. "It's the Sweet Harvest Sugar Company, but they don't know anything about harvesting anything."

"We met those people," Selke said.

"Where?" Judy asked, surprised.

"Right here in Huna's, Rhonda and I."

"Yeah, we talked to them a couple of times," Rhonda added.

"They were more interested in *gwisin,* Korean ghosts, than they were in harvesting sugar."

"Ghosts?" Judy exclaimed. *"Why?"*

"It started with those skeletons that were found in the mountains," Rhonda said. "Then Selke started scaring them with ghost stories."

"I was only talking to them," Selke said defensively. "I only started talking to them because I overheard them saying the word *gwisin*. *They* brought it up, and *they* kept asking."

"I know," Rhonda admitted. "I was only teasing, but they were really eating up your ghost stories."

"People tell ghost stories to scare each other, right?" Judy asked rhetorically. "Didn't you do that when you were kids?"

"Of course," Rhonda said. "But Selke had them going with those stories of ghost armies marching through the night."

"The marchers in the night, the *huaka`i-pō,* are a real part of Hawai`ian culture," Selke insisted. "People really have seen the 'spirit ranks,' the *oi`o* in the sky under a full moon."

"Tonight's a full moon."

The three women turned to look at the man in a ball cap with a television network logo who had made this observation. He was about their age, no longer a kid, but still with life left in him, and not bad looking, in a grizzled way and, he was the same journalist whom Rhonda and Selke had met the night before, and with whom Rhonda had later spent some quality time.

"*Hey Chris,*" Rhonda said. "I didn't see you sit down. You're sneaking up on me!"

"I'm sorry," he said. "I didn't mean to sneak up."

"But yes, you did," she said, giving him a kiss on the cheek. "What are you doing in here? With that rocket launch going on, I figured you'd be working."

"I'm just having a quick one before I head up to the press tent at the base. We have the camera truck all set up, so there's been nothing to do all day except wait around."

Rhonda introduced Chris to Judy and reintroduced him to Selke, and he politely apologized for interrupting what he observed to have been a pretty lively conversation.

"No harm done," Selke said in a friendly way. "We were starting to tell ghost stories and it's not even dark out. What time is your launch?"

"It'll be at 4:02 local time, about forty minutes," Chris said. "If everything goes according to plan."

"Why wouldn't it?" Judy asked. "Don't they have these things figured out?"

"Lots of moving parts," he said.

"Why would they launch their rockets during a full moon?" Selke asked. "Aren't they afraid of everything that can go wrong during a full moon?"

"These people are all science people," he said. "I don't think they're superstitious that way."

"I wonder how many of them checked their horoscope apps this morning," Selke quipped with a chuckle.

"I wonder," he said, smiling. "Hey, could I buy you ladies a drink?"

"Let us buy *you* a drink," Judy said. She'd had two by now and was feeling especially cheerful.

"She's with the distillery," Rhonda pointed out. "She makes the stuff."

"T-minus one hour and counting!"

Seven miles north of where the lady from the distillery was offering to buy a drink for the man from the network, the journalist from *Defense Up Front* glanced up at the clock in the PMRF Battle Management Interoperability Center. He felt a chill of excitement running up his spine.

One hour!

Dave Altbeck had been listening to these proclamations every hour on the hour for hours. Now, they were at the end. No more T-minus *hours*. They would now be in *minutes*—until they were in the final *seconds*.

This was it!

There was nothing left for Altbeck to do but scribble in his notebook and watch the countdown clock with its mesmerizing millisecond numerals which existed only as pulsating blurs. Mainly he looked at the hour slot on the far left. After more than twenty-six hours, it now read simply "00." His insides were knotted in anticipation.

He maneuvered around the BMIC, nodding to men and women whom he had gotten to know through the long days of his embed. He had come to be acquainted with quite a few of the people who came and went in this and the adjoining rooms. He found that most appreciated the passion of a gearhead like him, even if they thought of journalists as little more than amusing groupies.

At least he knew what they were talking about in their blizzard of technical talk. His readers would devour this like it was caviar, and this is why he had been picked to be embedded in this place. Even the networks did not have an inside man.

Despite the almost collegial familiarity, he had found the denizens of the BMIC reluctant to discuss a lot of topics today. Maybe they were being protective, and maybe they were a bit superstitious, but none of them talked to Altbeck about what could go *wrong*.

They all knew—and they knew that Altbeck knew—about what had caused failures with Aegis program RIM-174 missiles in the past. There was a fuse software design error here, a glitch in the missile navigation system there, and the time that a tactical seeker battery squibbed—and these were just the unclassified ones.

That said, the elephant in the room was the absence of a built-in hold, which underscored the bold confidence that had come over Admiral Kinkaide since the RIM-174 "G Models" with their new Mk109C rocket sustainers had arrived at Barking Sands on Saturday.

Suddenly, the admiral himself burst into the room, flanked by his entourage of captains and lieutenant commanders. Altbeck watched as the larger-than-life Admiral Hardgrove Kinkaide checked in with people it various workstations, gesturing and pointing to maps and data displayed on the huge AQUOS LCD displays. Then, he stood, turned and looked directly at the embedded journalist.

"Altbeck," he said firmly. "Grab your gear and come with us. I'm going to show you how we do things in the ballistic missile defense world."

Though he assumed he'd been seeing exactly this for the past week, Altbeck was eager to see whatever the admiral had in mind. He snatched his backpack and jumped into the wake that swirled behind the entourage as it swept out of the BMIC, down the hall, and into the brilliant sunlight.

The two SUVs that were used by the admiral's staff to dash from place to place at the twenty-four-hundred-acre base were waiting. The admiral took his place next to the driver of the lead vehicle, while Altbeck wound up crammed into the back row of the other one.

Little more than five minutes later they were at an open area surrounded by low trees near the beach. There was a structure that Altbeck recognized as a near clone of a Mk21 launch canister from the Mk57 Vertical Launch System that was found aboard guided missile destroyers. Perched atop it was one of the RIM-174G missiles Altbeck had seen being unloaded from a C-17 on Saturday.

"See that bunker over there?" Kinkaide asked, pointing to an unremarkable low concrete building with a slit opening. "On the launch stand, they're hardwired to the VLS, the Vertical Launch System. We transfer control to them at T-minus ten minutes for pre-launch sequencing, and it all comes back to BMIC for flight control and monitoring at the moment the missile leaves the launcher."

Altbeck scrutinized the bunker for a moment, then raced to catch up with the admiral as he led his entourage toward the slender, glossy white projectile that stood, with its launcher, almost as tall as a three-story building. This was the first time Altbeck had seen a RIM-174G SM-6 erected for launch. Imagining this thing streaking through the atmosphere at Mach four was a thrill for a defense hardware gearhead.

"Let's make this quick," the admiral said. "It's T-minus twenty and we need to be out of here in ten."

The expressions worn by some of his entourage suggested they should have cleared out of the launch area ten minutes *ago*.

Kinkaide waved the journalist over and began explaining the nuances of the missile, from its blast fragmentation warhead way up at the top, to the propulsion system at the base. Altbeck had heard it before, but the admiral's hyperbole was giving him some colorful copy. He decided that *Defense Up Front* would have to devote a whole issue to today's excitement.

Finally, the admiral brought his attention to the interface between the solid-fuel rocket booster, and the new Mk109C dual-thrust rocket sustainer that had apparently saved Vigilant Basilisk from being scrubbed before it happened.

"There you have the SM-2-IV first stage, with an unrefueled weight of 535 pounds, but this one's fully loaded with half a ton of solid fuel. You know what solid fuel means, right?"

Before the journalist could answer, the admiral charged ahead.

"It means no leaking liquid fuel line connectors that have to be repaired. All of us in the missile business have been through that. I could tell you horror stories about standing around with a quarter-million gallons of liquid oxygen and hydrogen fuel inside a ten-story thermos bottle while we had to troubleshoot a hydrogen leak. You know, what drives you crazy is that all of these damned nightmares seem to raise their ugly heads inside T-minus sixty minutes."

"I can understand your use of the word nightmare," Altbeck said sympathetically.

"With solid fuel, there's no leaks to detect," Kinkaide said proudly. "We're at less than sixty minutes and running smooth."

As he scrutinized the edges of the first stage and the rocket sustainer at the point where they came together, Altbeck saw something he did not understand. There were a lot of things in the world, even in the defense hardware world that was his life, that he didn't understand, but this seemed so elemental and so simple.

"What is it?" Kinkaide asked.

"What are you looking at?" Kinkaide asked again when Altbeck acted like he didn't hear.

"It's this," he said, pointing without touching. "Is this supposed to be like this?"

"Like what?"

"Like this. See how this sticks out about an eighth of an inch? Shouldn't this part be flush with that part?"

The admiral was now crouching down to look at what Altbeck saw, and his entourage was crowding in to look as well.

"There," the admiral said, turning to one of his lieu-

tenant commanders. "Is that supposed to be like *that*? See what I mean. Does that look right to you?"

"I don't know, sir."

"Then get somebody over here who *does*."

Other men, including some civilians whom Altbeck knew were tech people employed by the contractor, leaned in to look at the narrow interface between booster and sustainer.

"Can we launch successfully," Kinkaide said, his voice an angry growl, "with an eighth-inch gap like *that*?"

CHAPTER TWENTY-FOUR

TWENTY MILES to the north of Barking Sands, high on Pokuakini Ridge, a ghost army had been waiting all of Thursday afternoon in their splendidly camouflaged electronic warfare lair, a place of which no one across the entire length and breadth of the Pacific Missile Range was aware.

Like many others, they had downloaded the countdown app that the US Navy public affairs people had so generously provided. Waiting here in their nest, they had watched as the clock ticked past T-minus two hours.

To say they had been waiting patiently, or with the military discipline of a proper army, would have been untrue. There was an underling anxiety that affected each of the five differently. Neither Pak Mi-Rae, nor her fellow techie, Teddy Jong, had ever been anywhere near military structure. Meanwhile, former military officers Han jong-sok and Cho ho-jin who had lived and breathed this structure for over half their lives, had revealed themselves through the past few days as deeply superstitious men.

Ryu Myong-su, this army's *sajangnim*, its

commanding general, was a cool veteran of the Gukga Jeongbowo, South Korea's National Intelligence Service. He saw his role in the present group dynamic as a herder of cats. He recognized thin fissures now growing in the discipline that gave structure to his herd. Nevertheless, he was certain that they would make it through the last hour.

Ryu was about to unleash his own creation, a grand deception whose results could easily be globally catastrophic, and he didn't care. Even as Teddy had announced he *did* care, Ryu had found himself grappling with the question of whether he *should* care.

He also found himself grappling with the question of *why* he was questioning himself. There was something different, but barely tangible about the smell of this place. When they had arrived Pokuakini Ridge a couple of hours ago, Cho had been the first to comment of the subtle, but pleasing aroma he smelled.

"It was so stuffy in here on Sunday," he said, not realizing he was smelling the incense burned here that morning by *another* ghost army, the one of which no one else across the entire length and breadth of the entire Pacific Rim was aware.

"This agreeable odor is almost relaxing," Cho said.

"It must be off these flowering trees you see everywhere on this island," Rae had said as she first sniffed the air inside the tent. "Better than smelling the sweat of all of you for the next few hours."

Everyone but Ryu, the *sajangnim,* who styled himself as the mastermind rather than a mere technician, sat down at the consoles and began to methodically power up the equipment. Cho dialed up the 1RL257 and 1L269 broadband jammers which Ryu remembered were called Deadly Nightshade by the Russians. Han, meanwhile, leaned into their prize score from that Belarusian dealer in Busan, the 29B6 Konteyner—the same over-the-horizon VHF radar system used by the Russians to protect Moscow.

This gear had not come cheap, but after years with his fingers in the deep, dark bowels of international banking, Ryu's checkbook was very robust.

Rae's console had the most straightforward function of all. The R-330Zh short-range jammer would incapacitate every cell phone and two-way radio on this end of the island—basic comm devices so fundamental that they had no complex shielding mechanism to protect them. As Cho had said during an earlier discussion, "it pokes out their eyes and ears!"

She powered it up and sat back, waiting. For the moment, Ryu's gang needed their own cell phones to monitor the Navy's countdown app.

They each breathed heavily as T-minus one hour came and went, and the hour slot on the countdown clock rolled around to "00." Ryu stepped outside the tent to pace. As with Dave Altbeck inside the BMIC, his insides were knotted in anticipation.

In the center of it all, Teddy Jong sat pensively at his "Kitty," the heavily modified TPQ-76 Cloud Mirror system which he had explicitly created to generate illusions so real that those who saw them would be fooled into reckless action.

While the other workstations had crackled to life, Kitty's LG flat screens still remained dark.

"Get with it, Teddy," Cho insisted. "We have less than one hour."

"I fear this thing that we are about to do," Teddy admitted. "I fear the unsettled spirits of all those who we must kill. I fear all the *gwisin* who will rise up from the unnecessary dead between us and the devils of the DPRK."

"This is *necessary*," Cho insisted, as much to his own superstitious self as to Teddy's. "The real army of evil is the army on our border."

Cho was worried. On their previous visit to this place only four days ago, Teddy was effervescent with enthusiasm, and with his pride in his Kitty. Now he was enveloped in melancholy, and Kitty sat still and cold—though not as cold as Han, who glowered at Teddy with an angry expression.

"Power up your equipment," Han demanded.

"What if the American missiles fall short?" Teddy asked Han with a worried expression. "Pyongyang is only two hundred kilometers from Seoul. The immediately lethal fallout radius of a thermonuclear blast is estimated to be around half that, but *nobody* knows for sure. What if the angry *gwisin* are South Korean?"

"Start your machine," Han demanded. "Get it started before Ryu comes back."

"Before Ryu does what?"

They looked around. Ryu himself had just stepped back into the tent.

"Before Ryu does what?" Ryu repeated.

"Teddy is being slow in getting Kitty started," Cho explained calmly, trying to ease the tension.

"Don't fail us, Teddy," Ryu said unsympathetically. "Don't fail the Korean people."

Teddy could argue with Cho, and he could even argue with Han, but he was terrified of Ryu. Moments later, Kitty's monitors blossomed to life with only a half hour left to spare.

"I guess we'll be able to see the rockets from anywhere on the west side," Judy said as the two women settled up the second round tab and stepped out into the afternoon sun. Rhonda had left with Chris a half hour ago, leaving Judy and Selke to finish their drinks. "If you're interested."

"Not really," Selke admitted. "I've seen them before, and I'm not into weapons of war so much."

"Me neither. Make rum, not war, would be my slogan if I cared about slogans."

"You know…" Selke said, pausing to gather a thought. "What I'd really like to do is find those Koreans. You said they were going to leave the island soon, and I was hoping to run into them and ease the fear that I left them with about ghosts."

"Perfect subject for a sunny west side afternoon," Judy said, laughing.

"No, Judy. I'm serious. I had bad vibes that a couple of them were really fearful. The more I thought about it, the more I thought I should find them and help them understand that the spirit world doesn't have to be *only* a terrifying place."

"You are such a kind soul, Selke. You always have been. That's one of the things people really love about you."

"Thank you."

"Sure."

"Now, you worked with them," Selke said. "Do you have any idea where they might be on their last few days on the island?"

"They rented a house out toward the edge of town," Judy said thoughtfully. "I never went there, but I've seen that flashy blue Mustang that Mr. Ryu drives parked there. I know where it is. I have my not-so-flashy car parked over by Big Save. We could go take a look."

"That would be great," Selke said with a sense of relief. "Thank you."

Less than ten minutes later, as Judy cruised eastward, they spotted the Mustang. It was parked next to a tidy but unremarkable bungalow among other such houses in a downmarket area near the edge of town.

"I wonder if they're home," Selke said as she pulled back the flimsy screen door rapped on the sturdy back door.

"If they're like every other tourist on this side of the island today, they're out looking at rockets."

"I suppose," Selke said, peeking surreptitiously through a window.

"They had two cars," Judy said. "When they came out to see us, they drove a brown SUV. Mr. Han said they got it because it wouldn't show the dirt, but it was brown, not red like the dirt, so it showed the dirt. So much for thinking ahead."

Selke circled around the Mustang like she was expecting to find a clue as to where the Koreans were. She found no such evidence, but she did spot an item of interest lying on the ground near the tracks left in the soft red dirt when the other vehicle had pulled out. It was a notebook with a bright green cover, like the kind kids have in school, but a little more substantial, and with Korean characters in red and yellow printed at an angle across the cover.

"Look at that," she said, pointing. "They must have dropped it when they were getting into the car. See, they even ran over the corner of it when they pulled out of here."

"Well don't just stand there," Judy said. "Let's look and see what it says."

Selke picked it up, brushed off most of the dry dust and flipped through it.

"What does it say?" Judy asked eagerly.

"It's all in Korean. Here take a look."

"I don't read Korean," Judy said. "Do you?"

"No, but there's some drawings in here. This one looks like a pretty crude map of North and South Korea with a bunch of Xs on it."

"Maybe it's their distilleries?" Judy suggested.

"Maybe."

"What should we do with it?"

"We can't just leave it in the dirt."

"There's a mail slot in the door," Judy said. "Shove in through there. They'll see it as soon as they come back from watching the rockets or whatever they're doing."

"Wait a minute," Selke said. "What time is it?"

"It's twenty after four," Judy replied, looking at her phone. "Why?"

"Weren't these rockets supposed to go off around four?"

"Yes, they *were*. I wonder what happened."

CHAPTER TWENTY-FIVE

AN HOUR AGO, when Dave Altbeck mentioned the eighth-inch misalignment in the booster section of the RIM-174G to Admiral Kinkaide, he had no idea of the storm this passing comment would ignite.

Nearly every other passing comment he had made to the admiral about this component here, or that data display there, had been easily met by a confident and knowledgeable reply. Like no other flag officer Altbeck had ever encountered or interviewed, Kinkaide knew his missile systems down to the tiniest element. When the admiral was suddenly perplexed by something he had not noticed, it came as a shock to the journalist.

The mood changed abruptly. Suddenly, the captains and lieutenant commanders in the admiral's entourage were scrambling. Calls were being made and Kinkaide was running his own thumb across the eighth-inch dilemma.

"Tell launch control at BMIC that I'm calling an immediate 'unplanned hold,'" he ordered. "Now, check all four of our RIM-174Gs, and get this fixed. I want an estimate on fix time in fifteen minutes."

Altbeck had watched as the admiral and several of his staff jumped into one of the SUVs and took off in the direction of the Battle Management Interoperability Center. He might have raced to catch up, but curiosity kept him here at the launch site. He wanted to see what happened next. The gearhead in him wanted to see how they would fix their misaligned components.

The modified Mk21 launcher was surrounded by an open area about the size of a baseball diamond. Within moments, all the missile handling gear that had been pulled back in preparation for the launch, was returned. Cranes, auxiliary power units and other equipment were moved in. Big lights had also been set up. It was nearly five o'clock in the afternoon, and nobody was betting that the fix would be completed before sundown.

As he watched the crane start to lift the missile, Altbeck wondered when this could possibly be accomplished, and wondered if Vigilant Basilisk would be scrubbed entirely.

Chris and Rhonda climbed out of his Toyota rental car and walked over to the press tent. His network's camera crew would get the pictures, while Chris would get what he needed to write the copy for the online pages. He had already looked over all the unexciting handouts. Like Dave Altbeck, he was in search of color.

Chris had taken a rain check on the glass of rum and had invited all the women to join him for the press tent "funfest." The others had declined, but with obvious winks, they had insisted that Rhonda take him up on the invitation. She was happy to do so. She knew the fling she was having with Chris wouldn't last, but she was having fun with it in the meantime.

The funfest, as Chris had sarcastically called it, did have a festival atmosphere. Small clusters of journalists were mixed with locals standing around in sunglasses and beachwear waiting for something to happen. The Navy had set up a countdown clock near the podium at the far side of the tent, but most people were scanning the sky or fiddling with binoculars. One man had set up a telescope.

As Chris and Rhonda approached the tent, a group of people in Navy uniforms hurried out from a pedestrian gate next to the closed vehicle gate. Chris recognized the bulky form of Lieutenant Commander Irv O'Malley, the public affairs spokesman who had been giving periodic updates from this podium for the past twenty-six-plus hours.

"Ladies and gentlemen," O'Malley said as the microphone crackled. "I'm afraid I have some disappointing news."

"A sigh of disappointment and a murmur of confusion rippled through the crowd.

"On behalf of the US Navy Integrated Warfare Systems Program Executive Office and the Missile Defense Agency, I am advising you that we are currently in an unplanned hold at T-minus nineteen minutes. Admiral Kinkaide has personally ordered this hold, which was instituted for technical reasons."

"What were the technical reasons?" a journalist shouted.

"As this is still largely a classified program, I am unable to discuss specific technical issues."

"How long is the hold?"

"We are awaiting an update from the launch director, who is in contact with engineers on the ground, who are currently troubleshooting the technical issues."

"Will the countdown start back up today?"

"Engineers are discussing a plan for a resumption of countdown at this very moment."

"Are you going to call a scrub for today?"

"We'll have more information for you as soon as we get it," O'Malley said uncomfortably as he stepped away from the podium.

High on Pokuakini Ridge, they waited. The only sound other than the hum of electronics in their lair were the birds. It was late afternoon and they seemed to be coming alive. From the little red *i`iwi* honeycreepers, to the *elepaio* flycatchers, they were chirping, singing, flying around, and even audaciously perching on the tent poles of the human hideout.

The humans themselves had nothing more to say. Though Ryu had missed most of it, Teddy had said his piece and the other three knew where he stood. They also knew, or were sure they knew, that he and Kitty would do what was asked of them.

When he came back into the canopy tent from one of his walks, they all noticed that in his waistband, Ryu was carrying one of the Glock G17 lookalike ghost guns that they'd gotten from Karboli on Saturday.

Was this mere bravado, or had Teddy's griping roused a fear of mutiny?

Following the lead of the leader, their *sajangnim*, Han and Cho, who likewise had 9mm ghost guns, discreetly took them from their backpacks and placed them near at hand. The irony of there being a ghost army, as observed by Lauren Stahling that morning, armed with ghost guns, had occurred to none of them.

Rae had the countdown app running live and had her phone leaning against her R-330Zh console where the others could see it. Ryu was standing above her chewing his lip as he watched.

She would initiate the plan to shut down cell phone and two-way radio communication at less than a minute before T-minus zero, and Han and Cho would step into action immediately afterward, blinding the Navy Warfare Systems and the Missile Defense Agency as the missile were launched.

Next, Kitty would begin her deadly mischief.

All eyes watched T-minus twenty-one minutes come and go, then T-minus-Twenty.

Suddenly, thirty seconds into T-minus nineteen, the countdown simply stopped.

"*What happened*?" Ryu asked anxiously. "Did you start the jammer?

"I did nothing with the jammer," Rae said, tapping the screen of her phone.

Ryu took out his own phone, where he also had the app running, but it too had the same results. The countdown clock was frozen at T-minus nineteen minutes.

Han was feverishly tapping at his phone.

Finally, he stopped.

"I have the newsfeed from PRMF public affairs," he said. "It reads 'please stand by.' Something has gone wrong *down there*."

Everyone looked at everyone else in bafflement.

Ryu's face was red with anger.

It was nearly five o'clock local time when Dave Altbeck finally caught a ride back to the Battle Management Interoperability Center. He had seen enough of the frantic efforts to pull the missile down from the launch stand to be repaired. He knew that this was going on at three other sites around the base and he wondered what problems were being encountered in fixing the eighth-inch anomaly.

Inside the BMIC, the scene was nothing like it had been when he left with Admiral Kinkaide at T-minus one hour. Beneath the red numbers of a countdown clock frozen in time at T-minus nineteen minutes, everyone was scrambling. As so often over the past few days, the admiral was moving from workstation to workstation, discussing this or that with various people. He wore a brave and confident face as though it were a mask.

As Altbeck eased in close to eavesdrop, someone shouted to the admiral from across the room.

"It's Kwajalein, Admiral. They need a Sitrep."

Of course they needed a Situation Report. They were scheduled to launch a pair of ICBMs at T-minus zero and had been as taken off guard by the stand-down order as everyone else. They needed to know what the hell was going on here on the other side of the international dateline.

Kinkaide walked quickly to the elevated chair by his command console from which he overlooked the BMIC, the chair that seemed like a regal throne in better times.

"Hello General, this is Kinkaide," he said, speaking to the Air Force general in charge of launching the Air Force LGK-30G Minuteman ICBMs. After a few minutes of sympathizing with the general about the technical issues related to an abrupt unplanned hold to an ICBM launch, the admiral stood to make his announcement to the room.

"As some of you may have heard, we are go for countdown resumption," Kinkaide announced. "Reset the countdown clock for T-minus three hours and start counting. We'll launch at exactly 2000 hours, or eight o'clock for the civilians in the room."

There was a smattering of applause, which seemed natural after the firm emphasis of the announcement, but Altbeck also sensed some hesitancy. As he looked around the room, he saw concerned expressions on the faces of some of the people with whom he'd been having conversations over past days. The ones whom he had found most reticent to talk about the absence of a built-in hold yesterday now had "I told you so" expressions.

"Well, we have the countdown back on track," he said, sitting down next to the workstation of one of them.

"It might be a tad optimistic," the man said tentatively.

"Oh yeah?"

"The admiral obviously has a better handle on how the work on the booster sustainers is going, but I'm thinking they may not have taken the recalibration of the guidance systems into account."

"Recalibration?"

"If they're taking the missiles down from the stands, and manhandling them around them around, it's going to be worth it to check the guidance systems for possible miscalibration issues. Inertial Navigation Systems need calibration to make certain they're providing accurate data."

"As I understand it, only two of the four missiles are using INS," Altbeck said. "I was briefed that the other two are using GPS."

"That's right. Part of the test is to evaluate the two systems side by side. GPS is trickier with a moving target like these will have with the ICBMs."

"Right," Altbeck said. "That's what I heard. I guess they'll have to check both."

"They should if they aren't, but remember, guidance is only one of several systems that should be double checked. I'm not saying there *will* be issues with any of the systems. I'm only saying that I hope the people who are on-site at the launchers have allowed themselves enough time in the countdown for all the checks."

"Did the new countdown seem rushed?"

"Might have been, but that's above my pay grade."

"I think the admiral wants to get the launch in before the weather hits," a woman at a nearby workstation interjected.

"Weather?" Altbeck replied. "I guess I've been so distracted with what's going on here that I haven't been paying a lot of attention to the weather."

"That's because the weather's always the same on the west side." The man laughed.

"Seriously, though, there's a storm front stalled a hundred miles offshore," the woman said. "The current model shows it moving over the island early tomorrow. We can expect a lot of wind and rain with that," she explained. "When you're doing a test, you want good visibility and as little wind as possible."

While Altbeck was enjoying his all-access backstage press pass, journalists on the other side of the fence, like Chris, had spent the better part of an hour going round and round with Lieutenant Commander Irv O'Malley at the press tent. They were trying to get something—*anything* —more than what was on the press handout that everyone was given out at the time the eight o'clock launch was officially announced.

"Can you elaborate at on these so-called technical issues that caused the launch to be scrubbed?" Chris asked, getting him aside.

"The launch was *not* scrubbed," O'Malley insisted. "It was interrupted by an unplanned hold. The countdown is proceeding again. As we have been saying, we have a confirmed launch time of eight o'clock local time."

"What caused the interruption?"

"As I said, there were technical issues," O'Malley said succinctly. "We can say no more at this time. I'm sorry. We'll brief you the moment we have something."

"This isn't going anywhere," Rhonda said when O'Malley turned to someone else. "Why don't you offer to buy him a shot at Huna's?"

"That's not a bad idea," Chris said. "I doubt he's drinking anything this afternoon, but let's you and me go back there. There's a lot of press people at Huna's. Maybe somebody's heard something."

On a usual Thursday night, the scene at Huna's had an orderliness to it. It was mostly equal measures of locals and people from the base, with a handful or two of tourists thrown into the mix. Tonight, the crowd was predominantly journalists.

It seemed to Rhonda that Chris knew more people in here in her usual watering hole than she did. The media business can be like a club. People who specialize in reporting on a specific subject—whether that is the Kentucky Derby, race cars, or rocket launches—tend to know one another. If he hadn't gotten himself embedded, Dave Altbeck would have been here, and he would have known as many people as Chris.

"Did you get anything useful out of O'Malley?" Chris said, patting the back of a skinny man with a wire service press card in a lanyard around his neck.

"I didn't even try. He seemed like he'd be a dead end. Did you?"

"He *was* a dead end."

"Wish they'd give us some crumbs on the so-called technical issues that caused them the go into the unplanned hold."

"Heard any rumors?" Chris asked.

"They didn't deny the story that they were supposed to launch at the end of last week, but the old Mk109B rocket sustainer failed."

"All the press releases *since* Saturday call the sustainer Mk109C," Chris pointed out. "I heard that Kinkaide blew his stack and the contractor put a tiger team on triple time to make the new 'C' variant happen overnight."

"He's a real SOB. Nobody dares to cross Hard Kinkaide."

"*He's* the real story," another journalist quipped.

"*Hang on for an update*!" someone shouted from across the room, as the chirping and pinging of the updated information hitting a couple of dozen cell phones flooded the bar.

"What is it?"

"They just confirmed *another* new launch time," shouted the same voice. "Effective at one minute to seven o'clock local time, the countdown rolled back to T-minus *five hours* and counting."

"That's eight hours behind the original schedule," somebody else yelled amid the groans.

"That's one minute to midnight," Chris calculated.

"And there's a full moon rising," Rhonda added.

CHAPTER TWENTY-SIX

PAK MI-RAE WAS NOT Teddy Jong's big sister. She had never been *anyone's* big sister, and had never wanted to be, yet here she was, playing that role to a jittery tech genius who was arguably the keystone of the present operation.

On Pokuakini Ridge, twenty miles north of Huna's, where the media people were processing yet another recalculated launch time, Rae was in the emotional equivalent of playing with a hand grenade from which the pin had been pulled.

Three hours ago, when they learned that the launch had been pushed back to eight o'clock, it had only taken Teddy a moment to realize they would be in this place after nightfall. All afternoon, he had been in high gear, worrying about collateral fatalities in Korea, but now all he could think about was armies of *gwisin* rising up out of the darkness to march them all off into the netherworld.

Just before sundown, she had taken Teddy for a walk to calm him down. She wanted to get him out of the tent, which was still stuffy after the heat of the day, and the intensity of the four o'clock launch that did not happen. There was also that strange, but not unpleasant odor that pervaded the place.

With all of the emphasis on Teddy tonight, Ryu Myong-su had barely noticed that the other two men on his team were also becoming restless. Both of them—Cho more than Han—were troubled by the skeletons scattered through these hills, and by the restless spirits said to be hovering near them.

As the revised eight o'clock launch was announced, Rae had continued to monitor the Navy's countdown app on her phone, and she was the first to see that the Navy had pushed the time back yet again—to *almost midnight.* She knew that Teddy would really come unglued.

Rae gritted her teeth. Had it not been for the unpinned hand grenade of Teddy's high anxiety, this change would have been little more than an annoyance, but she felt the cold chill of an operation going off the rails.

She said nothing out loud but pulled Ryu Myong-su aside to show him the bulletin on her phone. His reaction mirrored her own. His forehead wrinkled and there was concern in his eyes.

"Don't tell Teddy," he whispered. "Don't say anything to anyone."

"In an hour, when the launch time comes and goes, they will *all* know," she whispered back.

"Don't say *anything*." he repeated.

"*Whatever*," she hissed quietly, rolling her eyes.

"T-Minus four hours and counting!"

For Dave Altbeck, the disembodied proclamation from the speaker on the front wall of the Battle Management Interoperability Center was déjà vu all over again. Hadn't that same speaker proclaimed that same countdown milestone at noon—*eight hours ago*?

Yes, it had.

The fact that *right now*, 2000 hours, eight o'clock, was the first revised launch time, once loudly proclaimed by Admiral Hardgrove Kinkaide, was lost on no one in the room.

Four more hours.

Out there in the night, under the lights that had been erected during the brightness of the day, crews were still working feverishly to repair eighth-inch gaps so trivial in appearance that they had gone unnoticed until it was almost too late. Inside the BMIC, meanwhile, there was almost nothing to do but wait. They couldn't even monitor systems accurately until the RIM-174Gs were back on their stands. They could watch the weather display, but the storm front was far away and stalled.

"Will they have time in this countdown for the guidance systems calibration that you were telling me about?" Altbeck asked, sitting down near the workstation of the man who had raised that issue earlier in the day.

"Theoretically," he said. "It will take an hour, or two to be on the safe side. I hate to be a pessimist, but when they set the previous countdown scenario, they were apparently planning that the booster-sustainer interface work could be buttoned up so they could launch by now."

"As of now, they've been at it for *three hours*," interjected the woman who was monitoring the weather. "I haven't heard whether or not they've finished with *any* of the missiles."

"I hope you won't quote any of us by name on any of this," the man said. Everybody was feeling the tension. "When they told us you were going to be embedded, they told us that whatever we said was just for background. Is that correct?"

"Um, yeah," Altbeck said uncomfortably. "They told me that I was not to direct quote anybody under the rank of captain. The admiral is the real center of this piece… the admiral and the RIM-174G itself."

For Admiral Kinkaide himself, it was the worst of times. As the COMABMPAC, the Commander of Naval Anti-Ballistic Missile Operations, he may have been one of the most powerful military men in the Pacific, but his power resided in his ability to deliver on operations of a monumental scale. Two scrubbed launches in one day in the biggest anti-ballistic missile exercise since he took over this job was an extremely negative moment in that career.

Only a spectacular success at one minute to midnight could salvage his predicament.

"Altbeck," the admiral shouted across the room in his stern, no-bullshit, voice. "Are you ready for another field trip out to the launch stands?"

"Yes, sir," he said, trying not to sound as eager as he was.

"Well, let's go."

Altbeck, in all his insecurity, did not know that Kinkaide had developed a newfound and indebted respect for him. It was Altbeck who noticed the eighth-inch gap that had derailed the first countdown, but Kinkaide knew that the journalist's noticing had very possibly saved Vigilant Basilisk from disaster.

They were headed toward the door when a young ensign ran up to Kinkaide.

"Admiral...*sir*," she said urgently. "You have an imperative call."

"Who is it?" Kinkaide answered with annoyance. "As you can see, I'm rather busy."

As she showed him the caller ID on the phone, Altbeck watched an already strained face convulse like it had been hit by a truck.

The caller was Admiral—as in *four-star full admiral*—Ronald R. Strettich, Kinkaide's boss. While Kinkaide commanded all anti-ballistic missile operations across the Pacific, Strettich led the US Indo-Pacific Command. He commanded *all* US forces across more than half of the surface of the earth.

"*Sir*," Kinkaide said, feeling himself subconsciously standing to attention. This was not something he was used to doing.

"Good evening, Admiral," Strettich said calmly and evenly. "How are things going out there? I've been briefed on a couple of hiccups you've had, and I wanted to get you on the horn for an update."

"Yes, *sir*," Kinkaide said as he hurried into a small windowless room where he could close the door and have some privacy. "We've had some issues with the booster-to-booster-sustainer interface, but the situation is well in hand. We just passed T-minus four hours and counting."

"I heard that you've readjusted your launch time *twice*."

"We pushed it back out of an abundance of caution," Kinkaide explained. "We want to be able to report a successful Vigilant Basilisk before start of business Pentagon time on Friday morning."

"That's why you picked one minute to midnight local time?"

Kinkaide could hear Strettich chuckling.

"That's how it worked out when we calculated all the factors."

"Are you fully confident of all your factors?" Strettich asked, no longer chuckling.

"Yes, *sir*," Kinkaide said, trying to sound confident. "We'll be go for launch at one minute to midnight."

"Good man, Kinkaide. You make us proud."

"Yes, *sir*."

For Kinkaide, Stettich's "make us proud" comment was equal part pep talk and a warning to not, *under any circumstances*, screw this up.

Message received and understood, Sir, Kinkaide thought.

The first thing Altbeck wanted to ask when Kinkaide stepped back into the BMIC was whether everything was all right. Obviously, the content of the relatively short conversation was not his to know, but when the last thing you hear a three-star admiral say to a four-star before he goes into a closed room is "*sir*...yes *sir*," you know that everything is *not* all right.

The best thing to do, Altbeck knew, was to avoid eye contact, as though he was paying no attention to Kinkaide's closed-room phone call.

Out of the corner of his eye, he saw the admiral's eyes flick around the room to assess how many or how few outside his small entourage, had seen him duck for cover. Not many, he thought. His invitation to Altbeck had been fortuitous. He was glad they were on their way out of the BMIC, away from the prying eyes of this room, and into the night.

Five hours ago, in the last minutes before the original launch minute, Kinkaide had first showed Altbeck this place, with the same modified Mk21 launch canister and the same RIM-174G soaring three stories above it. Ready to go, they all thought, but they were so very wrong.

Now, as they approached the launch stand, and as the clock edged toward T-minus three hours, the RIM-174G was not soaring. Cranes were lifting it slowly from where it has been lowered to horizontal to repair the booster interface.

Ready to go? No, but getting there.

By the time that the entourage reached the third and fourth of the launch stands, the missiles were vertical, and Altbeck dared ask Kinkaide the question on his mind.

"Admiral, with the missiles now erected on the stands, will they be able to get on with the guidance calibration and all the preflight checks?"

"That should already be underway," Kinkaide said with tentative assurance. "You remember how quiet the BMIC was when we left? How everybody was just staring at screens?"

"Yeah..."

"Well, I can *guaran-damn-tee* you they're scrambling up there *now*. We're on the move again."

An hour and a half later and a short distance away in Kekaha, Chris and Rhonda were on the move themselves. After discovering they had five more hours to wait, the crowd at Huna's was incorrigible. Grumbling had erupted as the journalists and their hangers-on all calculated the "minute-to-midnight" launch time. The man at the next table was imaginatively writing an online web post update with the headline "In the Midnight Hour." You put a press pool in a bar and feed them drinks all afternoon and you get creativity.

Rhonda's reaction was to tell Chris that she had a bottle of *pinot grigio* in her fridge at home. At some point after sampling the Italian wine, they had fallen asleep. At some point around nine-thirty, or 2130 Navy time, Rhonda had woken up.

"Chris, it's T-minus two hours and twenty, you better wake up," she said, thumping his hairy chest with the palm of her hand. She had become a rocket-launch-press-groupie without even realizing it.

"I better wake up," he said after a stream of unintelligible garbles.

They often say that Ernest Hemingway was quoted as suggesting that you should "write drunk and edit sober." Most writers know that he did not, but they all know it makes for a good anecdote. Whatever Chris thought on the subject, and how much he'd had to drink, he had at least gotten some exercise and a nap.

After they were dressed, and Rhonda had fed him a peanut butter sandwich, they decided to drive over to the place, just outside the PMRF base perimeter, where Chris's network's camera van was set up. This turned out to be a better option for the groupie and her journalist than plunging back into the drunk tank at Huna's.

The three men standing on the truck's roof platform waved them up. Even without the binoculars that were being passed around, they could see the four tall white things they knew to be missiles. Bathed in the brightness of spotlights, they each stood three stories tall on their launchers, though at a distance of a few miles it was their stark whiteness against the night that made them stand out more than their size.

Rhonda listened as they bandied about words and numbers that were utterly foreign to her, things like all these "marks," from twenty-one to fifty-seven. She lost track of why a Mk109B and a Mk109C were so much different, and why it matters. All this seemed trivial to her, but the experience was exhilarating. Their enthusiasm, while being a tad humorous, was infectious.

Then somebody shouted, "*T-minus two hours and counting...again*!"

The mood turned serious when he said "again."

Would this be the *last* T-minus two?

In the darkness high on Pokuakini Ridge, where the mood had been serious since Teddy Jong's last outburst hours ago, and where T-minus two hours was greeted as being like the threshold of an eternity, Ryu Myong-su stepped out from under the canopy tent. He walked over to his backpack, which was a few feet away, and opened the fasteners.

He rifled through the pack, trying to locate his notebook. With its bright green cover, it should be easy to spot, even in the dim light, but he couldn't find it. He remembered seeing it back at the bungalow. Maybe he'd left it in his hurry to get loaded up this morning. He *was* pretty distracted, especially by Teddy's superstitious muttering.

Ryu didn't actually *need* it, but he wanted it in the way that people reach for a favorite book of verse to calm them at times of angst. He felt like J. Robert Oppenheimer, who turned to the *Bhagavad Gita* on that night in 1945 when he exploded the world's first nuclear weapon. Oppenheimer had memorized passages from the ancient Hindu scripture, but Ryu didn't have to memorize the green notebook—he had *written it*.

Like Oppenheimer, Ryu wanted the reassurance of the familiar words of his manifesto, but what greatly haunted him was finding himself feeling the unexpected angst that demanded such reassurance.

The irony of the passage that Oppenheimer spoke out loud that night was not lost on Ryu. It read "I am become Death, the destroyer of worlds."

If he had known of it, Teddy might have chosen this line to quote.

CHAPTER TWENTY-SEVEN

SHE HAD THOUGHT about texting her father to tell him goodbye.

Lynsee hadn't seen him since Tuesday, and he had called only once in all that time. Vice Admiral Hardgrave Kinkaide had stashed his daughter in the Barking Sands admiral's quarters with all the creature comforts that a teenager could possibly want and had gone off to run an exercise. That's what he had always done. He stashed people who got in his way. Until this was over, he was too busy for Lynsee.

Her mother, whom he had routinely stashed in the family home in San Diego for years, had phoned several times from that place over the past few days. She called Lynsee, and she had tried to phone her husband to give him a piece of her mind about dumping Lynsee in a luxury suite and going off to shoot rockets. He told her that he was too busy to talk. He was running an exercise. That's what he said as he hung up. He had been saying this for all the twenty-some years she had been his second wife.

Lynsee figured that by the time this exercise was over,

her mother's lawyer would have the divorce papers ready to serve.

Lynsee didn't care. She had a plan. By the time this exercise was over, she and Anthony Karboli would have run away from all this and would be the happiest people on this damned island. She just kept running and rerunning all the romantic, passionate things he told her on the night they made love in that Korean guy's suite at the five-star Royal Pacific Resort.

She had thought about texting her father to tell him goodbye, and to tell him about the plans she had made in her mind for her future life with Anthony.

She had thought about texting her father but knew this was too impersonal.

At last, she decided to write him a note—with an actual pen, on actual paper.

All afternoon and into the evening, Lynsee Kinkaide had anguished over what to say and she had thrown away a half dozen first attempts. She drank a little gin from a bottle she found in the top of a kitchen cabinet. This made it even harder.

She fell asleep around the time that the sun went down and woke up with a headache. A couple of Keurig pods later, she felt better. She thought about this missile test that had everybody at Barking Sands in such a knot and wondered why she hadn't heard the rockets blast off.

She must have slept through it.

She looked at her phone, and at the countdown app she had downloaded.

It had apparently been delayed. Those idiots hadn't even shot them off yet. They still had another couple of hours. She could imagine that her father was seething. It was good that she hadn't tried to text him. He would have been furious.

With the coffee clearing her head, Lynsee went back to

writing her pen-and-paper letter to her father. It went much more easily now, and finally, she had something with which she was *almost* proud. It would do.

She told him about how much she loved him. She guessed she *did*—deep down—but she wasn't really feeling the love this week.

She wanted to say something about the good times they had shared, because that's what she had seen women do in movies, but the last time she'd actually had done something fun with him was when she was about ten.

When this part of her missive was written, she broke the news that she was moving on with her life. She had grown up, and the little bird was now a big bird and flexing her wings. She wrote that she was leaving with a petty officer with whom she shared the unshakable bond of love, and not just love, but *true* love. She did not mention Anthony Karboli's name. He'd find this out soon enough.

She shared some of what he had said to her and explained about how special their love-making had been, how rich and fulfilling their passion had been, and how they were two spirits who had become one. She did not tell him where she and her soul mate were going. Actually, she had not yet decided. He'd find this out soon enough.

She spritzed the note with a little perfume, put it in an envelope and left it on the table where he would be sure to find it. She addressed it simply, "*Daddy*."

Lynsee stared at her closet.

What do you wear to rescue the love of your life and run away for the rest of your lives together? It needed to be cool and sophisticated, yet seductive. It needed to make his heart explode with passion yet burn slowly with the enduring love which she knew would last forever.

At last, after a half hour of narrowing down, she chose the perfect dress. It was white and trimmed with lace, with a full skirt that fell just below her knee. Would it remind him *too much* of a wedding dress, or *not enough*?

Then she started folding everything else into her roller bag. She didn't have much to choose from, so she packed everything. She was glad she had overpacked when they came over to Kauaʽi. She had no idea back then that she was packing for the first days of the rest of her life.

Oh, sweet handsome Anthony. She thought about his blazing red hair and even allowed herself to daydream for a moment about the beautiful, red-haired babies they would share one day.

She was glad to see that the Lexus RX rental car had a mostly full tank. That would make things easier for her and Anthony.

She had not counted on seeing the main gate closed, but the guard enforcing the closed gate had not counted on seeing Lynsee Kinkaide.

"You'll have to turn around, ma'am," he said. "All gates are closed at this time."

When she did not comply, he demanded to see her ID.

Again, as earlier in the day, she tapped a nicely painted thumbnail on the surname line of her driver's license, while covering the line about her date of birth.

"Kinkaide? Is that…?"

"Yes, it is, and yes, I'm his daughter."

The man stammered and she continued.

"I'm on important family business which cannot be delayed," she said, bluffing. "If you need to phone my father to confirm this, I can wait…but *please* don't take long."

She knew that at this moment, her father was

unreachably ensconced in the BMIC. Meanwhile, she knew that the guard knew he could get his head chewed down to his shoulders for even attempting to interrupt an admiral at a time like this.

The guard, suddenly rammed between a rock and the very hard place of Hard Kinkaide's wrath, waved for the gate to be opened.

"Have a nice evening ma'am," he said weakly as she drove out into the night.

"*Uhoo-ooo,*" the owl said, gliding otherwise silently through the cool tropical darkness.

Sitting on the crest of a small rise at the edge of the koa forest, Lauren Stahling followed its unseen flight with her ears as her eyes caught it for a split second silhouetted against the rising moon.

"Did you see that?" she whispered.

"I did," Jim Hammer said quietly. "Pretty cool."

"Hope she has a good hunt tonight."

"I bet she knows *exactly* what she's doing," Hammer replied with a smile easily visible in the brightness of the moonlight.

"I bet," she said.

An obvious avian-human metaphor came into Lauren's mind, but she did not articulate it. She knew the only other human present knew what she was thinking. There was a lot of that between them. Some couples finish one another's sentences. These two finished one another's thoughts.

A couple of years ago, if someone told her that she'd one night be sharing a tropical aerie with *this* man and *this* most treacherous of adventures, it would have been the most distant thing from her mind.

Her mind drifted back to earlier memories, to the memories of the teenage Lauren, her face buried into the leather of his motorcycle jacket as she clung to him on the back of his Norton N15CS while the motorcycle careened down those Montana gravel roads under a full moon.

The addictive ecstasy of those endorphins, which had engulfed her back then, had lain forgotten and completely dormant for two decades—until *he* came back into her life. The excitement and adventure which he had experienced in those intervening twenty years made her realize that her own life had seen no such adventure, and she rediscovered how much she craved it. All of this brought to mind that famous quote where Marcus Aurelius says you should take what's left of your life and *live it*.

A little over a year ago, when she and he had found themselves tossed together as antagonists against a monstrous international human trafficking cartel, he had decided to take it down on his own. Would the Lauren of a few years prior recoiled in fear? Who knows?

All she knew was the Lauren of that moment who refused to let him do it on his own. *Why*?

Then she joined him, asking herself *why not*?

It was the same Lauren who stunned herself with how she felt more exhilaration than apprehension, and how her endorphin addiction hungered after excitement.

Perhaps the turning point came the night when she was threatened by a man intending to kill her. Hammer had seen this and had instantly erased this man from the world of the living.

This was the night, but *that* was not the moment in which Lauren realized the change in herself. This came a few minutes later, when another gunman, who dismissed Lauren as irrelevant, raised his weapon behind Hammer's back for an easy kill.

She impulsively, and with a steady hand, raised her father's old Colt .44 and squeezed the trigger. Her only thought had been that when someone threatens deadly violence against a man with whom a woman is uncontrollably in love, her first and only thought is simply to kill him.

This was the moment she crossed the line into succumbing to the excitement and adventure of *him,* and of his *world*. This was also the night when he first told her that he loved her.

This was the night that her attitude toward life changed. She decided to pursue the rest of her life wherever it might take her and *live it*.

She looked down at his back as he lay there in the moonlight with his binoculars. It was the same back as that of the long ago leather-jacket-motorcycle-rides, but a back now bare in deference to the warm evening.

He was lying there, studying the Korean electronic warfare lair on Pokuakini Ridge. He was just lying on the ground, so vulnerable to her lustful designs. She leaned down to lightly brush the back of his neck with her lips. His only warning had been her long hair falling upon his shoulders.

His reaction was that for which hoped.

As he carefully lay down his Oberwerk 10x42 HD IIs and rolled over to face her, nothing was said. Some couples finish one another's sentences. These two finish one another's thoughts—and one another's passions.

Despite their proximity to such a deadly enterprise, one about which the term "Armageddon" often came up in their conversation, Lauren and Hammer had spent the day in a most idyllic way. After their early morning visit to the Korean camp, there had been a quiet morning, a picnic lunch, some passionate moments, and afternoon naps.

Through it all, they kept their cell phones charged with their small high-capacity power bank chargers so they could monitor the Navy's Vigilant Basilisk countdown app. They casually made note of the changes which had caused so much angst and consternation elsewhere—from the Battle Management Interoperability Center to the Korean camp a quarter mile down the hill—on this island.

If you had to "hurry-up-and-wait," what better circumstance in which to do it?

They had watched the arrival of the occupants of the electronic hive on the ridge and watched as they fussed and fumed. With Hammer's binoculars, it was like they were in the next room.

They saw Teddy hopping animatedly, and Ryu Myong-su pacing irritably. From Afghanistan to Southeast Asia, Hammer had been on ops like this, with long waits before short and deadly actions, but never, until Lauren had inserted herself back into his life, had these waits been so agreeable.

With an almost comedic tone, Hammer had called play-by-plays as he read their body language with an experienced observer's eye, often with phrasing that had his companion trying not to explode with laughter as she grabbed the binoculars to see for herself.

He welcomed the one-minute-to-midnight launch time, in part because he knew the symbolism would unnerve their antagonists, and in part because what they had to do would best be done in full moonlight.

At last, she held up the countdown clock, and he nodded.

T-minus one hour and counting.

They pulled on the dark gray swim shirts and swim pants they had pulled off many hours ago, laced up their well-worn hiking boots, and packed their extraneous gear into a duffel bag they'd grab on their way back to the Taurus that waited at the anonymous parking spot.

This done, they stepped assuredly into the familiarity of a moonlit night very much like those in which they had navigated the Montana mountains on many hunting trips of other kinds.

CHAPTER TWENTY-EIGHT

"*T-MINUS ONE HOUR AND COUNTING*!"

Twenty-something miles south of Pokuakini Ridge, where one ghost army was waiting with intense impatience and another ghost army was walking with quiet care, Dave Altbeck of *Defense Up Front* was looking at a clock—*the* clock.

He had been listening to the proclamations issued from the speaker in the Battle Management Interoperability Center for more than sixteen hours, and he'd been through this countdown three times. The first time it was "goose bumps" exciting. Now, it was like that *Groundhog Day* movie where Bill Murray relives the same day endlessly.

As the countdown clock raced, with its mesmerizing milliseconds, and the hour that now read "00," all he could think of was what could go wrong—as he had been thinking this for much of a very long day.

Of course what went *wrong* or what went *right*, was really not his problem. He was embedded *into* this place, but he was not *of* this place. He was here not to launch missiles but to tell a story of their launching. Whether it was a success or failure, there would be a story. Of course, his gearhead readers liked reading stories of things that worked, so his preference tilted that way.

Also tilting him that way was the camaraderie he had naturally built up with the people in this room and around the base—because they were the *only* people with whom he had interacted for the past week, and because *they* cared.

"Guidance systems check. We are a go for launch," boomed the voice on the wall.

Altbeck whispered, "Check," as he looked across at the workstation of the man with whom he had discussed guidance system calibration earlier in the day.

He glanced at the slender woman who had shown him the weather front on the map. She was wearing a headset with a microphone. When the big speaker boomed next, it was with her voice.

"Weather is a go for launch."

Her voice through the huge speaker dwarfed her as an actual person

"The storm front is off shore and holding."

Finally, there was Vice Admiral Hardgrove Kinkaide, the COMABMPAC, the man of the hour, the man of *every* hour for the past week. He was the subject of this article, the name that would dominate the headline. If Altbeck succeeded in pushing the editors to do a full issue on Vigilant Basilisk, Kinkaide's picture would be on the cover. Whether he was pictured as tragic or heroic would be decided in the next forty-five minutes.

Of course, neither Altbeck nor Kinkaide, nor anyone in this room, nor on this base, nor it the great vastness of the Pacific Missile Range realized what was going on at this very moment up at the Korean camp on Pokuakini Ridge. Nobody who was not now on that ridge knew that there was hardware up there which could not only assure that Vigilant Basilisk was a failure but turn it into a mere footnote in a vast and overarching calamity.

Kinkaide was in his usual everywhere-at-once mode, leaning into workstations, asking questions, pointing to the eighty-six-inch AQUOS touchscreens and asking people to explain why some line of code read as it did.

Suddenly, he made eye contact with Altbeck again. As he had so often this week, he gave the journalist a follow-me wave as he led his entourage out the door. As they churned down the hallway to the doors that led outside, Altbeck expected another run across the base to one of the modified Mk21 launchers that held a RIM-174G.

Instead, when they burst out into the night air, Kinkaide made a right turn and led them up a broad metal stairway.

The balcony!

For a launch, this would be the best seat in the house. The four missiles, sitting on their launchers and bathed in floodlights were all clearly visible, and seemed almost close enough to touch, though the nearest one was almost half a mile away.

"T-minus nineteen minutes and counting. We have go for transfer to pre-launch sequencing."

The speaker works out here too, Altbeck thought to himself. *Is the time finally that close*?

Now he was really getting excited.

Back inside the BMIC, everyone not glued to their workstation monitors was staring at one of the AQUOS touchscreens on the walls.

Just as the speaker proclaimed "T-minus nineteen minutes," someone in the sea of workstations suddenly shouted.

"I got a monitor glitch," she complained angrily. "I tried tech support and got an error code."

"I'm having trouble too," someone else said. "My screen froze and I can't get it to respond."

"This is like troubleshooting grandma's new tablet on Thanksgiving," another man whined. "This is all so amateurish. What can be wrong here?"

"Try control-alt-delete," someone suggested, only half kidding.

"I just tried tech support on my cell phone," a man said desperately. "I have no cell service."

"Me neither," a woman shouted urgently.

"What a horrible time for the software bugs to take over," another screamed.

"Call the admiral!"

"*No*! Don't interrupt him, it's almost time for the launch."

"Yeah, wait on calling him," another man shouted. "None of our workstations over *here* are affected. Everything in this section seems to be working fine."

"Same here," came another yell from another part of the room.

A young captain stood, intending to be the voice of calm in this situation.

"Let's all take a step back and try to isolate which systems are *not* compromised by this bug," she said sternly. "Then we can reboot the others and work through this systematically."

The voice of reason was taking charge.

Nothing allays panic like a logical plan, and the shouting started to subside. However, what the logical planner and her followers did not yet know was that all of the systems and programs that were hardwired would be unaffected. Everything that was dependent on Wi-Fi, or any form of wireless data connectivity had failed completely. For the moment, no one had yet realized why some things worked, and others did not.

Far above the BMIC, and well beyond its soundproof doors, and away from the long hallway and the other set of soundproof doors, the people on the rooftop balcony watched a big analog countdown clock at waited.

They had no reason to call down to the BMIC. They could see what they assumed to be the whole show from this lofty vantage point.

If BMIC needed to report in to them, there were half a dozen two-way radios on the roof, and everyone had a cell phone. Nobody yet realized that none of those things still worked.

In contrast with the raucous disorder that had erupted in the hall of flat-screen displays within the BMIC, all was quiet, albeit tense, within the hall of flat-screen displays on Pokuakini Ridge. Most of them barely noticed the odd, but pleasant aroma that had been so conspicuous earlier in the day. They were all preoccupied.

Pak Mi-Rae's fingers scampered quietly and expertly over the keyboard of the R-330Zh Zhitel jammer. Operating across a waveband from a hundred megahertz to two gigahertz, it was swiftly assaulting and cooking both military and civilian communications and Wi-Fi connections across a fifty-mile radius.

She knew it was working, and she knew exactly *when* it wrought its malevolence. She had watched her own cell phone wink out. The countdown app feed was simply gone.

At Huna's Hideaway, the groundswell of irritated murmurs from the press corps angrily blamed the cell service provider. On top of the TV truck platform,

Rhonda was in the middle of trying to call Selke. She didn't know what had happened but shrugged it off. This was not the first time cell service had gone down in western Kaua`i.

As Cho ho-jin once said, the Zhitel "pokes out their eyes and ears."

It had now done exactly that.

Monitoring the countdown timetable on his analog stopwatch, Ryu Myong-su calmly announced "T-minus eighteen minutes" in English.

With the first phase of his plan behind him, he was trying to contain his excitement. He watched happily as Han jong-sok scanned the screen of the 29B6 Konteyner over-the-horizon VHF radar system that gave their operation an unrestricted view across the vastness of the Pacific. Within a few minutes, when Cho brought up the 1RL257 and 1L269 Deadly Nightshade jammers, the analogous BMIC radar systems would go off line, and the 29B6 screen would have to only such view anywhere on Kaua`i. Nearly everything that still worked within the BMIC would go down.

All was going according to plan—so far.

Ryu still held his breath as he watched his "wild child," the unpredictable Teddy Jong. When Teddy had first noticed the full moon a couple of hours ago, he had freaked out again. He stepped away from his Kitty, the modified Cloud Mirror system, and had begun ranting about ghosts and skeletons and armies of the dead.

Ryu was immensely grateful when Rae kept stepping up to calm him down again. Most of the time, Rae was cold and aloof, as one might expect of the only woman on a team like theirs, but she could turn on an uncanny talent for empathy whenever Teddy needed reassurance.

Out of one eye, Ryu watched nervously as the full

moon moved across the sky, slowly approaching a position where it was practically overhead.

Yet, everything was going according to plan—so far.

All was quiet as they waited. The only sounds were those of the crickets and of Cho drumming his fingers. In the quiet calm, that faint aroma was getting to him in ways he didn't understand.

While Ryu focused his worry on Teddy's part of the operation, he knew in the back of his mind that Cho was also superstitious. *At least he had the discipline of a military man*—or so Ryu hoped.

"T-Minus sixteen minutes," Ryu said quietly in English.

Soon it will all be over.

Suddenly, a loud and unexpected sound, a long and deep-throated howl, echoed up from the narrow valley below Pokuakini Ridge. Everyone held their breath. Even Ryu felt a chill at this eerie noise

It lasted for several seconds, then stopped.

Just as Ryu felt himself taking a gasping breath, it happened again. This time, there was a series of shrieks, made all that much more eerie by the effect of the sound echoing off the walls of the slender valley, which was more of a deep canyon.

They all looked at one another as the cries came in waves.

Ryu could see concern on the faces of Rae and Han, and fear in Cho's expression. With Teddy Jong, it was the look of utter terror.

Everyone present remembered vividly the descriptions by that strange woman named Selke, who told of the "night marchers," the lost souls who rise up from places where they died violently to pass through the night beneath a full moon. Even Ryu and Rae, who had dismissed Selke's words as pure fantasy, could not now help but feel uneasy.

"It's the restless spirits," Han said without a trace of sarcasm.

The otherworldly screams were now punctuated by the shouts of breathless human voices. They sounded like the calls of people in distress, yelling as they ran, but nobody could make out the words.

"Is this the sound of the *gwisin* herding humans through the gates of the underworld?" Cho asked, sounding genuinely worried.

As the howls continued unabated and became louder, Teddy leaped to his feet and ran out of the tent.

Standing near the edge of the cliff and facing into the canyon, he began shouting into the night in English, as though he thought he could communicate with these angry ghosts more easily in the local language.

"Stop it...*stop it please*!"

"Teddy, get back from the edge," Rae said, walking briskly toward him as she had twice before. "You'll fall off the cliff!"

"Rae, we have to make them stop," he insisted. "Shut down all the components...*now*. We can't go through with this. We must stop *everything*!"

"Take a breath," she said.

"*Listen*," he yelled, turning toward the canyon from which the painful shrieking was only growing louder. "Listen to me. We will kill no one tonight. There will be no skeletons because of what we planned...not in the vile north...or anywhere."

"Teddy," Rae said softly. "Just calm down. Everything will be fine. Just relax."

Even though he knew she was lying, her voice was comforting. She had a gift for this.

Yet when Rae reached Teddy and took his arm to try to calm him, he jerked away violently.

Slightly off balance, she took a step to steady herself.

Unfortunately, when her foot came down, her high-top skidded on loose gravel and her leg slipped out from beneath her.

With a terrifying scream, she slid over the edge and disappeared into the night.

CHAPTER TWENTY-NINE

THE GHASTLY *THWACK* of Pak Mi-Rae's body striking a lava rock far below was audible even between the ghostly cries that still echoed wildly from the canyon below Pokuakini Ridge.

Teddy Jong stood motionless in the moonlight, staring down into the dark chasm below the cliff to where Rae's broken body lay.

"Rae!"

As he called out plaintively to his friend, his mind was racing. He could easily picture her spirit leaving her lifeless body to join the unsettled souls in the spirit ranks that were even at this moment gathering for their march through the night.

All this had happened in the narrowest of slices of split seconds, but for the three men watching this almost theatrical tragedy, time stood still.

Han sat transfixed, not noticing that his jaw had dropped practically to his chest.

Cho stood and took a step sideways to his right, as he prepared to exit the canopy through the open flap. His impulse was to go to Teddy, though his non-impulsive mind had no idea what to do or say.

Ryu saw only his worst fear unfolding as things spun out of his control.

"It's over," Teddy shouted, continuing in English. "We must stop this now! I can hear Rae's spirit...she whispers that there can be no skeletons of anxious, haunted spirits. Hear that howling out there in the night? We cannot impose *this* on our Land of Morning Calm."

"Jong, I order you to return to your position *now,*" Ryu demanded firmly, just as another blood-curdling shriek, the loudest this far, reverberated up from the canyon below. "We have only a few minutes before T-minus zero."

"No," Teddy replied tersely.

Then, turning to face the edge of the cliff, he extended his arms.

"I'm coming, Rae," he shouted. "I cannot let you be alone. My spirit will join your spirit, and together we will face the afterlife, or..."

His words fell off as he stepped forward and his body disappeared into the void beyond the cliff edge.

None of them had any idea what they were hearing from below, but Teddy had bet his life that *he knew.*

He was wrong.

None of them could have guessed that the frightening sounds they were hearing were *not* otherworldly at all.

These very worldly sounds were those of young men hunting wild pigs by the light of the full moon!

Most people from off this island have no idea that it is customary on Kaua`i to hunt pigs with knives, and this is obviously a noisy, messy affair. When you are not expecting it, the sound of a two-hundred-pound boar being hacked to death incrementally, and often while on the run, can be horrific—and it sounds eerily like *human screams*.

"Han, take over the Cloud Mirror," Ryu ordered. "We needed Teddy to *build* it, but *you* can operate it. You know what to do. *Do it at exactly T-minus zero*. I thought I might have heard something nearby. I'm going to check our perimeter."

A second later, Ryu *did* hear something—for sure.

"Roger that," a male voice whispered from about twenty yards directly behind the tent.

Somebody was out there talking on a radio, and it was not angry spirits.

It must be the Navy.

How could they have found out? Why did they wait until now to initiate an ambush?

Ryu knew what to do. Through his years of covert missions with South Korean Intelligence, he had been in many tense, tight spots before, especially in North Korea, where they take no prisoners.

He was cool and confident, sure he could handle whatever challenges lay out there. All he had to do was distract whomever it was. All he needed was to buy time —just a couple of minutes for Han to engage the Cloud Mirror. He could delay whomever it was long enough for Han to start the dominoes toppling. Soon, and very soon, North Korea would be no more.

Ryu contemplated the tactical situation.

That *babo*, that fool, out there, had allowed Ryu to hear his radio transmission. It was a novice blunder, which meant that this was not a Seal Team, but probably just security cops like Master Chief Tony. Maybe it *was*

Chief Tony? Nobody else in the world knew about this place.

Ryu knew he could stop whoever it was. He had a fifteen-round magazine in the ghost gun and two more mags in his pocket.

As Ryu moved away from the tent in pursuit of the voices, and as Han moved to Teddy's chair to power up the Cloud Mirror, Teddy's "Kitty," Cho ho-jin stood dumbfounded just outside the right edge of the canopy tent looking at the spot where Teddy had been just a few seconds before.

He looked into the darkness, and as the shrieks grew louder and more frantic, Cho grew more terrified.

It was not that he had just seen two people die twenty feet in front of him. He had seen violent, sudden death before. He was a soldier.

It was not the horrible banshee wails from out there in the night, but the cumulative effect of the whole experience.

It was a feeling that had been awakened. It was a feeling that had lain buried within him until tonight. It was Cho's admittedly superstitious dread of *gwisin*, magnified by hearing the howling spirits of the anxious dead, blocked from reaching the afterlife and determined to exact vengeance.

As he stood there sweating, a lump growing in his throat, Cho now also heard a voice. It was a quiet voice, unlike the howls from below, and it was much nearer. He turned and looked to his right. Out there in the darkness, he thought he could make out a face.

"Teddy was right, you know," the voice whispered. It was the gentle voice of a woman. "You *know* this. You *know* this madness must stop before the irretrievable damage that you will cause."

He squinted in the direction of the voice, but the pupils of his eyes were dilated from the brightness of the monitors and screens.

He could barely make out this face. It seemed to be floating in the darkness. Was it human or *gwisin*? It had to be *gwisin*! He was certain.

As Cho had no idea about the pigs, he did not know that this barely visible face was that of Lauren Stahling, who was dressed entirely in dark gray, the shade of the night.

She was generously giving him a choice to stand down, but Cho the soldier reacted instantly by pulling his gun. It was an impulse. Drawing his gun had no practical purpose, but it made Cho the soldier feel better.

K'pow!

Just as drawing the ghost gun was useless, so too was squeezing off a shot into the darkness. Any fool knows that you cannot shoot a *gwisin*. You cannot kill a ghost. They're already dead.

K'pow!

Of course, Lauren Stahling was neither a *gwisin*, nor was she anywhere near where she had been when she had spoken to Cho.

A battle had been joined, and this one was a little like an Old West gunfight.

She had calmly and reasonably given Cho an offramp from a dangerous and deadly trajectory. He had replied by firing first. Lauren took this as deadly aggression requiring a deadly response. To mix in another metaphor, the gloves had come off.

As the saying goes, you can take the girl out of the Old West, but you can never fully expunge the Old West from a Montana girl who used to hunt coyotes at night with her father's old Colt .44 revolver.

Cho moved forward, his eyes gradually adjusting to the dark. Gripping the pistol with both hands, he turned this way and that. He saw no one.

The *gwisin* had evaporated like a hallucination.

Meanwhile, Cho's tangible adversary had dropped to the ground and rolled forward, not *away* from him.

When he felt his legs suddenly entangled in the very real arms of his assailant, a chill went down his spine. He was thinking *gwisin,* but there was no *gwisin* there. In the split second that it took him to realize this, it became too late.

Nothing prepared Cho for the excruciating, blinding agony that exploded *up his spine* as the long, slender blade of a razor-sharp boning knife was thrust into his lower abdomen, devastating the webs of ilioinguinal nerves there. Cho felt the unimaginable pain from the countless severed nerve endings through which the steel was passing. The blade bisected his femoral artery as it sliced through to his bladder. A shriek caught in his throat and the ghost gun tumbled from his fingers.

Han had been watching the Cloud Mirror come to life, and panicking to see the big LG screens flooded with blizzards of error codes, when he heard Cho fire two 9mm rounds into the night.

"What's going on?" Han demanded. "What do you see?"

Without answering, Cho suddenly collapsed to his knees with a groan. The injury was so severe and the blood loss from the punctured femoral artery so great that Cho had gone into hemorrhagic shock immediately and had not screamed in pain.

What was happening?

Han did not realize that the same person who had hours ago rearranged wires to bring Teddy's Kitty to her metaphorical knees, had just brought Cho to his knees—literally.

Han had only a matter of seconds to process this when his eye glimpsed a shadowy figure moving through the darkness.

When this being moved into the light, Han saw that it was a woman with a sympathetic expression on her face, not a ghost. She was crouching near Cho and staring directly at him.

"You can end this," she said calmly. "Your choice. Just step away."

What is going on? Who are you?

She made no threatening movements. She just looked at him, displaying neither anger nor fear.

Without taking his eyes off her, Han grabbed the gun he had placed on the table between the Cloud Mirror and the 29B6 Konteyner radar system.

Once again, it was a classic face-off scenario.

She had said, "Your choice," and so he made his choice.

As he traversed the gun to the right, Han's eye drilled into this woman's face, but even as his weapon moved rapidly, he found himself already staring into the muzzle of the gun which had earlier fallen from Cho's fingers.

Her hands were solid, with no hint of unsteadiness. One eye was closed, her other was looking directly at him.

This was the last thing that Han jong-sok would ever see.

While Han jong-sok was engaged in his interaction with Lauren Stahling and trying to comprehend what had just happened to Cho ho-jin, their *sajangnim,* Ryu Myong-su was many meters away, breathlessly listening for sounds from another direction.

Suddenly, he heard it—the slight crackling of a two-way radio. *Another newbie slip-up!*

This time, Ryu was ready. He prided himself on his hearing and his direction-finding skills.

He raised the Glock lookalike, aimed and squeezed off a round at the source of the sound.

K'pow!

He heard his round strike something solid, but that was it. There was no sound of movement, no yelp of pain. Ryu may have missed, but at least he had come close.

How much time was left? Ryu wondered to himself.

He didn't look, but he knew it was down to just a couple of minutes. He had to neutralize the threat and get back to the tent.

Then, another sound came. It was a crunching in the brush about two meters to the left.

As he waited, listening carefully and barely breathing, and trying to screen out the wails from the canyon, he heard three gunshots from the direction of the tent.

What is happening?

We're under attack! Who? How?

At the sound of the gunshots, Ryu's target was on the move again. He could hear someone moving in the brush.

Again, Ryu fired.

K'pow! *K'pow*!

This time, he placed two rounds in rapid succession about a half meter apart.

There was a sound of rustling foliage. He was sure he had scored a hit.

The self-assured professional, used to working against the Jeongchal Chongguk, the North Korean covert operations directorate, was relieved to be facing an army of amateurs. But he had to take them out quickly and get back to the tent.

He had to make sure that Kitty did her job.

It had not occurred to him that his assumption of rookie mistakes might have been deliberate misdirection.

It had not occurred to him—and there was no reason that it should—that his opponent might have spent more than a decade in the mountains of Afghanistan eluding and defeating the Taliban on their home turf.

On the scale of uninhibited cunning and ruthlessness, if anyone was farther off the scale than the Jeongchal Chongguk, it was the Taliban. Maybe his opponent was farther off the scale than the Taliban?

It had not occurred to him—and there was no reason why it should—that his opponent might have started hunting in the mountains of Montana before he turned eight and had learned to move through the most difficult of terrain without making a sound.

On the scale of possessing that defensive mechanism known metaphorically as "eyes in the back of the head," neither the Jeongchal Chongguk nor the Taliban are farther off that scale than a bighorn ram.

As a martial arts master, Ryu was the inheritor of centuries of the practiced skill. He had been taught that in combat, one achieves victory through exploiting an opponent's weaknesses. You moved with great speed and dexterous precision to implement this with incredible proficiency.

Of course, the key to exploiting an opponent's weaknesses is to *find them*. Ryu could not. It was as though he had become wrapped in two immobile tree limbs several inches in diameter.

Realizing he had not dropped his gun, he decided to use it. The weapon was not pointed optimally, but maybe the blast and recoil would cause his opponent to flinch, even ever so slightly.

K'pow!

Nothing.

Growing uncharacteristically desperate, he tried again.

K'pow!

K'pow!

Ryu felt his opponent moving, but the man's grip did not relax.

Ryu then felt a stinging pressure on his neck, followed by blinding pain.

He struggled and tried to move his own arms.

For Hammer, the titanium alloy scuba knife in his hand was comparable to his own Ka-Bar knife, with which he'd drawn much enemy blood around the world.

Ryu next felt the gun fall from his hand, but his opponent's grip still did not relax.

"I am become Death," J. Robert Oppenheimer had quoted from the *Bhagavad Gita* on that other night in another doorway to atomic fury.

Oppenheimer had continued with the phrase "destroyer of worlds," but tonight there would be no such nuclear destruction, nor even another gunshot, as Ryu left the world to join the spirit ranks.

Just as an opera can never end until the fat lady's final solo, one of Jim Hammer's wars cannot end until the head of the mastermind rolls.

As the endorphins flooded his body, Ryu began to

experience a calm, but nauseating dizziness. The last thing he ever heard was Hammer's deep voice breathing the word *"checkmate."*

Lauren Stahling stood alone just outside what had once been the electronic nerve center of a global catastrophe, but which was now just a canopy tent perched upon a cliff.

When she had heard the six gunshots twenty yards away, a million thoughts shot through her head, but she had little time to process them before a tall human form materialized out of the darkness.

"Is that blood on your shirt?" Lauren asked, trying her utmost to be nonchalant, though the slight quaver in her voice was a dead giveaway of the emotions that were bubbling up from inside her like magma in a Big Island volcanic eruption.

"Yeah," Jim Hammer said. "But it's the other guy's. Looks like you had some action down here, too."

"Yup," she said, not even bothering to glance back at the two blood-stained corpses.

Instead, she just grabbed the big man in her arms and pushed her lips into his.

For a moment which seemed like hours, they pressed their bodies into one another with all the emotion that came that knowing that the person in whose arms each was entangled, the person whom they loved, was *not* among the spirit ranks.

This entanglement certainly might have gone on longer, but suddenly the night was filled with the light of day.

They paused to look up as a RIM-174G streaked into the sky atop a sweeping white-hot contrail at an incredible speed that would increase to more than twenty-six-hundred miles per hour.

This was almost instantly followed by a second missile.

"There's your ghost riders in the sky," she said, looking up.

"When all at once a mighty herd of red-eyed cows they saw, plowing through the ragged skies," he replied, paraphrasing a line from the lyrics.

"Their brands were still on fire and their hooves were made of steel," she replied, continuing into the next line. "Their horns were black and shiny and their hot breath we could feel."

Two ghost armies had done battle that night on Pokuakini Ridge, though neither was exactly the kind of spirit rank described in Hawai`ian legend, nor in Selke's colorful narrative that night at Huna's. These armies had not come to this battlefield as an endless and boisterous band of chanting spirits, but surreptitiously—like ghosts. One army arrived so ethereally that the other did not know they were even in battle—until it was too late.

The whole war, one in which the stakes would certainly have included some form of a nuclear apocalypse, was over in less than nine minutes. When it ended, one army littered the battlefield and the other morphed innocently into a couple of vacationing mainlanders.

Nobody needed to know exactly what had happened on Pokuakini Ridge that night, and nobody ever would.

"If you wanna save your soul from hell, riding on our range," she said with a smile, playfully pulling his body close to hers again, "then cowboy change your ways today or with us you will ride…"

"Tryin' to catch the devil's herd across these endless skies," he added, completing that line from the lyrics.

"Yippie aye oh, yippie aye yay," she hummed as a third

missile arced into the sky and their lips returned to the pleasure of the earlier moment.

CHAPTER THIRTY

MASTER-AT-ARMS PETTY OFFICER Second Class Joel Dyallic was standing alone beneath the full moon at the Miloli`i Ridge Trailhead when the missile launches suddenly cast their brief, but witheringly bright glow across the surrounding forests.

He and his boss, Chief Petty Officer Anthony Karboli had spent more than sixteen hours up here in the mountains at the 3,900-foot level doing practically nothing until just a few minutes ago. Then they heard the sound of three distant gunshots from the direction of Miloli`i Ridge.

Dyallic had started to speculate about what this might be all about, but Karboli reacted almost immediately. Grabbing a MagLite out of their Humvee and subconsciously patting the SIG Sauer M18 pistol in his holster, he took off jogging down the trail.

All Karboli said as he dashed into the darkness was the offhand "wait here," that left the younger man asking, "*why*?"

Dyallic was wondering what might have inspired this sudden urgency when he heard three more faraway gunshots from the same direction—and then three more. The night had taken a sudden turn to the weird.

He looked at his phone. Whatever glitch had happened about ten minutes ago was still happening. He couldn't connect to anything.

Without the small talk he'd shared with Karboli all day, it seemed very quiet. Even the hissing of the crickets made the scene seem all that more forlorn.

Looking at his analog wristwatch, Dyallic recalled they had pulled into this parking area at 0754 this morning, but he quickly corrected himself. That was *yesterday* morning. It was Friday now.

When they had arrived, the countdown stood at T-minus eight hours, but through the day, the countdown had changed twice, finally pushing the launch time back to almost midnight.

Through all that time, only a handful of cars had stopped. Each time, Karboli had answered inquiries about the Miloli`i Ridge Trail by telling of an impending naval exercise. Each time, the parties doing the inquiring decided to hike elsewhere—with one exception. What was it about those five Koreans whom Karboli did *not* try to dissuade? Why?

Did they have something to do with the gunshots?

Why did Karboli hurry off so hastily, and with no explanation?

Dyallic knew that the "Second Class" in his rank meant he should not expect to be briefed on all the nuances of an operation, but after being on duty with one other guy for sixteen hours, he had assumed that some sort of camaraderie had developed.

He guessed he had assumed wrong, and this was one of many thoughts that coursed through his head in the lonely darkness.

After what seemed like an hour, but which was far

less, he caught a glimpse of a light flashing somewhere to the south. As he stood up from where he was lounging in the open doorway of the Humvee, he could tell that what he saw were the headlights of a vehicle coming up Highway 550 from the direction of Kekaha and Barking Sands. The headlights were slipping in and out between the trees as the vehicle made its way up the winding road.

He had seen no cars on this road for hours, maybe since around eight o'clock, and those had been headed downhill. People going home after a day up in the mountains at Kōke`e Park.

Dyallic stepped out to the road. He could tell that the car was coming faster than usual, and he wondered who it might be. He decided that he should move back toward the Humvee. He didn't want to get nailed if this motorist took the curve too wildly.

As it came around the bend, the car slowed, as though the driver was studying the sign in the moonlight. Abruptly, it lurched to a stop and turned in sharply to park near the Humvee.

Compared to the dark-colored Humvee, the brilliant white Lexus RX glowed in the moonlight. The figure who stepped out of the driver's side door glowed like a phantom, but she was a lithe young woman in a white dress with a flowing skirt. In the moonlight, she seemed almost surreal, like a vision from a movie or from one of those old paintings.

Dyallic was at a loss for words, but he finally resorted to the clumsy standby.

"Good evening, ma'am, can I help you?"

"I'm looking for Anthony," she said. "Anthony Karboli? I was told he was stationed up here today."

As she came closer, and as he smelled her distinct but subtle perfume, he thought he recognized her. Then it dawned on him. She was the woman who had taken such an interest in Karboli at Shenanigan's that day. She was the woman who someone had said was actually the *daughter of Admiral Hardgrove Kinkaide*!"

Again, Dyallic was at a loss for words, but he resorted to another clumsy standby.

"May I see some ID, ma'am?"

Almost immediately, he regretted what he'd said, expecting an argument, but she surprised him. She swiftly plunged her hand into her purse and brought out the requested document.

"Yes, sir, mister..um," she said, studying his name tag in the dark. "Mr. Dye..."

"It's Dyallic."

"Mr. Dyallic," she said with a smile. She had long ago given up on deciphering all the stripes and chevrons of Navy rank, so she called men in uniform "mister." This aggravated her father, but maybe *he* was part of why she ignored the nuances of Navy rank.

Dyallic flicked on his compact flashlight as she produced a California driver's license. As she had done at the beginning of this drive, she held it up with a thumbnail directing his attention to her surname.

"Yes, Miss Kinkaide," he said. "Chief Karboli is posted here, but he's actually gone up the trail to observe a forward location. I expect him to return shortly. You are certainly welcome to wait here."

"With *you*?" Lynsee Kinkaide said with a smile, unable to resist an opportunity to flirt. Though she was desperately in love with Karboli, she found Dyallic easy on the eye.

"Yes, ma'am," he said nervously.

"*Naw*, I think I'll surprise him and meet him on the trail."

"But Miss Kinkaide," he said with some urgency. "It's

dangerous to hike these trails at night. There are tripping hazards…"

"But under this beautiful full moon?" Lynsee sighed.

"You really shouldn't…"

"Don't worry," she said with a laugh. "I'm wearing tennies and you are going to lend me your flashlight."

Grabbing it from his hand, she gave him a finger-fluttering wave and skipped off down the Miloli`i Ridge Trail.

Her flowing skirts were visible for a few moments in the moonlight, and then she was around a bend, gone from sight.

Petty Officer Second Class Joel Dyallic was once again alone in the darkness and serenaded by crickets.

What should I do?

Karboli had told him to "wait here," but that was before the admiral's daughter had shown up and had run off down the trail. What if something happened to her? What if she tripped and fell? What if she broke a leg? What if she crossed paths with an aggressive wild hog?

If any of those things happened, and Dyallic was not there to render aid immediately, Karboli would eat him alive—and Admiral Kinkaide would guarantee that the rest of his naval career would involve scrubbing bilges.

The choice was easy. If none of those things happened, then nobody would know that Dyallic abandoned his post.

After quickly rearranging the orange cones to suggest that the trailhead was closed, he grabbed the other MagLite and the first aid kit from the Humvee and started down the trail.

She was fit and athletic, and could probably handle the trail with ease, but Dyallic was nevertheless sure he could catch up to the admiral's daughter—somewhere out there in the darkness.

CHAPTER THIRTY-ONE

AS HE JOGGED through the night, Chief Petty Officer Anthony Karboli had no idea what he would find.

After sixteen hours on guard duty with Petty Officer Second Class Joel Dyallic, he was ready for anything else. Small talk with Dyallic was exactly that—*small.*

Having watched the fiery contrails of the Aegis RIM-174Gs in the sky, he wondered what had happened to the depraved scheme of Ryu Myong-su. He knew enough about Ryu's plans to know he meant to disrupt the missile launch, but anything beyond that was open to question. If he meant to stop it, then it had not worked. If he meant to misdirect it, then what? Had he, or hadn't he?

At this point, Karboli was beyond caring.

He secretly hoped the impossible hope that the gunshots meant that the Koreans had wound up killing each other. That would solve a lot of problems—mainly *his* problems. There were five of them and there had been nine shots. That was a good sign, he thought.

After the Miloli`i Ridge Trail emerged from the deep

forest and into the open, it was easy to see in the moonlight, so he switched off the MagLite.

He remembered the place where the goat trail out to Pokuakini Ridge forked off the well-marked Miloli`i Ridge Trail. He found this again fairly easily, even though it was so indistinct as to be nearly invisible if you weren't looking for it.

Because of the jagged escarpment along the ridge, the approaches to the Korean electronic warfare site were in deep shadow, so he switched on the MagLite again and moved more cautiously.

As he came within reach of his destination, Karboli flicked off the light and inched forward slowly. He listened warily but heard nothing but the crickets. The caterwauling from the canyon had wound down a half hour ago. He didn't know what he had missed.

He could see the canopy tent up ahead in the shadows, but he saw none of the ubiquitous LED lights one expects with piles of electronics.

Suddenly, about twenty yards from his goal, Karboli stumbled on something.

Feeling around in the darkness, he realized what it was.

He had tripped on a human body, a bloody human body on which the blood was starting to congeal.

Taking a deep breath, he turned over the head and found himself staring into the lifeless, but wide-eyed face of Ryu Myong-su.

Karboli looked around. The world was still, except for the crickets.

He continued forward and reached the tent.

Everything remained quiet, quiet as death.

He thought he could make out another body amid the jumble of gear inside, so he flicked on the MagLite.

Directly ahead of him, he saw what would have been

the answer to his prayers—if he was a praying man, which he was not.

He was looking at the mortal remains of his nemesis. It was Han jong-sok, the man who possessed the long and dangerous video of Karboli in the carnal embrace of the only daughter, the precious daughter, of Admiral Hardgrove Kinkaide.

Now, here he lay, with a dim-witted expression on his fiendish face and a bullet hole in his chest, just above his heart.

A further search revealed the immobile body of Cho ho-jin, with his face frozen in a death stare. He had an immense bloodstain that covered the lower part of his shirt and his khaki trousers all the way to his knees. Karboli looked no closer.

On the tables above the bodies were the electronics as he remembered them. Finding them slightly warm to the touch, he flicked a few on-switches, but all of the machines were as dead as the humans. Hammer had earlier disconnected the solar panels from the batteries, and the electronics had sucked the batteries dry.

As he looked around, he saw no trace of either Pak Mi-Rae or Teddy Jong.

"What the hell happened here?" Karboli asked out loud, half expecting to hear one of them answer. "It's Karboli. Whatever happened...you're safe now. What *did* happen?"

There was no reply, so he circled the area, methodically searching for them, but saw no sign of Rae and Teddy. Gradually, he figured it out. In his mind, there was only one plausible solution. There had been a mutiny. The superstitious Teddy had gone off the rails and killed the others. Then he and Rae had run off.

Karboli figured that he must have passed them on the trail. They saw him coming with the MagLite and took cover. Then they kept going when he passed. That's it. This is the *only* solution. Karboli breathed a sigh of relief. Them he could handle, and they were irrelevant with all the others dead.

He walked back to the canopy tent. This time, he noticed they had pulled back the covering. He recalled that a storm was due in tomorrow, realizing quickly that tomorrow was today—it was Friday now. This place would get a serious soaking, but nobody was left who cared about all these thousands of dollars' worth of electronics. Karboli certainly did not. He'd be happy if all this was soaked and ruined beyond all possibility of salvaging.

Now, all Karboli needed to do was grab Han's cell phone and get rid of that damned video. He'd be home free!

He began his search calmly and methodically, starting with the obvious search of Han's pants pockets, and then his backpack. No luck. He searched the area under and around Han's corpse, then expanded his search nervously, but still methodically. He even poked through the congealing blood to search for Cho's phone, but again he come up empty-handed.

After a thorough search of the work area, he still had found *no* phones.

Then he had a brainstorm. Maybe the boss man had held on to all the phones! This inspiration ended badly. There was nothing in Ryu's backpack or within a ten-yard radius of the boss's haunting death mask.

What Anthony Karboli did not know was that Jim Hammer never leaves cell phones behind at a scene like this. *Never*. He even had those of Rae and Teddy, because they had left them on the table near the consoles. Cell phones often come in useful later, and Tim Tommis can give Hammer the magic decryption algorithms to break into any phone in the world.

As he searched for phones he could not find, Karboli realized that he had not seen the guns—the ghost guns that he'd supplied to this gang. They too were nowhere to be seen.

Karboli ended his search for the phones and weapons almost frantically, but without result, and decided that Rae and Teddy had taken them. He pictured the pair as a sort of K-pop Bonnie and Clyde armed with untraceable automatics.

He knew he'd better double-time it back to the trailhead parking area where he'd left Dyallic and the Humvee. Hopefully, he would catch up with them there. If not, he knew where they were staying. He would catch them at the bungalow. He could shoot them both and claim self-defense. A Navy cop versus two people with ghost guns? Self-defense would be an obvious conclusion.

He had just reached the main Miloli`i Ridge Trail when he saw something in the distance across the open ground between there and the tree line. Illuminated in the moonlight was a bright white object moving along the trail. Was it Teddy and Rae? If so, why were they coming *this way* rather than going toward the trailhead.

As he got closer, he could see that the bright white object was a woman in a flowing white dress walking toward him on the trail. What was a woman dressed for a garden party doing out here alone in the middle of the night?

She came in and out of view as she passed among the crests and swales of the uneven terrain, making her seem otherworldly and ghostlike.

Joel Dyallic also had eyes on Lynsee Kinkaide. Unlike Karboli, he knew exactly who she was and what she was doing out here. He was much closer to her, but because of his darker camo uniform, Dyallic was not visible to Karboli, whose attention was fixed upon the specter in white.

Finally, when Dyallic was within about fifty feet of her, she stopped and turned.

"I've been listening to you back there," she said, placing her hands on her hips. "I've heard you puffing and squishing in the gravel for a half a mile at least."

"I couldn't let you come out here…not *alone*. There are wild hogs out here. They're nocturnal. They're *dangerous*."

"Wild *hogs*, is it? Why didn't you say that before?"

"You were in too much of a hurry."

"You said that Anthony came out here," she reminded him. "So w*here is he*?"

"I don't know," he said, continuing down the trail to where she was.

"Are you lying to me, young man?" The seventeen-year-old enjoyed using that term when speaking to men in their twenties. Her therapist always criticized her, telling her that it was her way of "asserting dominance" over the opposite gender, and that this could get her in trouble. So far it hadn't. It had always worked.

"No," he said. "Chief Karboli *did* come out here on this trail."

"So you came to protect me from wild pigs?" Lynsee said, half in a mocking way. "How gallant."

For a moment, they just stared at one another in the quiet moonlight.

In that moment, through the hiss of the crickets, they heard a thrashing sound in the distance which they did not know was Karboli hurrying uphill toward them.

He could now hear their voices, but he was too far distant to make out who they were or what they were saying.

"What was that?" Lynsee asked, sounding worried for the first time.

"Could be a hog," he said, taking his SIG from its holster. "I'll fire a warning shot."

K'pow!

The sound of the 9mm round being fired reverberated through the nocturnal stillness.

Anthony Karboli immediately crouched low to the ground and reached for his own SIG. Already on edge by his failure to find Han's cell phone, he interpreted Dyallic's shot as someone firing at him.

Trained and experienced, Karboli was now able to close the distance between himself and the others without being seen or heard. It didn't hurt that the first clouds from the impending storm had already drifted in, and the moon had slipped behind one.

At last, he was close enough to recognize Dyallic. He didn't recognize the woman. The last person he ever would have expected to see up here was Lynsee Kinkaide. She never even entered his mind.

Karboli saw them both staring into the distance, toward the place where he had been when Dyallic had fired the first shot. He watched Dyallic raise his pistol over his head and squeeze off another round.

K'pow!

The woman covered her ears and jumped slightly at the sound.

Karboli used this distraction as cover to creep even closer.

He was about to shout to Dyallic to holster his weapon when the young petty officer lowered it and pointed it into the distance.

"No! *Don't shoot*," the woman screamed, grabbing for the gun. "Anthony is out there somewhere!"

Now Karboli recognized her voice!

As Karboli dashed toward them, they continued to struggle—with Dyallic's right hand and both of hers on the weapon. He watched as she grappled to get it away from him.

K'pow!

As he watched, she slipped and stumbled, leaving Dyallic standing alone, watching as she slowly dropped to her knees. As she did so, Dyallic unconsciously relaxed and lowered his raised right hand. As he did so, it looked to Karboli like he was pointing the gun at *her*.

Still agitated by everything that had transpired, Karboli acted impulsively, raising his SIG and squeezing the trigger in one single fluid motion—just as he had done at the range three hundred times or more.

K'pow!

He saw Dyallic's neck snap backward violently as his body toppled to the ground.

Karboli reached the pair just a second later and dropped to his knees next to Lynsee.

She looked so peaceful as she lay in the grass in her white dress.

Was she injured? He touched her neck and felt a pulse.

Whew!

She opened her eyes. They were filled with tears, but she managed a broad smile.

"I love you, Anthony," she whispered. "I love you more than…"

Her voice trailed off.

The softness of her voice reminded him of that night when they first met at the Royal Pacific Resort. She was so unbelievably sexy that he had never imagined her to be underage. He certainly had never imagined she could have *fallen in love* with him. How could this have happened?

As he picked her up, she felt limp and totally relaxed.

Then he noticed the huge bloodstain on her dress.

As she had struggled with Dyallic, the gun had gone off and the bullet struck her in the abdomen, ripping through a half dozen vital organs. He well knew that there was no coming back from a massive wound like this, and, tragically, she would not.

He touched her neck again. No pulse.

He lay her down gently and stood to survey the scene.

His own round had struck Dyallic squarely in the forehead.

It was an irrational shot he should never have taken, but he had. He had reacted to Dyallic pointing his gun down, toward her. It was impulsive, and it was *wrong*. Lynsee was *already* mortally wounded, though he did not realize this at the time.

Two people lay dead at the feet of Anthony Karboli. One of them was the admiral's daughter, the other a man whose death could easily be construed as second-degree murder.

He knew that somewhere out there in the world, there was a video of him in bed with the same pitiful teenager who lay here in the moonlight like a heartrending post-Raphaelite heroine.

How could he unwind this catastrophe?

He could not think of a way.

Anthony Karboli well knew that there was no coming back from what he had done here tonight.

CHAPTER THIRTY-TWO

DAVE ALTBECK WOKE up Friday morning in that same dusty, windowless anteroom where he had been grabbing a few hours of sleep every night for the past week. His head still spun from the chaos of the night before when everything had gone so terribly wrong with only minutes left before T-minus zero.

His wristwatch, which he'd set to twenty-four-hour military time, read 0531—an appropriate approximation of the proverbial "oh-dark-thirty," the military euphemism for "ridiculously early." The last time he looked at his watch, it was around 0300. He looked at his cellphone. Still no service.

As he had on all of those previous days, he pulled himself together, and after a visit to the head, he made his way to the BMIC, which had been the center of his world for all those days.

Today, the crisp military precision of other days had evaporated into a scene that looked like move-in day at a college fraternity house. Every workstation was a jumble of computer components and an impossible rat's nest of tangled wires as tech people scrambled to unwind a cataclysmic crash that no one had yet figured out.

Altbeck saw the man with whom he had been discussing issues from potential snafus to guidance systems calibration, over the past couple of days. He was staring at the techs tearing apart his workstation and nibbling nervously on his thumbnail.

"Are they getting things back up and running?" Altbeck asked, opening the conversation.

"Slowly…if at all," he replied without taking his eyes off the workstation. "But I guess there's no rush. Vigilant Basilisk is concluded. There won't be anything happening in the BMIC until the next time, whenever that will be."

"What's the official verdict on that epic fubar last night?"

"I don't think they've got an 'official' verdict, but unofficially they're saying it was a pretty sophisticated jamming attack. Please don't quote me on this, but I heard the electronic warfare types saying that a Chinese Type 039D Yuan-class stealth submarine might have sneaked in near here last night."

"I thought they swept for those types of threats *before* the launch," Altbeck said.

"They did, and since midnight, they've had destroyers out there searching everywhere and playing damage control."

"The sub will be long gone by now," another man interjected. "Those Type 039Ds can run at better than twenty knots."

"How could they have gotten in close enough to use a jammer?"

"Your guess is as good as mine."

"So, what's the *official* verdict on the test itself?" Altbeck asked. "What *can* I quote?"

"Don't quote *me*, but Irv O'Malley, the public affairs guy is holding a final press briefing at the press tent by the main gate at 0800, and you can quote him. Spoiler alert...he's going to call it a success."

"A *success*?"

"Yeah, a *success*. What was the objective of the exercise? To shoot down two ICBMs with RIM-174Gs of the Aegis Ballistic Missile Defense System, right? Well, they shot down two ICBMs with Aegis System missiles. They were the two RIM-174Gs with old-school INS guidance."

"Right," Altbeck said thoughtfully. "Since inertial navigation sensors are self-contained, they don't need radar or radio signals like GPS does, so they're not vulnerable to being jammed."

"Bingo. You've obviously done your homework. They were able to launch even though the electronics were scrambled because the launch control bunkers are hardwired to the Vertical Launch System on the launch stand, so it's all analog...like a landline telephone."

"I was up on the platform with Kinkaide last night for the launch," Altbeck said. "Everybody started freaking out when they learned that the electronics were crashing. He was trying to cancel the launch entirely. He tried to call a hold using the usual channels, but they were fried, so somebody handed him the land line that goes direct to the launch bunkers. It was almost too late; he only got through to the last one."

"The other three had already been launched."

"Yeah," Altbeck said with a nod. "I guess it's lucky that the one he stopped was a GPS-guided one, and both the INS-guided missiles launched."

"The GPS-guided missile that *did* get launched failed," the man said. "But it fell into the ocean hundreds of miles downrange so nobody from here saw it."

"Out of sight, out of mind?"

"That's what successes are made of," the man said cynically. "But don't quote me."

"Is that going to stay classified?" Altbeck asked. "Or can I write about it?"

"Probably you shouldn't ... but it depends on when Irv O'Malley says when he gives his briefing at 0800. Watch for him to tell everybody that Basilisk achieved its goal despite some glitch that fried everybody's cell phones and everything else. That can't be classified because everybody on this end of the island knows about it. Then he'll give Kinkaide credit for valiantly holding back one of the GPS missiles so the forensics people can pick apart the fried guidance to troubleshoot the cause."

"That rascal," Altbeck said with a chuckle.

"Oh, give him a break. Let him take the win."

By the time that Dave Altbeck passed through the main gate, anticlimactically ending his week of being an embedded journalist, the nearest cell tower had come back online. He checked his emails and found that his editor at *Defense Up Front* had forwarded one from a mutual friend at a popular aerospace blog. Could Dave give him a thousand words of an insider's view of the launch—and deliver it today?

Are you kidding? Of course! He was dying to start writing copy for publication.

Dave had tapped out the headline even before he set down his backpack.

"Backstage Behind Basilisk," he typed.

At that moment, Vice Admiral Hardgrove Kinkaide was on his way back to the PRMF admiral's quarters for a shower and a fresh uniform. The storm front that had been stalled out over the Pacific for the last few days and become unstalled, and the sky was already darkening.

Kinkaide was exhausted and worn down to a nub by a tumultuous week, but he was feeling pretty good. He had already gotten a congratulatory call from his boss, Admiral Ronald R. Strettich, commander of all US forces across more than half of the globe.

"Two-for-two, both ICBMs intercepted," Strettich had said, as though none of the things that went wrong mattered. Maybe Kinkaide's two-for-two success against the odds would play well with his career. Maybe it would be a step toward that fourth star that he coveted more than anything. The idea of a four-star Admiral Hardgrove Kinkaide was what he lived for.

Kinkaide had not set foot in the admiral's quarters since Tuesday morning. Like Dave Altbeck, and most of the Navy people who were part of the launch team, he had bunked in the same building as the BMIC. Kinkaide liked the example this set for the rest of the team. He liked being seen as a leader who led from the front.

The first things he saw as he walked into the place were the soda cans and pizza boxes that Lynsee had left lying around.

As he surveyed the scene, he realized he had almost forgotten she was even staying at Barking Sands.

He hadn't seen her or had a text message from her in days. *Damn it.* His wife was going to go more ballistic than an ICBM on him for this. But what could he do? He was the Commander of Naval Anti-Ballistic Missile Operations in the entire damned Pacific. He was a very busy and *important* naval officer.

"Lynsee," he said as he placed his admiral's cap carefully on its shelf. "Get yourself out of bed and get this place cleaned up."

"Lynsee," he shouted as he hung up his uniform coat.

"Lynsee," he repeated as he stepped into the kitchen to put a dark roast coffee pod into the Keurig.

As he paused, he noticed the envelope on the kitchen table.

It reeked of perfume and was labeled "Daddy."

He opened it and started reading it. There was something about a little bird flexing her wings.

What the hell?

Then she got into the part about a petty officer and true love and *making love.*

What the hell? Some damned petty officer is screwing my daughter?

"Lynsee," he screamed as he stomped toward the second bedroom. "Get the hell out her and explain this!"

He burst into the room like a dredge colliding with a pier and turned on the lights. The bed was empty. It was a mess, but it was an empty mess.

He tore through the rest of the house like a merciless typhoon but found her nowhere. He went back into the bedroom and opened the closet. All her clothes were gone except an old sweatshirt hanging half off the hanger.

He grabbed his cell phone out of his jacket pocket and tried to dial.

No service.

Damn those Chinese and their jammers!

Think, he told himself. *Where could she have gone? Evidently, she ran off with this petty officer in the middle of the exercise last night. That's desertion for him. If the Chinese were involved, that's desertion in the face of the enemy. This SOB who's screwing my daughter is going to the brig for the rest of his worthless life!*

Then Kinkaide remembered the Lexus that his wife had rented. He barged out the back door. It was gone.

Instinctively, he pulled out his phone to call security

but immediately remembered there was no damned cell service. He went back inside and reached for the landline that was hardwired to the Barking Sands base security command post.

No. He would simply *go there.* The Barking Sands base security command post was only about a city block away.

When he walked in, everyone present gasped in disbelief, but they were on their feet, at attention, and saluting no more than two seconds later. The unexpected sight of a three-star admiral in a bad mood did this to people.

Kinkaide glowered at the young lieutenant behind the counter, the first officer whom he saw.

"*Sir,*" the man said crisply. "What can I do for you, *sir?*"

"I need you to put out an APB or whatever you call it," Kinkaide said angrily. "My daughter has gone *missing!*"

"*Kidnapped,* sir?"

He hadn't thought of that.

"Possibly. I obviously don't know. She's just gone. She left a note about some petty officer. Didn't give a name. No idea who he is. She's underage, so that makes this pretty damned urgent."

"*Yes, sir.*"

"And one more thing, the Lexus that my wife rented was parked at the admiral's quarters. *It's gone.*"

By now, the captain in charge of the command post had emerged from his office. He approached Kinkaide, snapped to attention and saluted.

"At ease, Captain," the admiral said, and the captain took over from the lieutenant, asking, "Do you have a plate number for the vehicle, sir?"

"*No.* Who the hell knows the plate numbers for vehicles their wives rent?"

"Make and model, sir?"

"It's a white Lexus RX. Late model. She got it from Hertz at the airport. She always rents from Hertz."

"Lieutenant," the captain said, turning to the younger man. "Get the plate number from Hertz and get in touch with the Kaua`i Police Department *immediately* about an APB. Also ask them to watch the airport. Tell them it's the admiral's underage daughter and a possible kidnapping. That should get them off their tails."

"I know that this is going to sound patronizing, Admiral," the captain said, turning back to Kinkaide, "but try not to worry. We're on an island with a very finite number of roads and highways. There aren't many places to go. We'll track them down."

As Kinkaide left the command post, it had already started to rain.

CHAPTER THIRTY-THREE

DETECTIVE KAI NIALANI was at her desk at KPD headquarters in Līhu`e, spending Friday morning trying to catch up on last week's paperwork when Lieutenant Richard Faralaco leaned into her office.

"Kai, be advised, we just issued an Amber Alert, a *very* high-profile Amber Alert."

"A missing child?" Kai replied with alarm. "Was it from one of the resorts? Has Ocean Safety been notified?"

"It's not a beach incident."

"Abduction? How old is the child?"

"That's the thing," Faralaco explained. "She's seventeen. Initially, this came through as an abduction, but it looks like she may have taken a car to go meet a boyfriend."

"Okay," Kai replied. "That puts a certain spin on it. You said it was high profile?"

"She's the daughter of Admiral Hardgrove Kinkaide, the three-star admiral who was in charge of that rocket launch out at Barking Sands in the middle of the night last night. This happened during the countdown while he was distracted and she was alone in the admiral's quarters. She was last seen at a quarter to eleven last night exiting the gate at Barking Sands. The guard who opened the gate for her said it looked like she was alone."

"If he had the choice, why would the guard let a seventeen-year-old girl drive out alone in the middle of the night?"

"He's in deep hot water with the Navy for this, but he claims she played the 'daddy-is-the-admiral' card and she said it was family business. He obviously couldn't interrupt the admiral in the middle of that thing, so what could the guy do?"

"What do you have on the car?

"It's a Hertz rental...an almost brand-new white Lexus RX. We've already got the plate number."

"What can *I* do?" Kai asked.

"I'd like you to take a drive out to Kekaha and be out there where this all started if anything turns up," Faralaco said. "I've got other detectives doing the same on the North Shore and uniform in patrol cars everywhere else. Eyes peeled for a white Lexus. I've also got uniform covering the airport. The good news is that they're getting cell service restored after that big outage they had out there on the west side last night."

"I'm on it," she said, powering down her desktop computer.

Rivulets of rain were dribbling down the windshield as she reached her patrol car. The big storm that people had been talking about for the past several days was finally here.

By the time Kai Nialani reached the west side of Kaua`i, the rain was coming down hard, so when her phone buzzed, she pulled off Route 50 to take the call.

"Kai, this is Lieutenant Faralaco," He said, though he probably knew she could see his caller ID.

"Yessir," she said. "I'm almost to Kekaha. I've been watching for white Lexuses. No luck. What next?"

"Good news," he said. "They *found* the Lexus."

"Great. Where?"

"It's up on 550 above Waimea Canyon."

"Wonder what it's doing up there. How'd they find it?"

"The Navy was missing a couple of their security people. They were posted up at the Miloli`i Ridge Trailhead yesterday during the launch countdown. They were there because that's just past the turnoff for the missile range facility on Makaha Ridge. This morning, they discovered that those two never made it back to Barking Sands, so they went looking for them."

"Did they find them?"

"They found their Humvee at the trailhead, but there was nobody in it. The Lexus was parked next to it. Also empty. They think one of the two Navy people may be the boyfriend. The Navy has sent out a search party on the Miloli`i Trail. The state park people from up at Kōke`e are lending assistance."

"That will be challenging in this weather," Kai said. "Do you want me to go up and help out? I have my foul-weather gear in the car."

"No, I think they have it handled," Faralaco said. "They'll probably find all the missing people under a tree waiting for the rain to stop. But in the meantime, I actually have another missing persons case for you."

"It must be the full moon," Kai quipped, making a joke that she knew was lame as soon as she said it.

"This one is a little out of the ordinary."

"All missing persons are out of the ordinary," she said, being serious this time.

"This one comes in from Kekaha, so you're in the right place to take it," he said, ignoring both her quips. "There's a woman who owns a short-term rental. She rented to a bunch from a Korean sugar company. They were supposed to check out this morning, but their bags are all still in the unit, and the landlady's got somebody coming in this afternoon."

"That's being pretty picky," Kai said. "Why did she call the police for *that*? They most likely went for one last bit of sightseeing and got caught in the rain. They'll probably be back any minute."

"Between you and me, I think she wants some legal cover so that they don't sue her for touching their luggage if she has to move it out to clean the place."

"That's legal, isn't it? If they aren't out by checkout time?"

"Humor me on this, Kai," he said. "I'll text you the address and phone her to say that you'll meet her at the property."

"Yessir."

As she hung up, Kai breathed a sigh of relief that she would not be hiking in the red mud of the Miloli`i Ridge Trail during a downpour.

As Kai pulled into the muddy, unpaved driveway at the address, the owner of the property was waiting in her older-model Honda, which was parked next to a bright-blue late-model Mustang convertible. At least the top was up. She was a middle-aged woman with her hair tied back, dressed in jeans and a yellow rain slicker.

"Good morning," she said, extending her hand. "I'm Kathy Kehale. Thanks for coming out here so fast."

"No problem. I was in the area when I got the call. I'm

Detective Kai Nialani," she said, handing the woman her card.

"This is my daughter Kristin," she said, introducing a girl in her late teens who seemed apprehensive about meeting a police officer. "She's here to help me clean up today."

"Hi, Kristin," Kai said, extending her hand.

"What seems to be the problem?" Kai asked, turning back to the older woman. "As I understand it, you have people who are supposed to vacate the property, but they still have things in there? You know that if it's in the boilerplate of your lease agreement, you can put unclaimed stuff into locked storage, right?"

"Yeah. It says I can."

"Did they sign it?"

"Yeah."

"Where are you moving the stuff?"

"Into the garage over there."

"Then you're probably okay," Kai said. "I have a sense that you phoned us because you may *also* be suspecting some kind of foul play. Is that right?"

"I don't know. I've tried to call them yesterday and about ten times this morning. I called both the numbers they gave me. It goes to voicemail."

"Who are these people?" Kai asked.

"They're with a Korean sugar company. It's called Sweet Harvest."

"Sounds innocent enough," Kai said. "Does the Mustang belong to them? It does look like a rental."

"I'm sure it is. It arrived about a week ago. Hard not to notice when I was driving by. Four of them checked in a few weeks ago...they had a brown SUV. They said their big boss man was coming in later, so it must be his rental."

Kai asked for a description of the other vehicle and jotted it down in her notebook.

"I'm sure everything is all right," Kai said, using her reassuring voice. "In ninety-nine out of a hundred of these cases, the missing people show up the same day. But just to be thorough, I'd like to take a look around. Is that okay?"

"Sure. I've got a key."

Kai entered first, wiping her feet on the mat and asking the others to wait outside as she looked through the modest fifties-modern bungalow.

The first thing she noticed was a bright green school notebook that had been hanging on the inside of the mail slot when she opened the door. Kai picked it up and flipped through it. The entire thing was filled with neatly written Korean characters. No surprise.

"Does this belong to them?" Kai asked.

"I have no idea. If it was hanging in the mail slot somebody must have slid it in from outside. Good thing they did, too. If they'd left it outside in this weather, all that paper would be nothing but soggy mush by now."

Kai stepped into the living room. She counted eleven pieces of luggage stacked to one side. They were not jumbled or random but piled with neat precession. The kitchen was spotless, with the dishwasher emptied and no last minute cups and spoons in the sink. The only thing in the refrigerator was an unopened water bottle. The bedrooms and bathrooms were likewise squeaky clean, far more pristine than any hotel room that Kai had ever checked out of. The sheets and towels were in neat piles in the laundry room. A landlord's dream.

Kathy would be happy.

Kai did not say it out loud, but this level of cleanliness made her suspicious.

The whole setup was that of someone who would

make a five-minute stop, grab the luggage, and be off to the airport, leaving *nothing* behind. The notebook was the only thing conspicuously incongruous.

"Everything seems fine," Kai said. "You'll be pleased with how they tidied up after themselves. Before I go, I'd like to get the names and contact information for the people who were staying here ...and I'm going to take the green notebook. You can tell them they can ask at the front desk of the police station in Līhu`e. It's only about ten minutes from the airport. It's on the way. The address is on my card."

"Okay," Kathy said with a sense of relief. "Thanks again for coming out."

"I wouldn't be surprised if they come wheeling in here in the next half hour," Kai said, smiling. "But could you please phone me when they do. My number's also on the card."

Kathy said she would, they shook hands and Kai walked back to her squad car. She tossed the notebook in and paused long enough to take a picture of the Mustang's license plate.

CHAPTER THIRTY-FOUR

TUESDAY DAWNED BRIGHT and sunny on the North Shore of Kaua`i. Jim Hammer and Lauren Stahling were loading their gear into the trunk of the old silver-gray Ford Taurus which they would later park in the lot near the rental car lots at the Līhu`e airport where they had picked it up a month ago.

After three days of heavy rain, the weather had cleared brilliantly yesterday afternoon, and this pair of mainlanders had gotten in an invigorating swim from their favorite beach to the distant coral reef where the breakers broke. They wound up lounging on the beach until the sun went down. The last tropical sunset of their current adventure.

Through the rainy, stormy weekend, while they had remained housebound, they stooped to turning on the television set for the first time a month. They tuned in for the weather but wound up drifting into the news. All of the Honolulu local channels, which predominate the Kaua`i market, were throwing all their news team energy into the "admiral's daughter" story.

Early in on Friday afternoon, on the muddy Miloli`i

Ridge Trail, search parties had discovered the body of Lynsee Kinkaide. She was the seventeen-year-old daughter of Vice Admiral Hardgrove Kinkaide, who only the night before had commanded a spectacular and well-publicized missile test at Barking Sands—which the US Navy had already deemed a "success."

An article had just appeared in the online edition of a magazine called *Defense Up Front* which painted the admiral as heroic for his hands-on persistence in overcoming numerous technical obstacles to accomplish his mission. However, this same mission-driven intensity was spun the other way by other media outlets. They painted his tenacity as self-absorbed grandstanding at the critical moment when his own daughter was on her collision course with tragedy.

Lynsee's body was found with that of Petty Officer Second Class Joel Dyallic. Each of them had died from a single gunshot wound. The situation had all of the provocative elements of those heartrending stories which resonate with viewers, and followers of the "true crime" genre. There was the grand tragedy of a great leader losing his only child at his moment of glory, and the perennial poignancy of two young people who die violently in one another's arms.

Phrases such as "star-crossed lovers" cropped up in the coverage, and the phrase "Princess and the Petty Officer" became almost a headline trademark at one channel. Those who clung to the romantic notion of doomed lovers could not accept the murder-suicide theory that crept into the speculation. Both Romeo and Juliet *had to* remain tragic victims, not perpetrators.

However, even after several days, *nobody* had any clear idea of what exactly had happened beyond a young couple dead from gunshot wounds. For Hammer and Lauren, it was an uncanny reminder of Glenn Dexsen and

Gladys Mattochs, dead of gunshot wounds in those same mountains above the Nāpali Coast.

There was almost no mention in the early coverage of the fact that there had been not one, but two, petty officers who went missing on Miloli`i Ridge that night. Chief Petty Officer Anthony Karboli, who still remained missing, emerged as a plot thickener as journalists grabbed at loose threads to explain the mystery.

Where was he? Had he gone AWOL? Was *he* the killer?

Jim Hammer and Lauren Stahling knew somewhat more than anyone about the backstory to those questions. While picking through the cell phone of the deceased Han jong-sok, Hammer found the incriminating video of Karboli with Lynsee Kinkaide, and it had become clear that his cooperation with the Korean conspiracy was based on blackmail, rather than collaboration. It was also clear from the lustful, though naïve, expression on Lynsee's face that the petty officer who was the object of her affection was *not* Joel Dyallic.

Whatever had gone down in the shooting, and whether or not he'd even fired a shot, Karboli would have known that there was no chance of his going back to his previous life—especially not with the possibility of that video ever surfacing.

Hammer and Lauren had not made coffee this morning. They decided they would stop at the little café in that quiet little town a short distance down the road, the place where they had gone to the farmers' market on their first day.

The café was just opening as they rolled through town. It smelled invitingly of fresh-brewed coffee and freshly baked pastry. These were the smells that made them trade comments about staying on the North Shore for *another* month.

They ordered coffee and a couple of cinnamon rolls—no need for a big breakfast if you're going to be sitting all day—and found a table in the back, which was open to a palm-shrouded yard.

They had just taken their first nibbles when two people they recognized walked in. It was Rachel and Brandon, the schoolteacher and electrician from nearby Kapa`a, whom they had met at the tiki bar in Hanalei during their first week on the island.

"Hello," Rachel said with a smile. "Don't we know you...from Hanalei a couple of weeks ago. You had just arrived here on the island."

"Yes," Lauren said, returning the smile. "It's good to see you again. So happens we're just on the way to the airport after a whole month here."

"How was your stay?" Rachel asked eagerly in that way in which people who like where they live want to make sure that visitors have had a good time.

"We had some very lovely experiences," Lauren said, obviously not referencing the Korean camp caper. "We got in some good swims, and we hiked part of the Nāpali Coast Trail. We also did several hikes up in the mountains and out to the cliffs *above* the Nāpali Coast."

"We just got off a hike into the Kalalau Valley ourselves," Rachel said. "We were so muddled and pooped when we came out in the dark last night that we crashed with a friend here on the North Side rather than drive home."

"Everybody says the in-and-out all the way to the Kalalau Valley is a tough hike," Lauren said sympathetically.

"It was the weather," Brandon said. "We left last

Wednesday, hoping to get in and out before the storm hit."

"Best laid plans." Rachel shrugged. "That's what you get for doing something like that under a full moon. I don't want to go through that again."

"Nobody likes to hike the western half of that trail in a downpour," Brandon said. "But it wasn't just the rain, you know. It was the whole scene up in Kalalau."

"You know there's people who live full time up there," Rachel added. "I think we talked about this last time."

"Yeah, we did," Hammer said. "Since then we've talked to other people who've said it's the place for people to completely unhook from the world...people with nothing to lose but themselves, and they go up there to lose *that*."

"We were stuck there in the rain with them for a couple of days," Brandon said. "They've got a whole system up there. They grow their own food, and they've got tents and houses they've built. It's like an ancient civilization...or a science fiction movie."

"At least it was entertaining," Rachel added. "There's people up there who believe that the valley is visited by Pleiadeans, you know, people from up around the Pleiades constellation?"

"Of course," Lauren replied skeptically.

"There are people who think there's a vortex there that you can use to go to and from the lost continent of Lemuria," Brandon said. "Quite a lot of people."

"We met one of them on our hike to Hanakapi`ai Falls a couple weeks ago," Hammer replied. "I wasn't convinced."

"I'd never heard of Lemuria anywhere else," Brandon added. "But then I remembered reading that in ancient Rome they had this festival called 'Lemuralia' where they did rituals to chase away evil spirits and ghosts of the restless dead."

Hammer and Lauren looked at one another. *Ghosts of the restless dead?*

"I can see how it would be easy to start believing in ghosts and Lemurians up there if you've got people all around you believing in that stuff," Brandon continued.

"Of course, if you smoke enough weed, you can start believing in anything," Rachel interjected. "Power of suggestion, you know, and they do smoke a lot of weed up there. They've got it growing all over the hillsides."

"Grows like a weed," Brandon said with a laugh.

"When we were there, they had a guy show up sort of out of nowhere," Rachel said. "A lot of them thought he must *be* a Lemurian. Maybe he was. Who knows?"

"Out of nowhere?" Lauren asked.

"Yeah," Brandon said. "They were sure he hadn't arrived by way of the Nāpali Coast Trail, and there's no other trails into that place. He just staggered out of the jungle. He was all scuffed up from it and said he hadn't eaten much in a couple of days. He had a really nasty scrape on his leg. I think he came from somewhere up in the mountains."

"Who was he?" Hammer asked.

"He didn't seem to want to say," Rachel replied. "Which of course seemed perfectly natural to the Kalalau people. They just called him 'Red' because he had bright red hair."

Again, Hammer and Lauren looked at one another. *From up in the mountains? Red Hair?*

"Was he dressed like a hiker?" Lauren asked.

"He had pretty high-end boots, but they were all ripped, like he'd been walking on rocks without a trail," Brandon said. "He was wearing long pants, camo pants, and a t-shirt. Didn't have a backpack. With the camo pants and his fairly short hair, I thought he might be military, but he acted like he'd come to Kalalau to be part of their scene up there, like he was in some kind of trouble. He was asking where he could crash long-term. They'll take care of him. They'll adopt him like people adopt lost puppies. He's got it made."

"Except for his leg," Rachel said as a reminder. "Splashing around in stagnant water up in those mountains with a gash like that is a good way to get a serious infection. I asked him if he wanted us to report him to a doctor or EMS or somebody. He was adamant that he did not want that."

"He was all fired up that he didn't want *anything* from the outside world," Brandon added. "But they've got a bunch of herb healers up there who promised to take care of him."

"People die of untreated infections, Brandon," Rachel said sternly.

"What happens if people do die up there?" Hammer asked.

"They have a graveyard somewhere," Brandon said. "Not anywhere near where people live. Nobody wants to sleep around dead bodies, and with all that superstition swirling around, nobody wants to live next to a bunch of skeletons."

"Or all those unsettled spirits," Lauren added.

As the two mainlanders shared the closeness of their impending flight time and said, "We better get going," the foursome shared cordial alohas and promises to "see you next time."

As Annison Cutts discovered long ago, and as Lauren Stahling read more than a month ago in his 1888 book,

the centuries have planted mysteries in the valley of Hemolele`auwai. As Lauren and Hammer discovered firsthand, a lot of mysteries have also been planted in the surrounding valleys and ridges all across to North Shore — and they *continue* to be planted.

While the Taurus raced south, down Highway 56 toward their rendezvous with another 737-800 like the ones which brought them here, talk naturally turned to all they'd seen and heard in their travels. They'd heard a lot about unsettled spirits and ghost armies, and they crossed paths with a few—although they were not exactly like those described in Hawai`ian lore.

They spoke of some specific spirits. They spoke of Glenn and Gladys, truly star-crossed lovers, whose skeletons remained where they had fallen for most of a century. They spoke of Lynsee and Joel, whom the media narrative anointed as star-crossed lovers even though they were not. There was nothing more to add about "Red."

As she gazed out the car window, watching the deep green forests of the North Shore thinning into the open country of the populous area near Līhu`e, Lauren's mind was on the living. She thought about the thousands, or even millions, on both sides of the Pacific who might have faced obliteration if Ryu Myong-su's megalomaniacal madness had been allowed to play out.

Mostly though, she thought about the hundred-and-seventy lives in the airliner over Pearl Harbor that *definitely* would have ended a month ago if not for the man sitting next to her back then, and now, at *this* moment.

As she returned his glancing smile, he was thinking mainly of how glad he was to have her sitting there. Some lovers finish one another's sentences. These two finish one another's thoughts.

EPILOGUE

DETECTIVE KAI NIALANI glanced at the clock on the wall at police headquarters as she made her way to her desk. She was waiting until after 8:00 a.m. to make her phone call, and wondering whether the party she hoped to reach would actually be in his office this early.

She took the business card out of her desk drawer, the one Army CID Special Agent Zachery Preneu had given her on that Friday exactly three weeks ago.

How the weeks had marched on!

Over the last two of those weeks, though, all her earlier dealings with the US Army had receded to a back burner, having been wholly overshadowed by KPD's interaction with the US Navy.

The search for Lynsee Kinkaide and Joel Dyallic had been led by Navy personnel, but when they were found deceased, and *not* on Navy property, the case was turned over to Dr. Kimberly Graihr, the Kaua`i County Medical Examiner. On this island, only she had the jurisdiction and technical capability to deal with a homicide case.

Kai had been at the morgue next door to the Wilcox Medical Center in Līhu`e when the bodies came in, and she was there again when Vice Admiral Hardgrove Kinkaide arrived for the formal identification.

For some reason, maybe out of respect, he had worn his full-dress uniform with its ribbons and gleaming stars, with its sharply creased trousers and the officer's cap with the visor encrusted with gold oak leaves. He looked very imposing, but beneath his practiced military bearing, Kai could sense the deep melancholy.

The pictures of him wading through the reporters as he arrived, surrounded by his entourage of similarly uniformed officers, had gone viral, and were on every news broadcast out of Honolulu and even on the national news channels.

Inside, he left his entourage in the lobby when he went in to view his daughter for the last time. For some reason, KPD Chief George Audhus had picked Kai to join him and Lieutenant Richard Faralaco as official observers. She guessed she was picked because she just happened to be there when they left headquarters for the five-minute drive to the morgue.

When Dr. Graihr pulled off the sheet, it was obvious she had done a lot of cleanup work. The wild pigs had passed by, and damage had been done. It would be a closed-casket funeral.

Kai watched the stoic admiral, stiff at attention when he walked in, as he fought himself for a moment before crumpling tearfully.

"Lynsee...*Lynsee Lou*," he whimpered as he touched her battered cheek, and as tears rolled down his own cheeks.

Kai guessed that some part of his emotional display was the sad truth behind a narrative, widely circulating in the blogosphere, that the admiral had abandoned his underage daughter to her own devices in the admiral's quarters for several days and had not even bothered to check in. These rumors were essentially true, as were those that his wife had already filed divorce papers, although this had been in the works for some time.

Kai felt a little bit sorry for the admiral, but a lot sorry for Lynsee.

Kai didn't know what to think about Joel Dyallic. Forensics had just reported that it was a bullet from his gun that killed her. So much for the Princess and the Petty Officer romance myth.

Master-at-Arms Chief Petty Officer Anthony Karboli, Dyallic's boss, who had also been at the trailhead on that fateful night, had disappeared completely, and this had fueled all sorts of additional conspiracy theories—for a little more than a week.

Then, a couple from Kapa`a had phoned in, saying that they had seen a man answering his description up in the Kalalau Valley, the place where people go to never be found. It was hard, however, to hide a big guy with bright red hair.

By the time that the Navy and the park rangers put together a search party to go check out the report, it was too late. Chief Petty Officer Karboli had just passed away. As Dr. Graihr's autopsy would confirm, he had suffered a raging bacterial infection in a deep laceration on his leg, which led to blood poisoning, and ultimately to a very unpleasant death.

They recovered his body and confirmed his identity, and they discovered he had a SIG Sauer M18 concealed on him. In turn, this weapon was matched to the bullet that killed Dyallic. This solved the loose end of the missing petty officer mystery, and the mystery of who fired the other bullet, but it opened yet another chapter in the legend of the Princess and the Petty Officer.

Nobody would ever *really* know what happened up there on the Miloli`i Ridge Trail that night, and as time went on, there would be no end to the speculation, either in the conspiracy theories or the true crime podcasts.

———

As she glanced again at the minute hand on the old-school wall clock and waited for the top of the hour, Kai picked up the green notebook that was still lying in the pile on the corner of her desk.

It was a typical school notebook, with bright happy Korean language lettering and a jolly emoji on the cover. Kai had no idea what it said, but it looked light and cheerful. She flipped through it, noting the crisp, neat penmanship, and the intriguing diagrams with lots of arrows, and pretty well rendered sketch maps of the two side-by-side Koreas.

Though she was somewhat curious about what it said, Kai had not yet taken the time to phone her friend who was fluent in Korean to come by and translate it. There was a lot to translate, and she figured her friend may be too busy.

Kai had told Kathy in Kekaha to have the Koreans call her to pick it up on their way to the airport, but they had never left Kaua`i.

The case of the missing sugar company people was completely eclipsed in media coverage by the Princess and the Petty Officer, but KPD *did* initiate a search. They found their brown SUV at a turnout on Highway 550. It was only about fifty yards up the road from where Lynsee Kinkaide's Lexus and the Navy Humvee were found, but it was on the *opposite* side. It was in the turnout for the trailhead for the popular hike eastward to eight-hundred-foot Waipo`o Falls, so all attention turned to searching this trail.

After several days of intensive scouring of the

Waipo`o Falls Trail by KPD, state park personnel, and local volunteers, no trace had been found. After the earlier thorough search of the Miloli`i Ridge Trail on the *west side* of Highway 550 which had located the bodies of Lynsee and Joel, no one considered looking for the Koreans over there. Thanks to their own skill in camouflaging what became their final resting place, the site would remain unnoticed by human eyes as it was gradually swallowed into the native vegetation through the coming months and years.

Four of their passports were discovered in their luggage, and Chief Ardhus had contacted the South Korean Consulate in Honolulu with this information so families in Korea could be notified. At first, the consular staff were very interested in the case and in getting involved.

The fifth passport was not found, but the fifth name was on the rental car agreement for the blue Mustang convertible. A few days later, when Ardhus phoned the consulate again and gave them the name "Ryu Myong-su," the chief was met with a long silence. Eventually, someone came on the line to thank him, and to say that this missing persons case was no longer a priority for the Korean government. They would not be displeased if KPD allowed it to become a cold case. And so it would.

Kai Nialani had been through the dropping of cold cases business before, and the previous instance was exactly *why* she was patiently monitoring the big clock this morning.

At last, the minute hand clicked past the top of the hour and Kai Nialani punched in the number for the US Army

Criminal Investigation Division Pacific Field Office at Schofield Barracks, north of Pearl Harbor.

She was ready to talk, whether Special Agent Zachery Preneu would like to do so or not.

As she expected, she had to work her way through several layers of receptionists whose job was to not let her through at all. She persevered. She was no stranger to bureaucracy.

"Agent Preneu, this is Detective Nialani in Līhu`e," she said when she recognized his voice.

"Yes, Detective," he said with a thin trace of apprehension beneath a patina of annoyance.

"I'm calling about Captain Glenn Dexsen…"

"Let me stop you right there," he interrupted. "That case is closed. Done. Locked up, signed off and sealed off three weeks ago."

He remembered that his boss had demanded in the strongest of terms that the name Dexsen should never again be spoken.

"I know who murdered Dexsen and Gladys Mattochs," she said, ignoring what he'd said.

"*Umm*…what are you saying?" Preneu said after a long pause.

"I'm saying that I have the identity of the killer with a ninety-nine-point nine percent probability."

"How…"

"I know the killer *and* I have the motive."

"*What*…?"

"I know about Operation Terminal Showa. I assume you do as well."

There was a very long pause during which she could hear the squeaking of an office chair and the labored breathing of an uncomfortable special agent. Preneu had never heard that term, but he didn't say so. Whatever it was, he assumed Quantico had briefed his boss, Special

Agent in Charge Margo Motherwell, and that's why she had shut down the investigation.

"I need to know what information you have and where you got it," he said firmly, although he was bluffing. He was practiced in the art of drawing out information he did not have. "But I'm going to have to call you back on a secure line."

"No need," she said. "I'm moving on the *other* matter."

"What other matter?" Preneu now felt himself caught off guard.

"I need something from you as well, Agent Preneu," she said after taking a deep breath, and trying not to sound as nervous as she felt. She had been bracing herself all night for this showdown with this federal agent.

"I need the remains of Gladys Mattochs," she continued. "I need you to turn them over to me, so I can turn them over to her family for burial. Since you have closed *your* investigation, and I have concluded mine, the family deserves closure. I have no say in what you do with remains of Army personnel, but Gladys needs to come home."

"I can't ..."

"But you *can*," Kai said, seizing her moment to be firm. "You have the remains of a civilian from my county, which belong *here*. I have information that you want, and which you'd obviously like to see."

Preneu paused. He *did* want to see it, and he knew that if the subject ever came up again, Motherwell would demand to know what KPD. Preneu didn't want to take a chance that it wouldn't ever come up again, and he wanted to be prepared.

"You don't actually know who murdered Dexsen and Gladys Mattochs, do you?"

"Ummm...I can't say," he stammered, having been

taken off guard. She was right and she knew it. He did not know. Motherwell probably did, and she would demand to know what KPD knew—*if* she ever learned of this conversation.

"What I *can* say is that Dexsen's name must be kept confidential," he insisted.

She noticed he did not use the word "classified." She had never been in the service herself, but she knew enough about bureaucracies to know that the process of classification involves a lot of people coming into the know about the subject being classified. Obviously, this was something about which the fewest number of people possible could know.

"I suggest that we meet *here* in Līhu`e and make the exchange," she said.

"This is extortion."

"Not in the least. It's just an interagency transaction. I have some information about Dexsen to share with you... information which you may not have, including the name of his murderer. It seems that this matter is *so sensitive* on your end that you can't even talk about it over an open line, so hand delivering this information *in person* is the best solution. On the other hand, I'm sure that you would not mind doing the honorable thing and hand delivering the remains."

Preneu was stunned. What should he do?

He quickly thought it over, realizing that the detective was offering him key information at a very low price. All she was asking was the return of the bones. Army CID really had no legal standing to hang on to civilian remains. They could fight it, and maybe win in court, but if the point of all this was to avoid publicity, a court case would defeat the purpose. Meanwhile, Motherwell had explicitly told him she *didn't care* about civilian bones, so Preneu could agree to this demand.

If KPD got the bones, Nialani would tell him exactly what information she had on Dexsen and his killer. Meeting her in person would present an excellent opportunity to insist that she not let any of this go further.

Finally, after a long pause, Preneu spoke.

"Since this is a matter of great importance, I'll agree to your extortion. There's a flight to Kaua`i at least once every hour. I'll be on a plane around noon. I'll phone you when I land."

"I think we should meet in a public place," she said. "I'll be at the Starbucks at the Kukui Grove Mall, not the one near Target, but the one at the north end of the mall. It's right next to the parking lot. It's ten minutes from the airport. I'll be alone."

Special Agent Zachery Preneu found the place easily. All malls look alike and they're easy to find. So was the Starbucks. It was the one with the Ford SUV in KPD markings parked nearby. He turned in next to it and grabbed the black duffel bag out of the back seat of his rental.

He felt like he was making a ransom drop, and in a sense, he was. Nialani had something he wanted, including the identity of the killer, and probably much more. Preneu's mandate from the top, apparently from way above his boss's boss, was to make Glenn Dexsen disappear. Nobody outside the CID stovepipe was supposed to know about Dexsen, but somebody did, and she knew a lot more. Preneu was here to find out what and how much, and to stop it from spreading.

He saw Detective Nialani inside. She was in uniform and seated at a table near the front window sipping a large coffee. She smiled and nodded when she saw him.

He grimaced at the idea she would *smile* at a time like this.

"Thank you for coming," she said, still smiling.

"Of course," he replied tersely, taking off his aviator-style sunglasses. "Here it is. You can keep the bag."

She unzipped it and peered in but took nothing out. Nobody likes to see human bones spread around on a table in a coffee shop.

There wasn't much to see, and she knew what would be there. Inside were evidence bags containing fewer than half the bones from the body of a small woman. She knew exactly what to expect because she had collected and processed them herself. There was the pelvis, the finger bones of the left hand, many other small random bones, and, of course, the skull with the horrible bullet hole.

"Everything looks in order," she said. "I thank you, and the family would thank you as well, but I don't think you want your name mentioned, so I won't."

"Army CID has no further need for this material," he said. "*Now*, what do you have for me?"

She reached into a large canvas bag that was lying on the chair next to her and took out a manila folder. She placed it on the table, opened it and rotated it so that it was right-side up from his point of view.

"These are copies of microfilm from the local newspaper for June 1946. They are news reports of the disappearance of Gladys Mattochs *and* Glenn Dexsen. These are for you to take with you. As you can see, this was a big story here on Kaua`i that week. The Mattochs family was very prominent in those days. You will notice that I have highlighted all the mentions of Glenn Dexsen's name. Like it or not, this name you want buried was widely reported. Forgotten now, probably, but widely reported then."

Preneu could see this. There were multiple highlighter marks on every page.

"His name and his association with her and with that week cannot be erased," she said. "If someone...hypothetically, of course...wanted to start by erasing this microfilm, he could go to the main library and steal the 1946 roll. But there would still be a roll or two in the state library in Honolulu, and all of this material is backed up on ProQuest, the global information database that stores microfilm digitally so that anybody anywhere can read any newspaper from any year on any computer. As we both know, if it's on the internet, it *never* goes away."

"There's *nothing* in here about the classified operation you mentioned," he said with a relaxed expression after spending several minutes scanning through the microfilm printouts.

"I'll get to that," she said, taking out another folder, which she did not open. "I also mentioned that we've solved this double homicide. I know that you want nothing more to do with this case, but as a point of information and professional courtesy, I'll walk you through it."

He just stared at her hands, which remained folded across the closed folder as she spoke.

"You'll remember our drive to Barking Sands and that afternoon with all those musty boxes in that musty metal shed. You found Dexsen in the Transient Personnel Records, but you said it was all routine and you dismissed it. Then you ordered me to clean it up and put everything away while you went off to find a bathroom. Remember? Maybe not, you had more important things on your mind."

He looked away and started to roll his eyes.

"I did put *most* of it back in the box, and the box back on the pile, but I pulled out a few pages where I saw a pattern that got me thinking. You may also remember that the chief petty officer said those boxes were not Navy property, and he told us *both* that we were welcome to take anything we wanted. You didn't. I *did*. Take a look."

She opened the folder and showed him a photocopy of one of the pages he had tossed aside. Dexsen's name was about two-thirds of the way down the list. It showed him taking a vehicle out of the motor pool.

"So what?" Preneu asked when she pointed to Dexsen's name.

"So this date is two days before he and Gladys went missing. That car was found here in Līhu`e, so there was an assumption by the family that they had hopped an inter-island ship and eloped to Honolulu and beyond."

"Again, so what?"

"So now look at this," she said, spreading several sheets out on the table side by side.

"See here on these log sheets how all the names have a number which identifies which outfit each of these men were part of."

Preneu nodded.

"See how Dexsen has letters instead of numbers? See how it says 'OSS?' You know what that stands for, right?"

"Yes, I do," Preneu replied. Obviously, a CID agent would know about the Office of Strategic Services. It's a legendary organization in the history and lore of American covert services, but Motherwell had never told Preneu that Dexsen was part of the OSS. Nor had Preneu noticed it when he last looked at this page.

"Now, look here," Kai Nialani said, pointing to a line on one of the pages. "Here's another OSS man who requested a vehicle on the *same day* that Glenn and Gladys were last seen alive. He arrived at Barking Sands a few days earlier, and he flew out a couple of days later."

Preneu could see the name, but he had never heard of Lieutenant Frank Striden. Motherwell had never mentioned Striden, but apparently there was a lot that she had not told him.

"Obviously a coincidence," Preneu said weakly.

"I'm not through," she said, turning over the pages and digging deeper into the contents of the folder. "These are a few highlights from Dexsen's service career. I'm sure you've seen all this."

He had not, but he said nothing as she laid out more pages.

"As you may recall," she said. He wondered whether she assumed he did or was teasing him because she knew he did not. "Dexsen transferred from the 34th Division to the 2nd Ranger Battalion in 1942. As you can see here, two years later, he was assigned to a British secret plan to assassinate Hitler. That obviously never happened, but by now he had been noticed by higher-ups in the US Army as a pretty special operator. That's when he got transferred to the OSS and assigned to Operation Terminal Showa."

"That was the term you mentioned on the phone," he said, nervously looking at the sheets of paper with "Top Secret" notices on them.

"Your bosses haven't told you what Terminal Showa was, have they?" Kai said, needling him.

His expression, as he said nothing, confirmed her assertion.

"It was the plan to assassinate Hirohito in 1945," she said. "This also did not happen because Hirohito surrendered and the war ended."

Preneu nodded as he looked at the confirming paperwork.

"Apparently, when Hirohito agreed to cooperate, the Allies got real embarrassed about having sent people to kill him, and somebody at the OSS decided to start killing off everybody who knew about the assassination plot."

"Now, *that's* pretty far-fetched," Preneu said.

"Until you take a look at this," she said, pulling another sheet of paper from the files. "Among other things, I have Striden's own checklist from his own field notes."

Preneu looked down and saw orders tasking Striden with killing eight people who were listed below. All of the names had a check mark and a date written next to them in pencil—except the last one. The last name was that of Captain Glenn Dexsen. The date next to the name above was in May 1946, three weeks before Glenn and Gladys went missing.

"We know what happened next," the detective said, closing the file.

"Can I take that file?" Preneu asked.

"I think I'll hang onto it," she said. "It's really not my place to share someone else's classified files. They're federal government files though, so as a CID Special Agent, you ought to be able to access any of this internally."

What could he do? He couldn't complain that Motherwell would never allow him to access any of it. He said nothing more.

"I have no plans to share these files with anyone else, certainly not the media," she said. "That is, for the time being. On two points, I believe that you and I are on the same page."

"Which are?"

"I believe that we are of the same mind that this folder, which I've just *closed,* should remain that way, right?"

He nodded.

"And I believe you'll agree when I say you and I should never again cross paths."

Had she just told him to go to hell? He guessed she had.

They just stared at one another impassively for a long time before he finally nodded once and began to stand up.

For Zachery Preneu, the case was closed, and his nod of complicity with the intractable Detective Kai Nialani would keep it that way. If nothing else, he sensed her to be a woman of her word.

Despite the circumstances, he felt a sense of relief as he walked out into the warm tropical air. He would take the win. He knew more than Motherwell knew that he knew, and he had Nialani's promise that it would go no farther. He could go back to Honolulu and continue to follow orders.

For Detective Kai Nialani, the case was not quite closed.

She watched Preneu walk out to his rental car carrying the folder of newspaper clippings she had given him.

She watched him start the car and drive away without looking back. He made a left turn out of the parking lot and a right up at the main highway. He'd be dropping off his car inside of fifteen minutes and at his terminal gate shortly after.

When he was gone, she walked to the rear of the KPD car and opened the liftgate. Inside was an empty box she had gotten from Kim Graihr. It was the kind that the medical examiner uses to turn remains over to families. It was cardboard, but substantial and tasteful. She transferred the evidence bags with the bones from the duffel bag to this box and sealed it.

Ten minutes later, she was on that leafy street about a mile from the Kukui Grove Mall and was parking in front of the home of Cynthia Mattochs. The white-haired descendant of Gladys Mattochs was expecting her and met her at the front door.

"Are these them?" Cynthia asked, though she already knew the answer.

"Yes, ma'am," Kai said. "This is everything I was able to recover at the scene."

"And you recovered it yourself," she said, phrasing it as a statement, not as a question.

"Yes, ma'am."

"It's more than I had any reason to hope for," Cynthia said, feeling the weight of the box.

"I hope that this will bring some sense of closure to the family."

"Oh yes…you cannot possibly know how much this means…thank you *so, so* much."

"You're most welcome."

"I'm sorry, I'm being horribly rude." Cynthia said in that way society matrons extend hospitality. "Would you like to come in for coffee or something stronger?"

"No, ma'am, I've got to get back to the station." She remembered Cynthia making that same offer last time they met.

"I guess this means that the case is over…have you solved it? Do you know who murdered them?"

"Are you sure you want to know?"

"Yes, I do. I have wondered since you told me they were murdered."

"It was another soldier…Lieutenant Frank Striden. He was out to kill Captain Dexsen for other reasons, and I'm afraid that Gladys just got in his way. He would not have known who she was."

"That's so sad."

"Yes, ma'am, it is," Kai agreed. "But there is no way that the murderer could still be alive, so that part has closure too."

"I suppose."

"Yes, ma'am."

As Cynthia stepped inside to set the box on a table, the detective cautioned her.

"You should probably wait to open that box until you're with your funeral director, or whomever you're going to have prepare what's in there for whatever burial. It's pretty unsettling. You should have a professional person help explain what you're seeing."

"Thank you," she said. "I will. I appreciate your concern. I really do."

"Yes, ma'am."

"So this is it, then?" Cynthia continued. "This is everything?"

"No ma'am," Kai said. "I have this."

She reached into her uniform shirt pocket and took out a small envelope. It was an envelope that had been in her desk drawer ever since the day she got back from Hemolele`auwai Valley. She had not given it to Preneu when he had taken everything else to Honolulu. She handed it to Cynthia, who opened it carefully with slightly trembling hands.

She held it above her left hand and tapped it slightly.

Out fell a delicately intricate gold ring with a tiny, shimmering diamond.

"This was still on Gladys's finger when I found her," Kai said, her voice barely above a whisper.

It was early on a cold Montana morning several weeks later, and Lauren Stahling was dressing for work when the phone on the nightstand chirped.

"Dr. Hammer's office," she said as she always answered calls from Tim Tommis on Hammer's phone. It was part of a running joke they played.

"Is the doctor in, or is he lying to a patient?"

"Actually, he's in the shower."

"How was your trip to Hawai`i?" Tommis asked. "I mean, apart from your distraction with the Armageddon gang."

"Or the hijacking?" Lauren reminded him.

"Oh yeah…that."

"That deal actually came back to us when we were trying to fly home."

"What happened?"

"We were changing planes in Honolulu when a couple of suits from the airline intercepted us. They knew we were coming."

"Oh, oh."

"It wasn't bad," Lauren admitted. "They upgraded us to first class and hustled us off to the first-class lounge where there was a vice president or some such who gave Hammer a lifetime first-class pass."

"Hammer? What about…"

"I got one too…my own 'plus-one' pass. After that deal with the skeletons and the sugar people, we're ready to use them for a *real* vacation."

Tommis laughed.

"Then we got on the plane and there was the same flight attendant from the day of the hijacking," Lauren continued. "She gave Hammer a big hug and started introducing him around like he's a celebrity."

"He made a big impression on a lot of people," Tommis said. "He always does."

"And now the big guy is out of the shower ...it's Tim Tommis...for you."

"Morning," Hammer said cheerfully.

"I've got something you're both going to want to hear."

"You're on speaker, so go ahead," Hammer said.

"I know that you've probably moved on from all that stuff over in Hawai`i, but after I hit a blank wall with that guy named Striden who murdered those people, I couldn't let it go. It's a matter of professional pride, you know."

"We know," Hammer said, laughing. Tommis never rested when some fact of importance eluded him.

"Well, I kept digging," Tommis continued. "It was frustrating as hell...one dead end after another. I found a few references to Terminal Showa, but all of them buried so deep and inside unrelated folders that almost nobody *ever* would have come across them."

"Except you."

"Who else? So, anyway, Lieutenant Frank Striden of the OSS was like a ghost."

"We ran into a lot of *those* over in Kaua`i," Lauren interjected.

"Then what happened?" Hammer asked. "I thought Striden fell off the map."

"He *did*, but I kept poking. Last week, I was talking to a friend of a friend who works in a basement of a *secret* basement owned through a shell company by those characters at our favorite magic castle over in Virginia."

"We're all ears," Hammer said, knowing that the "magic castle in Virginia" meant the CIA.

"Well, suddenly I'm looking at pages and pages of stuff with Frank Striden on nearly every one."

"Wow," Lauren said.

"The rub is that it was filed in a completely erroneous

folder...for reasons that became obvious as I read through it."

"Okay..."

"It seems that your friend, Lieutenant Frank Striden... he became *civilian* Frank Striden soon after he was killing people on Kaua`i...built a cottage industry for himself working for the spooks as a contract fixer...and a cold, efficient contract killer."

"Can't say I'm surprised," Hammer quipped. "Anybody who could go out and murder eight people from his own team, never mind bystanders, is a heartless sociopath."

"He had an interesting career handling things out in the plausible deniability shadowland. All through the fifties, as the Cold War was heating up, he was all over the world from Berlin to Bangkok...from Istanbul, even to Irkutsk, and those are just a few I picked for the sake of alliteration."

"A real James Bond," Lauren said, laughing. "An international man of mystery."

"That's our Frank. Out there shaking and stirring." Tommis chuckled, using a reference to Bond's routine martini order. "It makes fascinating reading. There's a lot of highlights, but a few jump out."

"Hmmm," Hammer replied thoughtfully, knowing by Tommis's tone that there was a punchline coming.

"Well," Tommis said. "You'll never guess where Frank Striden was in 1963, specifically on the twenty-second of November."

IF YOU LIKED THIS, YOU MIGHT LIKE:

TERMINAL MEMORY
BY BRIAN DRAKE

SAM RAVEN BATTLES THE ENEMIES JACK REACHER'S AFRAID OF. . .

Three years after a daring escape from a jihadists' camp, ex-CIA officer Mara Cole is a target once more. She's alone, on the run, and in need of a friend.

Sam Raven is tracking Mara's hunters for a different reason – he's on a mission of vengeance. A man with dark secrets, bound to Mara by shared history, they join forces to fight back. Together, they play a deadly game of chess through the back alleys of London, to the bright lights of Marseille, and the desert hell of Afghanistan opium fields, risking everything as they move closer to the truth.

With each feign and attack, they find the answers they seek lie deep in Mara's memories of captivity, torture, and betrayal – secrets to a conspiracy at the heart of the US Intelligence community, and men who will do anything to protect their power.

From the author of the Scott Stiletto series comes an exciting new hero! Sam Raven is grittier, deadlier, and you better not stand in his way.

AVAILABLE NOW

THANK YOU

Thank you for taking the time to read *Ghost Armies of the Nāpali Coast*. If you enjoyed it, please consider telling your friends or posting a short review. Word of mouth is an author's best friend and much appreciated.

Thank you.
Bill Yenne

ABOUT THE AUTHOR

Bill Yenne is the award-winning author of three dozen books on historical topics especially non-fiction books on military history and hardware. His various works have been translated into six languages. He has contributed to encyclopedias of both world wars, and his work has been selected for the official Chief of Staff of the Air Force Reading List. Yenne has appeared in documentaries airing on the History Channel, the National Geographic Channel, the Smithsonian Channel, ARD German Television, and NHK Japanese Television. His book signings have been covered by C-SPAN.

Bill Yenne grew up inside Montana's remote and rugged Glacier National Park, where his father was the supervisor of backcountry trails. He spent his summers on foot or on horseback in the remote mountains, and his winters becoming a voracious reader and history buff.

www.ingramcontent.com/pod-product-compliance
Lightning Source LLC
La Vergne TN
LVHW041106080826
845145LV00007B/1703

* 9 7 8 1 6 8 5 4 9 6 3 8 8 *